"O God, I could be bound in a nutshell, and count myself a king of infinite space, were it not that I have bad dreams."

Shakespeare's *Hamlet*

"So that at the world's Omega, as at its Alpha, lies the Impersonal."

Teilhard de Chardin

"Thus one can state that not only is the soul (mirror of an indestructible universe) indestructible, but so is the animal itself, even though its mechanism often perishes in part, and casts off or puts on its organic coverings."

Gottfried Leibniz

To Mom and Dad,
Thank you for all of the opportunities, support, and wisdom you've provided me with along the way.

Carlo Schefter,
Thank you for asking the tough questions and helping tailor the dream.

And Sam,
You are the Trinity to my Neo (minus all the death and mayhem).

CONTENTS

Chapter 1: **ARIADNE'S DREAD** 9

Chapter 2: **DREAMSCAPE** 21

Chapter 3: **SORTE** 24

Chapter 4: **RAPTURE** 35

Chapter 5: **STRANGER IN MY OWN SKIN** 39

Chapter 6: **BREAKING EVEN** 46

Chapter 7: **SNAKE-HOLED KINGDOM** 51

Chapter 8: **OVER THE MOUNTAIN** 63

Chapter 9: **CYPULCHRE** 70

Chapter 10: **BABYLON** 78

Chapter 11: **BENEATH THE VENEER** 87

Chapter 12: **INTERVENTION** 94

Chapter 13: **UNCOMFORTABLY NUMB** 104

Chapter 14: **TOO MUCH SMOKE, TOO MANY MIRRORS** 111

Chapter 15: **HIVE, SWEET HOME** 128

Chapter 16: **ON THE VERGE** 137

Chapter 17: **THE DEVIL WITHIN** 143

Chapter 18: **PESTICIDE** 157

Chapter 19: **RAINBOW'S END** 167

Chapter 20: **PICKING UP THE PIECES** 176

Chapter 21: **LOST ANGELS** 188

Chapter 22: **A WORLD APART** 192

Chapter 23: **THE WALLED CITY** 200

Chapter 24: **GRAY MATTER** 211

Chapter 25: **GLITCH MOB** 219

Chapter 26: **HARROWING HELL** 225

Chapter 27: **HERE COMES THE SUN** 230

Chapter 28: **LAST RITE** 242

Chapter 29: **THE ELEPHANTS IN THE ROOM** 247

Chapter 30: **SABOTEUR WITH A SAVAGE CURE**.......................253

Chapter 31: **ASCENSION** 261

Chapter 32: **SHAFTED**...264

Chapter 33: **CORPORATE REUNION** 271

Chapter 34: **KOYAANISQATSI**...282

Chapter 35: **IN THE GARDEN OF GOOD AND EVIL**.................290

Chapter 36: **DEUS EX DOMUS**...296

Chapter 37: **SUNSHINE** 300

GLOSSARY..310

Chapter 1: **ARIADNE'S DREAD**

BESIDE THE BONE SAW, the orangutan breathes shallowly, forfeiting the shadows drawn into its wired belly. Its mouth contorts through irreconcilable expressions, and resets to an abeyant gape, as if all of its muscles have come unsewn.

Dr. Paul Sheffield administers Clonazepam and a custom paralytic intravenously. Stubborn like his predecessors, Kim fights the inevitable, tugging violently at the restraints. Dr. Sheffield holds Kim's head still so he cannot rip himself open on the cranial grips. The cuffs clink as Kim stills and his sinews stiffen.

Kim is no longer a threat to himself, insofar as he is no longer able to physically react to his increasingly-perplexing mental state. He's both a spectator and an agent in the non-consensual hallucination Paul's designed; a shade blurred to a blip in an all-consuming static of information and sensation.

Paul has successfully cut Kim's mental tether. This will most certainly kill him.

Now wading into the undiscovered country, the orangutan will be blessed with untold knowledge and understanding, and his mind, ballooned and powerful, will become too large to bring back indoors; too expensive, anyway.

Paul holds Kim's hand purposefully for a pulse. *Heart-rate is down, right on schedule.* The sense of *déjà vu* hits Paul, as does the second-hand mortal panic. Every other subject has died at this stage, where the mind, mediated through and by the exo-cortex[1], simultaneously synchs with both its off-board

---

[1] I.e. The brain cannot possibly store all the information assimilated in the CLOUD, so an exterior brain will be provided in the Outland Corporation's central server bank, which the user may user to store or access memories and data.

memory server (i.e. a memex) and the projected CLOUD environment wherein the avatar is actualized.

The CLOUD is cyberspace reimagined, that is to say it's constantly imagined by the minds occupying it. It is a hybrid, unhobbled by linear visual and aural focus. It is tasted, heard, seen, felt, and metaphysically witnessed, forwards and backwards through incarnated ideas. *That's the gist, anyway.*

Paul fears what it'll mean if this works—what it will mean if this ape's survival entreats others to join him. After all, discovery and extinction often go hand-in-hand.

Bah. Let the ethicists and lawyers worry. Today Sheffield plays god. *Today I cast our mute likeness into chaos.*

The spiderlike probe above Kim's exposed brain blinks yellow.

"Alright! That 'a boy!'" Paul murmurs through a gritted smile. He checks the ape's PET scan for activity. *It's off the charts.*

Somewhere there's applause. Paul turns to match the sound to action: a broad-shouldered geriatric metes out fleshy encouragement beneath the red of the EXIT sign. His wheezes overtake his clapping. "Good show, Doctor," exclaims Niles Winchester III, an Armani-clad, Frankenstein monster—stitched together with surgical plastic and cultured tissue.

Paul gulps, sending spit to drown the butterflies in his stomach. "Mr. Winchester! Had I known in advance that you wanted to monitor this case, I'd have found you better real estate."

"Nonsense!" He swats away Paul's suggestion. "Keep up the good work." Observing a moment of silence, Winchester winces over a smile. "I was surprised by the ambition you exhibited yesterday..."

Yesterday? Paul can't remember much. He'd been in one of his moods.

"Baby steps, I suppose," Paul replies.

"That's quite a large baby, Doctor. I admire your focus despite the Board's skepticism and all of the caltrops they've set for you. They simply can't comprehend the vastness and promise of this project. We're changing the world here…changing what it means to be human. These are exciting days!"

"Certainly…" *Winchester's presence is off-putting, like someone watching you while you take a leak.* "Would you like to look-on somewhere nearer the stage? Help me change what it means to be an ape?"

"Unfortunately, I have to run. I am determined to source inhabitants for your new world."

"Well, it's hardly ready and the Board made it especially clear that we can't go ahead with human trials for at least another four years…"

Winchester's eyelids flutter, beating away Paul's prospective negation. "I had a novel idea."

Vexed by Winchester's obvious aversion, Paul makes an effort to look interested, now micromanaging Kim's scripts on the medical tablet. "Oh?"

"An idea to put this project on the map. Ahead of the Cordoba peace talks, we'll get Mahir Khomeini and President Jacoby into this brave new world of yours." Winchester coughs, and wets his lips for another parade of ambition. "Like your friend, goaded into service, you'll see to it that they instantaneously download and experience each other's memories, psyches, and souls. All incommensurability will be thwarted. The Holy Wars will come to an end in *the region*, and Outland will have both publicly proven itself indispensable…" He looks to his hands, "And your noosphere ready for mainstream consumption. Peace, first, and then Los Angeles!"

"Sir, with all due respect…"

Winchester grips the railing, his century-old knuckles discolouring the meat gnarled about them. His eyebrows shuffle impatiently. "Yes?"

"There are a million variables. A hundred things can go wrong just synchronizing a basic mind with its exo-cortex." Paul looks at Kim's corpulent mass, barely moving. "The difficulty is only compounded adding a second person into the mix. Ego death is the least of our concerns right now, but it's a likely first-hiccup."

"Where has this doubt come from, all of a sudden? You seemed so sure when we last spoke."

"I suppose I was a little off…"

"Well, buck up." Winchester slams his hand against the railing. Re-collecting himself, he lowers his voice. "Dr. Sheffield, I have every confidence in your ability to…surprise and succeed. Besides, I have an idea of how *this*," he indicates Kim with a shaking point, "will turn out." The criticism seems to have had an exhausting effect on the tycoon. Wheezing more heavily, Winchester takes a draw from his inhaler, and smiles. "Good night, Doctor. Tell Rachel and the girls I said hello." He torpedoes out the side door on a rush of cool air.

BESIDE THE OPERATING TABLE, Dr. Paul Sheffield hammers away at his medical tablet, checking the monitors for surprises. Paul adjusts the broadcast frequency in an effort to synchronize the ape's exo-cortex with the prototypic CLOUD tutorial.

"Easy, buddy. Just breathe," Paul reminds his hyper-tense patient.

Like the nonlinear flow of aural, visual, and simulated-haptic (SIMHAP) sensations that Kim's currently exposed to, Paul's concern is virtual. Utilitarian ethic and curiosity purpose this calm mask of sincerity.

"No, not now!" Paul murmurs to himself.

In all of the excitement, only heightened by the boss's visit, Paul's lost his grip. His hands begin to tremble in the pallid circle of light shone by his medical monitor. An itch bids him scratch and he obeys. He tears off his glasses and scratches at the little cracks in his mask, at invisible trans-orbital veins rupturing his façade with anxiety and fear. His fingers find an aberration along his scalp above the hairline— *stitches. When did I get stitches?* He inspects his finger, and notices a blotch of blood.

"No-no-no-no!" He palms his accordioned forehead and directs muddled thoughts with his free hand. "Not here…not now!" He teeters on one foot, closing his eyes— already sandwiched between squished features. "God-damn-it!"

The rhythm of Kim's heartbeat fills the gaps in Paul's freak-out.

"Damn!"

The green-and-pastel tiles beneath his feet seem to melt away, one by one, darkening into an unreflective tar. Paul cannot tell himself apart from his surroundings or relocate the familiar monologic of a single, interior voice.

A COM-Disc tolls out, releasing the darkness' grip on Paul's mind and body. The little drone judders over, propelled by its concealed rotor and the promise of dialogue. Paul's eyes open, and focus on the source of the commotion.

In a monotone prompt, the drone targets Paul with a speaker, simultaneously firing out a hologram. "Playback message for: Dr. Sheffield, Paul. Would you like to see the message played back? Answer: *yes* or *no*."

Paul shakes his head. "Just give me two minutes, Korrel."

"Message postponed for one-hundred-and-twenty seconds." The COM whirrs to a higher altitude, and begins orbiting the stage.

Resuming his calm, Paul rummages through his pockets, procuring a white-plastic SIK bottle: anti-psychotic unifiers tailored to address schizophrenic episodes. He pops the top and polishes off three green-and-yellow triangular pills. He stares into the blackness past Kim, waiting for his sanity to catch up with him.

Ahead of the remedy comes a euphoric sensation. Paul, though vexed and tired, manages a rounded grin, letting the SIK bring him up within *normal* parameters.

A grinding-screech sounds above on the Observation Deck. Paul quickly hides the pill bottle. He abandons his suave posture over the de-localized ape to press greasy wires of his hair back into place.

Oni, a dark-haired, Japanese neurologist from the University of British Columbia, appears on the balcony: a whole note on a bar line. With her hair tied back, her face looks even narrower than usual, resolving with a neat little chin manipulated by a peach slice of a bottom lip.

She looks down at Paul, reverently. Paul's paranoia mutates her look of professional interest into one of hideous omniscience. The minute curvatures at the corners of her mouth hook into her cheeks, the colour of cherry blossoms, as well as into Paul. He's caught. She's no fool; quite the opposite, in fact. *She definitely knows the dimensions of my private insanity.*

"Kim seems stable. One-to-one loop is consistent," she informs the mad scientist below in Japanese.

Paul, having completely neglected the fact that Oni took her dinner upstairs—*that she must have seen everything*—mulls over what depravity she may have witnessed during his episode.

14

"Oni, how are we mortals looking from up on Olympus?" he quips in Japanese, striving to gauge her reaction to his unconscious conduct with an innocuous query.

"Very impressive, Doctor. We are proud of your ambition, and we accept your sacrifice." Oni laughs. "We'll have to check on Prometheus to make sure there wasn't something more besides light in his fennel stock."

Oni had downloaded and memorized *Bulfinch's Mythology* to keep up with Paul's extraneous naming conventions. *She likely has a better understanding of the depravity and fate of the gods than I've grasped over forty years of obsession and recital, not that she'd show-off.*

Paul nods, ushering in a clinical disposition, noting his assistant's unaffected, professional tone. "I wish! No luck where cheats are concerned." He checks Kim's heart monitor. "Start the timer. Six minutes until broadcast."

Oni smiles coyly. She rolls straight off the railing, and disappears into the Observation Deck's rear analysis room where the insipid light of computer screens envelops her.

Paul shakes his head. *If only they knew that the one authorized to draw and test the depths of the World's Mind could not find solace, boundary, or reason in his own.* Pleased that his mind is not open on the stage for analysis, he deludes himself: *maybe she doesn't know, either.* Grinning, delighted his body has not given him away, he deletes the video-surveillance evidence of his episode with a swipe on his tablet.

"Korrel, play-back message."

Korrel swaps-out its monotone for a recording, loud with ambient conversations and music: "'Paul?" Rachel's flickering presence fills the hologram. Brown hair, bright eyes, and a shirt-run ragged by a pair of messy munchkins. Copper pots and pans dipping in and out of the third dimension with Rachel's sporadic rocking back and forth place her in the kitchen. "'I tried your Monocle and your Vox, but you didn't answer…You know you're the only one still pinging satellites? Anyway, Pythia's fever has worsened and the MediPen's still misdiagnosing her with the weirdest cognitive disabilities. Last time it was Autism, now it's a congenital birth defect. Paul…I think I'm going to take her to the clinic first thing tomorrow morning. Pedro said he'd see us, no appointment required.'"

That was real swell of him.

"'Hopefully it's nothing. Maybe you can take a look if Pedro proves incapable…There's food in the freezer if you're still hungry when you get home, and if you're interested, the hatch is full of ration bars. Printer is jammed, though, so you'll have to find coffee on your way home. Oh! I almost forgot: there's a dot-gram sitting here from Outland; two invitations to the Summer Ball. Tell Shouta you're going with me. Three's a crowd.'" Crying off-screen catches her attention. "'Listen, I have to run. Love you.' Say yes if you would like to hear the message played again."

"No, thank you, Korrel. Re-assign to OD and assist Oni with the synch."

"Yes, Dr. Sheffield." The speaker retracts into its slot on the COM, and the projected interface minimizes.

Paul leans forward, and wipes flop sweat from his eyes. "Kim, you're doing great!"

His reddish-brown gamble offers a muted groan.

"Good, good," Paul reiterates. He places his tablet on Kim's chest, and raises his hands out, as if in benediction. "That's it."

The yellow light on the eight-armed, suspended mobile turns orange, and pulses. A black drive on the gurney beside the table beeps, and a stream of disordered data floods Paul's monitors.

"All systems synchronized!" screams Oni from the tech forest above.

Paul slaps his armrest. "Okay, Kim. Here's one for you."

He triggers a command via the ape's implant. Kim shudders. The input sends the bandwidth graphs mapped across Oni's readouts into the red. Data-blocks crest in waves of code in tandem with Kim's convulsions.

Cued by the ape's successful mental circuit, Paul dials a series of commands on his tablet, lending shape to the hybrid cyberspace. With a pronounced tap, he initiates the commands and joins Kim at his side.

"You're eligible for an Education One certificate after this, Kim." He flips a switch on the driver. A green light flashes on. Paul types furiously into the in-feed:

—HELLO KIM. YOU ARE SAFE. THIS IS YOUR FRIEND, DR. SHEFFIELD. I AM HERE WITH ONI. DO YOU KNOW WHERE WE ARE?

The cursor blinks in the darkness, alone. "God damn it. You better not be off looking for your male member."[2]

Kim jerks back and forth, and then relaxes.

Oni runs to the balcony. "The synch-loop's been interrupted."

"How?"

"A small power surge. Narrowed the broadcast for half-a-second. Without a linkage, we're looking at brain death."

"Blast!" Paul compulsively massages the short black bristles on his chin.

"What should we do? I can try resetting him," Oni suggests, frenzied—having reverted back to Japanese.

"I'm thinking."

---

[2] Every other ape's first inclination was to ensure their choice organs were intact. Upon unsuccessful searches, they almost all went into cardiac arrest. Kim, thankfully, was chemically sterilized, undermining such natural reflexes.

Kim's mouth widens, revealing purple gums and a skeletal smile.

"Don't you dare!" Paul yells.

Kim flat-lines. The computer terminals blink a motley of colours like rogue Christmas lights, while Kim's respirator chimes a morbid carol.

"Dr. Sheffield, we're ten seconds into the four-minute countdown. If not stabilized—"

ONE MINUTE LEFT. Paul rolls over to his desk, and grabs a hypodermic needle from a box marked DLCLZ. "Alright, buddy," he says, apologetically, with a handful of euthanasiac promise. He turns Kim's arm over, and runs his fingers up to its seat of veins, slowly cooling. Paul holds the syringe steady, and yells up to Oni: "I'm calling it. Series five, number fifteen. Mental death at—"

"Stop! Don't kill him. Doctor! Take a look at his PET scan."

Absolution beeps behind the slab. Paul's medical tablet clicks emphatically: it's a response from the dislocated ape. Paul turns to the sound, and reads genesis:

—*I AM KIM.*

Stamped with a foolish smile, Paul discards the syringe, and leans over the cuffed orangutan. He types a scrawl into the holographic query box leveled over the ape's chest, and then backspaces to simplify it:

—*HELLO KIM. IT IS NICE TO MEET YOU. I AM DR. SHEFFIELD.*

—*KIM CANNOT SEE DR. SHEFFIELD. WHAT IS WRONG WITH KIM?*

"Yes!" Paul bellows, throwing a triumphant fist into the air.

Not only has the synchronization conveyed Kim's mind into the CLOUD, but it has successfully impressed upon him an encyclopaedia's-worth of information.

—*NOTHING IS WRONG WITH KIM.*

Paul turns on the intercom, filling the rafters with his excitement: "Holy shit! Oni, are you seeing this?"

The COM rings again. Suddenly, all of the monitors cut to a warning error: "Emergency in neural-research lab."

A siren cuts the clinical quiet. One-hundred red lights start flashing, accenting the blaring cacophony.

Transfixed on the blinking cursor on the holographic query box, linked to a now-conversational, self-aware ape, Paul clenches his teeth. "*What now?*"

"Dr. Sheffield," Oni shouts down from the Observation Deck, "Dr. Katajima is trying to page you."

"So bloody impatient!" Paul hesitates over the query box. "Dammit!" He drives away from Kim on his chair, gets up, parachutes his lab jacket, and steps into the falling white fabric. He returns to the query box, his jacket flaring behind him. "What does he want?"

"He's having difficulties with an unscheduled test."

Paul lunges to the elevated terminal copying and storing lab-commands and functions, and requests a back-up. "Tell him I'm a little preoccupied right now. The fruit of six-years-worth of research. He's jealous, *that's what this is*," Paul points at Kim. "And he wants to rain on my parade."

"He says it is urgent."

"If it's so damn important, tell him to wake up Tesla. Hell, Winchester's still around, isn't he?"

Oni sighs, clearly not appreciating being the intermediary between two megalomaniacs. She huffs into the receiver, and nods. "Dr. Sheffield, he says he cannot have it on record."

Paul returns to Kim, and lays hands on his chest and forehead. He recoils to type a message to his very first Humanities student.

—*KIM IS VERY BRAVE. ONI IS COMING TO TALK TO KIM.*

"Oni, watch Kim. This is it. We're on the verge of a monumental medical and social breakthrough!" The doctor transfers lab-command to Oni via his tablet. "Vitals go down, localize him. Use the PILOT device. It'll take over Kim's basic motor functions and substitute-in for his medulla oblongata, so we won't need a ventilator."

Oni returns a knowing smile, bounds to the back of the Observation Deck, and shimmies down the ladder.

"Dr. Sheffield," she says between rungs, "Will you need any assistance in the neural lab?"

"No, thank you. Especially not if it's an unscheduled test. *Who knows what he's up to?* Just chat Kim up. See what he's learned. Figure out if he's integrated anything else— check the interface against his virtual camera." Paul runs his fingers through his hair, frantically racking his brain. "And keep him warm…Record absolutely everything. Thank you!"

Paul opens the door to leave, and regretfully turns to see Oni resetting the interface with the crumpled human counterfeit on the slab.

Chapter 2: **DREAMSCAPE**

PAUL SHEFFIELD's pedestrian volley crashes through the shiny, linoleum hall. As he needles toward the department's so-called *inner sanctum,* he's fanned through by swinging doors. The last set crack open to a large, moon-lit atrium. Katajima stands frazzled and bowed at the top of a mirror-arched staircase that cradles the e-meal printers on the ground floor, rowed and columned by the skylight.

Dr. Shouta Katajima's white hair is cropped back into a ponytail, smoothening his shiny temples. A doomed silver coif arrowheads one eyebrow, sloped into a pitiful look. Paul can read the failure written all over his colleague's droopy posture and sweat-soused face.

"Where have you been?" squawks Katajima, ostensibly on the verge of vomiting. "I called at least half-a-dozen times. I did not expect you to put me on track only to derail me just before arrival."

"You started?"

"Yes."

"*Well so have I.* Sort of in the middle of it, actually."

"Paul, I would not have called you if it was not serious." Katajima drops his gaze to compose his thoughts. "Our data was wrong."

"That's impossible."

Katajima sighs. "Regardless, we have encountered a number of set-backs."

"Oh, I bet."

"Your projections—the ones you sent yesterday…they do not apply across the board. You…*I* was made to think they would."

"You're out of your depth, Shouta. Get Winchester on the phone right now."

"We don't need a chaperone. We just need to fix this."

"No. You need a goddamn saviour…Couldn't wait for me, huh?" Paul rushes the stairs.

"You said…"

"I don't recall telling you to waste both Outland's resources and my time this late on a Friday night."

Katajima stabs Paul's path with a tablet, scrolling scans from the lab. "Allen and I both agreed that it looked stable."

Paul brushes by Katajima, and charges into the prep-chamber. "What does Allen know, anyway? Oni's findings demonstrated that it was too thin to walk on."

A red grid, stretching the area of the room, envelops both scientists, scanning for electro-magnetic signatures. The grid descends, giving off the appearance of a room leaking some red-surfaced but otherwise invisible elixir. "CLEARED FOR ENTRY" runs across the tickertape mounted on the archway, and the bolts on the heavy, iron doors retreat against powerful springs, back into their barrels.

"Paul, you never sent me that report."

Katajima swipes his wrist over the SECUR-console. The door's hydraulic arm grinds it forward into a passageway clouded by plastic curtains, draped in succession like ambitious cobwebs.

"Don't be preposterous. Of course I sent it."

"Paul, the issue—"

Slashing through the transparencies, Paul barks back to Katajima: "Is impatience."

"You are being awfully inconsistent."

Inconsistent? *He knows. He must! No. Nothing more than a blind jab from a desperate man; a hack-scientist with a crosshair on my back.*

"Listen, we thought we had enough hard drives linked."

"But?" says Paul, incredulous.

"Three failed to start on-time, and the surge took out the fourth."

"Surge?"

"Yeah. Anaheim reported a two-second surge across the Tri-Angeles Network, but indicated it was inside Outland parameters. I discounted it, especially with all of our graphene cells fully-loaded, but it was enough to interrupt the loop and short input-capability on all four. Only two of the drives fully recovered."

"And?" Sheffield stops.

Katajima shakes his head. "Even if they all worked, it would simply not be enough."

"All the tests have shown that our apes max-out at around three. Four elastic Hitachi drives should have been more than enough for a momentary insertion."

"Check the synch," exclaims Katajima, sheepishly, trying to keep pace with an infuriated Paul, wagging the tablet aggressively. "Please."

Paul, cutting-down Katajima's demand with a glower wrenched forward, parts the lab doors. "It won't be a problem with the synch...Which ape series did you use?" He seizes the tablet, and raps through medical updates. Stunned, Paul looks up. "Holy shit." The tablet falls with his arm, limp against his leg.

Katajima freezes beside him, and trades his shocked stare at Paul for the cruciform slab at the center of the lab.

Chapter 3: SORTE

NAKED AND MANACLED, the Shef-Ajima Project's Chief Creative Engineer, Allen Scheele, lays splayed on a deathbed he himself designed. An oxygen mask deluges him with cold air, muting his sporadic, involuntary bellows. His purple eyelids darken under heavy-wattage lights that displace the darkness, leaving a black halo that silhouettes both Paul and Katajima.

The engineer has become another John Henry. He lays with chest swollen and body broken after having played the machine and lost. Blood-sickles on his cheeks handle at his nose. *His body is paying the price of forced transubstantiation.*

"The Board was explicit in their terms: no simian return, no human trial."

"Allen was under the distinct impression that you were convinced we were ready…that I was ready."

The Creative Engineer's head bucks back into the table, making a wet clang.

Dr. Sheffield shakes his head in dismay. He points to the altar. "How long has he been screaming like that?"

Katajima shrugs his shoulders, which look like hanger-ends simulating form in an oversized coat.

Paul flicks the intercom switch. It fuzzes on. "Nurse?"

"Yes, Doctor?"

"I want Allen sedated."

"I'm afraid he already is."

Allen's screams treble into disheartening yelps.

"Then give him something stronger."

"Yes sir."

"Fools! I knew it was premature. But a human? *Allen?*"

"We were running behind schedule. You told me…"

"What did I *tell you?*"

Katajima's face grows even paler. "You are not yourself, Paul." He pulls a chair between them. "I have the message saved…"

Paul plows forward, casting the chair aside. "Liar!" Paul's voice rasps into an incoherent growl. "Kill Allen and defame me? I'll have your designation for this."

The scorned scientist worms his way back into a bay of holographics and LED screens, and throws out his feeble arms in defensive anticipation. Paul's upper lip curls back revealing a set of yellowed canines.

"Paul, Paul! Stop to think! For the love of God, we need to save Allen…"

The cautionary yellow beacon at the centre of the room turns red. Paul glances over, and unknots his fists. He returns his glare to Katajima, and hides his teeth beneath a fleshy veneer of civility.

"Reset the receiver."

Off the ropes, Katajima slides a broadcast deck out of a small server tower, and claws at the tuners. The broadcast beacon twinkles above Allen's uninhabited form, green potential patterned third in the sequence.

Paul rolls up his sleeves, and scales the stage to check the gauge on the eight-armed mobile suspended over Allen's head. With a finger-flick, the beacon no longer reads yellow-yellow-green, but instead offers up a solid red rectangle.

"Allen's hyper-stimulated." Paul keys into the gurney-interface and prompts a diagnostic. "His off-board memory— *his memex*—and his brain are incompatible."

"How?" asks Katajima.

Paul winces, mulling over alternatives to the unavoidable.

"I cannot run him through the main." An anxious edge cuts through Katajima's tight-knit lips. "It would crash the broadcast."

"Catch-22."

"Huh?" asks Katajima, sounding more like a gasp than a question.

"He's finished. If we were dealing with a located mind, we'd be looking at three-hundred elastic terabytes, or a single, solid LT-pentabyte. The kind of capacity he needs now...we simply don't have, and if we had it, we'd have needed it ten minutes ago."

"Say *we did* run him through the main," says Katajima, grasping at straws. "Copy his current partition and direct all neural traffic to a less restrictive space..."

"You'd be extracting one person from two places and storing him in a third. *If* he survived, he'd be an incoherent jumble in an immaterial prison."

Katajima dashes to the controller desk. Rejecting both his colleague's analysis and his computer's prognosis with a slap against its projection-sphere, he snaps up: "Cardiac arrest."

"Nurse!" bellows Paul, gesturing cartoonishly to the voyeurs biting nails in the rafters. "Get down here."

One of the catwalk-specters looking-on descends into the pit. She dislodges a trolley from its station, and rolls it over to an adjacent stage, similarly washed in antiquated florescence.

"Ever assist with a back-alley electroshock?" Paul asks.

The nurse nervously shakes her head.

"ECT's the only option on the table. Dr. Katajima will accept full responsibility for any and all consequences, so you needn't worry about any liability or losing your license."

Overhearing this, Katajima bites his lip and continues abusing his keyboard.

Sondra, denoted by the sloppily-penned tag on her tunic, ogles Allen. She's already sweated through her surgical green, and the sight of Allen overloading merely expands her pit-haloes. "Can we use paddles around the machines?"

"Let's find out." Paul feigns a smile so insincere that it disheartens the both of them.

"Paul!" exclaims Katajima. "If it is not the synch-up—"

"It's not…"

"Then we re-route him through his Oasis construct. It'll be familiar territory, and far more linear and cogent a virtual space than the alternative. Besides affording him an opportunity and a place to recompose his thoughts, it will give us enough time to desynchronize him—to *rain him out.*"

"The Oasis construct…"

"It runs off a separate, dedicated drive. Large enough to store him a hundred-times over."

Heads bob in agreement.

Sondra stands, a living picture of uncertainty, on the stage's rim, halved by competing light and shadow. "Should I inform next-of-kin?"

Katajima shakes his head, hoping Paul's too busy to have overheard the question.

Paul bulls through safety locks and emergency routines on his medical tablet, hoping to transmigrate Allen's de-localized self. He thumbs the sequence ready, and spins it into an offering. Katajima reaches for the tablet.

Paul holds on for an extra second, squeezing as much disdain and frustration he can manage through a grimace to his colleague. "Buffer the Oasis and hope to God it works."

Katajima yanks on the tablet.

Paul seizes Shouta's retracting wrist. "Remember: you fall alone."

KATAJIMA SKIRTS the medical terminals, alight with holographic glare. A malapropos melody tolls from one of the computers. He pivots, and coils over the dash.

"It's up," he says.

A red, green, and blue lattice forms above Allen's bloody husk, now at home in two realities. The holographic lines and colours fuse and morph, constructing a low-res visualization of the two-pentabyte Oasis construct. It's a photo-realistic virtual world, maligned by surrealistic architecture and fauna. Whereas the CLOUD is a space defined by the person or persons actively imagining it, the Oasis is bound to the set of laws Allen set for it. Paul imagines it's a close approximation to an acid-trip-inspired video game, not that he has any real experience with either.

This prototypic cyber world is an eclectic graveyard now housing Allen's dreams and nightmares, initially abandoned because of its restrictive linearity. Allen designed it to serve as a tutorial bay off the noospheric river; calm water, perfect for launching.

"God Almighty! What's all that?"

"Our lab rat has been busy." Katajima adjusts the color converter.

Sand-swept, naked, and alone, Allen lies in a fetal position under an angularly-impossible diamond building and a waterfall spouting from a tear in an azure sky. A vast, virtual desert surrounds him, populated by frivolous monstrosities, egotistically watermarked and gorily decorated. Like escaped creatures from a Dali painting, they lumber about on lanky legs unguided, trailing two-dimensional smoke, simulating a circumference to Allen's navigable field. *Despite the place's geometrical perfection, it's horrible…simply horrifying.*

Paul sighs. He looks to the nightmare's engineer, Allen, whose body is unable to reintegrate his mind, calm water or not. "Mirror current visual, aural, and SIMHAP (i.e. simulated haptic/physical) inputs." Paul futilely grasps Allen's shoulder, reminding himself that this man, though seriously flawed, was not horribly unpleasant, and was worth exponentially more than Kim and his subhuman predecessors. "Scale-back all inputs and page Oni. We need all hands on deck."

The shaking stops.

"I have him," mutters Katajima, relieved. Katajima opens a line to the Oasis, where his words thunder and resonate like divine revelation.

—ALLEN. *THIS IS SHOUTA. YOU ARE GOING TO BE ALRIGHT. PAUL AND I ARE GOING TO LOCALIZE*—

Allen intuits an interruption from his arid purgatory:

—NOT ALRIGHT.

On the holographic visualization of the Oasis, Allen stands up and looks around. His self-perception has taken creative license where his manhood is concerned, rendering him something of a vaudeville cartoon.

Paul pushes Katajima out of the way. "He's screwed," he exclaims, through a mouthful of saliva. "Look at this."

On the glowing medical report between them pulses a death sentence. Allen's EROS brain scan, centered by data-flows, reveals dying activity. His belfry greys and then darkens. The data stream Allen'd engaged in the CLOUD had exponentially increased his mental activity and virtual memory. *There is now no real correlation between the synapses previously routed and those required to run his new intellect.* Allen's brain can no longer fit his mind. If they localize him, the balloon will destroy the container or pop in the process of their trying.

Paul throws Katajima's tablet into a "confidential-articles" box brimming with other bad ideas. The clang alarms Katajima, and prompts more gasps from the rafters.

"Regardless of whether he gave consent, *you're* the authority here and *you* knew better. He was expecting a steady flow in cyberspace, and you obliterated him with a flood. This is…" Paul wags his finger at Allen, growing purple, "Mental rape, rape and murder."

"Do not throw the rule book at me, when it has yet to be written. Besides, you really are the last person here to pitch condemnation…"

"Call your lawyer, Shouta. Forget what we are outside of work. I simply cannot and will not sit silent."

"Do not tangle me in your hate-love relationship with the work we are doing here. Allen might be fine, after all…"

"Whatever you do—whatever happens—do not let him waste away in there. If Winchester consents, you can get Allen the space he needs, but by that time he'll already have become a vegetable. His nervous system is fried."

"So that is it then? Just type 'die,' then hit enter?"

"When it comes to it, erase him and wipe the drive. Hell, erase the entire Oasis construct. It's the humane thing to do."

Katajima stares helplessly at Allen's body, terrified and unbelieving. Paul pushes him out of the way and opens the query.

—ALLEN. THIS IS PAUL. GOOD WORK, YOU IMPETUOUS CHILD. FULL DISCLOSURE: I HAVE AN APE IN THE OTHER ROOM THAT NEARLY DIED LEARNING BASIC ENGLISH, AND FIVE SERIES OF CADAVERS I STILL CAN'T FULLY EXPLAIN.

—IMPETUOUS CHILD? THAT'D MAKE YOU THE IRRESPONSIBLE PARENT, NO?

—…

—DAMN.

—'DAMN' IS RIGHT.

—I JUST TAUGHT MYSELF SWARM PROGRAMMING AND ADVANCED CALCULUS. DOWNLOADED ALL THE AUDIO BOOKS THAT WERE ACCESSIBLE THROUGH OUTLAND'S DIGITAL MARKETPLACE. BECAME A RENAISSANCE MAN IN THREE MINUTES.

Paul covers his awe-slacked jaw with one hand, and directs Katajima to a different console with the other.

—I'M GOING TO HAVE TO RUN THE PILOT PROTOTYPE UNTIL WE CAN FIND A WAY TO FIT YOU BACK IN THIS PALE, FLABBY VESSEL.

—WHAT?

—WE CAN'T LOOP YOU BACK. WITHDRAWAL WOULD OVERWHELM YOUR BODY. THE PATHWAYS AREN'T THERE. IT'D SHORT YOUR MIND, AND THEN YOU'D BE SCREWED IN TWO PLACES. THE PILOT DEVICE WILL MANAGE YOUR BASIC MOTOR-FUNCTION AND ENSURE YOUR BODY'S OKAY WITHOUT ITS MASTER AND COMMANDER.

—CAN'T LOOP?

—NO.

—TRY, WILL YOU?

—KATAMJIMA'S WORKING ON IT.

—HE DAMN-WELL BETTER. WHY DO I GET THE FEELING I'VE BEEN PAWNED IN A GAME BETWEEN YOU TWO?

—WE WILL TRY EVERYTHING, ALLEN. IN THE MEANTIME, FIND YOUR BEARINGS. THINK RELAXED.

—DON'T FORGET ABOUT ME.

—YOU HAVE MY WORD.

—SERIOUSLY, DON'T LEAVE ME IN HERE…

—WOULDN'T THINK OF IT.

—GOOD. WHEN YOU HAVE A SECOND, SEND ME UP A FEELER OR TWO. ALSO GIVE ME ADMIN ACCESS SO THAT I CAN THINK MYSELF UP A GODDAMN PAIR OF PANTS.

—SURE THING, ALLEN.

—AND PLEASE TELL ISABELLE I'LL BE HOME LATE.

—YOUR GIRLFRIEND?

—MY FIANCE. SHE'S MY EMERGENCY CONTACT. HER COMM-DOT'S ALSO ON MY QUIKSCREEN. WHATEVER YOU DO, DON'T LET HER SEE ME THIS WAY.

—YOU GOT IT, ALLEN.

"Katajima, send him some positive SIMHAP and a visual anchor," says Paul, recoiling from the query box. "He's too far gone to worry about Stendhal Syndrome…"

"I put him on the mouse-pleasure circuit. He hits a button, he receives the SIMHAP."

"Good. And make sure the anchor simulates the regular passage of time."

"Wouldn't we want to slow it down or suspend it altogether?"

"You know what?" Paul throws his hands up. "You do whatever you want. That's all this is, anyway, *right?*"

Katajima breaks eye-contact and programs a micro-drive. He silently prints it, and inserts it into the spidery mobile dangling above Allen's head.

Paul backs-up Allen's medical scans and contemplates this empty sign—this rasping body kept alive by a PILOT device: it is as disconnected to the living Allen as a photograph is to the photographed.

"Sondra?"

"Yes, Dr. Sheffield?"

"Forget the paddles. We're actually going to protect his brain. Get whatever anesthetic you need to put Mr. Scheele into a coma."

TINGED A BROWNISH-ORANGE, Katajima's collar rises above his head which is tucked into the arch of his stomach. "What are we going to do?"

"You mean, what are *you* going to do?"

Katajima looks genuinely betrayed. "Sure."

"Nothing…Unless you've figured out soul-transmigration." A desperate laugh escapes him. "Either way, you're going to have to bury somebody."

Katajima slumps forward, and traipses over to one of Allen's medical monitors. "For the love of God…"

"Why do you keep saying that?"

"Huh?"

"You keep saying that over and over like it'll help."

"I have you to blame, Paul. Remember the translation app you synched to my Monocle?"

"No."

"The program that helped me with my English, also provided me with a number of linguistic ticks. 'For the love of God' was a teachable-phrase that just stuck with me. This is the first it has irked you; I know for a fact you have heard me say it before."

"I've just realized how goddamned annoying it is."

"Yes, well; like I said: it has become something of a tick…I also enjoy using 'tarnation.'"

Paul nods, indifferent and tired.

"Paul, there must be something. Some way…"

Clicking his tongue, Paul stands up. "Save his data. There's no way you'll get your hands on the kind of memory that's necessary in the time that he has left, if he had any to begin with—even with Winchester's juice. If you're feeling *really* compassionate, you can populate the Oasis construct with as many carnal delights as you're able to script before he's looped in without an origin or a brain to center him."

"How long can he survive in there?"

"Well, if you don't know, I imagine your only recourse is to ask God...or the Devil."

Chapter 4: **RAPTURE**

>TEN_YEARS_LATER

"Hey Paul."

"Who's this?"

"It has been a while since we last spoke."

"This is a restricted line."

"Allen Scheele died last night."

"Katajima?"

"Something inside the CLOUD disabled his PILOT, thereby suffocating his paralyzed body. Winchester believes it was a hacktivist trying to make a name for herself, or at the very least, a political statement. There are other rumours circulating...In any event, he is gone."

"What time is it?"

"Paul, I am sorry. It is really important that we not blame ourselves..."

"Jesus, it's four-thirty."

"You heard what I said?"

"Allen. Allen Scheele's dead. *Again*."

"Yes. And it is not your fault."

"That I've already convinced myself of. Although, I don't imagine there are many others who share my certainty."

"One perhaps, but she is a criminal. If it is any consolation..."

"He was interred *for a decade* in Outland Labs, resigned to digital death in a sand castle of his own making. *Trust me*, it won't be."

"If you recall, it was your idea to unplug him."

"Ten years ago, maybe."

"Well, he followed a different trajectory to the same result."

"The lot of you are insane...Outland's a mad house."

"Paul, that is certifiably untrue."

"Well, if he's off to hell, at least it's a better one..."

"We tried to broadcast him."

"Oh?"

"CLOUD's not the end of the world, you know."

"Shouta, no one said anything about it ending the world. It does all the good we'd hoped it would do, revolutionizing psychological therapies, diplomacy, and whatever else."

"Spoken like a proud father."

"Was Chronos proud?"

"Your mythology is lost on me as always."

"If the CLOUD is ending anything, it's the age of the individual. Our insidious spawn—this noosphere—is a dehumanized nirvana. It's other people, perdition, oblivion. It's no damn good."

"You have certainly not lost your knack for the melodramatic. I doubt that all those with Alzheimer's, Parkinson's, dementia, and Autism would share your views. Even your sweet Pythia benefitted, *no*?"

"Not from the CLOUD...*What is this*? Did you call to lecture me?"

"Paul..."

"I'm terming the hail. Goodbye."

"Funeral's Friday."

"..."

"At St. Monica's in the city. Winchester has cleared me to send his Dragonfly to pick you up as well as temporarily suspend your restraining order. You might even be able to visit Rachel and the girls...Are you still there?"

"Yes."

"The Dragonfly can be at your retreat at nine-thirty Wednesday morning, granted you temporarily turn off your air defenses."

"*Air defenses?*"

"You are enough coy to run an algae pond. The carrier-pigeon drone that my assistant sent your way with word of Allen's passing notified me of your rockets just seconds before being vaporized."

"Ha! I suppose that's why I missed the memo."

"…"

"I don't know, Shouta. I've got shit to do."

"*If* you change your mind, I strongly advise you to take Winchester up on his offer. He would be relieved to ease your way to common ground. After all, the Hyperloop sky-transit system is awfully dreadful, and I am told you have developed something of an antipathetic following in the wake of *your* creation's coming-of-age. Driving is similarly perilous with the checkpoints and the risk of a run-in with escaped PIT rats. The Dragonfly and the extra day are really your best option, and I, personally, would appreciate having some time to speak to you before the funeral."

"I'll let you know."

"For the love of God, take care of yourself, Paul. Notify me if you change your mind, especially regarding the proposed ride. I know it would make me feel a lot better. Oh, one more thing, I meant to call about it earlier: Winchester has voiced concern over your NEXUS chip being wonky. Worried about you breaching the terms of the settlement. You should probably look into it."

"Definitely."

"Well, goodnight. Sorry to be the bearer of bad news."

"Hold up—"

"Yeah?"

"When did you say Allen died?"

"Says here it was last night…Not much later than ten Pacific. Why? Why do you ask?"

"What did you do with his off-board memory? His memex drive?"

"Looped his memex to Outland archives, and wiped the drive twice-over. It was a standard procedure. What is up? *Paul?*"

"Nothing. Never mind."

Chapter 5: STRANGER IN MY OWN SKIN

THE VINYL FLOOR, compulsively polished, reflects the greens, yellows, and reds, from the lower shelves. It squeaks at Paul's tanker boots as he makes his way up the aisle to the UtilMart clerk station.

He pauses below a silent hologram radiating Commander Cromwell's dispatch from the southern RIM. The headline reads, "The inter-partition violence between Outland Defense Forces and PIT gangs has worsened, spilling this time into eastern Burbank and the North-Hollywood CBLOCKS." The projection orients to Paul's line of sight, pulling the visualized riots sideways.

A band of pulsing pomegranate text signs the play-by-play: "Thirteen dead, hundreds wounded. No arrests have been made so far. Outland Security has teamed up with the LAPD and NORTHCOM to identify and apprehend the agitators. Outland Corp. is offering an award of sixteen-months airtime and/or reinstallation in exchange for any viable leads regarding the identity or whereabouts of the assailants. Chief Constable Scott has warned that 'anyone harboring or sheltering a dissident will similarly be desynchronized and rained out, and those without implants will be tagged for Federal re-processing.' Among those wanted for questioning, Dr. O—" Paul swats his hand at the notice. The riotous-pomegranate swirl disappears. *At least they've kept their revolution south of the mountains.*

UtilMart is crowded with basic shit RIM ticks and part-time CLOUD flyers need to get by: brown and white-striped ration-putty cartridges for 3D-printed InstaMeals (chicken, beef, veggie, or fish); booze and drugs; augmentations and cosmetics; and air-time gift certificates.

Pacing down the ultra-lit aisle, Paul stumbles upon his intended purchase. He runs his finger along a row of SIK-branded medication bottles filed neatly on an aluminium rack.

"Ol' faithful," he mouths to himself, grabbing a turquoise bottle. *Anti-psychotics.*

Paul probably should have always been taking these triangular anti-psychotics. *Might have been the difference between Allen living or dying.* Prior to his scandalous ejection from Outland and exile to the wastes on the southern tip of the Mojave, Paul deluded himself into thinking he'd a pretty good handle on his mind.

Mood chips and chem-rehab weren't alternatives he would ever consider, even now. Part of his interest when first building the CLOUD was precisely that: to resolve negative thinking, nightmares, PTSD, cognitive malignancies, and mental illness, through influence and mental bridging.

Paul's lab assistant, Oni, had undoubtedly glimpsed his madness, at least once or twice, but the hierarchy binding them bade her defer worry, assume caution, and practice understanding. Katajima, Rachel, Pythia, and Angela, on the other hand, never saw an episode full-on. If there was something weird about Paul, something insidious or imbalanced, they'd written it off as a quirk of an intelligent, eclectic personality. Paul had hoped that he'd cure himself before they realized that he was unfit to cure others.

Paul makes sure he's taken the right bottle—*because sometimes they change the colours or the branding, and you've got to be sure.* "Close enough," he mouths silently, heading over to pay.

Behind two competing advertorial holograms (i.e. "holoverts"), a short, stout man with a mesh-back hat crammed full of sunken Mayan features stands motionless. His arms are both crooked at ninety degrees, framing the e-ledger with dehydrated fingers. In southern California, stocked with automatic kiosks and virtual salesmen, UtilMart's human clerk is as anachronistic and irremediable as Paul, pleasure-seeking in the non-physical world while his body operates on auto-pilot without him.

"Morning, Roddy," Paul grumbles, reflexively, placing the bottle on the counter.

Roddy's eyes meet Paul's, but there is no connection— no soulful recognition. Paul coyly checks over his shoulder, and wrinkles his forehead, looking at Roddy's insinuated point of focus: a water-damaged wall, gummed up by religious literature. 'BEWARE THE MARK OF THE BEAST' bleeds over a hack-artist's rendition of a cognitive-implant in the imprecise ink of yesteryear.

Paul waves his hands in front of Roddy's face. Smiling through impatience, he shouts his name. The aproned effigy doesn't flinch. "Ah, never figured you for an evap," Paul deplores. Paul thinks "evap" is *his* clever term for someone who's synchronized to the CLOUD, although it is used commonly throughout California.

A wave of sentience floods Roddy's face, and his cheek-muscles twitch alive. "Sorry, Paul," he whispers in a crackly monotone, adjusting his hat. A few greasy locks fall free. "How're those girls of yours?"

Paul tilts his head with a smile, unexpectedly pleased with the familiarity. "Ah, you know," *as much as I do, anyway*, "just keep getting bigger and bigger," Paul's shaky voice evens on the wake of nostalgia. "What's new with you?"

Grating his coarsely-bearded throat, Roddy surveys the room. He finally plots his eyes on the counter, refusing to share Paul's gaze. "Was just watching the game."

"Oh yeah? What's the score?"

"The score?"

Paul laughs. "Yeah, who's winning? Flames and Richmond Capitals're playing today, right?"

Scarlet spills across the clerk's cheeks. "Oh. Let me check." He swipes a new page onto his e-ledger and intuits his query.

Paul glimpses the inverted score: 0-0. *It hasn't even started yet.* This oily automaton was probably basking in one of the CLOUD's more nefarious SIMPHAP pleasure forums.

Roddy's finger hesitates above the score.

"It's okay. Forget about it," Paul says, offering Roddy an out, and pushing the SIK bottle forward.

"Cool. Did I link your receipt?"

"Haven't paid yet, friend. Just these and," Paul scans the shelves of hermetically-sealed cannaberette packs behind the clerk, registering his brand peripherally—*the red, pinstriped prism*: "a pack of Walruses."

Paul'd been addicted to cigarettes before the InsurWide Ban. Not so much the nicotine they promised or the multiplicity of diseases they threatened him with, but rather the simple act of spitting smoke. When social convention became law, he switched over to a heavy-handed heavily-taxed indica. The Walruses offer him the same draconic recreation as cigs, plus they help with the SIK-pill-induced nausea.

"Paying with credit or airtime?" Roddy inquires, handing over a pack of cannaberettes.

"Credit, thanks." Paul runs his wrist over the e-ledger and it beeps, consummating the transaction. "Keep your eyes peeled for RIM ticks." Paul points to the hologram. "There's smoke on the horizon."

Roddy deflates with a tinny laugh. "Yeah! I'll do that."

Paul smiles, awkwardly, and turns to leave, pocketing the SIK bottle.

The ledger fires a projection showing an imbalance, emphasized by two long beeps.

"Sorry, Paul," says Roddy.

UtilMart's front door bars-over.

"Huh?" asks Paul, breaking-down into an awkward pose.

"I can't sell you the SIK."

Paul edges over, wincing at the ledger. "That can't be right."

"I'll lose my license."

"Yeah? I'll lose a lot more. I have a prescription…" He angrily yanks the SIK out of his pocket and jostles it onto the counter.

"Well, says *here* your prescription is void."

"Sure that's me?" Paul tries to decrypt the backward statements projected above the counter.

Roddy recoils, discomforted by forced intimacy over his ledger. "Please refrain—"

Paul recognizes his overreach, and steps back. "Sorry."

"That's okay." Roddy recomposes himself. "Any chance your insurers got wise to your habits?"

"No," he draws-out in a sigh. Paul's head sinks between his shoulders. "I disabled the bowl app. Haven't got a PILOT or an implant…"

Roddy nods suggestively to Paul's Walruses.

"They've no way of knowing."

"You might not be synched-up, Paul, but a friend of yours, possibly?"

"No."

"Family?"

"No," Paul replies quickly, visibly frustrated.

"Hey, man. Anyone and everyone's a snitch. Heck, they've got access to my memex."

"But you're not giving *everything* away…"

43

"Privacy-locks keep out other users, but not the admins, not the bigwigs. Outland's got to be selling that intel to the corporations—to the banks, the insurance companies...*Hell*—ever since my accident, I can't have a beer without my insurance premium going up."

Paul pinches the ridge of his nose. "Jeeze."

"Even my neighbour! Made some minor modifications to his apartment. His landlord referenced my memex number in the petty lawsuit against him. Three-months-worth of airtime up in a flash. Poor guy."

"That's got to be a breach of trust...an invasion of privacy or something."

Roddy laughs. "Privacy? Shit. I don't know what to tell you, Paul. All I know is that if anyone's ripped bad Intel on you, you're in hot water." He folds his arms, satisfied with having completed his first cogent thought of the day.

"Alright." Paul pushes the SIK forward, hanging his head in half-realized shame. "Just the Walruses today." Eye contact. "But get your scanner checked. So far as anyone's concerned, I'm on the straight and narrow. There's no way..."

"Sure thing, Paul."

Shaking his head in silent protest, Paul peels the red tape on the pack and turns to leave. "Ciao."

"So long, Paul."

Paul simpers. "Enjoy the rest of the game."

"Huh? Oh yeah. Absolutely." Roddy hooks a half-smile, and leans forward, closing the e-ledger with a flick. Cheeks aflame with embarrassment, he sees Paul out with a nod.

Paul drags his feet, creating du-wops off the vitric floor. As the door sweeps back into its frame, followed by the crossbar, Roddy synchronizes to the CLOUD, leaving his body, once again, inert.

Turning one into the flame of his lighter, Paul Sheffield tucks the rest of the Walruses away. Heavy with the dose, he looks back slowly, through the wire-mesh, to see Roddy lean back into a morbid pose. *Bloody human wasteland.*

Chapter 6: **BREAKING EVEN**

PAUL CLAMORS into his '29 *Rapid* FürE, and slams the door shut behind him. He looks down the neon strip with bloodshot eyes to mesas hemming the blue sky. *Barstow, California—the northernmost tip of the RIM.* The rich, the elites, and paying Outland subscribers live in the Blue Zone, formerly Los Angeles central; low-tech, low-lives live in the hell-hole known as the *PIT*, squeezed against and under the mountains; and everyone else lives along the RIM, including Paul. In Paul's case, it's not by choice.

He once had a nice bungalow in the city, a twenty minute drive to his lab at the Outland Corporation's former headquarters. For the role he played—unwittingly or not—in Allen Scheele's death, he was exiled to this big-city satellite, a sand-carved settlement rife with crime and old tech.

Barstow is far enough away from the Los Angeles Blue Zone for Winchester to feel safe from the perceived threat of a technological riposte from a disgruntled former employee. The old technocrat's sense of security was doubly assured with the tracking beacon—an M-series NEXUS chip—buried in Paul's thigh. Paul couldn't go anywhere without his former boss knowing, which is precisely why he'd recently hacked it, dug it out, and chipped-it into one of his housemates. *Winchester has no business knowing mine, especially when my business is ultimately bringing down the CLOUD.*

Paul sets a waypoint on his GPS slat: a pay-terminal on the way to his retreat. He'd automate his payments, if it wasn't for the satisfaction he took in secreting money away to his family before his creditors took their share.

He pulls out of the UtilMart lot, and onto the main drag, corralled by sun-bronzed signs and holographic dancers kicking their pixelated legs over uninviting store fronts.

The fiber terminal Paul'd marked as a destination, decaled with some libertarian propaganda about the "age of state omniscience," waits ahead, off the side of the road, for his delinquent paychecks. It's surrounded by fuming, maglev transports.

With his truck idling behind him, Paul plods over to the pay terminal, stuck with the feeling he's being watched. He pulls his financial microchip out of his shirt pocket, and blesses the machine with a vertical swipe.

Over by the nearest transport, a man and a woman both wearing onyx exosuits creak on their reinforced legs, staring warily at Paul. Paul finds himself nodding to validate their presence *and potential threat.* He smiles, dumbly, and subtly thumbs the electro-blade on his belt, ignoring the transactions and debts tallied on the projection before him. With a SIK scalene or two, he'd have the stability to recognize or dismiss the voyeurs as a threat. Now, with trembling hands, he'll just have to wait.

The terminal queries Paul, demanding him to submit his most recent employment file. He'd written a script just for this purpose. He waves his wristband over the scanner. So far as the City of Los Angeles and the Outland Corporation are concerned, Paul is nothing more than a solar farmer, which is only half true.

Since going into exile, Paul's been supplementing his severance pay working odd jobs for a Navajo tech-dealer named Mansueito. The power cells he carts off to Barstow Energy lend credibility to his cover operation, and double to provide him with that *little extra* to keep him whole.

At first, he had considered becoming an experience-fetcher, grabbing interesting stimuli for all the CLOUD's voyeurs and the agentially-retarded. Venture somewhere interesting or do something extraordinary, and then sell the associated memories. Didn't pan out, though, largely because of his fear of unintentionally uploading personal information, not limited to his crazy thoughts and secrets. If the CLOUD ever got into his head, his fractured mind would clear him of the charges Outland doled out, but it would also make his subsequent criminal activity public record. *Not worth the risk.* The benefits of Paul's particular technological know-how are, therefore, inaccessible to the disembodied public.

Aware of his monopoly on this fringe of information and ability, Paul decided to market his rare skillset to anyone off the Outland circuit with a checking account. Besides, the tech he needs for his personal projects isn't exactly free.

Every problem, including visibility or a rogue android, has a tech fix or a final solution, and Paul can make it happen. Choke-collar CCTV blinders. Cowboy-tech. EMP knots. Headspace hacks. And, luckily for Paul, just about everyone needs a fix: RIM mercenaries, white-palace detectives, PIT hookers, wasteland slugs; you name it—they all have his dots. High tech for lowlifes for hard cash on a second's notice. It isn't a clean, lead-scientist position at Outland, but it certainly isn't starving.

Even with the dirty money he pockets subverting the G-Men, he doesn't see much at month's end. By the time the money makes its way into his pockets, the Outland-infiltrated government turns them out, lint and all, in exchange for services he won't receive.

After three court hearings and a private meeting with members from city council, Paul and *antiques* like him were ordered to pay Outland maintenance and tower charges, even though they were slumming it outside of the city. And although he used neither of the two services, the powers that be expressed indifference to his predicament, the majority of them having been backed and compensated in advance by Winchester. So long as you were within city limits (i.e. within the markers, haphazardly dropped throughout the sprawl), you were required to pay in full. The temptation to move further out of state was always there, but Paul wanted to be close to his kids, however estranged. And besides, his restraining order and parole didn't leave him much wiggle room.

Pythia and Angela get the bulk of his cash. They were just babies when he lost his Outland job—when Rachel left him. Now they're little cadets with big ideas. His monthly swipe ensures that Pythia gets the medical treatment and therapy she needs for her cognitive infirmity. The rest, Paul presumes, is for groceries.

Again, Paul puts money into the plate, without ever a hope of seeing any kind of redemption or return. His efforts are squandered to serve those rotting in the gutters, keeled over protein bars in caffeine houses, or glass-eyed in UtilMarts.

The fiber-terminal projects a graphic of his remaining balance. *No debt, no savings.* Paul sneers. If there's still income left after all the government dips, it'll go towards Pythia's upgrade: a pair of cochlear implants and a transmitter in her Broca's Area, none of which is still insured by Outland. Paul's not the first creator to get absolutely brutalized as a show of thanks for his beneficence.

Paul looks up nervously at the exosuits before pocketing his financial microchip. They're busy changing one of the magnetic harnesses on their rig. *You're so goddamned paranoid*, he scolds himself. He steps away from the fiber terminal, zips up his jacket, and heads back to his truck.

Inside the humming compartment, he marks his retreat as the endpoint on his GPS, and leans back, mind untaxed and ready to go to work. Dante Alighieri damned his enemies while living in exile; Paul's ready to go one step further.

Chapter 7: SNAKE-HOLED KINGDOM

PAUL PULLS OFF Irwin Road onto a gravel driveway about eighteen minutes outside of Barstow. The detour is neither numbered nor marked by any other kind of signage. It is not on any map, at least not plainly defined. Over the next fifteen grid-lined and pixelated miles fed by satellite imaging to Paul's dash, nothing stands out, no more than anywhere else in San Bernardino County. Just the same cholla- and creosote-speckled desolation, minus a kilometre-long, one-hundred foot mesa.

To a misguided motorist facing south, it'd look like nothing more than a ruin on a Cretaceous hill, humbled and worn by time. That is exactly the kind of characterlessness Paul needs to go about his business in exile.

Dirt and debris, kicked back by the maglev stabilizers, blossom behind the truck as it moans up the serpentine track towards Paul's retreat: an adobe, wood, and steel cottage, built into the mesa.

The driveway ahead bypasses a grouping of red boulders. The tallest ensconces a sensor array that's already decided not to pulverize the vehicle with a barrage of incendiary rockets. Paul buries the array in his orange wake and slows at the base of a sandy buttress—the last leg of the ascent—permitting the loosed sand to catch up.

Securitas, an artificial intelligence Paul had developed on spec for the military and later modified to sate his own domestic-security demands, recognizes the truck's transponder and retracts the spikes and magnetic caltrops camouflaged at the base of the incline. Paul floors the truck to get over the last hump, and eases-off at the sight of the weathered façade hewn into the shale, in transition from an egg-shell blue to the colour of rot. *Home, sweet home.* With one last depression of the pedal, Paul veers to the bitter end of the driveway, knotted beneath the front door of the retreat. He stops and turns off the engine.

He gets out to the sound of ticking and desert static; the former metred to the engine-block's cooling and contracting, and the latter, sporadic—one billion insects dopplered, rustling in and around windblown junipers and cottonwoods. Roddy, the UtilMart chickenhead clerk in town, calls it the "deafening silence."

"You listen hard enough," he told Paul, "and you can hear nature's basest commands." *Always wondered whose life-experience, uploaded to the CLOUD, informed Roddy's idea that day.*

Paul swings around to hook the truck up to charge. *Ff-fa-sh* goes the power cables, channelling energy to the battery Paul'd exhausted running errands, which had almost been a complete success. *Two out of three's not half-bad.*

Paul interrupts his inspection of the flat bed for items he'd forgotten or shouldn't forget to turn on his Monocle eyewear. The graphical interface flits across his iris and prompts him with myriad options. Amidst the star field of executables and icons, one figures prominently at the top-left corner of his vision: a prison-barred 'S'. It shakes, responding to Paul's intention—decrypted in a nano-second by the Monocle's neuro- and eye-movement sensors. The 'S' expands to a black screen, which is immediately replaced by a talk-to-text window addressed to Securitas.

"All clear?" Paul comms the AI, immersed both in the virtual and the real.

"Apart from an innocuous, natural perimeter breach at 11:46:32—which was resolved without force—Sheffield HQ is *pristine*." Securitas' diction and tempo is precise; as natural and efficient as Paul's parameters will allow. "Cerebus Secondary confirms diagnosis."

"Thank you, Securitas. Monitor the perimeter and scan the comms."

"Yes, Dr. Sheffield."

Paul disables the electrical reinforcement on the front door with a finger swipe on the adjoining scanner. The door swings inward, revealing a modest foyer overrun with polycarb boxes. Scribbles, robot designs, and other writ-on-tree wad the walls. He enters, knocking a pile of disordered thought over, closes and then deflates against the door.

Securitas' paranoid entry-beep rouses the attention of Paul's only remaining flesh-and-blood cohorts: a pair of mutts. Paul hears them on the other side of the retreat, bowling over one another, yelping and barking, and skittling across the floor.

"Hey guys," he yells, priming their excitement.

With tongues swishing, they both bolt out of the central hallway connecting the front foyer to the living quarters sequestered on the far side. The first, a German-shepherd/coyote hybrid—the colour of Boreal-forest decay—and the second, a bionic Rottweiler—painted in the traditional black and tan of his fierce ancestors—find him with noisome, albeit welcoming, kisses. Overjoyed about their master's return, they run circuits around him, yapping with their ears pinned back.

Oni had recommended that Paul find himself some canine company with Rachel gone and Outland sending him into quarantine. He'd hoped she would commit as *company*, but had to face facts and sewer delusion. She'd be promoted with him gone. In any event, Paul ended up with two dependents; the second to provide consistency to the first when he couldn't.

The dogs scramble back down the hall to the kitchen, this time with Paul in tow. He motions to turn-on the string of LED lanterns stationed along the passage, but defers, seeing ample rays gild his pups.

At the juncture of the hallway and the cliff-side of his retreat, Paul bows to open a hidden panel. A biometric scanner prompts him for his handprint. Certain with a high-five, it retracts, offering, instead, a button. Paul hammers it, and two purple energy fences sever the hallway behind him. Nothing can get through or past them. For some people, freedom is a tank full of gas and an open road. For Paul, freedom is being all-that-he-can-be in a well-stocked hole, out of reach and out of sight.

Paul skirts around the main floor, double-checking to make sure Securitas hadn't overlooked any unwanted visitors. The AI had already flubbed once, permitting an antagonistic android Paul'd been charged to reprogram to make herself at home. For its transgressions, Paul assigned Securitas a distinct, secondary awareness, codenamed Cerebus, to assure quality and scrutinize response at the most elementary level.

Satisfied with a somewhat-thorough look around, Paul enters the kitchen—a chaos of wires, small pieces of tech, and paper squares covered in various dot configurations. Paul summons up the dot gram sitting on the top of the pile.

He activates his heads-up display, rooted under his skin around the temple. This heads-up display, nicknamed *Monocle*, automatically draws a holographic file from the Net using the coordinates insinuated by the dot formation on the flap. Paul's Monocle privately projects the hologram ahead of him.

Coloured in bright 3D, Paul reads: "CYPULCHRE TOWER MAINTENCE CHARGES." The Outland Corporation logo—a brain, a cloud, and a pyramid—oscillates above the counter. He crumples the dot gram, terminating the related hologram, and whips it over-shoulder.

The balled invoice doesn't go as far as dramatic necessity would normally dictate, vexing Paul even further.

He seizes up the next dot gram in the pile. "OUTLAND CORPORATION; PRIVATE MEMO— SUBJECT: ANOMALIES, CLOUD; SCHEELE FUNERAL." Paul flicks the introjected screen, which scrolls the message: "HOPE TO SEE YOU. WOULD LIKE TO PICK YOUR BRAIN RE: URGENT MATTER. WILL MAKE IT WORTH YOUR WHILE. REGARDS, S. KATAJIMA, PhD."

An attached holographic of Allen, circa ten years back, appears, conveyed by the dot gram and projected by Paul's Monocle. Allen's brown irises make his shallow eyes seem deeper, drawing attention away from his disproportionately-large ears and his blotchy skin.

Paul closes his hand around Allen's apparition, nullifying the projection. "Persistent bugger."

The Rottweiler scurries over, scratches itself, and then barks at Paul.

"Not you, buddy."

Paul balls up the flap, hoping to outdo his previous subversion of Newtonian physics. Winding up, he notices a warning light on the Kay9 auto feed. The hopper's over-packed with food, all out of reach of the dogs.

"Oh shit," he says, surrendering the flap to the countertop. "I'm sorry guys."

The Rottweiler aggressively paws his leg.

"Chill out," Paul murmurs, circumnavigating the hungry dog.

For a split second, Paul's gloom is alleviated by the prospect of still being needed. He unjams the dispenser. A single kibble was jarred just-so, preventing the wealth dammed behind to issue forth. Paul smiles, and cranks the lever, watching the aesthetically-neutral sustenance bury Apollo and Zeus' bowls.

"Alright, rascals. I gotta go to work." Paul gently knees through the tangle of fur, and steps out of the kitchen—competitive consumption loud behind him.

He saunters into the living room, and trades his pack of Walruses for the coding tablet resting on the oak coffee table, asymmetrically planted out of leg's reach of the couch. He examines his last entry in a long scrawl of code, which—to a stranger's eyes—ostensibly has no logic or recurring themes to it. If it weren't for his computers' consistent and unanimous validation of his code, he would have written the project off as delusional fancy; chalked it up to what Rachel called a "coping mechanism." He blindly stumbles forward, obsessing over the next string of commands and mathematical if-then statements.

"Securitas, disable interior liner on Door Three."

The energy-field fortifying the deck-door crackles and dissipates, giving Paul access to the patio, which juts defiantly outside over his yard, piercing the cone of solar panels humming in the gulley with shadow. At its furthest, it's pillared to thirty feet above the incline.

Cluttered around the patio is a curiosity-shop's store of technological abortions, prototypical implants, and doodads, complimented on the side by two double-locked boxes containing a pair of plasma rifles with no trophies to speak of. Stacked neatly against the lacquered hardwood banister is a cord of Aleppo pine and a box of kindling—his last defense against the midwinter desert chill.

Paul opens the patio door, but waits in the vacant threshold, temporarily content to let his eyes skip across terracotta waves and rock the cradle of cotton-candy clouds weighed-low with the sun.

Returning his attention to the tablet, Paul carefully steps outside, feeling the warmth of the last of the daylight. He looks up without addressing the sun directly with a gaze, and notices a purple and pink cloud-formation separate. The ordinary illuminates the extraordinary: *A fragmentor! I'm going to need a fragmentor*, he realizes. The code rolling down his tablet's screen into obscurity cannot be completed; not now—not without destroying the device and erasing a decade's worth of work.

He bolts back into the retreat, excited about his potential breakthrough, leaving the door open in consideration of any prospective bladder-heavy dog. Paul opens the middle compartment on the pantry-cupboard straddling the divider wall between the kitchen and bathroom, and yanks on a wired-can of ration putty. He recoils from the shelf, clutching the tablet to his breast. There's a click, followed by the sound of whining gears. The cupboard pops up an inch, and slides to the left, leaving a gaping rectangular divot in the floor.

Paul descends into the darkness. The temperature drops, almost a degree by rung. Ten degrees down, he overextends his leading leg, kicking terra firma. With a reflexive twist, he flicks a switch, and a string of lithium lights powers on, washing the cramped tunnel, enclosed by corrugated white-washed walls, in a sterile-looking plum colour.

Preceded by plumes of breath, he ventures down the passage, careful not to bump his head on the piping and fiber-optic cables soldered along the ceiling.

"Securitas, update."

"Perimeter is secure. Comms are clear. Batteries have charged and solar panels are folding."

"Alright," Paul says in a wavering voice. "Cloak the gulley and jam all scans."

Content with having addressed his paranoia, only sometimes warranted, he presses into the tunnel's destination: a small, oil-stained room coned around a crooked desk, cluttered with computer screens, quantum-processors, pickled brains, and wiry mishmash.

A photograph of Rachel and the girls, compulsively thumbed at the corners, leans against a screen set lower in the spider's eye. Paul sits down and looks at it sedately. He hears their voices. The picture reaches out to him with context, undermining his resolve and handle on the past. He hears Rachel telling him to take his time and to relax. Angela's keen to tell him about her day, puppeteering also for little mute Pythia, who says nothing; he feels her silence, just the same. Born with a rare form of autism, she could only mime or sign her affection, always more genuinely than the other two mouths oiled-over with thumb prints.

Paul shakes his head, and digs into the top drawer. He pulls a SIK bottle out, and whips off the top. One scalene left. *Great for treating problems in the short-run, but like the corner-store glasses dad used to buy and wear, the short-term relief bares deleterious long-term consequences.* He pops it, tucks the picture of his estranged family away, and plots his elbows on the desk, covering his eyes with his palms.

"Get a grip, man," his slurs with conviction.

Via a Monocle prompt, he turns all of the screens on. Paul's tablet immediately synchronizes with the amalgam of other whirring, buzzing appliances, and ten-years-worth of code and obsession begin to stream on all monitors. Paul's world-changing Empty Thought varnishes the cave in shades of green.

Ever since creating the CLOUD, he knew he had to be the one to destroy it. That is, when it failed to accomplish what he had intended it to do. *When* wasn't important; *how*, on the other hand…

The Empty Thought started out as an anti-virus program Paul'd been working on in his Outland lab. By fate and with a little bit of tweaking, it became a data singularity *in potentia*. Isolate a malignant tool, file or script, activate the Empty Thought, and then *bam!* Oblivion for the targeted file and anything associated with it; well, anything with a virtual component within reach, really. *Electronic antimatter.*

Paul runs a diagnostic on his latest line of code, proving himself right. *It's as complete as it can be at this stage. What I need...a fragmentor and a cipher.* Easier said than done.

The Empty Thought cannot be contained in its complete form. After all, whatever would save or accommodate it would be ruined. With a data-fragmentor, Paul can conceivably finish the code in segments, and transport the segregated parts to wherever it is he needs them to go. With a fragmentor, the only thing Paul would need is a way of decrypting the code's activator—he'd data-locked it years ago thinking he was doing the world a service.

Paul yanks an old keyboard out of the second desk-drawer, and prompts the centre screen with a query. "FRAGMENTOR, FOR SALE, CALIFORNIA."

A short list of dealers and addresses appears. So far as sellers in the region go, there's an Astro Farnsworth in San Francisco, a Chris Kalnychuk in Anaheim, and an unknown seller in Los Angeles.

Paul queries his aural inbox for comms from Katajima, specifically, comms pertaining to Allen Scheele. One transcript appears, indicating the funeral is in L.A.

Looks like I'm going, after all.

Paul flits on his Monocle and comms Katajima.

Shouta appears. He wipes his face and smiles. "P-S, is that you!?"

"Yeah. Hope I'm not interrupting…"

"Nonsense. Dinner services action, not the other way around." Katajima crooks his head, attempting to identify the place fish-bowled around Paul. "Where are you?"

Paul'd forgotten to turn off the Monocle's visual link. "That's not important," Paul replies, turning off the camera feed.

"Have you considered taking me up on my offer?"

"I have, actually."

"Terrific. Then I will see you on Wednesday."

"Alright. Goodnight, Shouta."

"I am overjoyed—"

Paul terminates the feed.

He already presses his luck working odd-jobs for Mansueito—the man they call "Chief"—in order to bankroll his efforts on the Empty Thought, all of which is in violation of his parole, not to mention in violation of a long list of petty and criminal laws. *Going to LA on business would be suicide. To go there on vacation? An entirely different matter altogether.* Wasting this opportunity because of a ten-year-old grudge would be foolish. *I might be insane, but I'm no idiot.*

Barking upstairs unnerves him. He looks down the corrugated hallway, and back at his bug-eye of screens. With a fluid, finger's dance on the keys, Paul firewalls his invention, ensuring its secrecy and safety.

Apollo is waiting for him at the top of the ladder. He prods Paul with a wet nose before he's even made it out of the hatch.

"What are you on about?" Paul says, thumbing the hair down on the dog's shoulders.

More barking on the patio prompts Paul outside, Apollo following close behind. A magnetic disturbance shakes the house in tandem with a scorching sound. Paul's heard it before. *R50 afterburners on a south-western MAT[erial] transport.* Silt and dust, shaken from the rocky protuberances above, give dimension to the fingernail of light squeezed beneath a sky-full of purple cumulonimbus. Paul rubs his face clean of the speckles, and winces, trying to confirm his suspicion.

The transport thunders over the house and away, trailing heavy black smoke towards the city. A stylized "O," complete with the trademark pyramid, reveal its nature and purpose. *I knew it.* A Spirit Train, carrying with it men and women who've either invested to insulate and forget their physical prisons in order to live unimpeded in the CLOUD, or, conversely, been marked for reprocessing. Either way, they're headed to one Outland Outpost or another.

The Outposts were initially purposed only to hold and broadcast the off-board memories and data saved by California subscribers, permitting them to synch to the CLOUD wirelessly. The locals call them "cypulchres."

Winchester's cypulchres no longer serve merely as signal-boosting server towers. With time, the CLOUD has produced extremists and addicts. Not everyone can afford all the latest CLOUD tech, or the airtime necessary to synchronize in the first place. Most of the population synch from home or from Outland hospices. Those who can fit the bill frequently have their bodies interred in the Outposts, allowing them to evap full-time without worrying about physical maintenance. California's cypulchres, stitching the horizon to the Pacific, are catacombs housing the living dead.

The barking subsides, and the dogs lazily collapse into the sunlight. Paul walks over to the weapon crates, armoured with heavplast—a durable and bulletproof polypropylene—and unlocks the closest with a quick grind of the combination dial, worn-down by repetition. Inside the crate there's a pulse rifle, swaddled in egg foam, and, beside it, a revolver. Paul summons up the revolver, prolapsing its foam outline. He cranks the cylinder open to the side, and blows down the barrel. Jamming it under his belt, he grips the railing, and leans forward, inhaling deeply. "Back into the Blue." *It'll get worse before it gets better.*

Chapter 8: OVER THE MOUNTAIN

BLANK COW EYES find him, inverted in the water droplets rolling down the mirror. Paul breaks his stare with the sad, scared, and lonely animal screened behind his ambition and grizzle, and rinses his comb. He hesitates, looking at the wet hair embroiled around the teeth, and quickly returns the comb to its soapy mold on the acrylic basin. Past his hand he sees the waste bin, flush with bloody rags and dried flecks of tissue. Looks like a Satanist's hamper.

He'd been a naughty outcast, digging Winchester's NEXUS chip out like he had. Worse than the chastisement he'd receive if discovered is the diminished mobility in his left leg. The Outland surgeon was wise to clip it under the *vastus lateralis*, where it'd neither chafe nor bruise, but hitch on over time, requiring extraction by a trained professional. Paul could very well have done it professionally or programmed an android to do the same, but instead elected to electro-knife it out after drinking a bottle of bourbon. The rags remind him of his impetuousness and the resultant pain, and the pain alerts him to an opportunity for a diversion.

Apollo, scampering downstairs—abetted by a prosthetic leg and hip—made a wonderful, temporary home for Winchester's tracking device. It didn't matter if Paul's overseers could make sense of his galloping around or his tireless pursuit of round-tailed squirrels...*I'm insane, after all.*

Paul traipses into the living room overlooking the gully, and calls Apollo. Apollo heeds his beckon call—not to be bested by Zeus, who similarly bounds to the sound of his master's voice. Paul carefully retracts the tiny beacon from a groove in the Rottweiler's titanium thigh, and stows it away in his jacket pocket.

"Thank you for holding onto this for me," he says, patting Apollo, and then Zeus, in turn, for the sake of evenness.

The domestic moment is broken by a loud, singular screech—the retreat's air-raid siren.

Securitas immediately comms Paul. "An Outland Reduvius drone just laser-tagged the premises from thirty-thousand feet. Would you like to respond with force?"

"If they wanted me dead, they'd have followed-through already. I believe they're merely marking a parking spot. Prepare countermeasures, nonetheless."

An incoming comm flits across Paul's Monocle. *Katajima.*

Paul closes his line to Securitas. "Shouta…" he says shrewdly.

"Good morning, Paul. Your ride is on the way. Is there any cause for concern?"

"Pardon?"

"Reports show that your retreat's weapon system is active."

"A precaution, nothing more."

"Please do not give Winchester any more reason to question my faith in you."

"Fine," says Paul, nonverbally instructing Securitas to disarm.

Securitas turns off the anti-air rocket launchers and radar jammers, as requested. The cloaking mechanism blanketing Paul's desert-compound sizzles, and then slinks back. Such an inviting gesture as reintroducing earth to sky won't bring back the killdeer or the warblers, but will at least save Katajima's pilot some vexation.

Paul disables the patio's electroshield, and heads out onto the deck, closing the door behind him. He drops the patio ladder into the gully, which clicks into its scabbards rooted in the limestone below. He buckles the strap on his overstuffed duffle-bag across his chest, checks the revolver at his side, and then dips down steadily.

At the base, he recomposes himself and comms Securitas. "Electro-fortify all doors when I leave. The second I'm airborne, initiate Alcatraz Protocol. See to it that Zeus and Apollo want for nothing. That means preventing the Kay9 auto feed from jamming again."

"Yes, Dr. Sheffield. As you wish."

Some things cannot be left to chance. Paul forwards Securitas' orders to Cerebus via Monocle, quashing ancillary worry about the first AI's constancy. The inconsistency of his digital progeny is probably its most humanizing characteristic and quite possibly the only fault in its design.

The gears on the solar panels, crimped together like rose petals, whine as they force the structure to blossom, on schedule. Paul wipes silt off of one of the panels as he walks by.

"Incoming U.F.O.," Securitas warns.

"Yes, thank you, Securitas. I know."

A black, gnarled V looms on the horizon, warping the sky around it with heat haze. Paul's Monocle targets it with a scanning reticle, but is unable to provide make or model. *No need.* Paul knows all about *Winchester's precious Dragonfly.*

Paul wasn't the only egg Outland had poached from the DOD's Cyber Warrior Project after the War. A colleague who'd fancied himself a renaissance man—building unbreakable, light plastics and navigation systems for autonomous Cyber Warrior drones—custom built and printed the Dragonfly for Winchester. Whatever the reason he offered for naming it so either boiled down to a lack of creativity or a wicked sense of irony.

It looks nothing like a dragonfly, and worlds-more like an antlered-deer's skull, with turbo fans in the place of eyes, a cockpit fitted between the jaws, and multi-pivot wings wired behind the fuselage where antlers'd be. *If it weren't for Outland's insectum-based naming convention, the obvious choice would have been "Actaeon."*

Winchester's ship touches-down just beyond the cone of solar panels, scorching the Mojave yucca grouped around the retreat's buried septic tank. The pilot activates aft-shields to minimize the kick of debris Paul's way. Notwithstanding the shower of rocks and sand that manage through the shields, Paul trudges forward, one hand resting on his bag, and the other protecting his eyes.

The ship's canopy slides back, freeing the pilot's waving hand.

Paul approaches.

The pilot pulls off his trunk to speak. "Dr. Paul Sheffield?" he inquires with a Texan lilt.

"That's me," Paul shouts over the double-stacked turbo fans, thrashing asynchronously.

"Captain Peter Samkorsky. I'll be taking y'all to Los Angeles."

BELTED INTO HIS SEAT behind Samkorsky, sucking oxygen through an accordioned trunk, Paul watches the earth track backwards, pulling Barstow's neighbour, Victorville, in and out of view—still as low and suburban as it was half-a-century ago.

The San Gabriel Mountains rise before them, puncturing clouds and high-hanging smog. Samkorsky signals to Paul with a thumbs-up that they're ascending, *probably to avoid gunfire from the PIT rats slumming it on the peaks.* Paul can see them, victims of war and geography, bunched in their shanties along the wall, which halves Telegraph Peak like Ming's wonder.

Clouds engulf the ship as it arcs over the rocks. Paul holds his breath for the reveal as the last of the vaporous film curls by like an opening curtain. Smoggy outlines fill with Lotusland high-rises. Los Angeles takes the stage.

Gargantuan towers, windowed-obelisks, and hexagonal pyramids stand above magma-flows of hover-cars and terrestrial traffic, which permeate the Blue Zone and the RIM, hemmed-in and protected from the chaos to the east by the Partition.

Winchester's Blue Zone, home to Outland subscribers, California's elite, and tech-progressives, extends up the coast and dominates most of the old downtown to as far as the river. *High tech, high life.*

Its neighbouring sector, the RIM, is populated by upper and lower middle-class reactionaries and moderates. A porous border separates the two, comprised of checkpoints and magnetic markers. *It's a mixed bag, by comparison, boasting freedoms and tragedies unheard of in Winchester's fiefdom.*

Although most of the RIM's architecture is relatively unambitious and stumpy, it is checkered along its westernmost reaches by the infamous T-Blocks, which confound any aerial distinction between the sectors.

These vertical suburbs—jet black glass structures in matte-grey iron and titanium corsets—boast their own mayors and their own municipal services. They flicker with illegally-rerouted power and pirated water—pumped up external piping from the Toronto Syndicate's aquifers in San Joaquin. Paul appreciates their purpose, besides housing RIM ticks: a big *fuck-you* to their architects insulated in the Blue Zone.

The RIM runs from Anaheim all the way to the Mojave Desert, acting as a buffer between Outland and Military properties and the insidious third sector sequestered to the east: the PIT.

Like "RIM," "PIT" is a neologism that stuck, bereft of its initial meaning. Paul isn't sure, but presumes it stood for *People in Transition*, granted the area was repurposed to house undocumented refugees from the south the system didn't care to recognize or remember.

These days, people don't so much transition as survive in the PIT. It's an extremely dense, walled-city populated by refugee children and California's poor. The government and the military tend to leave it be despite the disease, the overcrowding, and the violence, allowing it to serve as an extreme counterpart to the Blue Zone—as a disclaimer for a life lived beyond Outland's blessings.

Separated from the RIM by the Partition—a strictly-monitored three-hundred-foot-high, twenty-foot-deep wall, freckled with guards and guns—the PIT is more of a prison than a city sector. Whatever decay and lawlessness exists in the RIM pales in comparison to the chaos present in the PIT's vertical slums or the subterranean settlements carved into Mount Baldy. The warlords who run it make Winchester seem benevolent by comparison.

With Pasadena below them, Samkorksy's GPS bids him roll west. Paul feels the g-force pull all the blood to his legs, and bats his eyes, trying to stay conscious.

"Jesus! A little warning," he slurs through gravity's pull.

"Sorry sir." Samkorsky evens the ship and slows their approach. "Sometimes, when the sun is shining and the ocean glimmers like diamonds on velvet, I just forget myself up here."

Attempting to keep last night's bourbon down, Paul returns his attention outside.

"Sure," he says staidly.

Paul spots his tax dollars at work at the centre of the Blue Zone: the Citadel—a windowless, flat-black behemoth, standing one-half mile above the city. It is Los Angeles' own cypulchre—an Outland tower brimming with half-a-million translocated minds stewing in the noosphere's primordial pools. *It's a bloody eyesore.*

The Citadel—the diadem in Winchester's crown—appears crossed by the Hyperloop's red mien, which carries blinking, civilian pods northward, past the Partition and shanty-encrusted mountains, to the Barstow Green Zone and beyond.

In addition to servers, translocators, and honeycombs of data, the Citadel boasts its own private army, nuke-proof shielding, and one-hundred-thousand-or-so permanent residents. Towering fifty storeys above the RIM's T-blocks as well as the tallest of the Blue Zone's more humble glass and metal skyscrapers—all latticed together by pedway bridges, dangling wires, and transit tubes—its shadow dials time on much of the city. Paul hates it; how imposing it is; the hubris of it—a Babylonic tower corrupted from the top down.

On the cloud-swept top floor resides Paul's former boss, Niles Winchester III, sitting righteous in his imperious and minimalistic, sandstone throne-room, watching the sun rise over the Pacific, living the *real life.*

Samkorsky radios to Paul, "One-minute till touchdown."

"Whereabouts, exactly?" asks Paul, fumbling with his headset.

"Your hotel, sir. The concierge will take over and I'll take my leave. Gotta charge this bad boy."

Paul chortles into the mic. "Well, I appreciate the lift."

"Dr. Katajima insisted that I refuse your gratitude."

Grinning, Paul looks out the window, watching the rooftop of the Grand Hotel magnify beneath the Dragonfly. "My word's no good in this town, anyhow."

Chapter 9: **CYPULCHRE**

A PASTY, ACNE-SCARRED bellhop unshoulders Paul's duffle bag and points to the ground, awaiting some sort of confirmation.

"Yeah, anywhere is good," Paul says, distracted, surveying the spartan hotel room.

The bellhop dumps the duffel bag and cracks the door open, feigning to leave.

"Hold on one sec," Paul says, forcing a smile and patting his pockets.

Sensing a potential exchange, the bellhop abides and closes the door.

Despite having pleaded to carry his bag himself, Paul intuits a reasonable tip via Monocle, and swipes his hand over the bellhop's. *There's something to be said for building positive karma, especially when out of your element.*

"Thank you," squawks the young man, undoubtedly double-checking the amount displayed over his iris. A surprised grin forces his cheeks up, pre-empting a deluge of withheld information. "I neglected to mention: the room should have everything you need. The most up-to-date *Home* interface, an InstaMeal printer…The Nespresso machine is beside the net-cube. All of the windows can be tinted." With a point, he continues. "Dial's on the wall beside the bed. Windows can also be converted into viewing screens."

Paul folds his arms, and scans the room, bobbing his head to simulate interest.

"And if you'd like to simultaneously synch to the CLOUD and take advantage of our athletics room, we can offer you a number of temporary PILOT inserts to regulate body function. Get your heart thumping while pumping your noggin full of virtual pleasure—SIMHAP and such."

"That won't be necessary."

"Not a fan, Mr. Kernel?"

Kernel? Katajima's evidently keen on downplaying Paul's return, ascribing to him this moniker for his own amusement.

"The creator, actually."

The bellhop flashes his piano-key smile, silently disregarding Paul's confession.

"Well…" says Paul, as if to punctuate their conversation's end, feeling the onset of his usual anti-social anxiety.

The bellhop makes a spectacle of turning off his Monocle. He leans forward, cupping his hand over one side of his mouth. "If you need anything off the books, you just let me know. The name's Fergus." He points to his ID badge, *just in case I'm hard of hearing.*

"Thank you, Fergus. I'll let you know if the need arises."

Fergus scurries out the door before the tip can be reconsidered or recalled.

Paul deadbolts the door. He'd prefer an electro-shield and a missile system, *but expectations regarding comfort and security are best left at home.* He picks up his duffle bag, and carries it over to the thin, heavplast desk set by the window. He unzips the bag on the desk and pulls out a stack of Yuan. *Might as well get what I came for before masquerading as the man they sent for.*

He closes the bag, stows it under the desk, and trudges over to the bed. Sitting down, he procures the NEXUS chip from his pocket. Scrutinizing it, he schemes how to get the fragmentor back from the RIM without raising any alarms over at Outland.

"I need my sleep," Paul lies to an empty room, planting the chip under the mattress.

PAUL RODE THE DECREPIT Metro to the end of the line, and flagged a cab to take him the rest of the way, paying with cash to avoid his name inciting any queries or interest. *The last thing I need is someone from the teacher's union, out of work because of CLOUD-learning alternatives, or some random, exacting their revenge...*

He greased the driver's hand with a little-extra incentive to circumnavigate the main roads and to steal by the checkpoints into the RIM.

To his credit, the driver was phenomenally efficient. He knew where to go and how best to get there, and he knew what to do when minor hindrances posed a threat to his master circuit. He also made a show of his familiarity by driving recklessly down alleys and across construction sites.

Paul steps out into a neon puddle. "Thanks," he says reflexively.

Counting his money, the driver tilts his ear Paul's way. "*The door...*"

Paul shuts it, and steps back to watch the blue and yellow cab accelerate to green and disappear around the bend.

The street is uncomfortably quiet. No laughter. No commotion. Just the sound of subdued quarreling and far-off car alarms.

On this tier of the terraced thoroughfare—outdoors but partly covered by makeshift awnings and plastic sheeting—Paul's virtually alone. He pulls his collar up to help block the exhaust from the air purifiers and the smell of battery acid leaking down from the mag-highway.

The street is bracketed by dark-windowed shops and boutiques shouldering glass and brick apartments that reach past the next tier into khaki-coloured soot. On the lower tier, dilapidated pre-war homes and their artificial palms lean to whatever light's strayed down with the highway exits. *They'd be better off gone than forgotten.*

Heavplast pillars and statues are reclaimed by vines and other bellicose greens. Holographic billboards advertise updates to the technology chipped and spread across the sidewalks. Street-side dumpsters full of chicken bones and rotten fruit indicate that not all of the living that goes on in the RIM is virtual. Notwithstanding this area's preference for the physical, Outland still projects an undeniable presence.

An emaciated woman with wax dripping from her chapped lips and desiccated skin quavers by the Newslink hub situated on the median halving the road. Her dark, jaundiced eyes—smoldering in their charcoal pits—snap alert to the presence of another sojourner. "Hey mistah!"

Paul pretends not to notice. *Rained-out junkie.*

"Mistah, ya've any airtime?" She lurches forward into the quill of light allowed by the marquee, legs shaking puss loose from hidden bedsores.

Paul shrugs his shoulders. "Afraid not. Old fashioned, I suppose. Nothing but flesh and bone." He hides his repulsion and hastens his pace.

Her eyes disappear into her down-facing disappointment. "Shit. Shit, man. That sucks." She stops mid-lane, boney arms jutting out like loose straw falling out of a piss-poor scarecrow.

"Don't know what to tell you. Sorry."

Paul crosses the road, leaving the wiry transient anchored in the real—a refugee formerly committed to the virtual, now returned to her original being, a prisoner of rotten meat and an atrophied brain. *The rapture's already come, taking up the rich and the obedient into the unloving arms of the leviathan.*

Paul aches with discomfort, with guilt. He's grateful that his daughters won't succumb. *They won't abandon their bodies willy-nilly.*

He bobs through an asphalt lot, past a smog-browned church—squeezed between nondescript brick buildings— that'd seen one-too-many votive candle go unanswered. *A vestigial place for a dematerialized race.*

Against a backdrop of pulsating solar bands and overgrown history, the church's daughterless Sophia offers a bronzed hand to pigeons fighting over a ration bar. Paul takes a three-step head-start and launches the bar with a straight kick. It fragments, and the scavengers flutter over to a safe distance; Sophia, naturally, unphazed.

Behind the kick lags a dull ache. It shoots through Paul, straight to his resolve. He hunches over. Stripped by lightning, thigh down to knee, knee up to hip. His muscles throb. The electric storm, sending bolts into places he'd forgot he sensed, immediately blemishes his disposition, already a distorted mess. Suddenly, everyone is an asshole, Shouta especially. *Holy shit, that hurts.*

What's Shouta want? What good does it do him, interrupting his luxurious fantasy, to tease an exiled Luddite stuck at start with the promise of reconciliation and purpose? "Fuck him."

Holding his leg as if it were about to come apart at the seams, Paul covets the SIK bottle he'd been denied and decries his foolishness. He regrets having dug the NEXUS chip out of his thigh, then suturing it up like some mafia doctor. Alcohol, anger, and paranoia: a last supper for this schizophrenic.

Paul is reintroduced to his surroundings by a nearby rumbling. Across the park, a Goliath security drone powers down the street. Its hind-legs lower it, enabling it to scan below the awnings. It inspects a gun store flickering behind an iron-barred façade, and clamors on, stopping before the next block of old buildings. It strews a solid-laser band down an exhaust-filled alleyway, scanning for subversives. The scan stops, turning the plumes of exhaust a deep carmine. The drone's lasers retract, and the Goliath returns to routine inspections—its taupe chassis absorbing the pale light around it.

The Goliath, like the rest of the state apparatus marching down the streets, offers nothing more than the illusion of control, or so Paul hopes. Won't do him any favours having the Goliath effectively lurking around looking for dissidents like himself.

He checks his Monocle to verify the location of the missing piece to his anarchical puzzle. According to the intel he'd compiled, the seller calls himself "Q," and runs a hackshop two blocks away in a cellar hidden beneath an augmentation studio, beside a Chinese restaurant. The Net didn't have much writ or background on Q, apart from a street-view image of the ramshackle, red-brick building apparently housing his illegal-tech toy shop, and a single comment: "Buyer beware." Paul is ready to negotiate with Yuan, and if it comes to it, the six armour-piercing-rounds-worth of caution at his fingertips.

Past a few more rain-outs coughing blood and tar—murmuring resentment between scuffed knees—Paul finds the Chinese restaurant. The windows are glazed-over with epoxy resin, darkly reflecting the Mandarin characters, "Good Eats," which flicker on the groaning sign, dangling on rusted hinges. There's a padlocked, wire-mesh door protecting a stairwell up to the augmentation studio, but no entry to or suggestion of another business.

Paul turns the corner to find another exhaust-filled alley. He coughs immediately, having dared a breath of the poison. Wiping his mouth dry with his collar, he squints binocular vision out of both eyes. An LED "Q" cuts through the amorphous grey; the glyphic tongue penetrating the circle points downwards to a set of stairs that disappears into the side of the building. *Hello, Q.*

Two shades emerge from the exhaust, finding form in the light of the LED sign. Paul quickly retreats around the corner, and peaks to confirm his suspicion.

The two figures are dressed in mechanized exo-skeletons. *Mechs.* Using the zoom-feature on his Monocle, Paul scrutinizes the insignia printed on their broad shoulders: "OS." *Outland Sentinels.*

Dismissing the presence of Winchester's cronies as coincidence, Paul reflects on any possible indiscretion on his part that might have tipped them off to his intent. So far as his overseers are concerned, he's napping in his hotel room, unless, of course, the room is bugged and monitored, in which case...*I'm screwed.*

One of the mechs descends the stairs into the hack shop, while the other leans against the exterior wall, smoking contraband with his visor up. Exhaling, the mech turns his gaze up the alley and sees Paul's face—or enough of it to know he is being watched.

"Hey! You there!" the mech bellows, throwing the cigarette to the ground.

Paul vaults off the cornerstone into a sprint, and bounds across the street in search of an out. The *click-crunch* sound made by the mech's legs sends more than a shiver up Paul's spine. His legs deaden with mortal panic.

"Stop!" bellows the mech, now at the mouth of the alley.

Outland Sentinels are notorious for being thuggish mercenaries, only facetiously referred to as *peace officers*. They're Winchester's fist; his imperial guard. Away without leave, papers, or a good reason for sector-hopping, Paul's dead to rights.

Scanning the storefronts for someplace to hide, Paul recognizes the Outland insignia again, this time on a maglev hover-car crackling his way. Without hesitation, he pulls into the nearest doorway. Red light encapsulates him. He turns to see the nose of the Outland car, and commits to whatever is dammed behind the door.

The entrance doesn't give at first, but on his second try, he collapses into the room—a soundproofed antechamber bound by steel bars and egg-foam, with a little wired window on the left.

Paul hears the *click-crunch* of the mech's boots outside. A muffled voice blares over a radio, and the mech belts back, "Giving you trouble, is he? Alright. I'm on my way." The crunches dampen until they're no longer audible.

Thank God.

Chapter 10: **BABYLON**

A GANG-BRANDED bouncer in mirror shades and a vinyl vest enters the antechamber from the other side on a wave of noise. He presses the door shut behind him, cutting off the cacophonic flood. The room, caged and egg-foamed, is now silent, save for the creak of his leather wrist-cuffs crotched under his bulging biceps.

Paul gulps, hoping he didn't trade a beating and incarceration for death. He can hear his heart race, creating a polyrhythm with the guardian's constant beat.

The bouncer unfolds his arms and silently motions to a sign posted on the frame above the small, barred window. On the other side of the bars is a converted coat check, now housing a gun closet manned by a blonde-haired and semi-skinned android. The sign reads: "NO WEAPONS OF ANY KIND. NO EVAPS. NO DIDDLERS. NO HACKERS. MONOCLES <u>MUST</u> BE SHUT OFF."

With his revolver burning a hole in his side, Paul opts for his *other* universal key: a bouquet of Yuan. He thrusts a fistful of cash out with a trembling hand. Looking past snippets of Mao's face, he studies the bouncer's for a reaction. The mirror shades offer nothing but a dark reflection of Paul's expectation. *His heart skips a beat.*

The bouncer cuts the tension with a grunt and grabs the wad of Yuan. Crinkling it into his vest, he nods to the gun-closet android. Exposed gears on the android's face grind. It winks back.

Paul looks at the two of them, locked in agreement over god-knows-what. *I could outdraw the bouncer and ring him twice before he got a grip, but the android…that's a gamble.*

Breaking its stare with the bouncer, the android delicately plays a keypad. The door clicks open, inviting the noise back into the room.

Avoiding his hopeful reflection in the bouncer's shades, Paul walks around the brute and into the realm beyond. *The ordeal of getting in here probably keeps the paranoids out and the sadomasochists chomping at the bit.*

He descends a staircase, which slopes under a decorative grid of laser beams and strobe lights, and heads into a long, prismatic hollow. The music making the floor tremor is electro mayhem: a sporadic series of *wahs* linked by a dissonant trickle of modulated chords, all floored through a dozen old, vacuum-tube amplifiers.

Although his eyes haven't fully adjusted, Paul can make out enough to know he's out of his element. It's a real-world SenseDen: a strip club where patrons plug their PILOTs into sensorial portals running CLOUD tech, and feel whatever it is they need to feel while watching flesh sweat and sway. The place is a rarity now, an antique, with the majority of California's hedonists synching and going straight to the CLOUD for all of their anonymous debauchery. *The popular shift to the completely virtual is a real surprise given the charisma and candour of places like this.*

There are several stages along the right side jutting out like saw teeth into the centre aisle. Opposite the stages is a bar, which runs the length of the club. The bottles and vaporizers tiered behind it are backlit, silhouetting and casting both the bartender and the middle section's constituents in earthy colours. The middle section services a motley crew of perverts, drooling with mouths agape at the staged men, women, and androids, writhing under multi-coloured LED arrangements.

Pathetic, thinks Paul, hesitating at the head of the aisle. *Place stinks of despair…of hopeless idolatry.* He sees an evap, bound, goggled, and unconscious in a chair off to the side. The evap's legs twitch like those of a sleeping dog.

Paul had frequently and publicly defended SenseDens, claiming they served an important societal function in the battle against human mechanization and automation. Despite his firm stance, he'd never been in one. Looking around, he attempts to reconcile his immediate disgust with his ideological stance. *Here, they worship an idea they've found reflected by shards of broken glass. In the CLOUD, reflections mirror reflections, cutting out the object and leaving only infinite emptiness.* He decides he can appreciate it without liking it.

Pressing towards the back, out of the way of the strippers and their obsessives, Paul catches the gaze of a femme bot, swirling behind a holographic screen simulating rain. She looks at him and smiles. The simulated familiarity is unnerving, especially since obscurity and evasion were the reasons for this detour. He pauses to glance at the human counterfeit, aping forward with one hand on the pole.

"Hey'ah Paul! Got some time for me, for old time's sake?"

Struck by disbelief and worry, he shakes a glower onto his face. *What the hell?*

"P," she says, shaking her hips and slinking down the pole. "Don't make me beg…"

Paul's eyes widen with fear and disgust, watching the femme bot's features morph. Her once pale, circuit-striped cheeks flush with pink. Her blue hair turns brown, and her eyes dial to blue. With a few more tweaks, she no longer looks like the silk-plastic geisha that had yelped for his attention. Now, she looks just like his ex-wife, *Rachel.*

"Man-up and give it to me, P," she cries, seductively.

Paul raises a trembling hand to his forehead and fights to contextualize what he can only hope to be a symptom of withdrawal from his daily SIKs. He ambles towards the back, greased with flop sweat.

Slowing his pace so as to avoid drawing unwanted attention to himself or to his discomfort, Paul takes a seat at the end of the bar. *Relax. Don't let some parlour trick upset you.*

The bartender, a tanned, Spanish woman in a low-cut, low-rise, silver dress—no older than thirty—struts over, picking up grime along the counter with a rag. She brushes the particulate she's collected off the counter, and throws the rag into a receptacle behind the bar.

"Afternoon *senor*. What can I do you for?"

"A beer."

"Cash or airtime?"

"Cash."

She smiles and bites her bottom lip, raising an eyebrow at the femme bot squirming behind Paul. "Not here for the arcade?"

"Not really, no."

"She got to you? Our Simone, here?" she asks, indicating the android with a nod. *It's less a question and more a statement of fact from one more observant than her costume and composure otherwise suggests.*

Paul stares at his empty hands rattling on the bar, and says nothing.

"Anyway," she digresses, picking up on his discomfort. She pulls a bottle of sloshing gold from under the counter and plants it between Paul's hands. "This'll help with the nerves."

"How the hell did she pull that off?" Paul blurts. His knee skids uncontrollably against the bar.

"Huh?"

"She knew my name. Re-casted to look like my...*never mind*." Paul summons up the beer and clears a gulp.

"Don't know what to tell you, *senor*."

Her emphatic use of "senor" has an aging effect on Paul. It forces a wince, which cracks his face.

"Simone is not blessed with these techs or talents; certainly not t'kind that calls out your name or changes to…" she pauses, probably consulting her Rosetta App via Monocle, "suit your cravings. That'd be a crowd-pleaser I could retire off of."

Getting nothing in return from their social exchange but dead eyes squeezed between premature wrinkles, the bartender motions to leave.

The very suggestion of being alone again with his morbid thoughts incites separation anxiety. Paul slides his empty bottle forward.

"Whisky?"

She turns to him slowly, adopting an insincere smile. "Ah, you've *the thirst*."

Paul's failed attempt at a smirk leaves him with a look of bewilderment. "I've got some time on my hands."

The bartender pulls down a semi-transparent bottle with a black stripe, and liberally pours a headache's-worth over a few ice cubes. She places the glass in front of Paul and cups his trembling hand. His first inclination is to recoil, but he fights the urge in favour of opportunity.

He looks to her full lips for the answer ahead of asking. "Why did you ask if she'd gotten to me?"

She rolls her eyes and squeezes Paul's thumb. "You seemed agitated around her, coming this way." She trades his hand for his empty bottle. "First round was on me—for Simone's *falla*. Just remember," she says, blurring from a wink, "I live on tips."

Paul ogles her silver skirt as it shrinks down the way of the bar, catching light off the holograms and LEDs. His retreating stare picks up on a specter descending the stairs from the entranceway.

"Dammit," he murmurs.

He takes a sip of whisky, and attempts a second survey of the room. A bulky man sporting a Mohawk and a suede jacket is headed his way. Twisted horns protrude out the sides of his head.

A raspy voice finds Paul's ear. "You should know that running won't help you."

"What?" Paul gasps, looking for the source of the advice. There's no one... *Keep it together. You're okay.*

Paul thumbs the hammer on his revolver, and sits nonchalantly with his other hand on his glass.

"You the doc?" asks the stranger, out of breath. He slams his hand on the counter beside Paul. "Well, aren't you?" His nails, chipped and bloody, are barely better-off than his arms—tattooed and marred by electrical burns. His horns vanish.

"Who's asking?" Paul mutters into his glass.

"Gibson. Booker Gibson. A mutual friend sent me to find you."

Paul turns on his stool, revealing his revolver, firm against the outside of his leg. "Sorry, *Gibson*. I'm not the guy you're looking for."

Gibson sneers.

"At the very least, not the guy you wanted to find."

The veins in Gibson's temples bulge, stretching and pronouncing the knotted pink scars etched along his ebon skin. Eying the gun, he reconfigures his sneer into a smile, outlining bared teeth. "You really don't need that."

"This guy you're looking for...would *he* need it?"

"You're embarrassing yourself. Just put that shit away before you get yourself thrown outside to the pigs."

"Gibson—it's Gibson, right? You're best-off telling your boss that I am not on his leash anymore."

Gibson lets out a thunderous chuckle. His posture liquefies, and he slides onto the stool next to Paul. He flags the bartender with a finger's point. "Good for you, Paul. I'm glad the stories aren't all true."

Paul winces at the mention of his name. The revolver wavers in his hand, but he retrains it on Gibson's belly.

The bartender leans over the counter, and addresses Gibson. "Hello, handsome. What's your poison?"

Gibson crooks his neck forward to inspect the contents of Paul's glass. "Whatever my friend here is having."

"And for you? Another?" she asks Paul.

The words disintegrate before making any connection. Paul's staring at a moisture ring on the counter before him. She breaks his trance with a knock on the counter.

"Oh. No thanks," Paul stammers. "My free time seems to have gotten away from me."

She reads Paul's posture like a basic line of code.

Gibson pipes up. "Just the one then, Miss…?"

"Miss Terry," she fires back, clearly having been asked one time too many.

Furrowing his brow, Gibson looks to Paul for a reaction, and then back to the bartender. "As in…"

"None of your goddamn business."

Gibson grins.

"I won't read you boys the riot act, but know: if either of you two do anything besides drink or yap at my bar," she seizes Paul's empty glass, "You'll be sharing your buzz with the rats."

The scientist and the stranger raise their eyebrows in tandem, both surprised and secretly delighted by the bartender's frankness.

Cued by the bartender's distraction—fiddling with ice and booze—Gibson reaches into his pocket. Paul lurches forward, gun ready.

"*Relax*," Gibson reassures, gently pulling out a holo-disc. He places it gingerly on the counter. Paul's Outland file appears in shimmering duotone, along with a recent orbital scan of his face. "Recognize this mug?"

Relaxing the hammer on his revolver, Paul reaches for the disc and tracks it closer. "Where did you get this? You an Outland detective or something?"

Gibson swats away the suggestion with his marred hand. "*Hell no.* I'm not some bitch living off W'chester's dime. That mother wants me dead and I wish him the same." He closes the hologram and tucks the disc back into his pocket. "I also couldn't give two shits about some chip in your leg or the empty coffin that's brought you here. This is a *professional* courtesy."

"I'm no longer acquainted with any professionals."

"Well, we got a friend in common who thinks otherwise, and is mighty convinced your life is worth saving."

"No kidding. Does this mutual friend have a name?"

Gibson leans into a whisper. "Less I say, the better. We can't bet on you until you're formally in the game."

Miss Terry puts a drink in front of Gibson. He thanks her with a Chinese tap of the glass on the counter, and waits for her to disappear down the rail.

"W'chester thinks you're a hazard—thinks you were the one who disconnected his lab rat."

"And you don't?"

"Don't what?"

"Think I did it?"

"I really don't give a damn." Gibson sips his drink, and looks straight ahead at the rows of backlit bottles. "Those that manage a care don't think it's you. In fact, *those that would* have been talking about bigger fish and choppy water round the bend."

"*This* I already know."

"A'ight, doc. Suppose you also know this'll be your last trip to the big city—your last trip anywhere, unless you do something about it."

Paul breathes deeply. *Is it possible someone could be more paranoid than me?*

Gibson continues: "Them metal pigs at the hack shop?"

"Outland Sentinels."

"Right. They take orders directly from W'chester and the Outland Security Board."

Meaning Katajima didn't send them over to Q's...

"There's more of them at your hotel."

"Shit," mutters Paul. *He'd rather it'd been a coincidence or a delusion.*

"After the lab rat's funeral, they're going to pick you up and charge you with espionage and cyber terrorism."

Winchester must know about the Empty Thought.

"Our friend said she wants you to finish your work. Said it'll help a lot of people. That means you gotta stay alive." Gibson drains his glass, throws a bale of greenback onto the counter, and stands up. "Camp Mud. That's where you'll find us when you've committed to play."

"Play? And who's *'us'*? Who is *she*?"

"Take a chill pill and give trust a try. We'll send the coordinates once we've vetted a secure comm. Until then, keep your head up and your eyes open." Gibson stops mid turn. With his face eclipsed by the bottles' browns and greens, he addresses Paul. "If you tell anyone about Camp Mud, you'll be killing your only allies in a city that wants you dead."

Chapter 11: **BENEATH THE VENEER**

AWASH IN THE RED light of the SenseDen's doorway, Paul watches Gibson strut defiantly down the street. *The enemy of my enemy is my friend.*

A chrome motorcycle whips by, reflecting evening orange. Gibson jumps on the back, and throws his arms around the helmeted driver. They veer off, disappearing down a highway off-ramp to the first tier.

But who are his *friends?* "Bah," scoffs Paul, disregarding Gibson and the vague alliance he proposed. *Trust is a fiat with no guarantor or regulator. It's a fool's currency, and I won't invest.*

Paul double-checks for any remaining Sentinels or Outland drones. *They're gone.* The street is quiet again and a little bit darker.

He pops his collar, and hurries across the street to the Chinese restaurant. The smell of lemon chicken floods out the door, now propped open by a milk crate. Past weary eyes trained on the gap, Paul presses around the corner and into the alley. Leading with his revolver, he sidesteps warily towards the LED 'Q'.

The door to the hack shop is ajar, welcoming in wisps of painted exhaust.

"Hello?" Paul shouts down the stairs. "Anyone in there?"

Silence, save for the faint whining of machines.

Paul descends the steps. A short hallway intermittently lit by a flickering florescent tube ends in a security door, also unlatched.

"Q?" Paul says in a strained whisper. "Anyone here?"

The whine and whirr of machines answers back. He aims his revolver where a head would be if someone took the corner quick. *Might have taken Q in for questioning.* Paul feels like King Midas, only everything he touches turns to shit.

Paul pushes back the security door. Two CCTV cameras, one on either side of the door, hang limply—their lenses sprayed with a black goo. Mech footprints have tracked the goo forward into the shop.

There is a small kiosk bunkered below crooked shelves housing monitors, hard drives, wires, and circuit boards. Behind the kiosk is a little door, both chipped and splintered.

There's a bell on the counter. Paul rings it. "Hello?" he says, more desperately than before, providing lyrics for the short metallic note.

A grating sound catches Paul's attention. Revolver drawn, he seeks it out. He heads down an aisle cleared between two rows of rusted storage containers piled to the ceiling. Some of the containers are missing panels, serving as shelving units—as cupboards. They're full of android parts (i.e. hands, eyes, plastic genitals) and a mishmash of other tech.

Clank. The grating sound announces movement again. Paul locates the source. It's an unlocked container. He rests his gun on the neighbouring shelf, and pries the panel open.

Two robotic eyes fused to a CPU and a modulator rustle on a mound of circuitry.

"Help me..." it murmurs.

"Jesus!" Paul yells, jerking back—both surprised and relieved.

The eyes cross, and train-in on Paul. "The creator…the creator has forgotten about me."

It's just silicon and metal, Paul lies to himself as he closes the storage unit and grabs his revolver. The piecemeal android's muffled cries dampen behind him.

"Help!"

Paul passes a few shelves burdened with stacks of PILOT grafts and drone-ware, and comes full circle to the kiosk. He plots his hands on the counter, and takes a deep breath. *All for nothing.*

He notices that the splinters on the little door behind the counter aren't there from age or accident. *They're bullet holes.*

Paul lifts himself over the counter. He pauses with one foot dangling on either side, giving his bum-leg a second to recuperate. With a heavy sigh, he slides over the counter. Feeling like Alice frenetically trying to catch that damn rabbit, Paul paws at the tiny door. It gives way to his touch, and creaks open a sliver.

"Q?" Paul whispers, raising his revolver.

The backroom is pitch black. It's warm. It smells of iron and mint. Paul runs his finger along the wall for a switch but finds nothing. He appeals, instead, to his Monocle. Activating night vision, he looks around. *Damn.*

Q, a dwarf by the looks of it, is at once home and gone. He's an island in a sea of his own blood. *They snuffed him out. But why?*

Paul sees the light switch. He turns off his Monocle, and flips-on the incandescent bulb at the centre of the room.

It's a small room, not unlike the secret basement at Paul's retreat. There's a dozen monitors attached to a NET cube, and pigeon holes on all four walls full of gear. Two black racks of servers hum on either side of the desk, blinking red at their designer.

"Crap," he says, looking at the little body.

They made it look like a suicide. Brained him and fitted the smoking gun in his hand. With all the signs of a break-in, they haven't done much in the way of properly selling their lie, but then again, they'd only have to convince another branch of law enforcement owned by Winchester.

Internal corruption can only be stymied by a third party or a noble insider, and the Blue Zone boasts neither.

Paul sidesteps the carrion, adjusts the height of the chair, and sits at the desk. He turns on the computer. The screens strobe on. Q's stock manifest appears on the bottom-left monitor. Letters track out in green over a fuzzy black background.

"ITEM SERIES A43H29: FRGMNTR.....PICK UP.....WEDNESDAY."

Q had fully intended to sell Paul the device. There was no need for him to bring his revolver; the Yuan would have sufficed. According to the manifest, Q had the fragmentor serialized and ready for pick up...*so it must still be around here somewhere*. Paul mouths the series number, and stands up—almost slipping on the shop-keeper's blood.

He walks the perimeter of the room, trying to bingo the intersection between *A* and *H*.

"A-forty-three...and H! Here we go."

Paul stabs his hand into the pigeon hole. It's empty, save for a few wet streaks of black goo.

"God-damn-it!" Paul blurts.

The opaque band around his arm flashes red, turning the pigeon hole into a demonic eye. Paul sighs, retracts his arm, and flicks his wrist, triggering Monocle. "Yeah?" A dark feed flits over his iris.

"Paul? Hello. Shouta here." A live image renders Katajima's likeness, sitting comfortably in an automated Thorium convertible with the top down, and San Joaquin Valley compressed in the background.

"Yeah, Funeral's Friday; we meet tomorrow. *I got it.*"

"Do you have time to meet me this evening?"

"Jesus, Shouta. I'm already giving you a whole day."

"I know."

Paul pounds his fist against the empty slot, and throws the rest of the pigeon holes a defeated look. "And I'm not exactly jazzed about any of this."

Katajima's contorted face suggests genuine bafflement. "Oh?"

Paul rolls his eyes. "You've got to be kidding me…" He tip-toes over the morbid mound, and bows out of the room. "No, I wouldn't say so."

"Oh, Paul. What has passed is the past. The future is undecided…it could very well be *ours*."

"The past is very much alive. I belong to it. It has me."

"I was under the impression that was all water under the bridge."

"Bridge got washed out in the process…" Paul exits the shop into the alley, and palms his mouth and nose to filter the exhaust enshrouding him. "What exactly do you want?"

"I would very much like to pick your brain over coffee. We have been seeing some pronounced abnormalities in the CLOUD. Nothing too serious, but we do not want to hazard a second Purge."

"Can't. I'm doing some sight-seeing."

He crosses the road, and takes the sidewalk in the direction opposite the SenseDen. The far-off wail of police sirens shakes him—forcing him to accept the reality of the tragedy he just encountered…*the tragedy I'm potentially responsible for.*

"I was under the impression you were at the hotel."

"Yeah, I am," Paul barks back, forgetting his Monocle is broadcasting his sightlines.

"Still prostituting yourself out to luddites?"

"My business is my own," Paul answers, thankful Katajima had missed the corpse in the background. His Monocle heeds his *audio only* intuition.

"Paul, you there?"

"Yes." He meanders past a time-worn red truck, idling with its driver lying on the rusted hood, smoking pipe tobacco.

"If you make an appeal to Winchester, you may no longer have to lie about your whereabouts. You might even be able to come back to Outland."

"Won't happen," says Paul, distracted by the acrid scent of the tobacco smoke.

"Oh, for the love of God. Digest your pride…Fine!"

Somehow, Paul knows Shouta can tell he's smiling, and that it's driving him crazy, just like the old days.

"Winchester has been talking about you. The less you communicate and the more you deceive him, the more suspicious he will become, and he is already quite suspicious…In any event, regarding tonight: it is imperative that we meet. I will remunerate you for your time and your inconvenience. Hell, I will vice the company for a sky-full of airtime."

"Airtime?"

"Yes, airtime."

"No need." Paul checks his pockets for his Walruses, knowing full-well he's out of SIKS. He's out of Walruses, too.

"Oh?"

Paul approaches the pipe-smoking man stretched out on the truck, and mimes "Can I buy a smoke?" The man, wreathed in white hair, leans forward, and pulls a cigarette out of his chest pocket. Paul forks out a few blades of Yuan, and nods with a smile.

"Shouta," he responds over his Monocle, jarring the cigarette in his scowl. "I don't have an implant, in case you've forgotten."

"Ha! Of course, Paul. That would be mental. Everyone knows you are forever grounded. Did not mean for you. No, no, no."

Shouta's build-up and sudden silence is emotionally excruciating for Paul. "Huh?"

"For Rachel and the girls."

Dead air. White adrenalin coursing behind the comm. "Paul? You there?"

Eying the idling truck, Paul throws his shoulders back, and pulls out all of the Yuan he has left—a few-thousand-dollars-worth, minus whatever he hemorrhaged at the SenseDen.

"*What about* Rachel and the girls?"

Chapter 12: **INTERVENTION**

PAUL CAREENS DOWN a street where he'd, on many occasion, strolled around his colic offspring. With the brakes on his new red rust-bucket squealing like pigs to slaughter, he slows into park at the mouth of the *cul de sac*, forty feet short of his former abode.

It's a ranch-style stone and wood bungalow joined to the road by a cobbled driveway, just far enough away from the downtown core to avoid its shadows. Nice house. Nice neighbourhood. Nice try at normality, at cookie-cutter comfort.

Now? *The place's a mental sinkhole*, suitable for a non-questioning, myopic, Outland exec with a penchant for forgetting—a role Paul wasn't able to perform indefinitely because of his pride and arrogance.

At his best, he'd been around but not actively present; an aloof automaton focused on results and the future. Now, after his future's come and frozen, his past holds onto him tighter than ever, like the wedding band he refuses to take off.

Two micro maglev-cars sit in front of the garage. One is Rachel's. Paul has no idea who owns the single-seater jammed behind it.

Thinking of what to say and what to do, Paul thumbs the ripped pleather on the steering wheel, eyes burning an imaginary hole through the front door to the house. *Rush it? Bull right through, snatch up the kids, and save them for their sake?*

He'd mulled over several plans of attack and all the different things he could say *en route*—he had plenty of time on account of having to detour all the way to Eagle Rock to avoid Outland's checkpoints. All that scheming, and he still has nothing. Nothing but an ulcer boring a hole through his resolve and a splitting headache fogging his heroic one-liners.

Dammit. They're in there with god-know-who doing god-knows-what. The more he thinks about it, the more his logic is confused and the angrier he gets.

Paul gets out of the rust-bucket, worth its weight in Yuan. Shoulders forward, he marches to his nuptial lodge, past faceless-neighbours' manicured lawns set with imported greens to satisfy expatriated northeastern colour palettes. His fists are unintentionally balled, and his mask of civility, chip-thin.

Doorbell. Pounding. The *cul de sac* closes around him. His solipsistic world only exists, in this moment, bunched up behind this designer-panel door.

"Rachel!" Paul beats furiously on the door and rings again.

A Firefly drone drops from the awning and paints a halo above Paul's head, IDing him. Paul seizes it out of the air and crushes it between his thumb and index finger. "It's me. Open up. Rachel?"

Something stirs inside. Metal on ceramic. Chair-legs grind on hardwood. Someone unbolts the door. It opens to a distressed and disheveled ex-wife.

Her eyes are white and pastel islands in mascara tar pools. Wrinkles have finally found her, pronouncing her scowl and marking Paul's fall on her forehead. Her bodacious figure is hidden but hinted at by her favorite mod-black bodice—*her prowling garb.*

"C'mon, tell me you didn't. Please, tell me you didn't...The kids too?"

"Paul," she sighs. "Now's not a good time."

Her body language, distant and anxious, reads 'I DID IT' in bold-fucking-letters.

"Are you out of your mind?"

Rachel purses her angler-lips, and throws a hand on her hip. "Oh, you're one to talk. It's *your* creation, after all."

"You can't protect them. Not in there," Paul says, pointing over Rachel's shoulder—unconsciously trying to control the dynamic with an unprecedented physical presence.

Rachel shuns Paul's point. "You know what I realized?"

Paul makes a concerted effort to demonstrate his frustration with an embellished shrug.

She pauses and takes a deep breath. "Maybe that, all things considered, you weren't right about everything."

Vexed, Paul tosses his head back, reloading for a verbal barrage, but decides not to waste the ammunition. "I just want to see them."

"Honey, something wrong?" says a man in a gravelly voice, secreted off and out of sight.

Paul peers in, over Rachel's shoulder. "Who the hell's that?"

"Did Outland let you leave Barstow?"

She doesn't get more than a grunt as a response.

"Paul, go home."

Rachel attempts to close the door, but Paul pushes it open and her aside.

"This *is* home."

Rachel scrambles to block Paul's passage. "Stop! Paul, Stop!"

"Pythia! Angela!" bellows Paul, incensed. He plows into the living room.

Rachel chases after him, clawing and yelling. Paul peeks into the kitchen where a horned man sits hunched over a ration pack and a steaming bowl of noodles with his back to the doorway.

"Get out. Get out! You're not supposed to be here," yells Rachel. She manoeuvres around Paul and steps into his way. "The Court…"

"Damn the Court. You've mutilated my children."

The man in the kitchen gets up and charges to the sound of the disruption. "Rachel?"

"It's him," she shrieks. "It's Paul."

"Yo dude, you can't be in here," *the substitute* declares, his illusory horns now faded.

Paul stops to check the living room for signs of adolescence, letting his substitute catch up with him.

"Dude!" barks the substitute. He catches up and prods Paul, "Asshole! You're upsetting Rachel."

Paul glares at his replacement. Completely disregarding him as a threat or otherwise, he turns and presses on, down the hall.

Whispers behind him give way to violent articulation. "He hit you?"

Paul runs from the territorial show, noticing how all traces of his involvement in his family's life have been completely erased. Pictures on the walls speak of a single mother and two beautiful girls. *Uncle-Stuffing-The-Wife* nuzzling Rachel in a strip of selfies. Smiles at the Grand Canyon. Six Mickey Mouse ears. Birthday parties. Science projects. But where is Paul?

Here, out of place and out of his mind with worry and anger. If anyone wanted his side of the story, they'd have to rely on his word, but that's no good, not anymore.

Paul turns to Rachel, catching up—face warped to a Picasso extreme—with her partner barreling behind her. "Rachel, where are they?"

The substitute steps in front of Rachel, and puffs his chest.

A real fucking hero.

"Listen man, I'm going to call the cops."

"You do that." Paul makes sure his revolver is tucked out of sight with a palm-swipe against his shirt. Satisfied that it is, he feigns a smile, and turns to Rachel with a look of manic eagerness. "Where are my daughters?"

"So this is the guy?" Paul hears the substitute inquire.

"They're in their bedroom, sound asleep. You're going to wake them if you keep on like a—"

"Like a what?" cries Paul. "Like a *crazy* person?"

Anxious quiet.

"Ha! Well, this *crazy* person," Paul indicates himself, "built this infernal house and fathered those kids you're so keen on butchering."

Rachel leans forward and whispers, "Coins and cum."

Fury etches deep lines into Paul's face. He mouths, "*What* did you just say?"

A sudden look of pity crosses her visage. She knows she's wounded him. "You're not yourself, Paul."

"B-bought it inventing the cleaver you put to their minds…Dammit!"

The substitute gives Rachel a knowing "I'm-going-to-do-something" look. In their trembling sockets, her eyes lock onto his fists balling-up. "Paul," she stammers, still gathering herself. "You need to calm down before you see them…I think it'd best that—"

"The hell you know," belts Paul. He opens a door to his old study, now mired with work-out equipment. He tries the next door, which opens to a pink and blue Disney abomination: the girl's shared room.

Paul's eyes quickly adjust to the darkness. He sees them both lying in their bunks. *Little wonders.* He feels a hand on his shoulder, warm and strong.

"Get out before—"

Paul turns and levels the substitute with a punch that surprises the both of them. The sub spins across the hall into a concealed tech cubby, and then to the floor—the cubby's contents spilling onto his exposed side. He wrestles to his feet, and lunges after Paul's legs.

Paul kicks frantically at his attacker, and yanks himself free. He whirs into the girls' room, and slams the door behind him. It fails to close. It's hindered by something soft. There's a corresponding shriek. Through the rift bridged by a red blotch, Paul sees the replacement keel backwards, gripping a bloody mess. Paul tries again and successfully gets the door shut.

Leaning against the frame, he checks again to make sure his gun's hidden so as not to heighten everyone's panic, and scans for any potential blockade. He pulls over the waist-level dresser and uses it to block the door. Satisfied with his quick-fix, he turns to four starry-eyes.

"Daddy?"

The little voice is a beacon in the dark, especially stark and airy against the white-noise machine grumbling beneath the bunks, deluging the room with a stale quiet. Apart from some muffled sobs and the faint sound of pawing, Paul's spectacle continues under the pretense of false calm.

"Oh, my princesses!" His face is so hot with rage, he doesn't realize he's crying.

He slowly approaches the bunks. Angela's sitting up, rubbing her eyes. Pythia is slow to rise, but rolls over, awake, similarly stunned.

"What's wrong, dad? Why are you crying?" asks Angela.

"I just wanted to check-in on you. Wanted to see my babies..."

They've grown up. They're not babies anymore. The video chats stopped about five years ago. Since then, Paul's only had pictures for reference—still images freezing his daughters' development, keeping them pure and naïve forever.

Rachel or the man, outside, is desperately trying to open the door. Probably Rachel; she has all of her fingers left.

"Don't you touch them!" she cries.

Paul, eying his daughters for any signs of affliction, asks in a trembling inside-voice: "Did anybody touch you? Did anybody…"

"Oh, daddy! We've the coolest thing to show you." Angela tilts her head, showing a small gap in her lustrous brown hair. "I'm a CLOUD explorer! Pythia too!"

Paul cautiously approaches, and puts his finger near the implant site. A hot jolt of white adrenalin pulses through his core and he recoils as if proximity-burnt. He picks up Pythia from the top bunk, and carries her over to the dresser. Putting her down, he steps back and turns-on the desk lamp. He shines the outlawed-incandescent bulb over his daughter's head.

With all the commotion outside and her disheveled father crying over her, Pythia starts to pout. She throws her hands up, defensively, unsure as to why she's suddenly the centre of her estranged-father's attention.

Similarly puzzled by—and perhaps even jealous of—her father's impromptu check-up, Angela tearfully asks, "What is it? What's wrong with Pythia?"

"One minute, baby…No. No. No…" He looks for a mark. "NO!" his finger finds what he feared the most: a cross section of little stitches.

"Pythie's okay," declares Angela. "She didn't cry when we went. The doctor even printed us dessert bars after!"

Paul shakes his head, speechless.

"And guess what!?" Angela points to Pythia. "She can talk now!"

Paul, dumbfounded, looks to Pythia.

"What did I do wrong?" It's no more than a squeaky chain of peeps, but words, words nonetheless, bearing with them a world of meaning, a universe of irrational hurt. *Thus spoke Pythia.*

"Oh my god."

Paul tries to smile. His lips, jaw, and shoulders shudder. Whatever expression he's sculpted unnerves Pythia, who begins to panic even more, pushing away her father's scarred arms.

"Baby…" Paul blubbers. The darkness has caught up to him, and apparently to his daughters too. "No…"

In an uncertain voice, Pythia begins: "Dad, it's okay. We're okay! Angie and I can take you to Calm Waters. Everyone relaxes there." She looks to Angela for moral support. "It'll be fun," she says dubiously.

A simulated-serenity forum in the CLOUD, no doubt.

Paul turns away from the dresser, his daughter still legged over the edge. He falls to his knees, and starts to wretch.

Hearing their mother bawling on the other side of the door, caving in with the substitute's intermittent charges, both girls begin to whimper.

"Shush, now. You're going to be okay, you hear me?" Paul says, wiping his mouth. He looks up to Pythia—*little mute Pythia. She has no need for our secret language now.* "We're going to take those implants out."

"But mommy says not to touch them."

The door behind Paul begins to cave-in. The other man is making use of some blunt and heavy tool.

Rachel's screams, no longer muffled, incite Pythia and Angela to join in.

"Why's mommy upset?" cries Pythia.

"Your mother doesn't know what she's done."

Part of the door gives way, and a bloody hand reaches in to feel for the handle. It finds the dresser first.

"You're talking, baby girl." Paul lets out a manic laugh, and grabs his head. "You're talking."

"What's wrong?" she asks, half-blinded by tears.

"Oh my god," Paul whispers.

"Did I...misspeak?"

"No, sweetheart."

"I've been practising for days now!" she says with a smile, out of place amidst her tears.

"Oh, child. You sound beautiful." He can't stand it.

Through the gap in the door, the other man shouts: "Open this door right now, Paul. You're only making it worse for yourself. The LAPD are on their way."

Paul gets up, slowly, and staggers, looking at his girls. *Full-fledged evaps. Talking. Happy. Damned.*

Paul kisses Pythia on the forehead. "I'll fix this, don't you worry."

"What's broken?" she inquires, marking the question with an anxious, tear-fed gasp.

He turns his head, loosing tributaries from the streams running down his cheeks. He picks her up, and carries her to her bunk.

Angela, frightened, has balled up in the corner of her bunk—sent there by the warnings her mother's issued through the broken door.

Paul tucks Pythia into bed, and reaches for Angela. "Baby, I just want a hug...hug your dad goodbye, will yah?"

She shakes her head, eyes wide with fear and glossed over with saline separation. She kicks the comforters up, trying to squeeze as far back into the corner as geometry and physics will allow.

Angela's face grows pallid, and her eyes beam red. *No.* Paul bites his lip. He's mid-episode. *I need out. I need fresh air.*

He slides the dresser out of the way of the door. The substitute and Rachel pile in. Rachel swats at Paul, in the way of the other man's offensive, and Paul squeezes past her and into the hallway. The *banshee and her minion* chase him out the front with hateful promises and warnings.

Stumbling into the street, Paul is welcomed by the sound of sirens. Two police cruisers make a V at the base of the driveway, scorching the grass with their mag-levellers. A third cruiser slides behind Paul's truck and immediately begins scanning his dot-plate, registered to a nicotine-yellowed RIM tick.

A bald-headed brute lumbers out the passenger side of the nearest police car and severs Paul's trajectory with an out-faced palm and the threat of a gravity mallet.

A second moustached officer, tightly harnessed into his exo-suit, approaches Rachel. "Mrs. Sheffield? Is everything alright?"

"Ms. Irhap," she looks over at Paul who's already resigned to the will of the bald cop and handed over a gun she had no idea he was carrying, "It's Ms. Irhap. And no, it's not alright."

Chapter 13: **UNCOMFORTABLY NUMB**

THE MOUSTACHED OFFICER cuts the restraints. Paul's purple hands fall free.

"You're good to go."

Here—cold, sterile, and glossed-over by bleach and florescence—is as good a place as any. "Huh?"

"Bail's been posted." The moustache audibly hinders the cop's enunciation.

Paul rubs his bruised knuckles. "By who?"

"No idea. Above my pay grade." The officer throws a transparent-plastic bag bulging with a jacket, car keys, revolver, and a wallet, into Paul's lap. "Car's not permitted in the Blue Zone. I'm guessing you don't have the paperwork handy…"

"It's a rental."

"I bet. Should be processed and ready to leave the lock-up any time now. It leaves with you, back to wherever you're from." His left pupil oscillates independent of the right, likely reading a Monocle brief. He nods, and jabs Paul's bag of belongings. "The license on that firearm is about to expire. See that you renew it or you'll being seeing me *real* soon. Confiscated the ammo, just so you don't try anything stupid. An eye for an eye makes the whole world blind, after all."

"And a black eye teaches a lesson," murmurs Paul.

"What?"

"Nothing."

The officer looks for resistance to snap at, but Paul gives him nothing. "*That's right.* We're also checking your piece against details regarding a cold case."

Paul's confident that whichever one of the twenty-or-so cases the cop's possibly alluding to won't thaw. He spreads the bag out on his lap.

The officer picks at his teeth, and mumbles a follow-up: "Barstow's where we'll find you, correct?"

"*Wherever* was more accurate."

Tired of Paul's attitude, the cop stamps his foot. Paul flinches.

"Got your attention now, do I?"

Paul whips his gaze upward like a scolded adolescent.

"Between the two of us," the officer rolls up his meched-out sleeves. "If we catch you over by your ex's house again, John Law won't be so understanding."

Paul nods in agreement.

"You need to do better than that, Mr. Sheffield." The cop crosses his arms, blue with faded tattoos and oversized veins. "Y'understand?"

"Doctor…"

"What?"

"Yeah. Sure."

Half-turning, the cop mumbles, "No point, anyway."

Paul plunks his belongings on the seat beside him and tears the plastic film to the point of tearing. "Sorry?"

The officer drops his shoulder revealing a poorly-hidden smirk. "They won't be there. Outland is putting them up in a protected residence until Sentinels can confirm they're safe. Somewhere nice downtown. Might even throw them in the Citadel. Princesses belong in castles, don't they?"

"Why the hell would they do that?" asks Paul, standing up—losing his head in one of the few places that could legally keep it.

The officer unfolds his arms, and steps toe to toe with Paul. "Customer satisfaction. Keeping RIM ticks away from decent people. *Charity.*" His eyes widen. "Di'look like I have a fricking crystal ball?"

Paul averts his look of disdain and plays the beta. "No. I just think…"

The officer thumbs Paul in the chest. "That'd be a nice change."

Murderous rage wells up behind Paul's vacant stare, which he rolls up. *Keep it cool.* "I just think that a guy should be allowed to know what's going on with his family." He steps back. "That's all."

"Well your family's going on without you, so drop it. *Don't* let me see you again—oh, that reminds me!" He zips up his black vest, revealing a chrome-coloured plastic badge pinned to the front. The lettering espouses virtue and justice for all.

"Yeah?"

"Outland sent a private dick to the courthouse to review your case. Memo said you violated a—hold on, I've got it here…" he intuits the message onto his Monocle, "You violated a privately-negotiated, legally-binding restraining order. Pretty serious business, Mr. Sheffield. Better hope a bounty hunter doesn't find you before the bigwigs figure out how best to proceed."

"Won't matter. The result will be the same."

THE AIR OUTSIDE STINKS like rotten oranges and barbequed kelp. It complements the other senses LA's unsurprisingly ready to upset. Whatever is making the Stars and Stripes shiver on the police station's poles isn't natural, and sure as hell doesn't look natural: a dense, yellowish fog billowing out of the city's split veins. *Another revolting night in the City of Angels.*

Shouta's Whipblade—a flashy, over-the-top Thorium convertible—hums in neutral at the base of the steps, pulled up onto the curb *like he owns it. And he—the potential inheritor of Winchester's noospheric fiefdom—might as well.* His wiry frame, angled at a nonchalant seventy degrees above the vented hood, is nothing less than a swastika against the headlights' xenon field.

Paul sighs at the sight of the spidery outline. "Should've guessed." He pulls his heavy arms through the sleeves of his jacket, squirrels the revolver behind his belt, and trudges down the steps.

"Beat your friends to it," chirps Shouta, half-bowing.

"Couldn't have been much competition." Paul's tone is as chalky as his complexion.

"Thought it would be a step towards repairing that bridge."

Paul buries his gaze beneath his furrowed brow, avoiding eye contact. Through weary slants, he concentrates, instead, on Shouta's knife-gash of a smile. "What do I owe you?"

"Nothing." The loaded word chips through his perfect, white teeth.

"Thanks, I guess." Paul half-turns, patting his jacket pockets—growing anxious with every unsuccessful feel. The pouches secreted behind the leather fail to yield the goods. "God-damn-it," he mumbles.

Observing his debtor's vexation, Shouta nimbly pulls a pack of premium cannaberettes out of his satchel, and stabs the offering across Paul's frontage. "Thought you had quit."

Paul's mug transforms with relief at the sight of the trademark pinstripe design. *Walruses.* The trenches arrayed across his forehead and under his eyes smooth and shallow. He looks past the depressant to its donor. "And I know for a fact you don't smoke."

Shouta's smile cuts to bulging cheeks.

The man's a penchant for thinking ahead. "Carrying those just in case I drew empty?"

"I had a sense you might feel like relapsing and relaxing...in excess."

"Did you really?" Paul demurs in an audibly stale Japanese. He snatches it up and picks it in the corner of his mouth. Shouta lights it reflexively with an Outland-branded lighter.

"Well, you're damn right."

"Please do not mention it. Besides, this is a vacation of sorts, however morbid the cause for your coming. You should enjoy yourself."

Like it's my last. Paul sneers. "Yeah, like I said: *thanks.*"

He circumnavigates the convertible, and throws his hand up futilely, praying for a cabbie or a sky scoot with telescopic vision. Although legally able to repossess the red truck in the police impound, Paul's sick of the bureaucratic waivers and slip sheets. *It's not worth the headache.* A police hover-car whips by, bleeding red and blue light through the smog.

Shouta waits for the siren to wane before speaking again. "No need, Paul. I will take you to wherever it is you need to go."

Paul looks down the empty street, striated by LED lamps that sop-up moon beams with counterfeit daylight. "No roads where I'm headed."

Shouta laughs. "Good lord! Try not to be so macabre." He taps the broad-faced watch affixed to his wrist, and throws open a holographic map. Spreading his fingers and pedalling them, as if on a keyboard only he had the benefit of seeing and hearing, Shouta zooms into a store-front image of a road-side café, buried beneath gargantuan-corporate towers. Lime neon, alloy stools, smoke-stained bay windows. "How about that coffee?"

Paul sniffs, and stretches. *If I didn't have a small audience, I'd collapse and weep.* "What exactly do you want?"

"I told you: just to talk."

"Is this about the message from Allen?"

"What message?"

"I didn't mention it?"

"No."

"The night you called—the night Allen died—I received a comm from someone purporting to be him. The message was virtually blank."

"Hmm. That was probably just a delayed comm; nothing more than a digital artifact scripted to play by a dead composer. After the Purge, we got that kind of cross-chatter all the time from digital ghosts until we patched it over and updated the system. Chalk it up to lag."

"Then whaddya want?"

A cop strolls out of the station and hastily pulls an inhaler out of his pocket. He looks down at Paul and Katajima, pauses—taking a moment to rationalize blind service to addiction—and decides to huff a cylinder anyway.

Katajima shakes his head. "Thought we might be able to help one another."

Quailing, Paul snaps back, "Oh, I bet."

Shouta crooks his neck, clearly penning his frustration behind his fleckless, professional façade.

Paul recognizes that unmistakeable tick. A sudden rush of guilt and hope finds him, both coupled with a memory: a climber once told him that *any crimp's worth gripping when climbing in the dark.* (Not too soon after, that wise and harried consultant fell to his death.) Paul makes the leap: "You think you can change Rachel's mind?"

That loathsome smile makes its way back across Shouta's narrow gab. "No, we both know I could never...but I could certainly work on Pythia's and Angela's."

Paul scratches his chin, unintentionally showcasing his consideration. *And turn back the clock? Reverse cataclysm and dull error's blade?* He draws, illuminating his look of incredulity. "Where're you thinking?"

"I know we had agreed to meet tomorrow, but I figured we could zip over to Ruby's tonight so I could get some perspective and a little bit of a head start. Ruby's off Old Temple Street, just a hop-skip-and-a-jump away."

Caving slightly behind the amber glow, Paul closes his eyes, and concedes in a cloud of smoke. "Ruby's would be great...if this were an exotic Outland luncheon."

Shouta quickly internalizes the criticism, and this time fails to conceal his exasperation. "And given that this is not an *Outland luncheon*?"

"I'll do you one better: Indian in the Cupboard. You know it. Might seem like a half-remembered dream, but I know you know it. A few more blocks down. Far more private."

Shouta gestures to the car. "Privacy at the cost of security."

"Something like that." Paul strides over to the passenger side and rests his elbows on the window frame, pleased with the Walruses' ability to let him sense so much, and feel so little. Not quite his SIKS—serving to destabilize rather than level—but something to help mute his demons and focus on the *real.*

Shouta pantomimes Paul's posture, driver side. "I am truly sorry about what has brought us together, but nevertheless glad to see you."

Unexpressive—his face a dead plate of nerves—Paul snaps the roach. "You sure've a knack for leaving and finding me at my worst, Katajima."

Chapter 14: TOO MUCH SMOKE, TOO MANY MIRRORS

THE INDIAN IN THE CUPBOARD is a low-life, low-tech hangout run by a Navajo trader with whom Paul is quite familiar. Paul had written some security algorithms for him back in the day, among other things. Manuelito, or "the Chief," owns several dives throughout the RIM as well as some PILOT chop shops (off the books). The Cupboard is headquarters.

The Indian in the Cupboard was initially a veteran's clinic after the War, but now it's a licensed black hole, popular with RIM ticks with central access as well as with shady Blue Zone types whose business requires privacy—the kind afforded by four Harpocrate jammers. Manuelito brokers, overlooks, and blesses Paul's Barstow dealings in exchange for the odd favour. Paul knows he can count on the Chief to keep things quiet if a deal ever gets out of hand and to get him deals if things ever get too quiet.

Contraband-cigarette smoke is thick in the air around them. It serves to soften the creases at the fringe of Paul's mouth, suffusing soft, colourful halos around the antique-neon beer signs that flicker above a booth underscored by photoluminescent braces.

A grizzled bartender carries over two steins dripping condensation. Paul pushes aside the candled bell-jar planted at the centre of the knotty-wood table, making room for the frosty delights. The bartender, standing awkwardly—incongruous outside of his coop—looks around with one eye twitching. Evidently unsuccessful in his review, he slams the steins between Paul and Shouta.

"Er, thanks Frank," Paul slips, reflexively, staring at the moisture and froth cascading over the lip of his stein like amber comets, side-lit by the candle.

Shouta raises an eyebrow at Paul's familiarity, having previously entertained the belief that Paul'd behaved and stayed north of the mountains.

"Sheffield," Frank pronounces coarsely, as if a question by itself. He drops his gaze to stare at Paul's bloody knuckles.

Paul looks up to Frank's porcine chin-set, and tucks his hands under the table. "Yeah?"

"Long time no see."

Paul looks across the table to Katajima, who lets Paul know he's no fool with a big Cheshire cat smile. "Yeah, a few years, at least."

"Huh? Yeah, sure. Have you seen Max?"

"Maxine?" Paul surveys the bar. "Nope. She supposed to be in tonight?"

Frank clicks his tongue against his teeth and breaks into an oafish stretch. Along with his hairy belly, he exposes fresh cyborg elements. The combination of body odour and unhealed flesh hits Paul like a silent freight train. Satisfied with a cartilage pop, Frank turns.

"Bitch is fetching on Manuelito's dime, I just know it," he mutters.

Before Paul can piece together a response, Frank's crunching across the peanut-shelled floor. He disappears into the lime and red haze.

Both Paul and Shouta perseverate on their drinks. Shouta interrupts their trance, seizing his glass. He poises to offer a witty toast, but Paul's already a gulp in. Undercut, he sips, then lowers the cup—his gentle convention disemboweled by Paul's.

"Quite the cheery place," Shouta determines, aloud. He sets his beer next to the jar. "But it will have to do."

"That's right. It will."

In an overzealous attempt to down his drink all-at-once, Paul sends a torrent down his neck, into his shirt. He quickly grabs a napkin, and pats himself dry. With Shouta ignoring his former colleague's little accident, Paul bashfully fans out the napkin on the table, noticing a penned scrawl bleeding all over the inside: "HEADS UP. YOU HAVE COMPANY. SENTINELS."

Paul crumples the napkin, and scans the room. Nothing out of place...except for two bulky Japanese men sipping on Saki tins, backlit by the jukebox's incandescent oranges.

What is this? "You gaming me?"

"I beg your pardon?" says Shouta, still smiling.

"Who're your friends?"

Shouta chuckles. "I see you were unable to outgrow your paranoia. It is a well-documented fact that those smokes of yours inflame such delusional fantasies. Are you still taking SIK-greens?"

"Don't screw around."

"You know you can have your chemicals balanced. It is a really simple procedure. Painless, too. Cheaper than your prescription in the long run."

Paul gets up to leave.

Shouta grabs his arm. "Relax, Paul. I am not *gaming you*. You have my word and my honesty."

They sit back down in tandem, despite Paul's certainty that Shouta's "honesty" is yet another one of his words that's no good.

"Those men are not my friends. They are my employees." Shouta points: "Haruto, the man on the left—he runs my personal security detail; a wonderfully-loyal import from Tokyo. The man on the right...my sister's stepson. Slow, strong, and sedulous—very much like a bull. By the way he drinks and spends his free time, perhaps Kobe beef." He makes a self-satisfied grin. "Since neither of us will be in any condition to drive, I have arranged for Haruto to retrieve your *new* truck from the police impound once we have finished here, and for my nephew to fly you back to the hotel."

Observing the finger point, Haruto nods in the doctors' direction.

"Whatever," Paul says, blushing. "Would you like another? On me?"

"I am fine for now, thanks," *says a man so beyond the need for charity, the notion of reciprocity likely seems alien.*

Paul drains his stein, and waves at an animate shape near the bar, double-checking for any possible Outland spooks.

"You have something for me to look at? You mentioned an aberration of some kind?"

Shouta raises his hands as if readying to slow down a runaway mine cart. "I do not mind troubleshooting your domestic issue first."

"No, that's fine."

Paul intuits-on his Monocle, and a glitchy, parti-coloured visual flits over his eye announcing "NETWORK DOWN."

"Shit!" Paul growls.

Shouta throws Paul a flat stare.

"I forgot that we won't have access to the Net in here. Harpos…"

"No need. I saved a recent snapshot of the event." Shouta fumbles around in his satchel under the table. He pulls out a tablet, and shakes it. Three holograms emerge, especially vivacious against the haze.

"Jeeze."

"What?"

"Those the read-outs for CLOUD data-trees?"

"Yes," Shouta states, very matter-of-factly.

"Unbelievable how they've grown."

"Oh yes. But it is just business as usual, *as intended*."

The other holographic depicts an ocean of waveform, ebbing and flowing across a gargantuan grid of 3D-clustered bars, depicting innumerable, individual data stores and transfers, with colourful beams depicting regional energy consumption.

"Those're all the blue zones across the state?"

"God, no. That is just Los Angeles inside the walls." Shouta shakes his wrist and intuits a command. Another hologram actualizes. "This is the Tri-Angeles Network's CLOUD. LA, Anaheim, and the Military grid for San Diego North."

Paul gulps, and slouches back, absolutely stupefied. "It's huge…it's," he leers at Shouta, "untenable."

"Now, remember, Paul: it has been a while…Outland Corporation now has the reach; it has the means."

"But when this goes multigenerational—shit, man."

"That gives me an idea." Shouta closes his eyes, and a pop-up running scripts and codes peels across the holographic projection.

Key by key, Shouta's query appears telekinetically: "RACHEL, PYTHIA, ANGELA [SHEFFIELD/ex/custody_transfer:IRHAP]…LOS ANGELES, CA. SECTOR 000000043…" Their profiles appear, followed by shortcuts to financial statements confirming their CLOUD synchronizations. Three PBN sorting numbers hover above their entry-images, indicating PILOT activity and one shared pentabyte of active memory. *The family plan.*

Paul pushes forward, grasping at the holographic ghosts. "That's them."

"Yes, Paul."

"Can *just anybody* find this information?"

"No, I have a dual admin-exec account giving me access to pretty much everything. This kind of clearance does not exist at any lower echelon."

"So you can rain them out?"

"I wish, Paul. There is a ridiculous amount of red tape and privacy measures enabled to keep hackers from dropping clients willy-nilly."

"But you're no hacker—you said you have admin-exec access."

Shouta shakes his head and sips his beer. "If, by sheer, relative capability, I am a Herculean demi-god, then Winchester is the *Zeus with the juice*." He seems satisfied to have finally assimilated Paul's preferred mythology.

"*He* could…"

"Secreted in the corner of his office is the only device capable of accomplishing what you are asking for: the Baal Deck storm machine. Only his biometrics can turn it on. With it on, any or all subscribers could be rained out—maintaining connection with their exo-cortices, of course."

"So he can!"

"But he will not; not if he can help it."

"And when he passes the torch?"

"I guess you will have to ask the next bearer."

"Haven't I, already?"

Shouta sits back silently.

Pythia and Angela's faces glimmer on the haze. Paul's trembling hand falls through the hologram. "There must be a way…Some sort of alternate fail-safe besides Winchester's—an ejection algorithm…You've got to protect your subscribers."

Shouta sighs, reading the piteous look chiselled into Paul's face like a disposable pamphlet on a rare disease. He exhales—*not to be mistaken for a sigh*—and intuits-closed the

Sheffields' profiles. "Prior to the Purge, we had individual reset options. The problem was that the resets were approximate, and—granted the plastic and erratic nature of the human mind—also prone to error."

"What sort of error?"

"The reset algorithm would often mistake pre-CLOUD stimulation and memory for data obtained whilst synchronized. It is, after all, nearly impossible to impose such distinctions on the human mind…Anything from cherished childhood memories to basic motor function could be lost. We learned our lesson, unfortunately, from one-too-many mistakes."

"For crying out loud." Paul hunches over the table, crowning himself with flat-palmed hands. "God-damn-it."

"There was also the matter of assassinations. If a hacker got a hold of your reset codes, they could erase your sentience. Why use a bullet to accomplish what you can do with an idea?"

Paul tries to fully comprehend the horrible concept. "Assassinations." His voice sinks into a forlorn drone of despond.

"We retained a mass-reset function, should an Extinctive Event be discovered or forecasted."

"An Extinctive Event?"

"We are calling it an *Anomaly*." All emotion vacates Shouta's face, and his eyes seem especially clear.

"An Anomaly?" Dread dictates Paul's posture. "Not anything like the one you brought me here to see, huh?"

"Well, old friend; that is exactly it: I am not completely sure."

Paul keels forward. *Shouta has too much pride to admit ignorance, unless he's really screwed, and by that point it's already too late.*

"And that is precisely why I would love it if you would take a look."

Angry yawps exhale from the kitchen, tucked behind the bar. Select words amongst the quarrelling bass and mezzo-soprano find Paul. "'Bitch', 'fetcher', 'thief'."

Shouta rolls his eyes at Paul, whose posture has hardened around the resolve to intervene.

"Tell me, *old friend*," Paul says, feeling the testosterone rise on the heels of the overheard bawling.

Shouta tilts his head, receptively.

"Will I catch hell for this? I've already breached the terms of my restraining order..."

"Consider all bad-blood leeched." Katajima tries to hide his hesitation behind a sip of beer. "Outland cannot be compromised. This Anomaly has to be stopped. Winchester will see it in his best interest to clear your slate, now or after."

Interesting phrasing. "And if he doesn't?"

"If he cannot concede that point, we will have to work on our solution privately, without his knowing or his blessing."

Shouta intuits a new query, which bands across the hologram: "SCREENSHOT 4302: EPIC, DELOCALIZED DATA TRANSACTION>>>..." On the grid, towering above all the other 3D clustered bars on the graph, stands one labelled: "UNKNOWN SYNCH."

Paul leans in. "What's the measure, here, terabytes?"

"Decabytes."

"That's impossible." Paul spins the hologram to get a better sense of scale. "Empty data?"

"No."

"It's got to be some kind of data-mining group. Hackers...or a super AI."

"My team is absolutely certain that it is not an AI. As for hackers..."

"Yeah?" Excluding himself, the list of people Paul's aware of with the ability required for this sort of attack has been narrowed down over the years by bullets and overdoses.

Shouta wipes his brow, and sips his beer. He thumbs the condensation on his stein thoughtfully. "After the Purge, we went after the hackers, *big time*. Spies, oligarchs, and saboteurs—the lot of these so-called *noosphere gods* had forgotten about their meat. Now, it was not as simple as sorting them out at one of the cypulchres; most of them synchronized remotely. It would, after all, be foolish to subvert Outland whilst living in an Outland Outpost. Nevertheless, we managed to restrain what was sleeping, and publicly relished in their Titan-fall."

"Outland Security took 'em down?"

"Outland Sentinels, the military, cyber mercs. A lot of private detectives retired off that pay-day."

How'd I miss that memo?

"Remember, Paul: everyone is invested in the CLOUD. Anything with a mind to threaten the whole needs to be *lobotomized*." Shouta traces a window between them, and his Monocle quickly side-projects a criminal record into the prepped-space. "Including our old friend."

A photograph of a slim-chinned, raven-haired woman with mascara spikes cutting to her cheeks appears on the porous screen.

"Is that...?"

"Oni Matsui, PhD. A highly capable hacker and an ideological extremist. Followed your example and made a fuss when leaving Outland. We ascribed her radicalization to a personal loss she blames on CLOUD tech. Only, instead of whistle-blowing like her predecessor, she blew up your old lab. We have kept bad company, you and I."

"Did you *get her*?"

"No. We subpoenaed her memex for review, but she scrambled the file and then rained-out. Clever girl."

Hiding his satisfaction, Paul responds only with a guttural "Hmm."

"Fortunately, we got most of the others. Key targets, anyway. Outland tracked down and secured their air strips, waited for them to land, and eliminated them with extreme prejudice."

Uncertain if he's hearing things, Paul cuts Shouta off. "Hold on—when did you transform from a limp-dick scientist into a warlord?"

Shouta makes his dissatisfaction over Paul's statement known, shuffling his jaw side to side. "Necessity. It is not like they had forgotten to pay their bills. They threatened to destabilize everything we have worked for. Everything *you* built."

Paul drowns his skepticism in a glut of beer. He'd written-off the Sentinels at Q's as a Winchester initiative, but now he's not so sure.

"Regarding this Anomaly, we are looking at a completely different genera of malignancy."

"But if this new problem plighting the CLOUD isn't hackers or gods…"

"It is a data bubble—a heavy store—with a sentient director. It is constantly growing, replicating all of the available user data—memories, stimulation, knowledge…Think Moore's Law, just apply it to a virtual conquistador. At the current rate of expansion, this *thing* will be globally wired—hooked into everything with a wireless signal or a hardline—by the end of next week. The internet of everything will have one master, and we do not know who or what it is."

"Why'd you say sentient?"

"It is not a bug, a script, or a virus. It has an epicentre, a definitive pattern of behaviour and specific foci, and it manipulates the feed in ways our AIs simply cannot or will not. It is a hacker unlike any we have ever encountered."

"And at this rate," Paul says with his hand in the hologram, "It's going to overload your infrastructure."

"Forget the infrastructure. Like I said, it will have control of both worlds by the end of next week. Government and military secrets, passwords, launch codes…you name it. It can effortlessly turn off our taps, burst our dams, turn-off life support on Europa, or hijack battle bots; anything with a feed, whether it be pinging the net or the CLOUD, is fair game."

"Jeeze."

"For all we know, our food extruders might be printing poisoned meals."

Or cancelling SIK prescriptions…"This *is* an Extinctive Event…" It hits Paul. "Oh my god*, my girls.*"

"Relax, Paul. Like I said—"

"To hell with 'what you said'. You've got to track this thing down and dump that data. Somewhere, someplace, someone's synching, and you have to ice 'em."

"We are working on it."

"Bullshit."

"We have agents in 190 countries breaking-down doors and dropping nets, and there has yet to be any sign of the enemy. Whatever is doing this does not have a digital footprint because it walks with the feet of others. It does not even cast a shadow."

Paul's eyes widen. "Oh dear lord."

"What?" asks Shouta, timidly.

"If you're asking me, you must really be in trouble. What's the military doing? The government?"

The sound of crunching shells alerts both doctors to a tall, red-haired woman, buckled into a black leather skirt and torn fishnets. She gracefully anchors her glowing-blue jackboots, and hammers two beers through the hologram to the center of the table, hiding the wet rings left by their predecessors.

Shouta looks to Paul. Together, they simultaneously adopt the same fake smile.

In a warm and lyrical voice, the waitress addresses Paul: "Ay love, just a heads-up: Manuelito's ending all lines of credit. It's not personal; it's politics. We're only taking yen and rubles now."

Paul concentrates on her bright xanthous eyes, striking in their war-painted coffers. "Sure, Maxine." He ratchets his mirthless stare downwards, trying to sustain his plastic grin.

Her face lights up. "Paul!" she exclaims, deviating from her script. She clasps his neck affectionately. "Man, it's been a while."

"Glad to see you've stuck on the right side of the wall."

"*You know me.* Always looking for something to steady me so I don't get lost in the rest of it."

Paul's plastic grin slackens to a genuine smile. "Was that your alter ego who served us earlier?"

She giggles. "No, I just hadn't yet thrown my face on." She strains a mischievous smirk and leans forward to grab Paul's empty glass. Bending over, she looks Katajima dead in the eyes.

"Say hi to Frank for me," Paul mumbles, noticing the attention Maxine's giving Shouta.

"Sure, sweetie," she says, turning to Paul. "P-S, comm me when you have the time. I want to run an idea by you." She winks at him, and swaggers back to the bar, tracking the forest of eyes trained on her.

Watching people watch Maxine, Paul shakes his head, and returns his attention to Shouta.

"Military and government are searching for the person or group responsible. They have thrown resources and money my way to devise a counter attack."

"And here you are," Paul whispers.

"Here I am." Shouta looks around, as if readying to divulge some hot gossip. "The Empty Thought, *P-S*."

"Huh?" Paul sputters, clearing his throat. *Shouta remembers or he knows. Either way, I'll have to walk on egg shells from here on out.*

"Your virtual black hole."

Paul mouths 'black hole'. "Yeah, great help it'd be if only Winchester hadn't deleted it when he gave me the boot."

Deleted what he thought was the only nearly-finished iteration. I copied the Empty Thought. The version Shouta's referring to attacks an entire data tree and destroys it, whereas my beefed-up version back at home will destroy any data it comes in contact with. Forget data trees; my Empty Thought will fell forests.

"Delete? Heavens, no. I am not even sure that is even possible. Dr. Matsui saved it, notwithstanding internal protest. It has been quarantined ever since."

"Ah-ha!" Paul flattens his palms on the table. "Good for her...So, what are you waiting for? Give it a try."

"I have, or rather I would, but you never finished it."

Amused, Paul raises his eyebrows, tauntingly. "But you did try?"

"Yes. Would have been nice of you to inform me you had encrypted it. Destroyed my ciphers, not to mention wasted hundreds of man-hours."

"I encrypted the activator, is all. And I did the world a favour. The Mossad and the CIA wanted to use it for regime change. Hieronymus would have used it to reset the lower class' credit scores…I guess that if you haven't cracked it, the government's still stuck murdering the old-fashioned way and the poor are still poor."

"Even if I could play around with it, I would be hesitant on account of having absolutely no idea what it is capable of…no idea of how to employ it properly."

"You bring it up thinking it might be a solution to your extinction problem?"

"*Our extinction problem.* Yes."

"Say I helped you. Say I completed work on the Empty Thought, found a way to transport it and decrypt its activator. What then?"

"We target the Anomaly."

Paul furrows his brow. "How much collateral damage are you willing to incur?"

"Why? Can't we specify a target? Would it damage the CLOUD?"

Paul can't tell if Katajima is playing his cards close to his chest, or if he simply doesn't know. "Well," Paul turns his glass to distort the candlelight, "It might, but that doesn't matter."

"Why?"

"You've got two problems in addition to the execution of whatever end-run the Anomaly has in mind."

Katajima sighs. "Well?"

"The encryption poses a lot of problems. I locked myself out."

"Oh, for the love of God! Any idea of who could open it?"

"No. Nobody."

Shouta leans back and rigs an imperious pose. "That is too bad. I was really hoping we could help each other." He looks over at his men, still standing by the jukebox.

"No, no. I'll still be able to help," Paul yells, erupting into a panicked excitement. "It's just a matter of time and access."

"I do not know, Paul."

"Now I *know* you're gaming me. This Anomaly is going to destroy the CLOUD, kill god-knows-how-many people, and cripple your business." Paul pushes the stein out of his way and tents his fingers at the centre of the table. "We wouldn't be talking if you didn't need me. And here we are."

The taught-faced mogul opposite Paul grinds his teeth and tilts his head.

"If you guarantee successful resets for my girls and the prevention of all future attempts on their part to synchronize, then I'm your man."

"You mentioned a second problem."

Paul leans back, and regains his composure. "Transport. You need a data-fragmentor to transport the Empty Thought."

"No problem. I can find one, or I will have my team build one."

Paul wants to ask Katajima whether he'd paid Q an anticipatory visit, but would have to explain what *he* was doing there. "Then we finish it, we transport it, and, assuming we've found some way to decrypt the activator, we let it do its thing."

"And the CLOUD? It'll be left intact?"

"I guarantee you: the Empty Thought will destroy the Anomaly before the Anomaly has a chance to destroy the CLOUD."

Shouta gives a subtle nod, then, clasping Paul's hands, an emphatic one. "I am overjoyed to have the opportunity to work with you once again, old friend."

"Speaking of which, let's get to it," Paul says, upright and attentive. "What operating system are you running at the lab? It might take me a few minutes to adjust for future shock."

"Oh, no, Paul. You need your rest. Besides, there are matters I must attend to first, including disinhibiting you by clearing the charges the police are currently trying to nail you with. We have all of tomorrow to ready your Empty Thought, but will take more time if more time is required."

"Allen's funeral?"

"We'll ferry to the funeral on Friday via Dragonfly." He wiggles out of the booth, and stands up, throwing an intentional glance to Haruto. "Paul?"

Paul looks up keenly.

"My nephew will take you to your hotel room. In the morning, we will convene at your Barstow residence and get to work."

"Why my place?"

"Quiet. Secluded. Safe, knowing you, and off the grid, yes?"

"Yeah. I've a solar farm and a small aquifer. Some jammers and a magnetic band to throw my net address."

"Excellent."

"Why can't we use the Outland labs?"

"On the off-chance Winchester cannot see past your bad blood to his best interests, you and I will have to proceed as planned. We cannot afford any obstacles at this point in time, political or mortal. I will bring what you had finished of the Empty Thought over."

No need, I finished it already, Paul wants to say.

"And secure a fragmentor while I am at it."

"Well, if we're flying, it won't be so inconvenient…"

"My apologies. You will have to drive yourself out there. We will fly back together for the funeral."

A paranoid streak chills Paul from the inside out. *Katajima's being awfully inconsistent.* "Drive? The other day you said it was too dangerous to drive."

"It would be doubly dangerous to make Winchester think we have gone behind his back. Suspicion turns friends into enemies, and enemies into corpses, after all."

"Alright. If I set out at sunrise, I can be ready to work by noon."

"Splendid."

"You'll come alone?"

"Yes. The fewer involved, the better our chances of surprising the Anomaly, whatever it is. Now, remember: the walls have eyes, the darkness ears…Best avoid the Anomaly until we have decided upon the equation that best suits us."

Paul, face afresh with hope, shakes Shouta's hand. "Empty thoughts and full promises."

"Yes!" Shouta exclaims. "The former released, the latter kept!"

Chapter 15: HIVE, SWEET HOME

THE CLOSING DOOR CROPS Katajima's nephew out of sight. Shuffling outside deals silence upon the elevator's ping. Paul's alone again, his chauffeur en route to the roof parking lot.

He mag-bolts the door, and plots his head against it. *Hangover's come early.* The cold steel repels him into the darkness.

With a well-coordinated triangulation, he switches on the hotel's density field, and populates it with data direct from his Barstow retreat via Monocle. It's fuzzy and pixelated on account of Paul's security software. Securitas, of course, requires more than one code to verify identity and intent, so Paul confirms with an incoherent string of alphanumeric.

"Good evening, sir."

"Securitas, status?"

"All systems normal."

"Great work. Unjam the feed. Let me see my boys."

Securitas decrypts the data, and directs it over to the *Home* interface that Fergus had mentioned. The data, filling the field, clarifies and conforms to Paul's perception. Paul stumbles through the projected-blue fog, reflexively avoiding the hotel room's hidden obstacles.

He summons a live feed from his retreat's 3D CCTV cameras. The frolicking forms of his dogs appear, first as digitally-corrupted, two-dimensional objects, and finally as hi-def, full-volume projections.

"Zeus! Apollo!" Paul shouts.

The dogs respond to their master's voice—one crooks its head sideways—but are unsure as to its authenticity. They take turns shaking loose hair over the only carpet in Paul's Barstow retreat.

"Hey, y'little bastards."

Having dutifully tended to one another's nether regions, they bound committedly towards Paul's voice and reciprocated hologram. Their ears slacken from their initial points. Jaded, however, by the absence of their owner's odour, the dogs slough back off-screen, ears pointed once again. The smile that'd slipped onto Paul's face at the promise of affection flattens.

He traipses through the hologram of his Barstow place, and opens a Net search screen within the *Home* interface. The flickering graphics on the floor-to-ceiling organic-LED projection highlights Paul and his decadent, old-fashioned furniture with a periwinkle varnish. He turns the screen's opacity down two-thirds, letting the Blue Zone's shimmering cityscape outside the hotel room burn through the lettered polymers.

Across massive towers and over the Hyperloop's red aura, Paul's Net query lists likely answers, most of which he's already familiar with.

He swipes away the results, intuiting, instead: "IMPLANTS, CLOUD TECH."

The Net query refreshes, this time visualizing the resultant data-tree across the wall as well as against the city behind it. Trunks of code and branches of crypto-glyphs telling the story of the CLOUD's construction stretch down the Blue Zone's skyscrapers and take root below the Partition. The *Home* interface in the foreground makes sense of the Net results, pulling data and simplifying wiki-rhetoric into an organized spiral around Paul.

Outside the hotel room window, an ad-barge penetrates the horizon, jetting slowly across the screen. It fires out a bigger-than-life hologram of a sperm whale bordered by tickertape, which reads, "AQUARIUM OF THE

PACIFIC—BE THE FIRST TO SEE THE LAST OF THE GREAT SEA MAMMALS."

Paul tweaks the opacity of the screen to diffuse the ad-barge's distracting lights. He filters his results over the faint outline of Los Angeles' downtown, this time checking against what he already knows, as determined by the *Home* interface's buffer. The data-tree shrinks to an artifact-ridden acorn, and begins to grow again.

Impatient but certain that this most-recent search will prove to be the most interesting, Paul heads to the mini-bar for research supplies. He finds and wrestles off the cap of a bottle of rye. Snatching a glass from the cupboard, he pours a shot, downs it, and then fills the glass past the precedent he established, indicated by a thumb-deep watermark. With the brown tincture sloshing in hand, he clumsily trots over to the couch at the end of the bed, opposite the minimalist desk.

"The Outland CLOUD," he reads, the words blurring—worsened by the room's apparent spin. "Developed by the Outland Corporation, was trial-released to the public...after the proven popularity of nano-tech HUD displays in the early 21st Century. Introjection capabilities of this variety were first tested at Berkeley and at the University of Toronto by the Katajima-Sheffield team, who eventually defined the parameters of the CLOUD."

A holovert emerges, bevelling the article. Despite Paul's coding, one or two eventually get through every so often. Two scantily-clad and anatomically-complete androids writhe over some pathetic, clunk-head colonist. *Apparently, under all his mech and tech, there's still cause for sexual desire.* It takes two or three tries, but Paul manages to intuit the pop-up off-screen.

Already cognizant of most of the encyclopaedic history and rationale of the CLOUD, Paul reads on, hoping the solution to his domestic strife is simpler than finishing his masterpiece and turning society upside-down. He hopes it is emboldened in a crisp serif, hiding in plain sight.

"A number of prestigious scientists and sociologists hailed the so-called 'evaporation stage' as a monumental step in human evolution. Nobel Prize winner Johannes Freidman argued that, with popular access to the CLOUD, the 'Omega Point [is] within grasp.'"

Paul sips his rye, silently repeating "Omega Point" again and again to himself. *The Anomaly might not necessarily be a malignancy; it could very well be an evolutionary catalyst.*

Nominally satisfied with at least one takeaway, Paul slouches forward, summoned by the growl of his stomach, and remote-controls the bean-encrusted extruder in the corner of the room. With a non-verbal demand for meat pie, the little machine jostles back and forth, making a variety of beeps and blurps, incarnating Paul's four a.m. treat.

"Senator Niles Winchester III's Katajima-Sheffield team developed a mind space. This mind space is incomparable to early millennium media, as it offers users the option to pursue and engage in both linear and non-linear free-flows of visual, aural, and simulated-tactile experiences over a local network. This alternate reality, where minds and data converges, was deemed the 'SHEF FIELD,' named-so after its chief engineer, Dr. Paul Sheffield. After a scandalous breakdown, forcing Dr. Sheffield to retire from the project and Outland indefinitely, the project's code-name became its official moniker: the CLOUD.

"Owing to the unhindered transit of the mind through ideas, images, experiences, and at a later point, memories, CLOUD interaction destroyed barriers erected consciously and subconsciously by bias, geography, politics, language, and the myopia trained by subjective experience. The very first instance of its efficacy was demonstrated at the Cordoba Peace Talks where world leaders, having downloaded and shared the experiences of one another, found an agreeable diplomatic solution in record time."

Paul scans down, mumbling, "Blah, blah, blah." A segment on *dependency* jumps out at him.

"Recognizing the need for ways to give the human brain assistance in mediating all of the data experienced in the CLOUD, the Outland Corporation implemented server/broadcast towers (bomb-proof, high-security, ninety-storey fortresses full of active-flow hard drives) wherein CLOUD experiences could be stored. It soon became apparent that the invention and implementation of these data towers or 'cypulchres', simultaneously supported the human brain whilst rendering it an indefinite dependent."

Unsatisfied with the regurgitation of known-information, Paul resets his query. "CLOUD CONNECTION; PROCEDURE."

Thousands of results stream across Paul's wall. He selects one at random. Several holograms beam out before him, depicting individuals receiving implants in bright, sterile rooms. A dozen other windows escape their frames, showing organic interaction with the implant in a hypothetical brain.

"User receives implant at an Outpost station. This quick and painless procedure will result with an Outlander Z-Series fixture inserted into the brain. Three days after the insertion, the user must return to ensure that synthetic dendrites have formed along the implant barrier and have created linkages with the pertinent elements of the occipital lobe.

"User negotiates a long- or short-term health plan with BiAnima to assure against mid-stream death, loss, or injury. Depending on the user's preference, BiAnima can provide a PILOT device that carries out basic body functions on the user's behalf while he or she is de-located. Some insurance plans enable the PILOT to perform menial tasks automatically while the host is mentally in the CLOUD. Deluxe packages also enable multi-processing, whereby the user can technically be aware and present in both the CLOUD and the material world simultaneously. The PILOT device also services an interior function: it indicates the day and the time to users in the CLOUD, additionally providing an in-feed from the outside.

"Upon showing proof of a BiAnima subscription or V-insurance, the user can choose to pay for one, six, twelve, thirty-six, or forty-eight months of broadcast time in advance. Lifetime subscriptions will be honoured, but family and/or any dependents must be consulted first. Usually for lengthy subscriptions, Outland will insist on housing the subscriber's body at a cypulchre or at an Outland hospice.

"Once the user has reported proof of insurance, PILOT activity, and subscription, they are admitted access to the CLOUD.

"Hot tip: prior to receiving the implant, select a memory, a special word, or a remote trigger, that you can use to prompt synchronization.

"Upon synchronization, the implant is triggered. A feedback loop is created between the implant and the user's exo-cortex, remotely stored in their local cypulchre. Their exo-cortex, or 'memex', is similarly synchronized with the CLOUD and their living-breathing self, completing the mental triangle."

Sprawled on the couch with an empty glass heaving up and down on his belly, Paul humours his self-pity. He closes all the windows on the wall-screen, and intuits a picture of Pythia and Angela. *Should have stuck to cannaberettes. Rye always makes me weepy*, he reminds himself.

With a swipe of his hand, the Net-wall's opacity drops to zero. Paul puts his glass down on the floor, and walks over to the window and into the embrace of the city light.

Between Paul's hotel room and the Blue Zone stretches an embankment of border-properties. Partyers from the Blue Zone come over to enjoy the unrestricted pleasures of the flesh that the RIM offers, provided by RIM ticks who keep their heads down and earn their keep. One building in particular catches Paul's attention.

On a rooftop across the gap from Paul's, twenty or so yuppies roll off each other, glistening under holographics depicting a primeval California. Their projections of giant redwoods and sequoias reach about thirty feet above the rooftop before dissolving into the smog and exhaust threading through this part of the skyline. Drunk and undoubtedly high on smuggled SIMHAP, the tech-junkies lunge about their shared dream—scouting the nooks and crannies of the illusory forest.

That's how it ought to be, Paul concludes in his personal court. *Tech to live, not live to tech.*

A police hover-car drifts between the redwoods, trawling a red-laser scan for bottom feeders, refugees, or any other kind of criminal who'd think a rooftop along the BZ/RIM border would be a good place to let loose. Likely prompted by a surprisingly dull scan, the car's off, leaving the redwoods, waving in the exhaust, to reform. The partyers resume their imaginary romp through the woods, Johnny Law's presence no sooner gone than forgotten. The drugs that were anticipatorily ditched over the edge will soon find users in the sky-alleys. *Nothing is wasted here, except for life and freedom.*

Paul steps out of the blue light, and heads for his bed. He sits on the edge, and digs his NEXUS chip out from under the mattress. Wobbling, he scrutinizes the basic, mean tech in the half-light.

He can't help but feel responsible for his daughters' plight. Sulking in a sweat-stained costume, with alcohol and

THC coursing through his veins, he is the rotten extreme they'll leave behind. Their bodies will shrivel up as their minds balloon, and they will become gods, or, conversely, helpless slaves. *No better than the hybrid rouging the back room at Q's.*

What will become of Pythia, with her newly-acquired power to speak and the mind to command? In all the circumferential hurry to converge and connect, she will either rise about the herd or else schlep into some deviant archetype on the fringe, where she'll ultimately be erased in the name of communion.

Angela, loved and understood, will become a follower; a nodule on the leviathan—a nameless fleck on a beach, washed and rounded into sameness, oblivion. He'd wanted better for her, but...

Rachel. *She'd sacrificed them. My daughters. Why,* after she'd agreed to protect the girls from the dangers of the noosphere? The notion of letting the world access their perfect little minds was anathema to the both of them. *Why the sudden change of heart?*

Someone got to her, just like someone got to Q—like someone cancelled my prescriptions to derail me. Someone manipulated her, made her think the CLOUD was something besides the hell her ex-husband tried to seal-up. Someone with juice and avarice and intent.

Katajima? Hard to say. Brutus had been pronged by a latent guilt. *Why would he go after the girls? Leverage? Why'd he go after Q? Control? What good would a fragmentor be to him without the finished code?*

Winchester, Paul knows for certain, would prefer to see him lowered into the ground with Allen. *But then why go through the trouble of destabilizing my family and driving me mad?*

Perhaps the better question would be: *who doesn't want to screw me over?* If he was theoretically capable of inflicting damage on or destroying the CLOUD, there'd be a mob with pitchforks lined-up at his door.

Shouta and the man who called himself Gibson both claimed to be allies. *Tomorrow, I narrow down the list.*

Something beside the bed beeps. Paul falls back into the embrace of the plush, hypoallergenic comforter. *What is it now?* The beeping persists.

Paul looks through ruffles of blanket. It's the hotel comm.

"Yeah?"

"Play message for Mr. Kerner. *Yes* or *no?*"

"Sure, what the hell."

"'Hey Mr. Kerner. It's Fergus. Couple Outland 'Sels came by asking about you. I said you were out. Thought you'd approve.' Would you like to hear this message played back?"

"No it's fine." *Nice kid. Hopefully doesn't see any blow-back for helping me out.*

Paul closes his eyes, wishing he could have his life played back differently.

Chapter 16: ON THE VERGE

MORNING SUNLIGHT licks the Outland Citadel, which dwarfs the rest of the jagged Los Angeles skyline, similarly sinking in the rear-view mirror. Someone's found Q by now. *Called it in as a suicide.*

Across town, Rachel is getting dressed for work, assured that yesterday was a bad dream. *Whether or not she believes it herself, that's what she would have told the girls—that is, right after bandaging her partner's brutalized hand.* The Citadel disappears, virtualizing all of the tragedies dialed under its shadow.

A red projection flashes a warning on the dash. "HEED LOCAL TRAFFIC LAWS, SLOW TO ACCEPTABLE LIMIT: 50…" With a boot heel steeped in Q's blood, Paul kicks the accelerator—what his generation still calls "the gas." The old truck's tires wrench back the asphalt, unraveling Highway 15 into the kaleidoscopic, desert wilderness, barbed with mesa, dunes and unyielding greens

With the soldered-on maglev panels stabilizing the drive and with the shitbox's governor disabled, Paul careens past the last of the signs for Partition checkpoints to the PIT. *It'd have been nice for Shouta to have at least sent me back on a charter under another pseudonym. Kernel, Colonel, Kurtz. Whatever. Suppose beggars can't be choosers, but I'd rather beg for a quick flight than have to drive for six hours.*

A two-speaker system with a subwoofer, embedded beneath the hood, simulates the growl of an old, gas-fed engine. It plays a gross, synthetic lullaby through the dash. Paul is comforted by the sound. It offers him something besides his lonely, acidic thoughts. He meditates on its gravelly crescendos, and reacts in turn with heavier depressions on the pedal, flooding the engine with charge.

His knuckles are swollen and roughened by a bloody crust. He grips the wheel harder. The pain fires a renewed focus back up his arms. Paul shakes his head and glances out the side, glimpsing a man crucified to a MAXIMUM 50 sign. He double-checks, but the man is gone. Paul's sanity usually finds him whenever he's stationary, sitting in his safe room at the retreat or anchored on a barstool. The last few days have already taken their toll—knocking him around like a pinball in a scoreless game. Granted his current rate of speed and trajectory, his sanity is likely not catching up anytime soon.

A volt of turkey vultures corkscrews in the distance. The spiral breaks, and a swarm of Wasp drones power through the gap. They glimmer for an instant in the morning orange, and disappear again into oblivion. Paul shifts into a higher gear and watches the vultures collect again, and funnel to a pinprick.

The faux-engine sound now competes with the grind of his molars against one another. *What to do with a virtual pansophist? Pray to it? Author another?*

Paul leans into the steering wheel, thinking on his pending meeting with Katajima. He lapses as driver and lets the tires trespass over the yellow divider. Drumroll.

"WARNING," announces Paul's deep-voiced dashboard co-pilot. "ALIGN VEHICLE TO ROAD. CHECK: FATAL SEQUENCE OF EVENTS."

An animation of the car flipping plays on loop in flashing green and red.

"Sounds about right."

Paul grips the steering wheel tightly, creasing the cultured leather, and pulls back into his lane.

On the seat next to him: an animated photo of his family as it was before the Fall. *Anything for them. Anything.*

A staccato beeping in his ear seizes Paul's attention. Securitas' atonal voice fuzzes through his Monocle: "Perimeter breach."

The AI attempts to pinpoint the intruder, scanning camera views, one by one, sending screenshots straight to Paul's heads-up-display. The camera input blurs slightly, catching reflections off of the solar panels decaling the natural walls outside of the retreat, as well as the glint off of the active-camo LEDs simulating continued desert floor.

The security program announces a successful scan with a digital flourish and zooms-in on several Outland Sentinels skulking around the house, knocking over shelves and tearing apart furniture. Paul's dogs run nervous circuits around the intruders, barking and growling. One figure approaches the camera, raises a spray can, and bam! The feed cuts out to popcorn-like static.

"What!" Paul whispers, returning his attention to the road ahead. *Either Katajima's got a death wish, or Winchester's tapped his Monocle.* "Deploy incapacitating agent. Protect Zeus and Apollo. Initiate Alcatraz Protocol."

"Defenses remotely deactivated. Cannot accomplish task."

"Log feed," Paul orders the security system, "and send a copy to Dr. Shouta Katajima."

"Video file sent."

Paul comms Shouta's link, but the Monocle projects an "Occupied" message.

"God-damn-it," he says, frustrated.

He draws his revolver, and plops it on the dash. Paul could give a damn about the house, save for the almost-finished Empty Thought hidden-away in his cellar. His dogs, on the other hand...*If someone lays a finger on them,* he'll go nuclear.

THERE IS SMOKE ON THE HORIZON—mammoth pillars of black teased eastward by the wind. Although he knows his mind is playing tricks on him, Paul nevertheless shudders at the sight of the devil spreading gloomy wings above his retreat.

He pulls to the side of the road. *The only friends I have left are in that inferno.* He'll save them or he'll avenge them. Regardless, Paul fully intends to spill blood. He checks his revolver to make sure its cylinders are plugged, and pulls back onto the road, lightning quick.

A wide, tan maglev van whips by him with the Outland pyramid on the side. *That's them*, Paul concludes, watching the tan box shrink in his rear view. *Whatever they came for they've found.* He badly wants to pursue them, but is holding out for the possibility that Zeus and Apollo are still alive and need his help.

He veers up the secret side-road to his retreat, and parks behind a thicket of creosote bushes. He closes the car-door quietly, fearful the retreating van left someone behind, and runs into the gulley, just below the patio. The windows above hiss and pop at the heat as fire carves improvised exits through the second storey.

The patio ladder is still locked into place. Paul mounts it, but hears footsteps above. Someone's still here. *Not for long.* Quietly and quickly, Paul ascends the ladder. He peeks over the top rung, and sees matte-black boots, reinforced with titanium strings. Paul looks up—it's one of the mechs from Q's.

Before his mind can catch up to his reptilian impulse, he's already plotted his revolver beneath the armor at back of the mech's head.

"Nice place you got here, Sheffield," says the mech, stiffening.

"You were just leaving."

Paul pulls the trigger, painting the patio in CLOUD tech.

He immediately turns, and kicks the French doors in. Covering his mouth with his collar, he charges through the smoke and flame. During thunder storms, Apollo and Zeus would hide at the foot of Paul's bed. *That's where they'll be.*

Struggling over to the base of the stairs, Paul entertains the remote possibility that they're o-k. *God, they'll be happy to see me.*

At the top of the stairs—now sporting bonfires for banisters—he sees them. The mechs overturned the room looking for something. Two still forms lay in the tracks left by their search. Apollo's sprawled over on Zeus, cast in a defensive position like a lava-rock Pompeian.

"I'm so sorry, you guys," Paul babbles, weeping. Despite the carbon monoxide choking him and the flames blistering his skin, Paul drops to his knees, and slams the floor with his hands. "No, no, no…*my little ones.*" His tears don't track far before evaporating in the hellish heat.

One of the reinforcing timbers cascades into Paul's bed, obscuring the little bodies.

"God, why?"

He crawls backwards, down the stairs. Fiery tornadoes consume his possessions and throw out flurries of cinders. Waves of blue and red flow across the ceiling like an inverted tidal pool. The retreat is caving in, piece by piece.

Paul feels dead inside. Like an automaton, he reflexively opens the passageway to his secret lair, and shimmies down. He bolts down the tunnel, yanks up all the hard drives and data slips that he'll need to deliver the Empty Thought, and hurries up and out.

Passing the mech bleeding-out on the patio, Paul puts down his armful of gear, and grabs the mech by the lid of his helmet. Furious and fresh out of opponents on which to exact his revenge, he drags the mech to the edge of the patio, and flips him over. The crunch of the saboteur's bones against the gully floor doesn't make Paul feel any better, but it also doesn't make him feel any worse. He grabs the gear and slides down the ladder, away from his premature funeral pyre.

THE MESA CONTINUES to heave black into the blue. Paul, caked in soot like a coal miner, watches the destruction through teary lenses, sitting in his newly acquired red shitbox—his alternative transport, the '29 *Rapid* FürE, having been rendered defunct by a volley of plasma bursts. *Winchester is going to pay*, he promises himself. *Katajima too, if he had any hand in this.*

An incoming message turns his wristband red. Monocle plays it for Paul. "Couldn't make it out, Paulie. I'll be at my place in San Joaquin."

Shouta.

Paul replies, "See you *real soon*, old friend." *Empty thoughts and empty promises.*

Chapter 17: THE DEVIL WITHIN

PAST GUILDS of rusted grasshoppers pumping out dregs of oil from under parched Californian skin, the GPS on Paul's Monocle bids him pull up an ostentatious side road. The cracked yellow sides are soon replaced by vineyards, wetted by little hydro-drones. Like a question mark, the road bends, and then hooks in front of a large concrete wall. Glint off the centre of the wall catches Paul's eye. Paul zooms-in on the glint.

"There you are," he mumbles.

Bumps in the transition off the highway push Paul's revolver into his side. He grunts, adjusts his belt, and accelerates forward along the compact mix of sand, gravel, and retired asphalt.

Paul's Monocle indicates another incoming message from an unknown caller on his visual feed.

"Put it through," Paul orders his Monocle. He slows the truck just enough to make his divided focus manageable.

The caller opts for audio-only. It comes on fuzzy, with a lot of background noise. "Glad to see you made it out of the fire. Now, about the frying pan..."

"Gibson?"

"Yeah, doc?"

"You knew about the fire and didn't warn me?"

"Our *mutual friend* had me clip your security system for updates. By the time I knew, you were already playing cowboy..."

"Comm me later. As I am sure you know, now's really not a good time."

"Tell me about it. You have any idea what's going on downtown?"

"Call me back in an hour."

"Listen up, doc. The super AI's taken over the CLOUD. Anyone who's synched today is trapped—they can't get back to their flesh."

Paul swears, and slows the truck down. "It's not an AI," he says definitively.

"Pardon?"

"Assuming you're not the one master-minding the CLOUD-takeover, I think we can help each other and get the Anomaly responsible."

"Anomaly? How's that?"

Sucking his teeth, Paul deliberates on how to deliver the Empty Thought if he ever manages to get his hands on a fragmentor. "We'll need someone with access to the Citadel."

"That's a tall order…Maybe ask to borrow Katajima's executive deck."

Katajima's deck is hypothetically one of the few devices outside of Outland Labs that can remotely interact with and manipulate the CLOUD.

"We'll see. Look into alternatives, anyway…You send me the coordinates to your place?"

"Camp Mud? You bet I did."

"Alright, well, I'm currently working on a solution. Let our *mutual friend* know I'll be in touch."

Paul terminates the comm.

The glinting structure—a gap in the one-hundred-foot-tall concrete wall—is a grey gate, initialled "S K" in heavy steel. A guard house flattered by a double roof, all corners curved upwards, is situated off to the right of the dip in the wall. Paul pulls up to it, and leans into the horn.

Outside, there is a loud, crackling sound. Paul opens his window, and pops his head out. He scrutinizes the air just above the barrier. It sizzles, with little white specs revealing not all is what it seems. A majestic albatross appears out of nowhere, and flies unperturbed through the crackling air.

"Well, isn't that something."

Haruto, the large, ogreish man who'd shadowed Shouta at the Indian in the Cupboard, shuffles out of his aspiring pagoda, decked-out in dragon-scale armour. The armour is painted a cobalt blue, offering a contrasting background to his white, custom-assault rifle. He bows, ever so slightly, and approaches the passenger window, which Paul powers down, halving his inner monologue to possibility.

"Good morning, Doctor," Haruto routines to Paul in an affected movie-English with a Japanese lilt. "Dr. Katajima is currently occupied. You might try calling him or come back later." This dismissive lie animates the curled wings of his thin moustache.

"He was very clear about wanting to meet me today. Was actually supposed to come by my place this morning."

Paul's words fail to affect the guard in the slightest.

"His world is going to come crashing down if I don't help him shoulder it..."

Thumbing his lip in the shadow of the gate, Haruto shakes his head. "I'm sorry, unless you have an appointment."

"I do! 'Bright and early', his words..."

The ground trembles beneath the car, jostling Paul from side to side. Silt and sand rain down from the pagoda's valleys. Similarly thrashed by the quake, the guard recomposes himself against the side of the truck, rippled forward in its tracks. He regains eye contact with Paul, and attempts to hide his frustration.

"What the hell was that?"

"Perhaps an omen, sir."

"Yeah, or the Big One...Mind just letting Shouta know I'm out here? *Trust me*: he won't mind the interruption...We have serious business to attend to. Lives depend on it."

Looking over Paul's mask of confidence and charred clothing, the guard poises as if to speak, and then hesitates. He ticks with a visible change of mind, and redraws his lips. "One moment, please." He turns to whisper into his feed.

Paul eyes the guard's rifle. Fully automatic, armour-piercing, heavplast extrusion. *Shouta's not fooling around.*

The guard's monitor fuzzes back a prompt and crackly order. With a surprised look and a shot of indignation, he bows again to Paul. "My apologies, sir. Dr. Katajima will be delighted to see you. One moment, please."

"S" and "K" separate, freeing to sight the long, winding driveway hemmed behind the iron. Paul waves out his window to the guard, and accelerates down the Gatsbian parade. In Paul's side mirror, behind the shrinking blue and white figurine, a gargantuan Locust drone uncloaks, standing guard with enough firepower to harrow Hell. Paul cracks a nervous smile, thankful he hadn't played it tough at the gatehouse granted the *bad omen*.

Encircled by the concrete wall is a spectacle of green and glass sublimity: a seeming Shangri-La; an oasis blessed by a man-made and controlled micro-climate, teeming with myriad species of flora and fauna. Giant birds thrash the canopy, and well up into the zenith of the fantastical compound. Stabbing the feathered swarm, built on a hill in the very centre of this splendid ark, is Katajima's stronghold.

It looks as though it'd once been a neoclassical mansion that was later swallowed up by functionless, Gehrian forms. There's a splash of red brick shadowed maroon beneath curvaceous sheets of crystalloid glass that seem to defy gravity. The sheets—at points bending to form tubules—cord around the structure, and flow out, rolling down and around the hill like tentacles, blurring natural/inorganic distinction.

Sequestered in the deciduous forest behind the mansion is a tall, black tower, braced by metal supports—

Shouta's own cypulchre. *Even the CLOUD has a first class.* A long glass hallway stairs down the hill from the mansion, cuts through the canopy, and connects with the tower.

Paul, committed to the task at-hand, stops salivating over the beauty of the reserve—*plenty of room for Apollo and Zeus to explore*—and disembarks. He leaves the car running just in case he has to make a quick exit. He strides past the garage doors to the right of the garish staircase, and up to the vaulted front door, curiously left ajar. Paul pushes the door open wider.

"Hello?"

An operatic male voice trills off in the distance, and somewhere a drawer slams emphatically. In the lull of the song, a frenzied yell trails on, mimicking and distorting the melody.

"Shouta?"

Paul ventures into the building. A little Mosquito drone flies over and past Paul, taking pictures and scans.

"Piss off!" Paul says, irritated, swatting at the little paparazzi. It takes off, loaded with genetic information.

Feeling like a tourist—some voyeur skulking through the home and life he'd surrendered—Paul covets in broad visual sweeps all he'd never possess: awards, antiques, busts of prominent scientists, and eclectic placarded inventions. The spoils of unfettered scientific exploration litter the foyer, tiled with veined black and white marble. Every nook and cranny speaks to Shouta's love for scientific progress and himself.

Pictures line the walls, half-a-dozen or more showcasing Katajima brandishing canines with powerful personalities, including Winchester III, President Jacoby, NewsLink's David Danson, and, in a glossy capture, high-ranking members of the military and Congress.

Figuring prominently among the miscellany is a defunct Tesla coil, raised on a wooden pedestal. At the sight of it, Paul keels ever so slightly, his sadness translated into a peptic fissure. He'd given the relic to Shouta as a birthday present—a playful and expensive riff on living on the fringe of scientific inquiry. Now it's a dust-covered testament to the homeowner's comprehension of what was lost for the sake of his gain.

Behind the coil stands a large Samurai statue: a helmeted buke with an electric sword in one hand, glowing blue, and a gross-looking plasma cannon in the other. Judging from its composition and the oil smears around its joints, the armoured buke is probably a prototype for a battle-mech of some sort, now a toy for Shouta's collection. *Katajima's hobbies have not changed, but his financial ability to pursue them certainly has.*

Shadowed and neglected mid-centre on the alcove behind the massive coil and the buke is a small digigraph looping a video feed of Paul and Shouta ingratiating one another, spilling expensive wine in celebration of their newly-funded Shef-Ajima Laboratory, looked-on by a class photo of technicians, engineers, surgeons, and staff, Oni Matsui and Allen Scheele included. Paul bows his head in grief at the sight of a man named Sheffield, happy and relatively unbroken.

His moment of reflection is upset by cynical-sounding cackling ahead. Paul stands his ground, ready on black tile like a righteous knight from Carrollian fantasy.

"Hey, Katajima! Is that you?"

The cackling stops, followed by the operatic voice—cutting off as if the needle'd been dragged across his dramatic finish in protest. Footsteps reverberate in the long hallway, marking the presence of another in the labyrinth. Paul's not too worried about what shape or mood the Minotaur should arrive in. He steadies his hand over his revolver.

Ambient creaks and hums submit to the volume of an Italian tenor who has resumed belting on the heels of the bass.

Katajima, white-haired and smiling, turns the corner, wine from his glass carrying on without him. Red splotches across the grid.

"Oh damn it!" Katajima looks at the red splattered on the marble, and up at Paul.

"Shouta?" asks Paul, pulling his hand away from his gun.

"Still haven't got the handle of *this thing*! Oh well. *Such is life*."

Paul notices something odd about Katajima's demeanour. "What the hell is going on? We were supposed to—"

"Oh, hey Paulie. Surprised to see you."

"*I bet*. Met one of your colleagues at my place. A real empty suit." Paul grits his teeth. "Killed my dogs." He sniffles angrily. "Burnt the place to the ground."

Katajima notices Paul's hand fidgeting at his side, and wrinkles his face with a disingenuous smile. "Wasn't my doing, I assure you. Just caught word of it now. Someone's put it into Winchester's head that you've something to do with the *Anomaly*. Haven't had a moment to sort him out."

"'Just caught word'?"

Katajima twists his wrist, and draws out a hemigram of an Outland memo. "Let's see. Tim Archer. Delocal ID: *ba de buh*, six-nine-zero-zero-two-eight. PILOT report says he's dead as a doornail. Last signal was—let's see here—your patio."

"Winchester, huh?"

"Uh huh," grumbles Katajima.

"You seem a little—"

"Off my game?"

Paul was going to say "possessed."

"Oh, Paul." The white haired lab-rat-cum-magnate makes a sucking sound with his tongue against his teeth, and

149

swaggers a few steps closer. "Please make yourself at home." Katajima pirouettes—arms indicating the splendour around—and unwittingly spills more of his wine. "He's done considerably well for himself, wouldn't you say?"

Paul discounts this rudeness as a symptom of low tolerance. "Listen, I waited…"

"Ha!" Katajima interrupts. Flailing his arms erratically, Katajima steps into a pouty face. "Must have been absolutely terrible!"

"We agreed…"

Katajima throws his wine glass into the shadows encroaching on the seeming chess board, and waltzes within breath's warmth of Paul. His nose is bleeding. "How was that?"

Paul takes a step back, transfixed on the blood dripping from Shouta's nose. *Either he's recently taken-up snorting cocaine, or someone's been tinkering inside his head.* "What?"

"Waiting, hours on end for someone—for something that'd never come. The thought of it makes me downright sick! Poor Paulie."

"*You* are sick, you know that?" monotones Paul, sweating anger through his shirt.

"Hmm?"

"You climbed over me to get out of the quick sand, and I didn't say a bloody word. I ask you this one time—just this once—for help…You owe me," Paul yells.

Katajima cups his chin and feigns interest. "Mm-hmm."

"Pythia and Angela—we need you. And, unless you've forgotten: *you need me. You* and the city of Los Angeles."

Striking another melodramatic pose, Katajima addresses Paul: "It's an awful thing to lose family; even worse to be unable to help. Really a punishing kind of impotence, wouldn't you say?"

"At the Indian—"

"I said…" Katajima rolls his eyes into their pinkish folds, and back again, "I'd help you get them back."

"Yeah." Paul tries to recompose himself, still unable to get a read off of Shouta's amorphous tone and form. "But first," he strains, "we have to figure some way to get me into the CLOUD without actually synching."

"The Creator cannot enter his creation. That'd just get him crucified."

"This thing has to be stopped. For all we know it's the very same tech singularity the government eradicated the Watson D-series to prevent from spreading."

Shouta sighs, ostensibly bored.

"For fuck's sakes, *you're* the one who came to me. You're the one planning to take it down."

"Was I? Am I? Oh, Shouta, Shouta, Shouta. I've recently had a change of mind. Bad for me, bad for you. Oh yes, and your Empty Thought? I was compelled to destroy the program. Felt it was more dangerous than the problem it was designed to resolve."

Paul waits for a punch-line. Without one, his face turns bright red. "Is this some kind of messed-up joke?" Paul screams into Katajima's taunting smile, saliva coning outward. The gun feels especially heavy on Paul's side.

"Forgive me. The funeral's been on my mind. I know you know the kind of toll guilt can take on a man. It's given me a lot to think about…*Do you* ever think on your sins, Paul?"

"Enough with the goddamn games!"

"Indulge me, Paul. Do you remember our adventures? Do you remember our old lab? Do you remember Allen? Or do you need some SIK tabs to jog your self-awareness? "

Katajima's mirth begins to unhinge Paul's moral restraint. "Of course I remember."

Katajima nods, thoughtfully.

"I remember how you killed him," Paul continues through clenched teeth.

"You convinced yourself that I did, when in fact, you cleared him for entry and encouraged *me* with doctored reports and data."

Paul shakes his head.

"C'mon; if anyone could have saved him, it was you, right?"

"I had nothing to do with his death."

"You mean you washed your hands of his fate?"

"*My hands* were never dirty to begin with. What the hell does this have to do with anything?"

"Could have grabbed a few Hitachi drives and reintegrated him. Ol' Winchester would have cut down all his money trees to help keep things quiet—to keep things running smoothly. Shit, he'd have splurged on a new circulatory system and a neural map if that's what it took. But your self-righteousness interfered."

"You opened the door before I could equip him with a parachute. I told you it was premature."

"It's not just what you did, it's what you didn't do."

"I tried everything."

"Wrong, wrong, wrong. Don't lie to me, Paul! Can't you remember? There's still history beneath all of that snow!" Shouta's face concretizes in an ecstatic smile. "*You* opened the flood gates! *You* got all up in arms about the CLOUD. *You* drew too much heat, too much attention. The Board wouldn't take the chance bringing poor Allen back from Oasis with everyone watching or blemish the CLOUD further with a casualty. No one wants to try to be a hero if failure paints him the villain! If he died, then the project was caput. You threw the baby out with the bath water, buddy. And someone lost everything because you wanted everything your way. You and your overblown ego…"

"That someone was me," Paul yells. "*I* lost everything. Look around, Shouta. My loss *is* your *everything*. I got two dead dogs, a burnt-down sanatorium, and a family—*that hates me*—marching to destruction…How *dare* you?" Paul bites his lip, attempting to suppress his fury. He surrenders the attempt. "I swear to God, Shouta. If you don't help me…"

"You'll what? You'll hurt me?" He widens his mouth to mime an 'o'. "Kill me?" Katajima playfully runs his finger across his neck, and twirls into the umbra of the skylight diagonally gridding the chess board. "Abandon me in the dark recesses of the noosphere? C'mon! Talk dirty to me, baby!"

Paul can feel his fingers gravitating towards the cold steel cutting into his waistline.

Katajima notices Paul's hand twitch towards his belt and recoils. "No, Paul. It's not right that you should have all the fun…" Katajima jaws into his delivery, smiling at Paul. "I mean, that's what this is all about. Ridding myself of all and any debtors before moving on, moving forward. Peeling off this base weakness."

"What's wrong with you? The Anomaly tune-up your mind or something? I'm not asking for the world here."

"Oh, I disagree on the basis of relative meaning. You're asking for *your* world back."

"Does this get you off or something, you sick bastard?"

"Little Pythia. Wow! She's a tough one to crack."

Paul's eyes widen. "I swear, Shouta. One more word…"

"And boisterous! Now that she's bunking at dear ol' Winchester's, she's evaporated twenty-four-seven. My lord. Talk, talk, talk, talk, talk."

Tears trail across Paul's soot-masked cheeks. *He'd have killed Katajima simply for touching his dogs. Going after Pythia?* Hot adrenalin pitches through his veins.

"Now, she likes you a whole lot more than that other one; Angela, is it?"

Paul pulls his revolver and aims it at Katajima. "Shut the hell up. Just shut your mouth."

"Her ego, my ego. Can you hate me, if she's a part of me? Can you bring yourself to kill me then, *daddy*?" Katajima laughs.

"*You*…What have *you* done to my daughters?"

Katajima paces around Paul, articulating into the barrel of the gun. "Here's a little food for thought: perhaps what's taken your little family doesn't give a damn about what happens to them, and is more invested in watching you suffer."

With explosive judgment seated under his thumb, Paul asks in a shaky voice, "Is it you? Are you doing this?"

Katajima's smile pronounces his cheeks, mocking Paul in advance of his answer, "Ah, both excellent questions. In short, no, on a technicality! And yes!" He steps back and curtsies, coinciding with a swell in the background instrumental.

Paul thumbs back the hammer on the revolver.

"Why?"

Resuming a rigid, upright posture, Katajima tilts his head, squeezing air-snaps out his vertebrae. "Don't ask stupid questions, Paul."

"I'm not leaving until I know."

"Well," Katajima throws his hands up, and grabs his cheek-skin taught, "good luck with that." Partly muffled by his stretched embouchure, Katajima declares: "Hey Sheffield, I know what *would* cheer you up!"

Ahead of Paul's wagging gun, Katajima pulls the flesh free from his own face, laughing, stringing sinew and dripping blood.

"How do I look, Paulie?" he chatters through an excavated mouth.

Paul lurches back, aghast, as Katajima's fat, teeth, and musculature are revealed.

Katajima's fierce laughter turns to a rattle, interrupted by gurgling sounds. He claws again and again, pulling at his hair, skin, and eyes. No longer identifiable, the sadomasochist tears at his chest without pause—without instinctive objection—*as if possessed.*

"What are you doing!?" screams Paul, tempted to shoot but otherwise stupefied. "Shouta! Shouta!"

Katajima's form falls to its knees, skeleton-baring through the gore. What remains of the esophagus and voice box manages a burbling "Ha-ha-ha-ha," and the body crashes forward.

"Oh Jeeze..." Paul cannot finish his thought, as it fragments into a million little inconsolable anxieties. He vomits off to the side.

Wiping his mouth clean, he looks askew at the bloody stump of what used to be a man. He approaches the body, gun still drawn. Parts of it—fingers, mainly—twitch involuntarily. Paul turns the body over, and checks for a pulse. *He doesn't stand a chance.* The carotid vein Paul would check is not even in the right neighbourhood.

Paul grinds his teeth and looks around for witnesses, help, *for anybody.* The great hall is quiet and still. He crouches and rips open Katajima's tattered shirt, exposing a PILOT device with a small sensor board flashing a red-alert indicator. Although his suspicion was right—*Katajima was not of sound mind or in control of his body at all*—it doesn't amount to any great conclusion. Paul pulls the PILOT insert, and interfaces it with his Monocle.

Paul mouths bits of the diagnostic as it scrolls in front of his iris. "'Outland Override; Redirect Command to:

Unknown User. Inhibit Re-Entry. Enable Window Feed.'"

Jesus. Whoever hacked into Shouta's personal cypulchre and then commandeered his body via his PILOT device made him watch... Paul intuits a prompt: "Ping user location."

"LOCATION NOT FOUND."

"Trace origin of override."

"TIER 3, MEGA-CLUSTER. RESTRICTED, CLOUD SYSTEM V1.341."

Off in some back chapter of the mansion, the operatic record twists forward announcing its finish with intermittent cracks and hisses. Clk-clk-ce-buh.

Paul, sick of watching Katajima's blood checkmate his corpulent mass, pockets Katajima's PILOT insert—a dead-man's key—and jogs towards the back of the mansion in search of Katajima's executive deck.

It has to be here. Shouta would never be more than fifty feet away from it: a custom piece of hardware that they designed together. It interfaces with the CLOUD in such a way that the user can effect virtual and cognitive changes without actually evaporating. It's Paul's best chance at saving his girls and delivering the Empty Thought remotely, that is, without getting an implant and doing it in person.

At the end of a wood-paneled side hall draped with tapestries is a small metal door. *In a place where nothing is small or simple...* Paul courts over, and cautiously opens the hatch. *Bingo.*

Chapter 18: PESTICIDE

SHOUTING ERUPTS in one of the antechambers. "Dr. Katajima! Oh my goodness!"

Japanese. Haruto knows. Haruto, the guard with the big-assed gun.

Comm chatter, beeps, and "roger-that's" ride on what Paul surmises to be Haruto's grief and anger-filled wails. "You bastard! You'll pray for me to let you die before this is over!"

"Shit," murmurs Paul, noticing blood on his hands.

Beyond the hatch door is a small room. Exposed-brick walls, seemingly pixelated in the glow of a low-hanging LED chandelier, surround a metal table that could easily double as a medical bench. On it, Katajima's deck, a half-finished bottle of Saki, and a steel briefcase.

Paul taps the deck—a book-sized screen with executive access to the CLOUD's backend. *Now I can address the Anomaly remotely. Link the Empty Thought and destroy both the Anomaly and the CLOUD forever. Will have to rain everyone out first, or they'll be* destroyed *as well.*

He cracks open the briefcase. Enveloped in foam-padding is a fragmentor. *Q's, no doubt,* Paul tells himself, unsurprised.

Encircled by sleek-silver is the core of the device: a thumbnail-sized processor designed to encrypt, atomize, and suspend data.

Katajima's deck's no good without the fragmentor. Paul's Empty Thought would destroy the deck, and any other device it came into contact with while cohered as a complete program. *Gotta upload the fragmented Empty Thought and figure out a way to then decrypt it on the other end.*

Paul throws the deck into the briefcase, clasps it shut, and turns to go. Ahead: a corridor that could stand-in for any of the Louvre's. Katajima's dead body actualizes it—anchors it in the real.

There's a loud bang. Paul stops.

Mid-way down the corridor, the windowed side-wall caves in. Instantaneously, glass, stone, and drywall tear through the gaping divot. A cloud of dust and debris unfurls over buckled marble, finding and hiding Shouta's body. A second bang rocks the foundations, as if the hill's evacuating into some infernal chasm. *Is this fortress' existence tied to its master's?*

Paul grips the small doorframe for stability. The ground continues to shake, and with it, the crystal LED chandeliers dangling along the corridor. Pillars bearing memorabilia and scientific artifacts bear over, and ceiling fragments cascade down like wavering flakes of snow.

Some unseen force splits a seam along the ceiling. Rubble loosed from the upper floors rains onto its invisible form, defining its contours. Its light-redirecting cloak scales back, flickering as it retreats and revealing the destroyer underneath: a Locust drone.

The Locust drone stands twice as tall as its shadow, which reaches Paul, three metres away. *It looks like a bus-sized cricket on steroids.*

Its two forelegs respectively sport a 50-calibre undercarriage, which are fed ammo belts from a chink in its conte-red chassis. Paul can only assume that the brown stumps with frontward-facing holes built into its collar are rocket launchers. Its thorax is complimented by rows of serrated-blades that run down to its owner-interface.

It looms over Katajima's corpse, running a quick autopsy with its faux-mandibles. The Locust's eyes—or rather, its self-illuminated configuration of sensors and radars—narrow and cycle through shades of green.

"Shit." Paul quickly surveys the room behind him for a way out.

The Locust sonar-pings the room, which sounds like a whale song. Its green-hued eyes rotate, the ocular disc spinning them—analyzing the room and all of its variables.

With nowhere to go but forward, Paul pulls out his revolver, and advances. He ducks behind a fallen pillar, and sneaks a peek at the terror ahead.

The little Mosquito Paul'd swatted at the front door buzzes through the Locust's improvised entranceway. It darts over to the Locust and scans it. With a beep, it sails down the hall, and ascends to within feet of the ceiling. It spins wildly firing a red laser.

Paul's eyes widen. "Perimeter scan." *Damn.*

Another beep marks the completion of the scan, undoubtedly bad news for Paul. The Mosquito scoots over, indicating and accusing Paul with its laser.

"God-damn-it," whispers the accused, barely keeping it together.

With all six weaponized legs in agreement, the Locust hammers forward, bowing its head out of the way of its shouldered firepower. Paul peeks over the pillar, and sees the dark blur of the insectoid marauder grow.

The Locust's mini-guns start to spin. The metronomic whining sound of accelerating hammer clicks and whooshing barrels underline its intent.

Paul blind-fires over the pillar, accomplishing nothing but noise.

"Inago! For the love of God," a man yells in trebly Japanese, no doubt emulating his former master by using his favorite turn of phrase. "Open fire!"

"Hey, hold on! Call off the dogs! This is a mistake," Paul cries into the fleeting vacuum before the barrage.

The Locust crawls forward. With a thud, the inhibitor releases the guns. A thrashing sound, like nailed-down plastic flapping in a hurricane, fills the room. Paul keels forward as his cover receives the first, fluid volley of large-caliber rounds.

The air smells like gunpowder and is noticeably hotter. Each subsequent hail chisels more off the pillar, eroding its former illusion of permanence and cutting nearer Paul's failing reserve.

RED SEARING PAIN.

"Gah!" The shock grips him before the pain finishes its circuit. Paul can see a parade of blood mapped out before him. Possible bone fragments—what look like fish scales—are caught in the cuff of his pants. He moans, and sets his head back, forgetting the threat that had him hunched over to begin with.

More rounds pound his cover, serving as a reminder—some arcing over and chewing up the far wall. Inarticulate worry meets his lips and sounds as vexed murmurs. Paul's cold fingers probe the wound. His jacket is frayed. His skin, peeled back, no longer hides the torn musculature above his collar bone. He cries out in vain.

"You—" Haruto declares in shaky English, competing with the volume of the mini-guns, "you killed a great man!"

The Locust pauses. In this moment of reprieve, Paul can only hear his pulse and the clinking of spent shells. Shaking—stricken with animal panic—he rattles around to see Haruto, standing with his assault rifle slack at his side.

"Ch-ch-check the surveillance feed," Paul pleads, burdened with the clarity of a dying man. "I didn't. I swear to God, I didn't."

"He was more than a great man. He was my friend."

Don't expect a trial, here. Paul resets to his caustic factory setting. "Friends don't live in guardhouses."

Blinding Paul with dust, the guard opens fire on the nearly-decimated pillar and advances between the drone's legs. He sees Paul's gore painted on the marble opposite him and smiles.

"Inago, for the love of God, hold fire and position. Suspend surveillance uplink for five minutes," Haruto commands the steel beast in Japanese. "This is off the record."

Stooping as a sign of recognition, the Locust aligns itself with the hall, and laser-marks the pockmarked pillar.

"Listen, will yah?" Paul's right arm slumps over, fingers twitching on their own accord. He seizes the revolver with his left, and wrenches the hammer back with his thumb. He gestures to stand.

Incoming bullets nip the motion.

"For God's sake. I didn't kill Katajima."

"You'll have to excuse my disbelief...and my intended cruelty." The guard plinks a few more rounds over the pillar as a sign of control.

Paul, covered in chalk, blood, and marble dust, glimpses another fallen pillar on the other side of the hallway, within reach of a shattered window. *C'mon, you son of a bitch. Get up.* The courage fails him, but so does the mental message coursing through his body to stop. He bolts towards the pillar, but the Locust severs his trajectory with a rocket.

FEAR.

Paul's skin is warm and blistered and pimpled with shrapnel wounds. He can't feel his right arm. He hatches his bloodshot eyes, and sees the guard, face eclipsed by the barrel of his rifle.

The whoosh of Inago's mini-guns picks back up.

"Inago, for the love of God, hold your fire," bellows Haruto. "Paul Sheffield, is it? So-called friend of the late, great Dr. Katajima." He crouches, and jabs Paul's massacred shoulder with the hot muzzle of his gun. "Even if I let you go,

161

the depleted uranium nested in your chest will render you blind and dumb by week's end. You're already dead."

Paul's fading. *I've failed the girls; failed myself.*

"You die without a shred of honour."

Paul's revolver didn't make it over with him. It's jammed in a groove of destruction in the line of fire. The briefcase with the fragmentor and Katajima's deck, on the other hand, is within reach. Paul paws the cold marble for its handle.

Haruto tilts his gaze and connects the dots to Paul's prize. He steps on Paul's grasping hand, looks at the case, and distorts his face with a knowing smile.

"Inago!" Haruto yells in Japanese. The Locust's eyes turn green and widen. "For the love of God, keep an eye on the target. Continue to hold your fire."

The guard gets up, and walks over to the briefcase. He slams it down on a bullet-ridden pedestal, and clicks it open.

Paul nods his head and prays. He prays that it won't hurt. He prays that the Anomaly or whatever evil genius controlling the CLOUD wished him dead will have mercy on his family. He prays that his soul will survive his body...*for the love of God.*

The Locust's eye-plate stops spinning, and the lenses revert to red, framing Paul.

"Inago, for the love of God, break a rib or two," Haruto says, laughing and shuffling forward.

Paul reacts to the order, and attempts to roll over, out of the way. Inago catches him mid-movement. Its pincers puncture his sides. Inago holds Paul upside down before its ocular disk, and scrutinizes every last detail.

"For the love of God, Inago, send him over here!"

Inago whips Paul past the guard. Paul crunches against the marble floor and slides near Katajima's gnarled corpse, tracking blood along the way.

The guard turns Katajima's deck and shakes his head. "Is this really worth dying for? Worth *killing for?*"

"I didn't…" Paul babbles.

The guard tip-toes over Paul, reviewing his file via Monocle. "Says here, you speak Japanese." He turns to Paul with an inquisitive look. "Is that true?" he says in his native tongue.

Paul sits up into a fog of pre-death. "A-a-after the war, I spent some time in Fukuoka," Paul replies, manufacturing an accent. "Picked up what I could. *What I needed.*" He half-slumps over. His faculties are failing him.

The guard smiles, and looks up at Inago, glaring red over Paul. "Life is a lamp flame before a wind." He ejects his spent magazine from his print, and paws his belt for another. "Understand?"

"Sure," Paul grunts, thinking on the importance of Katajima's favorite turn of phrase.

"Inago and I are the wind."

Paul interrupts, sitting up. "Inago? For the love of God…"

With attentive eyes-turned-green, the Locust skews its head sideways. Haruto looks to Inago, and then to Paul with a marked look of confusion and panic.

It's a command prompt.

"No!" yells Haruto.

Paul cracks a smile. "Kill Master Haruto before he utters one more word."

Inago's ocular-disc spins, this time framing the guard.

The wings on Haruto's moustache veer down, "No! Inag—"

The Locust slings one half-dozen high-calibre rounds into Haruto, cutting him in half.

Sliming backward, Haruto whispers, "For the love of God…"

The last of the hot casings clinks behind Paul. Trained on the bodies, similarly gutted, Paul gulps. He falls over, the smell of iron misting around him.

"Monocle, medical status report," he rasps.

Paul's Monocle flits-on, blurry and mired with digital artifacts. "Critical condition. Seek immediate medical attention."

"No shit."

SIRENS AIR on the breeze threading through the divot in the wall. Like a bedside alarm, they wake Paul from his painful stupor. *Fight the temptation…*

"Inago," he yells through prison bars of spittle. "For the love of God, slow down any units dispatched to this residence."

Inago's steel musculature flexes behind its red shielding.

"I prefer you use non-lethal force," says Paul, leaning against the pillar, issuing more blood than syllables.

The Locust, domineering and terrifying, pounds the floor, and bounds out through the void, trailing dust and debris.

Inago's new commander closes his eyes. *Holy shit.* Deluding himself into thinking it'd all been an episode, he reopens them, hoping for something to evidence his insanity. *No such luck.*

Doubled-over his broken ribs and charred flesh, Paul snatches-up his revolver and the briefcase, and stumbles down the hall to the front foyer.

Venerating the Tesla coil with a wince, Paul looks over at the photograph of the Shef-Ajima launch-party, and takes pause. "I don't get it. I just don't get it."

Falling concrete and sparks in the hallway break the image's spell on Paul. He presses out the front door.

His getaway vehicle is now a bullet-ridden pretzel of metal and broken glass, sinking on melted tires. Again, Paul's not even the slightest bit surprised. He walks up to it, just out of reach of the tongues of flame licking the corners of the hood. Paul admires Inago's handy-work, and stops.

"The Empty Thought!" He bolts around the wreckage, and peers into the flatbed. "Ah Jeeze!"

The heavplast container with all of his gear from the retreat is fire-licked, but hasn't yielded to the heat.

"Ah, god-damn-it" yells Paul.

Paul places the briefcase down on the cobbled-driveway, and wrings his left hand through the cuffs of his shirt. *I'm going to regret this.* Paul throws his barely-protected hand into the trunk, and throttles the container loose of the molten flatbed. The slick of melted plastic burns through his cuff and eats away at the top-layer of skin around his finger nails. He bellows, hand knotted into a yellow and red ball.

"Shit!" Paul yanks the container over the side, and drops it, fighting to free himself of his blood-soused shirt.

An alarm sounds from Shouta's compound. His personal cypulchre quickly buckles under armoured plates. The halo of exotic birds above the compound stop dead in flight, and fall down en masse—ended by an anti-air force field.

Wincing through the pain still charging along his charred digits and high-caliber graze, Paul mumbles, "If I don't hurry up, I'm going to get sealed in Pharaoh's tomb." He flicks his wrist, sending globules of blood flying. Monocle flits on. "Open transmission to Gibson."

"SUBJECT NOT RESPONDING…"

"Gibson, I don't know if you'll get this…" He coughs, probing the black cavern in his shoulder with a marred hand. "I'm in a bad way. Going to try to head to the RIM…to the coordinates you sent." Paul tilts his head to look past the truck's sinking wheel for threats, and notices, instead, Shouta's garage, tucked to the side of the driveway. "You wanted me to find you, but you're going to have to meet me half-way. RIM. Somewhere near the Foothills Partition. I have the solution for our problem. Find me."

Paul picks himself up, leaving damp genetic impressions on the cobbled way. He grabs the briefcase—its cold steel handle tricking his nerves into thinking they're taking continued damage—and stows it in the heavplast container. Bunching the fabric from his torn-shirt around the container's melted handle, he hooks-in with protected fingers and drags it over to Katajima's heavy-metal garage doors. Paul takes a knee before the security panel at the side of the garage.

"For the love of God, please open this bloody door."

Clanking gears and a drilling sound forerun the reveal. Jet bikes. Motorcycles. Cars. Maglev transports. *The works.* Paul chuckles, happy to have known Katajima well-enough to rob his grave.

The closest vehicle, and ostensibly the Cadillac of this car show, is Katajima's lancer jet, the Titan VI.

"This will do."

The driver's door on the Titan VI locks behind him. Paul flicks on his Monocle and sends the coordinates Gibson gave him to the Titan's GPS system. The engine hypes and the vertical jumpers glow. Paul slouches back into darkness.

Chapter 19: **RAINBOW'S END**

RAIN, RAIN and gaudy lights. A decrepit T-Block carpeted in faded laundry leans overhead, dripping wet ash. Paul's made it to the RIM; *a field hospital, by the looks of it.*

Sunken cheeks on the misshapen faces on either side of Paul do little to hide the skeletal frames secreted underneath. Between the gurneys and the monitors, bags inflate and deflate, sustaining the other medical patients' weak grips on their even weaker bodies.

A frayed and weathered canvas flaps, enclosing the sickly space. The medical tent's ceiling—torn off by sand, wind, and shrapnel—has been replaced by the RIM's cognac-coloured sky. LA's downtown skyline jags up and down along the medical tent's ragged edges, like a haywire cardiogram. *The RIM or Purgatory.*

A blurry, raven-haired nymph leans over Paul. "Not much honey left in the hive, eh?"

Paul coughs a bloody retort, shaking free the rain pooling under his eyes.

"In any event, welcome to Camp Mud."

Oni Matsui.

THE MORPHINE DRIP, or whatever approximate Oni's used to dull Paul's pain, has sent him tumbling into the annexed archives aback his mind; scary, irrational places, full of repressed memories and fractured ideas. And so much unbridled, paranoid fantasy.

Niles Winchester III.

If he wasn't after Paul in the name of Outland expansion, then what did he send his merry band of assassins to accomplish, apart from killing a lowly tech dealer, a pair of dogs, and an Outland Exec? *The Anomaly?* Could he have mistaken Paul for the rogue saboteur? Did he think Shouta was in cahoots?

This paranoid streak doesn't ripple Paul's façade. On the outside—the only thing that counts in the RIM—Paul's soused in sweat and rainwater, strapped with rough, brown leather bands to an elevated cot.

A rotund brown-haired woman, vice-gripped into medical garb, barrels from one of the pallid patients siphoning plasma nearby over to Paul. She immediately synchs her tablet to Paul's case file, and plots the tablet at his side. She yanks two latex gloves out of a drawer beneath the cot, and snaps them on. Finding the ends of the finger portals, she analyzes both Paul's exposed shoulder and the tablet's MEDBOT conclusions.

"Dr. Sheffield, this might hurt a bit," she says, out of habit, smirking at Paul's lack of reaction—trapped behind still, burnt flesh.

The large woman peels back the glue-tack applied to Paul's chest, shoulder, sides, and arm wounds, and scans the micro-diagnostic plates to make sure the mechcrophages have repaired the veins and capillaries Inago had handily obliterated. Satisfied with the little devices' progress, indicated by a promising green-status bar on the tablet, the woman turns to consult the full-scale holographic replica of Paul's insides, vertically oriented and slowly spinning at his feet.

Paul, lurking somewhere in the viscous dark between consciousness and nightmare, feels the pressure spike down his forearm. His eyelids flutter, and he feels the agency pipe up his spinal column. Still unable to see, he reaches out. His fingers find warm flesh.

The large woman spins around and motions to smack Paul's arm, but remembers her oath. She seizes Paul's hand, and folds it over his chest.

"Now, Dr. Sheffield," she says—her voice sweet, calming music to Paul's ringing ears. "We are trying very hard to take care of you. That might prove to be quite difficult if you keep-on in *this manner*."

Paul mumbles something, and one of his eyes opens independent of the other.

"Try to get some sleep. Should be easier now that the rain's stopped. Father Ed will be around to close your wound, and make sure that your ruptured—ah," she checks the hologram, "well. He'll make sure your shoulder and sides are back to where they ought to be, and that everything's doing what it should…"

"Appreciate it…" Paul says in a quavering voice, now cosy in his stupor.

ONI PUSHES the plunger. The adrenalin ambushes Paul's system. She retracts the needle, and steps back into the fold. With her: a white-collared man in his mid-sixties; Booker Gibson, dressed in the same suede-trimmed flak jacket and scars he had on at the SenseDen; and two women strapped into medical garb, including the woman Paul'd unwittingly assaulted.

Gasping, Paul reels forward, no longer fettered by his leather straps.

"Jeeze!"

"Amen," says the old man, stepping forward. "I'm going to get my introduction out of the way now, because that nasty wound of yours is just begging for sepsis…"

The very mention of his wound has Paul searching his body for shrapnel and missing parts.

"And normally I'd shake your hand, but under the circumstances…" The old man points to Paul's arm, as if asking a question.

Paul nods.

"Father Edmund Barros. People around here just call me Ed."

Paul sees two dark little eyes grilling him behind the pastor. He leans back, and bungees a smile.

"Nice to meet you Father. I'm…"

Oni steps forward, her eyebrows umlauting a serious stare. "They know, Dr. Sheffield."

Edmund pulls a wheeled chair over to Paul's side, sits down, and unrolls a cloth-burrito-full of surgeon's utensils on his lap.

"I don't remember ever being so popular," says Paul, gulping at the sight of the blades and derms, Oni's intensity warming his legs. "Oh shit," he startles, "Allen's funeral…Have I missed it?"

"Cool your jets," Gibson says, calmly. "Y'barely escaped the need to haunt your own. *Relax.*"

Oni nods to Gibson. She takes a breath and then a pause. "These are important times, Paul," she says with a soothsayer's confidence. "We all have to decide what we want and what we're prepared to do to see that happen."

"How'd you know about the mechs following me?"

Oni sighs and bats her eyes. "Someone at Outland wants you dead, and for the first time in a long time, they're not being subtle about it. Not even securing their comms."

"Why?"

"Why do they have it out for you *this time*?"

"Yeah."

"Not exactly sure," she blows a rebellious wisp of hair out of her eye-line. "But it probably means we need you alive more than Gibson and I had first imagined."

Paul wishes it'd all been a bad dream. *All of it.* "Crap," he whispers, staring blankly past the tent's frayed ramparts to the LA skyline. "But I'm not even at war with Outland. I'm a non-player."

Gibson pipes up: "Granted your history, I'm not so sure. Regardless, Outland's at war with you."

In the light of the hologram depicting his insides, Paul can make out the raised etchings written across Gibson's face, documenting pain and loss.

Oni throws a dagger of a glance to Gibson. "Paul wants his family back." She sits at the end of Paul's cot, and turns her gaze to his brutalized face. "We all have problems. And all of them start with the CLOUD."

"Yeah? What's your problem?" Paul says dubiously.

His disbelief knocks her in the gut. She tilts her head, just-so, enough for Paul to glimpse her pain and guilt. "It's taken something from all of us, Paul…My principle problem has been our lack of a solution up until now. *Look around you.* I'm cleaning up my mess. *Our* mess. I'm finishing what you started a decade ago."

"What are you talking about?" Paul asks, genuinely interested in hearing an honest answer. His sides hurt more with his newfound vigor. "Damn," he wheezes.

Edmund pushes Paul back, and applies a localized anesthetic. "Calm yourself down, son."

"You fought Winchester on pushing the CLOUD to the domestic market. You knew what it was capable of doing…" Oni continues.

He can't feel Edmund's blade, but Paul shivers at the sound of his skin separating—the sound of a Ziploc bag being resealed. "I don't know if you've noticed, but I didn't exactly win that fight."

"Booker, here," Oni indicates Gibson with a light flick against his lapel, "Doesn't know who he is. Doesn't even know if *Booker Gibson*'s his real name. Name's all it said on his pod."

Paul feigns a sympathetic nod.

"Ed and I found him two months ago in a Spirit Train that was headed to the Citadel. Was shot down by RIM-tick privateers. According to the script on his pod, he was on his way there to be de-synchronized for violating Outland protocol."

Gibson's pursed lips dam silent agreement.

"Stole XP and intel from the Yakuza or something like that. Has more of their memories than his own. Some mechs from Tokyo were looking for him. Some experientialists too."

"So they want him dead. What's *he* want?"

"CLOUD destroyed him, whatever he was. CIA agent…Hacker from the Yukon Sprites. Orientalist. Who the hell knows? Now, he's just fragments of different types. A ghostly mosaic."

"What does that mean?" Paul turns to Gibson. "What *do you* want?"

"To stop running."

The scars mapped across Gibson's face now make sense to Paul. He could have easily and cheaply had them corrected by a cosmetician's laser, but kept them. *Wanted to maintain some connection with his past, even if that meant wearing his incomplete and violent biography.*

Paul laughs. "I wouldn't pray for immobility. Chances are, you'll be surprised by fate's misinterpretation." He notices Edmund coating the wound with a variant of heavplast—one that crumbles if peppered. "That's a neat trick."

Edmund shuffles his eyebrows in agreement.

"What's your deal?" Paul asks the priest.

The old man pauses, holding his tools above Paul's wound as if readying to eat a meal. Serious reflection contorts his face. "Well…" he says wiping his forehead with his gloved wrist. "I suppose I'm just trying to help."

"Great," says Paul, "I've got Shouta's murder on my ticket. Gibson's a fugitive being hunted down for whatever sparks he's got left by *more than one* paramilitary death squad. And," he continues, pointing this time to Oni, "you've gone full-Mother-Theresa with Ed, here. Doesn't sound like a playable starting-line. *In fact*, I can't imagine what this team could start, if anything. I'm thinking the lot of you will bring a bunch of heat and attention down on my efforts."

Edmund squeezes together the lips on Paul's wound. *No numbness there.*

"Jeeze, watch it will yah?" Paul says, sucking in air around his clenched teeth.

"Efforts? Which are? What exactly do you plan to do? Picket out front of the Citadel? Outland Sentinels are everywhere looking for you. And, Dr. Sheffield, no offense, you've never really been in any shape to fight them alone."

Paul looks over at Edmund's reaction. *Cool as a fish.*

"You want your family back," Oni reminds Paul.

"Obviously."

"Tell me how you plan to get them out of the Citadel's protected residences. Tell me how you plan to desynchronize them without Outland coming after you or severing their exo-cortex leads."

He conveys his frustration by throwing his head sideways into the pillow. "I'll figure it out."

"Before the Anomaly assimilates them?"

Paul's silence affords Edmund's chair an opportunity to squeak uninterrupted. He tongues the roof of his mouth. "You know…?"

"I found out independent of Dr. Katajima's discovery. Gibson hacked Katajima's Monocle to confirm my thesis. It took a few hours to draw the correlation between the spike in evap mortality and the data stockpiling, but once it grew large enough to stand out, I knew it'd be a problem. Those who've died already…They were assimilated; their minds, anyway. It's vacuuming sentience and data and power. It's far too late to go on the defensive. We need to attack this thing with everything we have. And when we do, we have to make sure that there's nothing left of the CLOUD."

"Cyber-terrorism?" Paul balks. *Oni's on the right track*; Paul's looking for innovation by teasing out the discrepancies between their respective plans.

"Liberation," answers Gibson.

"Tell me how crashing the CLOUD will be any different from letting the Anomaly consume everyone?"

"We want a hard rain, not a genocide." A new mask of seriousness tightens around Oni's features. "Whoever's behind the Anomaly is out for destruction and power."

"Right. And remind me: you want destruction and…?"

"I've turned it around, Paul. I'm helping people now. Eddie, Gibson, the staff, and I—we're working all day, every day, to help those the CLOUD's shorn and rendered helpless."

Gibson winks at Edmund, who's looking up, exasperated.

"The CLOUD and the so-called Omega Point that Winchester was always on about—they have to go. But not before everyone is extracted safely. This thing, *whatever it is*, will kill everyone synched to the CLOUD. And it won't stop there. If it's after power, then it'll hardline out. Drones, the Net—anything with a receiver or an electric signature will be fair game," says Oni, sporadically dipping from English into Japanese.

Katajima couldn't have put it better. "Then I guess you're running out of time."

"Listen, asshole," barks Gibson. "You came to us. She fixed you in good faith, thinking that you'd buck-up and consider not being such a chickenhead. *You're* the one out of options."

Oni gets up. The mud left by the rain slurps at her boots. She grabs Gibson's arm, and turns to go. Without looking at Paul, she says coolly, "Let me know if you want us to take a break from treating symptoms in order to help you with a cure."

Chapter 20: PICKING UP THE PIECES

FATHER ED CUTS the twine gridding Paul's wound, and dabs the puss collected at the corners. "Sorry about your family," he says somberly.

"It's not too late," Paul convinces himself.

"Never is." The priest winces, squeezing focus and accuracy out of his vision. "There!" he exclaims. Edmund lays a transparent binding tape on the oozing trap. "Blasted printer is jammed, so I can't graft you anymore layers, but the lace will hold and the wound'll heal...so long as you don't pick at it."

"Then I guess I have to think of something better to do until it scabs over." Paul lifts his shirt, stained a brick-colour, and he runs his finger along the alien skin lining his arm and side.

"Ah, yes! I decellularized the patch to lessen the chances of rejection. It will naturalize to your colour once the blood starts flowing again."

"Thank you."

Father Edmund smiles. He takes a look at Paul's holographic, and shuts it down. "You're a lucky man, Paul."

Paul slides off the bench with a grunt, squishing his face into a clownish look of disbelief. "How's that?" he replies, checking the cleric's handy work. "Besides you finding me when you did?"

"You've something left to lose. That's rare outside of the Blue Zone."

"I suppose I still have that to be taken away from me."

"Well, count yourself blessed. As for Booker and Dr. Matsui, this is it. All they have are dreams of justice and revenge."

"Oni didn't say what she'd lost…Shouta'd mentioned something about the Purge."

"I found their names on the memorial downtown…*Her family.* She was so excited about the CLOUD, that she enticed her brothers and her mother to buy-in. They were among the first victims of the data collectivization—the Purge."

Paul sighs.

The Purge was a fatal programming error that took out a few thousand early subscribers. Outland had tried to curb excessive bandwidth-hogging by assigning barriers to high-intensity users. Instead of sectoring and limiting noospheric activity, Outland had effectively lobotomized all their frequent fliers. Should have been the end of the CLOUD, but the blame was ascribed to hackers and anti-tech groups. *The CLOUD wasn't ready for consumption then, just as it isn't now.*

Paul had no idea Oni had lost family, let alone that she had had family. He massages his brow, regretting his earlier response.

"Your family is not the only reason you're lucky…"

Paul jerks his head, physically bidding the pastor continue.

"Your osteo-implants—"

"Spidersilk," Paul interjects.

"Kept you whole. Could have been a lot worse."

Pulling his shirt back down, Paul winces—the morphine's effect now waning. "No doubt."

"The contortion marks on the scar tissue we removed while you were under…" Edmund turns Paul's holographic doppelganger back on. "The only instances where I've seen marks like those before were on amputated limbs or on hanged men."

"Sticks and stones, unless you've a little help," Paul throws his shoulders back into a stretch, tweaking for the strength wrapped around his core.

Father Ed snaps off his latex gloves, and tosses them into a bin overflowing with bloody rags. "And you," he pivots, and strides over to a little coffee maker squeezed between ventilators, fuming from the hood, "Have had a lot of help." He turns to Paul with twin tin cups. "Drink this. Whatever's next is going to require all the energy you can muster. And try to keep the weight on your other leg."

Paul looks down past his knee. There is a heavplast band around his ankle.

"We threw in a micro-rivet to reduce joint tension. You're going to have to take it easy for a while, but it should last you until you cross the finish line."

"Sure thing."

"Before I forget, I managed to scrounge up two bottles of anti-psychotics. Your file stressed their importance, and for whatever reason, someone cut your line to supply."

"There's a full cast of potential suspects."

Edmund hands Paul the SIKS. Paul ravenously wrenches the lid off of the first bottle, and pipes-down three triangular tabs.

"Thank you. I was seeing things…hearing things. Thank you."

Paul pockets the bottles, and throws out his hand. Smiling, Edmund takes it and grips it.

"A second chance."

"You're a life-saver, doc…Y'have a preference?"

"Pardon?" Edmund asks, returning Paul's hand to him.

"Doctor or Father?"

"Goodness. I guess that depends on the nature of the saving." Edmund's grin widens, and then flat-lines. "Now I've a question for you."

"Alright, shoot," Paul blurts out, feeling the quick flush of SIK-induced euphoria relax his shorted nerves.

Father Ed thumbs the handle on his mug, and steps into his query. "Spidersilk. A Monocle. Juncts. Subcutaneous orthopedics. You seem to be on board with all the latest tech…"

"Yeah?"

"But you're drawing the line at noospherics? The CLOUD?"

"I'm interested in improving life, not illusions, Father."

They both sip with fallen gazes.

"And I'll be forever damned," continues Paul, indicating the rain-outs tabled around the clinic, "for my hypocrisy—for distracting people from what really matters."

PAUL HOLDS A SECOND cup of Edmund's coffee against his chest, feeling the rising steam soften his prickly chin and wet the bandages greased across his swollen face. He watches Oni, on the other end of the medical tent checking the med-regulators on one of her patients. She squeezes the saline bag above the closest blanketed body, and wipes her brow with her palm. Sighing, she corners a blade of hair behind her ear. If an ant under Paul's current magnification, she'd burn.

All that time I'd pinned her a mouse in my lab, when she'd actually been a lion.

Another one of Oni's nurses startles Paul, scanning his arm without an introduction or warning.

"Jeeze!" yelps Paul, gripping his chest and embellishing his scare.

"Nope, just Emily." Emily, in a tight, gridded leather jacket, with hair pulled back into a bun, whose saffron curls strike a surreal contrast with her drab, pastel surroundings.

"Whaddya want?" Paul grumbles.

"Dr. Barros asked me to double-check to make sure he didn't miss anything when mending your wounds. Shrapnel or the like. Now lean forward." Clearly not the waiting type, she unabashedly pushes Paul forward, and continues her scan.

Paul coughs, and then capitulates to her warm handling. "You guys aren't too keen on bedside manner, huh?"

"Would you prefer I ask you 'how's your day going?'"

"No," Paul grunts, half-resisting the nurse's grip. "That's fine."

"Dr. Matsui is a very strong woman. Very courageous. Deserving of respect," she says.

"What?" Paul pulls his arm free of the nurse's clutches and stands straight.

"You were watching her work."

"Oh, is this that bedside manner we decided against?'

Emily leans in closer, pocketing her scanner. "But she's not invincible. So long as the CLOUD's up, she's in danger. We all are."

"Wow, you guys are relentless…They put you up to this?"

"No."

Paul scratches at the heavplast concretized around his wound. "I have a mind to put an end to it. Just not much of a team player," Paul says. "But that doesn't mean I won't play."

Emily crooks her neck. "At least with a team, there's someone to pick you up when you fall."

One of the nearby rainout's monitor beeps. Emily communicates goodbye with a squeeze of the arm, and scurries off.

Something about her pisses him off, Paul decides. *Her sincerity? Her outmoded good nature? Something about her interest in Oni—in my interest in Oni? Maybe she's right. Oni, too.*

"Hey, one of you two mind giving me a hand over here?" yells Oni, fingers lost in a bramble of circuitry, wires, and flayed flesh.

Paul looks around for one better-tasked, only to see Emily busy massaging some loser's heart.

"Sure," he answers, placing his coffee on the bench. "What's up?"

"This one is synched to one of our rehab Sandboxes. *Think along the lines of the Oasis construct.* He's in withdrawal, and fading pretty fast."

Paul meets Oni, leaned over the gurney, and surveys the sweat-encased subject. "Where're you backing up his memex?"

"Elastic drive inside the terminal; one pentabyte plus a shared floodgate. Mind running a diagnostic?"

"Sure." Paul circles the rainout.

Swaddled in white sheets, the patient—no more than twenty-years-old—exhales and shudders. His heart rate is recorded on the hologram above him. It tracks across the graphic, slow and faint.

Paul intuits-on his Monocle, and severs the hologram with a swipe of his hand. The projection adjusts to his perspective, and offers up a command prompt. Intuiting a script, the computer's tentacles, wrapped around the young-man's head, click-ready. Paul intuits a comm box.

—HELLO.

—OH GOD, OH GOD, OH GOD.

—PLEASE CALM DOWN. I AM HERE TO HELP.

—WHERE AM I?

—YOU'VE LOST ACCESS TO THE CLOUD. OR RATHER, BEEN DENIED…A FRIEND IS EASING YOU BACK INTO YOUR BODY. YOU NEED TO STAY

CALM, AND HELP HER RE-PROCESS YOU INTO THIS SANDBOX SIMULATION.

—IS MY WIFE OKAY?

Paul looks around the tent at the other patients. Three men and a sealed body bag.

—WE'RE LOOKING INTO IT. PLEASE JUST RELAX AND LET US HELP YOU.

Paul closes the box, and recoils from the projection. He approaches Oni, busily writing code at a console.

"He doesn't know."

"What?" asks Oni, tonelessly and preoccupied.

"Your patient. He doesn't know his wife is dead."

Oni looks at the swaddled cadaver. "Jane Doe couldn't reintegrate. The husband doesn't need to know, especially if we're not certain he'll make it for knowing to matter."

"Right." Paul shuts his eyes, feeling the SIK's security blanket unweaving.

"He should reset nicely with this reboot algorithm," Oni announces. She emphatically taps to complete her code, and turns, elated, only to see Paul looking crushed.

"Dr. Sheffield?"

Paul stands silent.

Oni inputs the algorithm into the rainout's terminal, and steps back. "We'll check-in on him in an hour."

"Great," Paul drones.

"Here," Oni says, grabbing Paul by his grafted skin. "Your belongings—the briefcase…"

"You have them?"

"When we found you, we brought everything in. Mag-pulsed anything they could use to track you here…Traded the Titan in for favours."

"Outland?"

"Who else? Judging from their comms and flows, you're a high-priority find. Body of the mech at your place legitimized my suspicions."

"I never got the chance to thank you for sending Gibson to warn me..."

"You'll find a way, I'm sure."

She hands Paul an old-toothed metal key. "Your gun and clothes are in the locker room. Right through there, past Eddie's quarters. Room's locked, so you'll need this code." She intuits it over, from her Monocle to his. "Your briefcase is over by Emily, under the bench in Tent Two."

Paul's conscience has found him. "I just don't know how we'd go about it."

"What's that?"

"The CLOUD."

Oni conceals the hope that's rushed to her cheeks in shades of red. "You and Katajima had hatched a plan..." She turns to Paul. "Judging from the list of bodies turning up in hack shops and missing fragmentors across the state, something to do with the Empty Thought?"

She doesn't miss a beat. "How do you figure?"

"You mentioned it while you were under. You were debating next steps...with yourself. I didn't mean to eavesdrop, but...anyway, I did some digging, and cross-referenced possible delivery systems and sellers. Once I hit coffin wood, I knew there had to be a connection."

Paul sighs. "Yeah. Fragment the Empty Thought and deliver it via Katajima's deck."

"We intercepted an Outland log saying Katajima had ordered the Empty Thought to be destroyed."

"I have a duplicate."

Oni smirks. "I figured you were either working on an EMP in exile or versioning the Empty Thought."

"Problem is, I haven't the faintest on how to decrypt it on the receiving end. Even with Shouta's deck, I'd still have to manually extract my girls."

"Why just your girls, when you can save everyone with a massive reboot?"

"Katajima said it couldn't be done."

Oni's happy disagreement creases her eyes. "What he meant is that *he* couldn't do it." She yanks one of the patients' med-tablets and types away, knowing full-well her multitasking will piss-off Paul. "There's one who can."

Go on.

"Winchester..."

"You're going to convince a man unabashedly sending men to kill the both of us—whose entire empire depends on the CLOUD—to just turn it off? All because you asked nicely?"

"Winchester's Baal storm machine...the Empty Thought...your family; they're all at the Citadel. Even if you don't have the mind to do what needs doing, we still have a destination in common." Oni has more on her tongue, but she is cut off by a sharp and metallic hiss. Hurriedly she finishes her thought: "Besides, how are you going to target an amorphous enemy with Katajima's deck if you can't pin it down? It'll have to be done in person."

The green and backlit-black on the rainout's monitor flickers. With a fizz and a quiet snap, all of the electronics blink off and on, and then off again.

Beeping. Technological meltdown. Sparks stream out of the modulators beneath the gurneys.

"Shit!" swears Oni, slamming her fist into an open hand. "It's the generator; it's overloaded."

She darts outside the tent and around the corner to the breaker affixed to an old telephone pole. With a *pkt-pkt-pkt*, all the electronics are off.

Cardiac monitors running independently off battery packs announce doom. Soulless and unaided, the rainouts begin to twitch.

Emily bursts into the tent, panting. "Dr. Matsui! Where's Dr. Matsui?"

Oni runs back in, knocking over a weapon case propped against the front flap. "Emily, help me stabilize the patients."

Emily opens a reserve-charge pack, and pulls out an octopus of wires. "Routing to Sandbox server. We're going to need to synchronize one at a time…"

"Paul," shouts Oni, grabbing one of the wires from Emily and affixing it to a SAT anchor. "Do you think you can restart the generator?"

"Where?" Paul says, adrenalin-fed alacrity displacing his darkness.

"On the other side of the compound, just inside the perimeter fence."

Paul readies to run.

"In the direction of the Citadel, away from the T-Block."

"Alright."

Hurrying around the compound, Paul's Monocle stops him with a glaring red "INCOMING" prompt. He slows to listen to the coded transmission, apparently from the CLOUD.

"Daddy? Daddy, it's Pythia." It's not her voice, but rather a computer's toneless interpretation of her thoughts. "I'm with Angela and mommy—she's no longer angry at you, *I don't think*. Also, your friend is here. He explained what's wrong with you. Don't worry. I still love you. Anyway, your friend is giving us a tour of the most beautiful spatial renderings! We just saw Venice fetched through the eyes of an opera singer. Going to anchor to a Madagascar feed next. So

185

cool! He says for you not to worry, and that Mr. Shouta sends his regards. Don't tell mom I messaged you! I got to go. Bye."

Paul's stomach immediately knots-up. He can't decide if the transmission is a threat, but is certain it's bad news.

"Monocle, prep message for reply."

His Monocle chimes back, "No return C.I.P. given."

I'm coming for you, baby girl.

He bounds forward, recommitted to the mission at hand.

ONI HADN'T MENTIONED that the generator would be guarded by eight mechs. The second Paul sees them, taking the corner—all congregated around a smoking, pulsed generator with machineguns locked and loaded—they've seen him too. *When it rains it pours.*

"Bogey, dead ahead," one belts, raspy, through his respirator.

A human orbital and frontal bone is grafted across his kabuto-style helmet, offering a second pair of empty eyes. Paul gulps, half-turning to reference the distance to cover— *to an exit.* His window's closed.

For the love of God...

One of the larger thugs clears the ejection port on his pulse rifle and advances. Paul stands his ground. He can think of no other option.

"Hi there," Paul says, sheepishly.

The thug stops within a foot of Paul, rifle pointed at his centre of gravity. "You," he says, his respirator modded to drop his voice an octave and grizzle it. "Identify yourself."

"It's not him," says the skull-plated thug, closing in. He circles, and grabs Paul by the neck. He waves his free hand over Paul's dome for a quick scan. *Whatever they think they're scanning isn't in there.* He shakes his head at the other thug. "Sheffield. Paul Sheffield. Where is he?"

Paul's bandages, blemishes, and swollen features are evidently enough to throw off the mech's personnel scanners. He counts his blessings and savours the mechs' ignorance.

"You better tell me where he is and where these savages've put Katajima's belongings."

"I don't know."

"Bullshit."

"Just off him already," hollers a mech sporting a red helmet.

"I just got here," Paul confesses. "I'm...*a patient.*"

"Right," says the man sporting the orbital bone. "Judging by the DNA all over Katajima's ruined mansion, Sheffield is too. You're keeping dangerous company. The lot of them are abetting a known-terrorist."

"Just kill him, Cap'n," repeats the mech in the red helmet.

"Don't know *the lot of them* from Adam." Paul sees himself reflected in the thug's reflective mask. Dark, as always, but a version of himself he thought he'd never see. *The world's pinball.*

The skull-plated thug squeezes Paul's neck harder. "We're just here for Sheffield and the deck. We don't want any trouble."

Paul, sick of watching his panic version on the thug's mask, forces bravery *ex nihil.* He smirks. "Hence the machineguns."

"They're for our safety."

"Listen, I have no clue—"

The skull-plated thug looks to his red-helmeted comrade and to the other black sheep gathered around the generator. "Then why don't you just shut the fuck up?"

Lights out, *again. If it can be fixed, it can be broken.*

Chapter 21: LOST ANGELS

GETTING UP SLOWLY, Paul quickly realizes he's gotten-off lucky. He pats the back of his head, making sure it's still there, and returns a bloodied hand.

The thugs are no longer gathered around the generator. Judging from the mournful screams and crying coming from the other side of the camp, it's clear why.

Paul opens a comm to warn Oni. Glitchy bits flicker in front of his eye. *They've really done a number on his head.* "Damn it."

He runs around to the medical tents, but is too late.

Thick black smoke billows out of the nearest tent and broils across the compound. Oni, in the midst of the carcinogenic broth, is trying to close the recently widowed-patient's neck, hemorrhaging dark blood. Beside her, Father Ed is trying to resuscitate one of the rainouts who's been ejected about twenty-feet too far from stabilizers and his respirator. *'Trying' being the key word on both accounts.* Oni falls back, defeated, and Edmund finally crosses the rainout on the forehead.

A dozen or so of Camp Mud's other patients and in-house humanitarians are strewn across the clearing. The singes along the periphery suggest a pulse grenade. *For the thugs' safety, of course.*

Someone pinned the red-helmeted mech against the old telephone pole using a piece of rebar. Paul staggers over. He touches the end of the rebar, and looks around for the pile driver. Still dozy from the attack, he stares up into the thug's inert ocular implants and whispers, "Not safe enough."

A wet thump alerts Paul to movement behind a pile of knocked-over containers. Turning the corner, he sees Gibson straddling one of the other thugs, punching his face into a porridge of gore. Gibson senses the presence of a possible threat, and rolls off the thug's corpse with a round ready for Paul in the chamber of his gun.

Paul immediately throws up his hands. "It's me! Relax!"

Gibson lowers his gun, and pulls himself up by one of the containers. "Where the hell were you?" he yells, wildly.

"Went to the generator and got knocked out of commission. What went down?"

"They took them. Emily and Constance. They took them," Gibson says morosely. "And that fucking briefcase of yours."

"Who? Where did they take them?"

"I shouldn't have given you the coordinates. I shouldn't have brought you here. This is all my fault."

Oni, having given up on saving the recently widowed patient-cum-Pez-dispenser, limps over to the sound of Gibson's voice. She pats Edmund on the shoulder as she sways forward. He holds her hand, and bows his gnarly head of white hair to finish reciting Last Rites.

"Paul!"

"Oni, I'm so sorry."

Oni releases Edmund, and pulls her hair back revealing plasma burns across her cheeks. "They came to stop you," she looks at the sky antagonistically. "To stop *us*. Gibson was trying to boost the signal inside when they started shooting. Ambushed them, giving me a chance to crack out my RPG…"

Paul points to the rebar, while addressing Gibson. "So I gather this was you then."

"No. That was Eddie."

"Jesus." *Doctor by trade, cleric by vocation, and apparently a warrior when the shit hits the fan.*

Gibson chimes in. "Ed saved everyone in tents four and six. I suppose they thought you were in two, because they killed all the men…By the time Oni and I got to tents one through three, they'd gotten wise to our counterattack. Ending up taking Emily and Constance hostage in order to escape."

"Are they alive?" asks Paul.

Oni shoots a mournful look to Gibson, and shrugs her shoulders.

"They'll be sold for parts in the PIT," says Gibson.

Oni shakes her head, "Outland won't waste time selling to PIT rats."

"Not unless they want to get out alive," Gibson corrects her.

"Why go to the PIT?" Paul asks.

Oni turns, crouches, and lugs up a muddy rocket launcher. "Nicked them as they took off. Their pilot tried for the Blue Zone, but the engine gave out, sending them zig-zagging right into the PIT."

Oni approaches Paul. "They also got your briefcase," she whispers.

"Yeah, Gibson told me. Briefcase was solid, but who knows if Katajima's deck is still any good."

Anxious quiet.

"So what's the plan?" asks Paul, clawing his itch for retribution.

"I'll go," suggests Gibson.

Oni shakes her head. "And who's going to protect the survivors in the event they return?"

"You and Ed and Paul can handle yourselves."

"If the Yakuza find you in the PIT, we'll be down a man and a mission."

Paul doesn't care for bickering couples. "Emily and Constance will be the first of many if I don't get Katajima's deck and the fragmentor back."

"I thought the fragmentor was in your heavplast case…" says Oni through a wisp of raven hair.

"No. Those are just the drives housing the Empty Thought, broken down into scripts and executables. I need the fragmentor to package it—to weaponize it—and I need the deck to deliver it."

"You barely made it here, Paul. We have to figure something else out."

"You want your friends back, and I want my girls back. At least here," Paul says, prompting a glare from both Oni and Gibson, "the solution is simple. Nice and low tech. Where's my gun?"

Chapter 22: **A WORLD APART**

ONI, HOODED with her visor jutting out, leads Paul through a maze of twisted fences and dilapidated shacks. She takes him to the largest bramble of razor wire and spikes along Camp Mud's perimeter hedge. With a wave of her hand, the bramble crackles and disappears. *A hologram.*

"Strongest point's usually an illusion, anyway." She'd probably smile, but is still in shock. "Through here," she says to Paul, following in tow.

The overgrown fence on either side of the apparition clanks and buzzes behind them.

Paul watches Oni's hair bob as she deftly navigates the rubble. She takes a knee, and peers around a corner.

"Okay, we're clear." She bolts across a day-lit intersection, back into shadow.

Paul mimics Oni's paranoia, and double-checks the corner. He looks up into the black of the pock-marked warehouse ahead, consumed by weeds and sand. He lunges forward as if dodging a sniper's mark, and careens into the darkness. Inside, an unseen hand grabs his battered wrist and pulls him over. Paul gives himself up to the other's pull. He finds himself squatting with warm breath on his face.

The specter whispers in a familiar voice, "They're cannibals…"

"What?" Paul whispers back.

Oni jostles something out of place, opening an aperture in the wall beside them. Two figures traipse by, mumbling in Spanish. Paul makes out a machinegun before Oni plugs the holes again.

"The Partitions do as good a job of keeping demons in the PIT as they do keeping ticks in the RIM. Cannibals, deviants, gangs…every day they trek into our neck of the woods looking for food, tech, and whatever else they can get their hands on. Every day is a battle."

"So why don't you get out of Dodge?"

Oni pulls Paul to his feet, and leads him onward through the warehouse.

"This is where we're needed the most. And it's as far away from Outland's mechs I can get without actually being *in* the PIT. This is the fault line between the RIM and the PIT—a divide between Purgatory and Hell."

Oni lifts a grate, and guides Paul into the earth. Without question, he shimmies down a ladder slick with mud. Oni seals the mouth of the tunnel behind her.

Together, they slog along a wet, rifled barrel, towards a soft-white light. Paul, mole-blind, follows Oni to the end of the tunnel.

"Wait!" whispers Oni. She places her hand against Paul's chest, preventing his progress. "Careful," she warns, indicating the fall ahead.

She uses her obstructing hand to feel around the mouth of the tunnel. She finds what she's looking for: a wire. With a tug, a second ladder falls, nearly guillotining her.

Up the ladder, there's a slim path that navigates the cliff-side, which juts out like an inhaler-addict's teeth. Below them: wires, a couple-hundred hazardous catwalks and cantilever bridges, all reaching to the other side of the gulley, unguarded. The other side appears to be a twin, an industrial neighbourhood similarly shorn and interrupted by the chasm.

With a grunt, Oni leaps across a divot in the path. An old refrigerator, toppled-over with its door open, marks a waypoint that—judging from Oni's look of recognition—means they're close. She mounts it, sits, and swivels to the side.

Paul similarly leaps across the divot, and joins Oni on the fridge. Across the gulley, encrusted in piecemeal barbwire fences, ruined cars, concrete, and rebar, a metallic carpet of urban decay lines Mount Baldy. Swarms of drones course through the air. Tracer fire illuminates the smoke stacks, pillared along the horizon, penned behind the wall.

"This is the backdoor to the PIT." Oni turns her wrist and activates a holographic map of Paul's destination. "Gotta wait a few minutes until the border patrol's passed. It'll be quiet at first, but once you're street-side…it's FUBAR. Don't trust anyone and keep moving."

Paul nods, transfixed on the unhappy sight. Rolling blackouts make the vertical slums twinkle like tangled Christmas lights. He squints to focus on the shelves of humanity—*encapsulated rot at war with ruin.*

"I'm sorry about Emily and Constance. Any chance that they're still—"

"No. They're dead. Two more links in a very long chain," Oni says casually. She shakes her head, and tosses a glance Paul's way. "Sorry, that must have sounded callous."

"You're just being honest."

"Suppose I'm just tired of lying all the time…Massaging atrophied legs, telling over-stimmed dead men it's going to be okay…I'm so sick and tired of it, Paul."

"I get that."

"Then you also *get* that we have to destroy it," she declares sternly in Japanese.

Paul gulps.

"The CLOUD, I mean."

Biting his lip, Paul turns to Oni. "Yeah." He exhales heavily through his nose, announcing his aggravation. "*I know.* But I've got to get the evaps out first. *All of them.* Only then do we go after the Anomaly, and with the Anomaly, down goes the CLOUD. My goal compliments yours…"

"What do you think it wants?"

"The Anomaly?" Paul watches Mount Baldy flicker. "It's infinitely more knowledgeable than you and me. Who knows what something with all that data at its command might want or need? What we do know is that it is growing, most likely in order to survive. Given its current rate of expansion and assimilation, I'm doubtful it still has a targetable centre, if it had one to begin with."

"If you can't kill the dreamer, kill the dream."

"*Precisely.* Katajima showed me some holos of Outland's data flows. It's imperative that I...that *we* destroy it as soon as possible before it makes the leap from CLOUD tech to the Net and into our lives." Paul remembers Pythia's comm. "*Damn.*"

"What?"

"Before the raid...The Anomaly's gone after my family. She called it a 'he'. *He's* taking them on a tour of the CLOUD."

"Who called it a 'he'?"

"Pythia, my youngest daughter."

"The Anomaly is assimilating minds left, right, and centre, but stops to play virtual flaneur with your kids?"

"I don't know..."

Oni's eyes stray across the sand-swept ruin. "Paul," she says excitedly. "There *is* a way to eject all of the evaps en masse."

"You were saying before..."

"Yup. Winchester."

"Shouta had also mentioned it."

"It's in the Citadel." Oni flicks her wrist, and intuits a bookmarked query. Hemigraphic blueprints depicting a stilted device projects above Oni's bracelet. "Right in his office."

"The *Baal Deck*."

"That's the one," she rejoins, excitedly.

"Assuming I get Katajima's executive deck and the fragmentor back, we'll have ammunition without a gun."

"Sucks that your version is encrypted too."

Paul shrugs his shoulders. "When I duplicated the program, I also duplicated the encrypted activator. Everything else is good to go."

"Then what's the fragmentor for?"

"It fragments it so I can deliver it, but I need a way to remotely decrypt it on the other end to deploy it. Before he died, Katajima told me he had a team working on breaking the encryption. Didn't make any inroads. Was going to have me take a crack."

Oni smiles thoughtfully. "Please tell me you didn't overlook our greatest asset—Outland's best cipher of all?"

Palms up as if to give a prayerful offering, Paul replies: "I don't follow."

"The CLOUD. It can take a madman's jumble of loose connections and make sense of it. If you were to take the fragmented code into the CLOUD with you—whether stored on your exo-cortex or chipped-into your PILOT—you could Trojan horse it. The CLOUD will decrypt anything and everything it considers relevant to your synch."

Katajima wouldn't have considered letting the CLOUD open the self-addressed weapon of mass destruction. Not as a first course of action, anyway.

"How do I get the Empty Thought onto my memex, assuming both that it's me who goes in and that I can get a memex?"

"Someone will have to transfer it to you on-site. All of the memices are locked up in cypulchres around the state."

An ulcer sends acid crawling up Paul's throat. "I suppose it's less coincidence and more providence that Winchester's storm machine and a host of available memices should be stowed-away in the same place."

"The Citadel is the best-protected building in the state. I know it's been a while since you were last there; it's no longer a glorified corporate skyscraper. Ever since the RIM ticks attacked it on the first anniversary of the Purge, and..." she smiles, "my fire incident, it's become a fortress. No one's getting out of there alive."

"Not without this, anyway," Paul says, holding up Katajima's PILOT insert. "An all-access pass to Outland's Holy of Holies."

Oni furrows her brow. "That's barely enough to get in. And even if you managed to get in—and that's a big *if*— they'd figure out pretty quickly that dead men don't meddle with top-secret devices. There'd be no way of uploading the program to your memex and getting to the storm machine in time."

"Which is why I won't go in alone."

Oni rolls her shoulders, disapprovingly, "It's suicide."

Paul shoots Oni a look of worry.

"Don't worry, Paul. I'm onboard, one-hundred percent. But that doesn't mean I have to like it."

"Well, like it or not, it's what needs to be done."

"And you don't have what you need to get it done, unless you're willing to open your mind for some CLOUD gear." With an exaggerated sweep of the arm, Oni taps the back of her head.

"I don't imagine you have yours in-tact?"

"My implant?"

Paul nods despondently.

"Outland mercs crop-dusted a rally I was at with mycotoxins. Synchronization would kill me."

Paul's eyes widen. "Nuts to that," he vents. "I can't."

"You can't or you don't want to?"

Silence.

"Then you absolutely need to get that deck back. Katajima's executive, remote-access is your only alternative for successfully delivering the package. With the deck, you can go it alone—steal into Winchester's, rain everyone out, and then upload the fragmented Empty Thought. Hell, with Katajima's deck I can upload the Empty Thought from here while you're off and about."

Paul turns to face the gulley and the human wreckage built into the mountain. "And then there's the matter of getting in…"

"We'll figure that out when we come to it."

A heavily armoured Border Patrol gunship blurs by. All of the bridges and wires wag and whine in its wake.

"That's it, then."

Oni turns off the hemigram blueprint with a bandaged finger and re-projects the PIT-map holographic. Two pale dots strobe amidst the yellow and green lattices.

"So where do I begin to look?"

"I told you the girls were dead."

"Yeah?"

"That's only half of it." Oni turns the holographic of the PIT and thumbs their current location. "We can track any PILOT device we've logged-in at the camp." The hologram presents a vivisection of the PIT. Oni zooms into a three dimensional map of a densely-populated junction at the base of the mountain. At the center of the depiction, two dots pulsate."

"Is that Emily and Constance?"

"Past-tense. They're not moving. I didn't want to tell Gibson. It'd send him over the edge. I knew it would be less a rescue, and more a salvage run…Take this to track them down."

Oni unclasps her wristband, and the hologram disappears. She hands it to Paul, who adjusts it to fit around his scarred forearm.

"Hopefully…" Oni's mirthless stare cuts through Paul, "If you find their remains, you'll find Dr. Katajima's deck. If they've survived the crash, they'll hawk it as their first order of business. *Fingers-crossed they didn't survive.* In the meantime, Gibson and I will figure out a way into the Citadel and tweak Dr. Katajima's insert to at least get you through the gate. Can't race if you don't pass go."

The Partition appears particularly ominous. Paul spots devils dancing on the distant shore. He fiddles around in his pocket, and procures a few SIK tabs to quell his satanic fantasy. "Come back the way I came?"

"If you can. Otherwise, head for the rooftops. I'll track your signal." Oni angrily points at the mountain lying beyond the Partition. "Kill anyone or everything that gets in your way. Those monsters are beyond mercy."

Paul flicks his wrist, bringing up the map. He swipes it closed, and jostles his revolver out of its groove. "We all are."

"Let's say you make it out…"

"Yes, let's," Paul says, cracking a grin.

"Then we'll figure out the rest."

Paul's laughter breaks the tension. "A kinder, gentler destruction."

Oni fails to fight a smirk, which transforms her scowl. "Right…"

Chapter 23: THE WALLED CITY

PAUL'S NEVER BEEN to the PIT. The metaphors he heard thrown around and used to describe it weren't lost on him, though. In his twenties he'd been stationed in Detroit. There he got his first taste of despair and chaos. That was bad. *Really bad.* But it wasn't really big *and* bad.

The PIT had grown outside its original constraints, largely as a result of the '27 Migration. No one wanted to be near the Mexican border until the War of the Americas died down or until all of the factions had massacred each other or run out of drug money, so most people got out of southern California. Only the immobile and the mad remained in the ravaged desolation that remained.

By spring, refugees doubled the population of both Los Angeles and Anaheim. By fall—around the time that the military evacuated San Diego in order to turn it into a pivot-point for NORTHCOM—the region's population quadrupled.

The eastern-LA refugee camps couldn't hold all of the migrants, but economics, politics, and paranoia prevented them from expanding, forcing them to adapt. Since reactive, proto-partitions were already in place, the refugees and their hosts were forced to build their walled-city both skyward and away from anchored, moneyed folk, into the mountains.

There's no shortage of nick-names for the resultant territory, but only one really stuck: the PIT. *Supposedly 'Hell' was taken.*

Of course Paul has seen pictures and holograms, and heard tall-tales spun by colleagues who'd gone in for a scare— a popular remedy for those privileged Blue Zone blues. Whether they'd ever own up to it or not, anyone who came back had taken every imaginable precaution and would only have travelled with the most reputable thano-tourist outfit.

One of Rachel's old friends from the Academy, Braedan Becket, had gone in on "safari." This *hunter* retained a small army for a hefty sum to make sure he wouldn't be chased while slum-running. His guards, in turn, greased palms PIT-side using a fraction of their charge. This kept PIT rats off their backs and guaranteed Becket's safe passage. Whereas Becket had a small army, Paul's got a revolver and a schizophrenic's temper.

"Oh, I could never!" Rachel protested, laughing flirtatiously.

"It's darker than even the best de-sensitization tank," Becket had bragged, "So much so that those who can scrape the change together buy themselves night-vision goggles or implants. They wear them 24-7 over there. I can't even imagine: no natural light at the lower levels! Really caught me off guard the first time."

"It *really is* another world."

"The goggles, I mean. There I am, crossing one of the make-shift wood bridges connecting the slum-scrapers, and all of a sudden there's ten, maybe fifty homunculi with huge bulging eyes closing-in on me."

"Oh my god! What did you do?" Rachel'd cried out with real concern in her voice.

"Well, I didn't have a weapon, as per my security detail's terms, so I activated my energy bubble and waited for backup. My guards dispatched with them, naturally."

Becket had gone again for his fiftieth birthday and never returned. Paul smiles to himself, thinking maybe he'll find Becket, the dapper world traveller, vacuum-sealed into a hazmat suit with green, bulging eyes. "I'd have to dispatch with him, *naturally*," Paul says to himself, grinning like an idiot.

Paul leaps from the last of the precariously-strung catwalks swaying above the chasm onto the flatbed of a burnt-

201

out two-tonne truck balanced on the far-cliff's edge. He winds himself on landing. The truck squeals, Paul having dislodged one of the tires. It bucks back. Panting, Paul scrambles to his feet, and monkeys over the truck's cab, which no sooner is under him, then over the side. With dirt climbing under his fingernails, he holds on for dear life, waiting for the crash below. *If Oni's watching, she's going to lose hope for the mission before it even begins.*

Emily and Constance's champion grapples with an exposed root belonging to a tree long-gone, and pulls himself to safer footing. He turns to wave triumphantly at Oni, but she is already gone, off to figure how to break into the country's most inaccessible fortress. He can't see Camp Mud from the wind-swept ledge he's toeing, just the Blue Zone's bright and marvelous skyline and the Hyperloop sky-transit system running red, parallel to the chasm.

Paul gives up on waiting for Oni's validation and presses into one of the cliff-side factories, torn asunder—spilling its contents into the rift—and through to the other side. Old strung-up traffic lights creak, while the rest of the façade picks a dissonant metallic chord.

Behind the cliff-side ruins, there's an impassable wall, preventing Paul from walking straight down Main Street, USA. 'Wall' might be a misnomer. It is part of the north-south barricade that eventually becomes the Partition proper, built with a dual purpose: to hide the interconnected, eighty-storey sin-shacks on the other side from civilized eyes, and to make mobility between the two worlds next to impossible.

Paul was just a kid when it first went up. Back then it was a reflective, chrome-colour. *Keeping LA, the States' southern-most gem in the imperial diadem, pure and safe.*

Paul mulls about, looking for another illusory strong point that he could disappear. He nearly stomps a rat as he carelessly ambles along the wall's skirting irons. The pathetic, hairless pest—grotesquely disfigured by bald tumours—turns and hisses at Paul's tanker boot, and then scurries away. Back at the retreat, Paul would have simply shot such a pitiful rodent, but he's instantly glad he didn't.

The rat takes a sharp turn along a drainage pipe. It scampers up the pipe into what Paul initially mistakes for another concrete aberration jutting out of the wall. Paul pursues the quantum-leaping rat to the juncture between the wall and the pipe. It hadn't vibrated at the atomic level, but had rather made use of a man-grate mounted just above the pipe. Thankfully, the bars sealing the sewer channel have already been laser-cut. There's fabric and spittle in the metal fingers, curled away from the laser incisions. *The fastest way is through.*

The smell of excrement overpowers Paul. He takes a deep breath, and then clamors in. *If shit's what comes out, what do you call what goes in?*

Nearing the end of the sewer tunnel, he looks back to savour the last glimmers of natural light. *It only gets worse from here.* He pops his head out of the tunnel mouth, and, although more or less blind, senses for threats. Satisfied no one is laying in ambush, he gasps for air, the quality of which has certainly not improved. He hops out, and slips. Slime makes its way into his boots. It soaks his socks. It finds his wounds.

"Damn!" His swear echoes, stirring bats and rats and other grotty creatures.

Paul intuits-on his Monocle and prompts it to provide visual assistance. Prefaced by a faint hum, the Monocle pings the room, determining depth and dimension, and then factors artificial colour into the heads-up display for Paul's benefit. The night vision doesn't reveal much, but then again, there's not much to see.

He's ass-backwards at the end of a canal in a slurry of body parts, nameless fragments, inhaler canisters, android features, and human waste. The canal, stretching-on for miles, is lined with gargantuan pillars that reach up to support the PIT's lower levels. Looks like an evil, industrial version of an old-Provençal country road, but instead of trees for shade, the canal boasts an entire city.

Paul gets up, slowly, and wipes his hands off on his jacket. He waits for his Monocle to visualize the path to the coordinates specified on Oni's wristband. It privately fires an arrow through the viscous black and hooks up a scuffled pillar a couple minutes down the line. With a flick of the wrist, Oni's holographic map is fizzing in front of him in glorious orange. The PIT's scaled-down re-presentation is reflected like a monadic vision in the muck sucking on his boots.

SCRAWNY HUMANOIDS sway along the canal's shores. Paul can't decide whether they live off of refuse and drippings from the ceiling, or if they've been sent down here to die. He notes how the mopey, swaying luddites intentionally avoid one another. *Maybe they're sick. What's that say about the slime spreading down my pant leg?*

One of them looks up to the sound of Paul, trudging through the grime. Its eyes flare-up red on Paul's Monocle. Though partial to pre-emptive attacks, Paul knows not to start firing slugs, else all of Babylon should descend on him. The red eyes flash down, back to the miserable waste coursing by. *Good thinking.*

EVERYONE'S COUNTING on him, Paul reminds himself as he reaches the base of a corroded ladder off to the side of the canal. *Even if they don't know it yet.* Rung by rung, he contemplates what needs doing and who's got to do it. Katajima's deck seems all the more important, now that it's down to the wire.

To Paul, climbing into the hornets' nest after two dead girls, a fragmentor, and a deck makes perfect sense, especially if the alternative is letting *his* girls die or letting someone stick a piece of hardware in his soul's eye, pimping it out to everyone else, including his enemy-at-large. Paul knows what it's like to have his psyche tested, tried, mutilated, and stretched threadbare...

He hadn't shied from the CLOUD's predecessors in immersive tech, and, as a result, found out firsthand just how impactful they were. He'd experienced ego-death on more than one occasion just running SIMHAP while surfing the deep Net. It's the same with people, he reminds himself. Only, *there's so many layers of skin and convention between persons that you can actively sieve what influence you are willing to accept. To let that influence run free in your head turns every interpersonal connection and data exchange into a gamble, and every time it's individuality being raised.*

About one-hundred rungs up, he's made it to a catwalk that feeds into a cement stairway carved into the load-bearing pillar. He feels like he's walking through a dim dream with only the rudiments for mobility present.

The entrance to the stairwell is unlit and camouflaged by graffiti and posters. "'QUINCY MARKS IS A DEAD MAN'...'#79041 HAS THE BEST CANISTERS ON THE EASTSIDE'...'FUCK THE REPUBLICAN GUARD'."

It certainly isn't kids who're coming down here to decal walls unseen by virgin eyes. Paul can't figure out who'd author the subversive writ, nor does he want to.

Upstairs, there's a heavy black oak door, chipped around the edges. Paul pushes it slightly, and leers out at what of the world beyond the sliver has disclosed: a dark room, full of dusty iron-work, gears, and blanketed boxes. Leading with the barrel of his revolver, he leans into the door, and then into the room. *Empty.* The silhouettes of pipes and metal mesh show through the tarps nailed over the windows. Faint and subdued colours filter through in bursts. *Must be sub-street level.*

The enclosure is more or less hollow. Brick walls girded with heavplast and steel. Hooks and chains dangle from the ceiling, catching the muted oranges and pinks from the street. There's more graffiti, this time almost all cryptoglyphs.

Paul searches for a subtle way out. *Here, any attention is unwanted attention.* He finds a double-door. One side has been boarded shut. The other is latched-closed, but the lock on the latch isn't. Paul wipes his feet against the concrete and pops his collar, and then throws away the lock. He opens the door. The stale air behind him rushes out like an eager ghost to a haunting.

The street is abuzz with old, bio-fuel-fed cars and bicycles. Bulging eyes everywhere. Hemigraphic and neon signs authored in every imaginable language and dialect purr, alluding to businesses and consumption penned up within the brick and adobe frontages. He walks to a sidewalk, pretty much indistinguishable from the street—designated more or less with a coat of grey paint—and attempts to orient himself.

He can't make out any identifying features above, owing to the sea of umbrellas employed by the freaks and geeks sauntering up and down the way. Before he can fully articulate the question, "Why umbrellas?" the answer hits him in the head, wet and stinky, explaining away the fetid stench. *How medieval.*

Paul'd imagined that when he'd got to the PIT, he'd find a stagnate pool rippled by the occasional massacre. This first-look dispels his assumption.

The PIT is booming with activity. Somehow electricity makes its way along the chaotic weave of wires threading together the buildings, the pulsating Chinese characters, and the old neon brand names. Somehow there's water routed to the dives, SIMHAP dens, and whorehouses lining the streets. Somehow there's garbage pick-up. Whether it's a warlord who benefits from this modicum of civility, or some fat-walleted and big-brained NGO, the traffic keeps moving, and bodies aren't left out too long to rot. As for Becket's goggled specters, there're plenty.

Paul waits for a gap in the line of cars, mopeds, and bikes, and hurries across the road. He's almost decapitated by a hover-scooter making a b-line for the off-ramp leading to the second tier.

"Watch it!" Paul yells. His bark can't compete with the volume of the traffic.

Heeding the arrow provided by his Monocle, Paul deviates from the street, and turns up an alley. It's more of a tunnel, really; the buildings on either side converge about ten stories up.

"Ten blocks over, three blocks north," Paul reminds himself. He breaks into a light jog, but is accosted by a rotund man in a wrinkled suit, standing over a food printer wired to an old car battery.

"Hey, you t'ere!" he blathers, spraying Paul with cholesterol.

"Let go of my arm," growls Paul, in no mood for a lecture.

"You ain't allowed t'rough here."

Paul pulls his arm free of the fat man's grasp. "*Yeah*, okay. I was just leaving."

"No. Not okay." The fat man directs Paul's gaze with a finger point to a flayed body strapped to the fire escape overhead.

Jeeze. As Paul realizes his mistake, the fat man turns to the door ajar behind him, and screams something in Russian.

The free fly doesn't stick around to debate the spider.

Paul throws all of his weight into a punch. His knuckles slide across the Russian's temple and catch his brow, sending him wind-milling into the door. Paul instantly realizes why anything works in the PIT: *fear and movement.*

He runs out of the alley, and barrels through the next street on the other side. The mirror on a three-wheeled cab catches his shoulder, knocking him to his knees. A van smashes into the back of the cab, and another car side-swipes the van. The drivers disembark, rolling-up their sleeves and screaming vulgarities. Paul staggers to his feet, engorged in a concern of cusses and horns. He glimpses the Russian and two other men emerge from the alley. *Damn.* He back peddles from the mob of angry commuters, and resumes his course.

The alley, continued on this side of the road, looks as miserable and as dangerous as the last one. With the Russians in tow, however, Paul has to carry on. He decides to improvise on Oni's directions, and enters the flow of traffic. Brushing shoulders with daunting figures adorned with spikes and furs and pig leather, Paul knows to be on his guard. He does not, however, discount his own ferocity. He has something left to lose.

Feeling his pursuers close-in, Paul ducks into the doorway of a dimly-lit diner. The street-side windows are boarded up from within, but the sign on the door says OPEN in toxic blue-green. He shimmies into the joint. Leaning against the door closing behind him, he takes a breath. Outside in the street, amidst all the noise and confusion, he hears yelling. Angry yelling. In Russian.

The diner's empty, except for a stark-white Chinese man, face flush with cybernetics, snoring and encircled with empty cola bottles, and an android tending bar. It's a dingy place, but you could find no better in Anaheim or in New Sacramento. Like the neon sign outside, the colour scheme is white and turquoise. Pock-marked turquoise walls. Turquoise booths. White and turquoise stools. The countertop would likely be turquoise too, if the android, who someone thought would look better without facial-skin, hadn't compulsively buffed the colour out.

"What can I get you?" it asks Paul, its metal skeleton baring through synthetic musculature.

"Huh? Oh, nothing for me. Just wanted to get out of the—" Paul wants to say rain, but he doesn't want to get metaphorical with an andy.

"Sorry," says the android, ocular implants turning a burgundy colour in their micromesh coffers, "No solicitors. No visitors. No police. *Paying customers only.*"

Not wanting to anger the PIT droid, Paul reluctantly answers: "Beer, please."

"Sorry, sir. Mr. Akbari does not permit alcohol in any of his establishments."

Vexed and tempted to retire the hunk-of-junk, Paul concedes defeat. "A cola, then."

The android reflexively yanks a bottle from under the counter and thumbs-off the cap. "Will you be paying in Yuan or US dollars?"

Paul jostles around in his slime-filled pocket for a *tenner*. "Here," he says, throwing the damp bill at the droid. "What's the fastest way to get to Gladstone Park?"

The android stashes the bill away in an antique register, and tilts its head back.

Paul waits for a response.

The sleeping man jerks forward, knocking a bottle over. The clank incites the hammer back on Paul's revolver. Noting the man's sustained languor, Paul holsters his piece before the droid can register him as a threat, and walks over to right the bottle.

Snapping back, almost excitedly, this time with green eyes, the android answers Paul: "By foot."

"Great," Paul says snidely. "Mind if I use the backdoor?"

"No. Watch your step," it replies, gesturing to the door lit-up by a turquoise holographic of a root-beer float on the other end of the diner.

"Thanks. Hey, if anybody comes in here looking for someone matching my description, know: he's a solicitor, and he means Mr. Akbari harm."

"Duly noted." The android goes back to scrubbing the countertop.

Paul heads over to the backdoor.

"Sir?" the droid calls out after Paul.

Paul stops, and half-turns.

"It is reportedly dangerous past Occam Street. Exceptionally so. I advise you to avoid it, unless you are affiliated with the Sangre de Dios."

"*Duly noted*," replies Paul.

Chapter 24: GRAY MATTER

THEY AREN'T CANNIBALS. Cannibals wouldn't waste so much meat.

In the seats of melons halved, between wet, useless tendrils thrown in locks to the carnage, each victim's temporal lobe was tongued-out methodically. Their assassins' kinky fingers worked with special care around the thalami where Outland-Corp's tripwires had been said to be hidden. *In the PIT, at least past Occam Street, life's a fiat currency.*

The kinks, all three of them, loom above their victims in a repurposed market square, formerly Gladstone Park, nestled at the bottom of a tall, narrow hollow.

Had the victims blinking on Paul's borrowed wristband still the faculty, they'd be staring up into the guts of the grid—at a web of severed stairways, pipes, wires, and catwalks, criss-crossing above, all silhouetted by LEDs, make-shift neon, and holograms—digesting glow in perpetual conflict with the creeping shadow. The structures alluded to by the tiny portals and balconies lining the hollow extend back into a forest of vertical slums that towers to the heavens, *blocking out both the sun and the Son, cursed twice-over with darkness.*

Here, on the filth-stained bottom, these scavengers prey on the fallen and the messianic, or whatever else weeps into the abyss. There is no cavalry, no hope, and no second chances. And if there are, they certainly don't make their way into this region of the PIT.

The square is spotlighted by sodium bulbs, which, sapping energy from forgotten and unattended battery cells, flicker orange-yellow. Appended to the dying street lamps are dated holograms advertising: "A-FRICTION TRANSPORT. ONE WAY TO MEXICO CITY: $28/¥1530." In synch, they depict a maglev transport scorching past white, sandy beaches on repeat. Exhaust from the upper levels funnels onto the floor, throwing extra dimension to the cancerous blossom and the repeating promise of leisure and escape.

A large red-and-white metal sign for "Bob's Deli," with a Yakuza tag, hangs crooked behind the bodies formerly occupied by Emily and Constance, contextualizing this butchery in other forms. Pacific waves crash against the exhaust, splashing a little bit of colour on Bob's wholesome cartoon smile.

Looking-on through jagged glass teeth at the three murderers as they pick and pluck, Paul actively suppresses his flee response. He maintains a sniper's placidity despite the nerve-fed acid's slow climb up his throat. The second-storey apartment's charred floorboards evidence Paul's presence with a Styrofoam hiss and squeak.

Paul's too late, again. He hadn't believed the android, but wished he had. *But if my wishes were any good, I'd wish this all away.*

The Outland mechs crashed into an apartment complex, one block over. At least one's survived, leaving Emily and Constance with the highest bidder, *just like Booker said they would.* Paul's sure that the girls had died slowly, as part of the deal, simply for wasting the Sentinels' time.

Get the case and get out, he reminds himself.

Like the ramshackle building secreting him—pressured askew on its pilings by the monoliths of glass and metal grown around—Paul is out of place, out of his element. *No, I'm out of my goddamned mind.*

Through his aperture in the Atlassian wall of stucco and wood, he watches history repeated: more stats heaped on a pile of chalk-outlines and derms.

Above vacant eyes, slack jaws, and mouths forever silent, the ring leader of this carnivalesque slum-show candles the night's loot: two in-tact Outland implants. *Noose knots for noosnauts.*

Below, a look of satisfaction crosses the scavenger's face, yanking taut the acne-scarred skin around his eyes and the wrinkled gang tats snaking down his neck.

The harder Paul looks, the more the scavengers look like demons, pricked with horns and devilish flare. He pops another SIK pill, not that his delusion has really changed anything.

"Nothing on this one's mind," says the ringleader with a sneer. He stashes Emily and Constance's implants and swings forward a brain stem like a limp croquet mallet, freeing it such that it plunks between his lackeys. "Shame, seen? Although renk and sipple, these would've made I and I a pretty coin Shanghai-way. Sexing robots wets tongues for the real thing."

His cronies shift anxiously, rattling the bones threaded and dangling about their shoulders.

The ringleader's facial skin loosens, and bunches-up into a frown. He scrapes the remaining occipital lobes off of his salvage. "Just two's no good." He turns his back to them.

One of the two lackeys, a wraith-like woman, steps through the mulch and bends over one of Oni's dead. She flicks active her wristband, and scans their PILOT mechanisms for synch IDs.

"Yan nuh see, Whitney?" she says waving the probe over the steaming meat. "S'more around to sweeten the pot. Just a minute."

"A minute's waning."

Paul shakes-on his Monocle and zooms-in on the bandits. A stream of data filters across Paul's iris, detailing armaments, vital signs, heat signatures, etc. *Definitely not demons, at least not in any literal sense.* The Monocle-scan throws a reticle around a metal object, buried beneath the bodies. "UNKNOWN" flashes in red.

That's gotta be it. That's got to be the briefcase. Paul recycles his only option, praying for a revelation—*for anything*. Bartering credit or airtime for the implants would make Paul complicit in this bight of a long string of brutal murders. There is no deal on the table. No negotiation to be had.

His revolver, cold and heavy in hand, feels purposed somehow, fated even—a hammer weighted to fall on the nails below.

Fuck it. Desperation and amorality make uninhibited bedfellows. Paul sequence-blinks off his Monocle. He knows where he's got to go and what he needs to do.

He shuffles across the chipped and weathered floor. Heeling into a feigned tip-toe, he pops constellations of glass shards en route to the rot-iron staircase. Half-way down the broken helix, he jostles one metal step against the stringer. With the creak, he pauses.

A sudden quiet floats the interruption, and washes away the alley-curate's sense of solitude. Biting his lip and palm-muting his heavy exhalation, Paul focuses on the threat. The banister frames a bloody triptych.

Alarmed, the ringleader reels back towards his lackeys. He hastily wipes gray matter off on his pant-leg, and hands the trodes over to the wraith-like woman towering at his side. Yanking the front lip of his crusty coat open, he jerks loose a sawed-off. With a nod to the third in his party—nothing more than a feral boy—he creeps forward into the tangerine corona of the square.

"Shit," Paul murmurs, gripping one of the balusters tightly. The whisper and the fear spiriting the bane seem to urge the demons closer.

The ringleader fires a random shot into the second floor.

"Nice try," Paul sneers, recomposing himself and numbering his targets with the barrel of his firearm. He needn't preserve their skulls' contents.

"D'be in there?" the ringleader shouts at the façade. "Yah might wonder what d'is you saw. Come out now, slow-like...Jah knows there's no need for ketch up."

The child, in tow, scratches at an invisible menace plighting his tangle of hair, and bares his teeth in Paul's direction. Though ostensibly a voiceless abductee from prehistory, the boy paroles a few words of caution: "Just rats, Whitney."

Paul quietly descends the remaining stairs. *At least they don't have infrared shades, although they undoubtedly have a sixth sense for fear.*

Turning his wrist outward, as if in a Kohanic blessing, the ringleader suggests the non-importance of the gun, trigger finger uncurled. "S'okay, see?" he lies to Paul, still crouched in ambush.

Paul sees right through the bullshit to the sadist's burgundy worm pies. Paul is judge, and his will, action.

The low-weighted trigger gives to his pull with a *whomp*. In the blackness of the dilapidated first floor, the revolver rocks back in Paul's hand. His manic smile, illuminated only for an instant, fills the feral-boy's head with more fear than he can shut his mouth around.

Paul fires again, pressing his way through the broken door and into the square behind his .44 Anaconda. The sonic snap waves up the hollow, ejecting hybirds from their nests and ushering misshapen voyeurs to their balconies. Screech Owl drones and news probes whizz down, capturing the violent pornography for the defensively entombed.

In competition with a cacophonic choir of PIT dogs starting to bark, the wraith-like woman eulogizes: "Whitney, no!" She steps forward, miming absolute terror at the sight of her perforated captain.

Screaming, the feral child bolts down the alley into fuzzy-orange orbs carved by lamps into the grey exhaust.

Paul shoulders past the wounded ringleader. At the head of the alley, he annihilates the small marauder with a double-snap. The boy somersaults uncontrollably into a cruciform pose.

The tall wraith, strangely shocked by another's brand of savagery, drops the trodes onto the mangle of bodies. She sidesteps the carrion, palms flat and hands high in defeat.

Paul bolts to the centre of the square, and takes aim.

"Ease up! You don't need your cannon, boy," the wraith says, scouting a seductive tonality. She forces a smile. "Sekkle. Let me be one to your own."

Paul shakes his head. His sight outlines the woman's shaved dome. He pulls the trigger.

Empty.

She winces at the impotent click. Paul pulls the trigger again, but to no effect. The convict tilts her head as he announces another empty chamber.

"Dead hoods get no special treatment," she says, brimming with confidence. "*We'll be back for you.*"

Paul takes a step forward, displacing her Cheshire-cat smile into the darkness. The tick of her boots against the pavement echoes, intensifying to a clamorous boom. Paul tells himself she's not worth the sweat or the ammo.

Discordant caroling begins above as the hive resumes its dysfunction. The ash and embers from one-thousand rushed cannaberettes flake to the floor. Paul's lost his audience. *Thanks for all of your help.*

Mulling over loose ends, Paul pivots to the sound of a metallic crack. The sadistic ringleader, gurgling upright, alludes with an index point to the shotgun at his feet, tarnished by a Fibonacci curl of vitals.

Paul strides over to face the ringleader, still standing. Noticing Paul, his teeth wall up into a red smile.

"I and I," he says. The syllables stain his chin red.

"Save it." Paul sticks his finger into one of the craters in the ringleader's chest. "The both of you're going to burn."

Doubting his mortality, the sadist paws at his breast with a shaking, limp hand, only to find Paul's arm spearing him. With what sensation his fingers still report, he reads Paul's extrajudicial verdict. He shakes his head in disbelief. Paul steps back, leaving him to sway.

Staged between his coat's waist flaps, the thug's stomach strains with parts missing, parts out of place, parts surrendering to the earth. He glimpses one last sight of the inverted hell he leaves behind, and his eyes retreat into their fleshy folds, as if looking for a solution. With a thud, he crumples to the ground, without one.

Cannon empty, Paul salvages the double-barrel and some shells from the former ringleader's bandolier, and heads back for the briefcase.

"Where the hell is it?" Paul mumbles to himself.

Ah-ha. He spies it, half-buried under one of the bodies, and hunches over to grab it. Paul pauses to pay a moment's respect to the disfigured shapes. He can tell by the scrubs that the nearest form belonged to Emily: a sweet lady who got wasted, wasting time rehabilitating wasted people.

"Jeeze," Paul sighs, acid staining the invocation.

In the fold of her torn blouse, an ID card spells out her empty signifier: *Emily Bishop; just another nice kid who'd promised serenity to rain-outs suffering withdrawal. Someone who offered reality in the place of pleasure circuits, nirvana, data flows... the CLOUD. Should've known you can't help someone who doesn't want to get better.*

Paul can barely make out the freckles on her face, yanked back from the incision like a latex mask. Cringing from the sight, Paul notices her windbreaker—shiny, black angel's wings fanned out over cracked pavement. He lifts her arm to pull it free, and enshrouds her with it.

Constance is worse-off. Unrecognizable as an individual or a human being. The only reason Paul knows it's her is by the simple math. *A bloody shame.*

He pulls the briefcase free, and unlatches it. The case is bullet riddled. Egg-foam flowers indicate at least three penetrations. One round clearly decimated Katajima's deck, evidenced by the countless shards of silicon and plastic.

"Damn-it!" Paul yells. He sends the deck flying through the holovert sunset.

The fragmentor is tucked away in the foam padding. Paul pulls it out carefully. *It's still good, at least.*

Paul quickly sandwiches the fragmentor in foam, and tucks it away. He smashes the girls' trodes, making sure no one benefits from their murders. Once again finding himself surrounded by death and destruction, he pauses to lament his involvement and the hell consuming his world. A modicum of perseverance finds him. *Anything for Pythia and Angela. Anything.*

Chapter 25: **GLITCH MOB**

PAUL's SURROUNDED by four bodies. Two that mattered, de-animated before their time. The other two? *Scum to muck.*

With Q's fragmentor tucked away in a pocket full of shells, Paul presses on. At the alley's end, he shoulders one corner for cover. *Outside of this labyrinth, there's more than one monster.*

The alley contributes to the PIT's asphalt river: Interstate 210-x. Unregulated and unpoliced, the 210-x runs through the PIT, blocked on both ends by the post-war partitions. It's hugged on either side by pock-marked and grid-cast buildings that feed the peak-time smog with plumes of steam. Ahead, a few-hundred shadows zombie the highway in the penumbral cast of an LED baldachin, running myriad holoverts, abstracted by the haze. Little fires fuming along the surrounding-buildings' bases key-light and silhouette the specters.

A holographic commercial overhead for workers' PILOTs cuts to an Outland Security PSA, projecting an image of Paul. It's an old render, taken back before he settled into his post-termination, Grizzly-Adams look. Projected beside it is a more recent image of him taken at the UtilMart. In a robotic voice, another dimension is lent to the decree:

"HAVE YOU SEEN THIS MAN? HE IS EXTREMELY DANGEROUS AND DISTURBED. IF YOU ENCOUNTER HIM, DO NOT APPROACH HIM OR MAKE ANY CONTACT. CALL O.S. OR THE LAPD WITH TIPS. SUBSTANTIAL TIPS WILL BE REWARDED WITH CLOUD BENEFITS."

"*Dangerous,*" Paul chaffs through a broken smile.

He cracks his adopted shotgun, and thumbs the yellow eyes. Latching it on his forearm, he intuits-on his Monocle.

Higher ground... The Monocle reveals a fire-escape that ascends a good forty-storeys or so on the other side of the Interstate. He tries hailing Oni, but the signal is too weak. He sends a message with his coordinates attached anyway.

"Hey, I've got the fragmentor. Deck's gone. Going to try to make my way to the rooftops. I have a sneaking suspicion it's going to get ugly..."

With a grudging brush at his shirt pocket, Paul produces a cannaberette. He awkwardly lights it—still juggling his gear—and pauses, letting the smoke rip through him. *The hell I care about paranoia when everything is out to get me.* His frame- and heart rate drop off. He's taking everything in on a different scale, according to a different meter.

Above the LED net enshrouding the 210-x are hanging towers—huge, peopled stalactites—and multi-story bridges, twinkling out of reach of the vermin, the thugs, and Paul. *If she doesn't show...*

Destabilized one step further, Paul locks the shotgun and struts into the street. If he was a fetcher, he could retire off this foray into the abyss.

Irises blossom in the darkness, alerted by the looped Outland summons to fresh blood, their hopeful nutrient.

Paul scans the asphalt horizon. It's littered with forms: burnt-out cars, shopping carts, bodies, and abandoned luggage. Unlike the crammed and bustling streets he'd first crossed, this one's dead.

"*Come on, come on...*" he says, hoping for a reply from Oni.

"HAVE YOU SEEN THIS MAN?" prompts the Outland announcement.

The sound of syncopated boots on gravel behind him propels Paul further into the Interstate. He waves his adopted gun around like a blind man'd his stick. Whispered arguments and hisses answer from the pockets of humanity surrounding him. More footsteps, somewhere nearby, force the singed hair on the back of his neck erect.

"*Ahí está!*" shouts a gruff Judas. "*Otra mosca en de tela de arana.*" The faceless accusation is cocooned by laughter and shrill agreement.

Paul's Walrus, canoed with ash, beads embers past him. Prompted by the warmth on his lips, he flicks it forward, its dying red observed by the circus ranged 'round.

The intensifying footsteps are close enough to be his own. Paul can't afford to bluff or negotiate. He offs a volley into the charge. The instant wet, crunch of bones is the only indication he's made his point.

Incensed cries spread from specter to specter. The inarticulate, antagonistic shouting grows in uniformity.

"Ah shit." Paul feeds the shotgun another shell.

A behemoth appears against the fires beyond, just out of range of Paul's salvage. "You're going to wish you stayed home today, hombre," it barks.

As if replicating, Paul's dark foe is joined by a dozen others. Spearheading the opposing advance is the wraith-like woman, this time brandishing an electrified scythe.

Paul clenches his teeth and flexes those muscles his body can remember. Encircled, he spins, exchanging glances with the brutes closing in. He can't help but laugh. *Did Emily or Constance, with friends crying and options absent, laugh?* Blood trickles out of his mouth as he grinds his teeth to daggers. *What's my family worth?* Paul wonders. *Three lives? One hundred? A genocide?*

Paul snarls behind the double barrel, filled with a sudden rage. He bellows: "You don't have enough friends, asshole."

He fires a shot, cleaving the head off the one who'd addressed him. Paul fires a second load, and throws the defunct weapon into the crowd. The bodies pile forward, eclipsing Paul with their murderous guarantee. His fragmentor is safely tucked away, but he can't say the same for his body.

His flesh—pressed, pinched, cut, and twisted—is indistinguishable from the rest; his person's being assimilated into their pain, which now shoots up his spinal column, wreaking havoc on his shoulders, head, and neck. Everyone wants a tip for their reward. *Everyone wants a souvenir.*

Among the little pre-death insights flaring before Paul's mind's eye is the realization that Hell'd never been that far away. It'd been smuggled into his Outland utopia, undetectable thanks to his pride; suffered by the guinea pigs he'd lost; discovered, industrialized, and interfaced by those who'd melted his wings; and loosed on humanity by a so-called humanist. It was loneliness in a crowded room, cold beside a fire, society abstracted to the heavens. The CLOUD: his greatest achievement, and humanity's ultimate damnation.

Suffocating in the binds of the mob, Paul resigns to his fate. *I'm sorry, Pythia...Angela. I'm so sorry...* His unspoken apology is interrupted, as he is lifted above the scrum by his neck. Paul's head feels heavy, his body light, and all his hope, wasted.

Oni's wristband blinks, lighting up the demonic faces squeezing the life out of Paul, as well as Paul's motionless form.

Horns, horns, horns, in the dark, congested slums of Old Pasadena.

Halogens wax over the hump, actualizing all the shapes lingering on the sidewalks and pooling in the Interstate. The buildings hemming the lynch mob climb above their shadows, stretching and exposing hybrid pueblo and metal elements.

The demonic rainout holding up Paul's torn body like a ragdoll turns to the magnificent echo, receiving and becoming the message: his face is pulled through the back of his skull. A high caliber round. *Oni.*

Paul falls to his knees, gasping for air.

Oni, hanging out of a hover-van's passenger window, sprays bullets from her compact assault rifle.

Still recovering his vision, latent behind a wall of blood, Paul's localized by the sound of fabric catching depleted uranium and the jangle of death and dying. He fumbles over fell bodies, and mucks through the muscle of the tough-guys who, a moment ago, had his number. He plots his hand in small puddle. Ripples guide his eye to a reflected jig-saw of a face: the wraith, *sans Cheshire-cat smile.*

The transport carves through the massacre, and air-brakes hard beside Paul. Paul feels the heat waving off its reaction jets, melting the corpses piled beneath them.

Father Ed, whose torn clerical collar shows through his horned lapels, kicks open the rear hatch. Edmund's angry yowl to the mob is pierced and thinned by his litany of cannon-fire. He hemorrhages .50 Action Express from his modified Eagle into the shadow league's chaotic retreat.

Paul crawls towards the thunder, clink, and gas smell of the preacher's deliverance.

Atop the herd's slower victims, Edmund commands Paul over. "Let's go, son. Enough time messing around in Gomorrah."

Paul fights to nod, but his neck, chaffed and lacerated, is too badly strained. The old priest tugs him to his feet, and helps him into the back of the transport.

Oni signals to Gibson who's piloting the van. He bashes a button on the dash, closing the hatch behind Edmund and Paul. Gore pelts the sides, as the stabilizers ignite and spin the transport. The thrusters flare, melting the past and tunneling the future.

In a faint whisper, Paul grunts, "Quite the service, Father."

Edmund laughs. "Should have seen my ten-o'clock." He corrects his collar.

The transport rolls on a magnetic bulge, and accelerates towards the Partition.

Chapter 26: HARROWING HELL

THE HOVTRAN'S a basic commercial job. Metal chassis, sliding side-door, rear-hatch, built-in workbench, and a cooler containing liquid courage. *Pretty much an old work van with maglev stabilizers and a quad-vented jet engine.*

"Good to see you, Paul," Oni monotones from the front. "Smelling you, on the other hand…"

Paul crooks a riven, bloody smile. "Didn't think I'd be worth the trip."

Gibson, yells into the rear-view mirror, "Emily? Constance?"

"They're gone. I'm sorry." He takes off Oni's wristband. "Here." He throws it up to her.

"And Katajima's deck?" Oni asks, clasping-on the wristband. She doesn't really need to ask, though. Defeat is marked on Paul's brow.

"Got the fragmentor, but the deck…I'm going to have to break my rule, *after all.*"

Gibson looks to Oni, and raises an eyebrow. Oni pantomimes receiving an implant in the back of her head.

Paul observes this silent summary, and feels the darkness inside ebb. *It's fed well today.* He closes his eyes, and sinks into lonely fantasy.

"EDDIE, if you lose any more blood…" Oni says, concern weighting each syllable.

"I'm fine."

Paul slumps forward and opens his eyes. *The rescue wasn't a dying illusion, thank God.*

"Can't say the same for him." Edmund's voice disentangles from Paul's subconscious, growing warmer and clearer. "You gonna be alright, son?"

Paul, balancing himself, makes a tinny, raspy sound only he could intuit to be a laugh. "Should've seen me after the divorce."

Edmund gives him a knowing and directed nod. Paul mirrors Ed's eyes' focus, and brushes off the undammed blood on his upper lip in broad strokes.

"Thanks."

"They went and ripped my handy-work? Do they have any idea how much a good skin-print costs? Those godless monsters…"

"He's alive," mumbles Gibson. "Could have gone a whole other way."

Edmund nods. "Paul, try to get some rest. It'll be a while until we're back at Camp Mud. Gibson's avoiding the checkpoints. Going to try to buck over the wall."

"Make sure the countermeasures are good to go, Ed," Gibson blares from the front. "No use holding back."

Oni laughs to herself, likely still in shock. "We're one big, broken, and unhappy family!"

Paul's too tired to disagree. He lights up a Walrus, and rolls his eyes. It sits defiant in its groove, completing his preferred look—the one invented by grain-fed luddites from an earlier time: the dirt-eating, skull-stomping, bad-ass trailblazer, programmed to fight to the death…for justice! *Those silver screen cowboys never seemed to get cold. Never cried out for respite.*

Without looking up, Edmund coughs. "What do you think you're doing?"

Holding in a toke, Paul tilts his head "Huh?"

"We'll each get a contact-high. Besides, those things'll make you psychotic."

"Yeah? Katajima said the same thing, and I outlasted him." Squinting his blood-shot eyes, Paul draws deep. A current of warmth sweeps over him—through him—

mutating the twinges in his bones and frayed flesh into a more-tolerable tingling. His heartbeat resets to the dictate of his Monocle's internal clock, and he leans back against the enclosure's cold steel.

The priest coughs again, and strikes his chest, as if to dislodge whatever prompted the contraction.

"Everything okay back there?" inquires Oni in a matronly tone.

"Peachy," wheezes the priest. He coughs again, this time dribbling blood all over the floor.

Teetering on the bench, Paul furrows his brow at the sight. He ashes the cannaberette on his pant leg. "Hey, I'm sorry…" Paul silently inquires as to the gravity of the wound.

"Guess I tore the micromesh in all the excitement." Satisfied with his fib, Edmund throws his shoulders back into a kingly pose. "The both of us'll patch up at the compound. All we need is in the clinic."

Assurances given should not be taken on faith alone. The same look of pity that'd blemished Paul's complexion in Camp Mud, once again creeps across his visage.

"So, Father," rasps Paul. "I don't imagine all this was in the job description."

Edmund frees the magazine from his gun, and begins thumbing-in new cartridges. He shakes his head.

"Not worried about sin or whatever?" Paul punctuates his question with a cough, inquisitively-toned.

Edmund laughs. "Guilt's a dessert, not an *aperitif.*"

Smirking at the priest's scant, humorous response, Paul leans back.

Father Ed pulls another SIK bottle out of his pocket, and taps three pills into his crimson palm. He extends the offering out to Paul. "Take these and rest awhile. Shouldn't have smoked that garbage. We need you stable and ready-to-go."

Paul scrapes the tabs out of Edmund's hand and swallows them in one fluid motion.

Edmund also jostles Paul's revolver out of his jacket. "Thought you might want this back."

"Thanks, Father. Chances are I'll need it."

GUNFIRE CRACKLES outside the van. Several dimples appear in the chassis beside Paul. Edmund, unperturbed, gets up and readies the countermeasures.

"What the hell is that?" yells Paul, now warming-up to the notion of surviving *this gong show.*

"Relax, son. You're going to need your strength."

Paul nods like a child who's been chastised for his own good.

"Release the countermeasures!" orders Gibson, from the front, pulling the throttle as far back as it'll go.

Paul topples over, along with the cooler, as the HovTrans pitches back into the jump. Edmund pounds the chaff out a tube penetrating the van's side. The countermeasures divert the first pack of heat-seeking missiles, which, misdirected, still manage to shake the van.

"Who's shooting at us?" bellows Paul.

"RIM anti-aircraft cannons and missile launchers. The real issue is whether or not we can jump the wall."

Another boom sounds, this time closer, with shrapnel raking the sides. Edmund falls back.

"Eddie!" cries Oni, turning in her chair.

"I'm okay," he mumbles, getting up to plug more countermeasures into the tube.

The cooler slides forward. *Gibson's taking the ship down.*

Paul tumbles to the front of the van, banging right into the dash. He half-consciously grabs Oni's ankle, and looks up her tightly-laced boot to her smile. "Didn't think I'd see you again."

"I didn't humor any doubt. After all…" She buckles up, bracing for turbulence. Her smile shepherds her cheeks up, wrinkling her eyes. "Heracles paved the way…"

Paul reciprocates with a smirk, and strains an appreciative nod, bloodying his shirt even more. He tries to get up. "Didn't turn out well for him, if I recall correctly."

"It was never about him," says Oni.

Gibson adjusts the van's nose, returning equilibrium to the cockpit.

"What about us? Where are we with the plan, if we're down Katajima's deck?"

"Huh?" she grunts, distracted by the van's chromatic HUD. "Booker and I have come up with a few ideas of how to get into the Citadel. But first, we're going to need to get you a PILOT. Thankfully you've an insert already."

Gibson pushes Paul's shoulder out of the way of the maglev button. "Pardon the reach."

The ship's stabilizers kick on, keeping the van from catching on any debris or magnetic disturbance ahead. The stabilizers pulse, going *wah-wah-wah-wah*, with the occasional hiccup in the bass-heavy cycle.

Oni, face marred by concern, grips Gibson's headrest and looks down at Paul. "You're fine saving *them* for a world you won't be a part of?"

For all the inconsistency and irrationality Paul's mind is prone to, the answer is there, surprisingly clear and sincere, enthroned above worry and any last-minute second guessing. "Yes. They'll be better off…and so will I. *Let's do this.*"

Chapter 27: **HERE COMES THE SUN**

PAUL CAN'T SLEEP, despite his best efforts. Not with the morphine. Not even after a combo-pack of high-test Walruses and SIK tabs.

Oni put him in an apartment off the locker room with computer access, across from Father Ed's quarters, where stray light from the Blue Zone couldn't find him. His thoughts don't need light to grill him over the details. All he can do is think, and all he can think about is the plan.

Momentarily satisfied he's memorized every turn or shortcut on the map—every obstacle and every nuance—he starts running over it again silently on his sweaty cot. The plan's not complicated, but given the hazards and stakes involved, Paul wants to complicate it as much as possible in order to suss out any invisible variables.

"WORSE-CASE scenario, we ride outside one of the pods and rope-claw over where the Hyperloop passes the Citadel," Gibson suggested.

"And what?" chided Oni, icing the fresh lacuna and stitches at the back of Paul's head. "Cut through four metres of blast-protected steel and glass without raising any alarms?"

"I still think," Paul interrupted, leaning forward, "that Winchester might just let us in…"

"Paul," said Oni, "*Keep it together*. We have no time for your 'darkness'."

"I'm serious," Paul pledged. "His entire empire's about to implode if the Anomaly continues on the way it's been going. He's got to know by now he's out of options."

Oni threw her gloved-hands on her hips, and looked to Gibson for a silent, second opinion.

"And," Paul continued, "If they haven't made a move already, the military's going to get involved. The Anomaly has proven itself to be power-hungry and malicious, and has shown no sign that it'll stop at the CLOUD. Katajima is proof of that. You think for one second that the USAF is going to risk their drones turning on them? That they'll risk Armageddon over some noospheric dream?"

Oni made her disagreement physically obvious. "Hi Mr. Winchester, remember me? I'm the former employee who blew up your lab. *O-K*? And here's the guy who tried to blow up your reputation. *O-K*? We're here to help."

"He hired me. Thousands of applicants, and he hired *me. Personally.* He knows I'm capable. He knows I can do it."

"You don't think I could?" asked Oni.

The competitive inquiry caught Paul off guard. "What? I didn't say that. You—"

Oni nodded, but was unable to shake loose her scowl.

"Sure you could. But I invented both the CLOUD and the Empty Thought."

Gibson threw up his hands. "W'chester doesn't know how desperate he is, otherwise he'd have rained everybody out already...which means he's got bad Intel. For all we know the Anomaly is messing with his mind too."

Paul and Oni nodded in agreement.

"He's half-andy, at this point, anyway," Paul remarked. "The Anomaly could take him over without having to route through his PILOT."

"He doesn't have a PILOT," Oni explained, hastily. "A good drug dealer doesn't do his own drugs."

"Maybe," said Booker. "Either way, the guy's not of sound mind, and is most definitely not letting you into his cypulchre without a little *wild west*. Thankfully you two've a handsome black ticket into the Citadel."

Paul looked cock-eyed at Gibson, who feigned an air of self-importance.

"Booker," objected Oni.

"No, it's not what you think," Gibson reassured. "I'm M.I.A., remember? When you found me, I was *en route* to the Citadel to be reprocessed and *dealt with*. Which means they'd let my unconscious meat suit in to have it pressed and folded. *Overdue process.*"

Oni nodded, having joined Gibson on the same page a chapter ahead of Paul. "We still have the G-suits from the crash. Might have to update them a bit…"

"Pardon?" interjected Paul.

"So," Oni carried on, despite Paul's confusion. "Eddie and I transplant your PILOT to Paul, get him ready to jack-in, and then sneak him on the air bus to the Citadel."

"O-K," Paul rejoiced sarcastically, both eager over the prospect of an actual plan, but also completely lost—the Walruses having impeded his ability to process much.

"Here's where it gets a little messy," said Gibson, ostensibly exasperated. "Oni and I did ourselves a little research while you were PIT-side. The system that oversees and manages all of the memices tethered to the CLOUD…"

"The MOS," interrupted Oni. *"Memex Overwatch System."*

"Right. The MOS is on the eightieth storey. At first we thought we'd have to remotely commandeer you a memex and then manually locate it in the honeycomb in order to download the Empty Thought. Not the case. All we've gotta do is hack into the MOS station, locate your memex in the system, and transfer the Empty Thought program to you. Don't have to find anything; we can do it direct from the station."

"The fragmented Empty Thought," Paul corrected Gibson.

"You eggs figure that one out. Know that the MOS is guarded by three or four of those s.o.b. Outland mechs, maybe more, depending on the time of day and who's in the central server bank."

Oni levelled-out an adhesive pad against Paul's implant scar, and tapped him on the shoulder indicating she'd finished. He pulled forward and rejoined: "So we go in packing."

"Granted. Trick's W'chester lives and works on the top floor. One-hundred-and-thirty-first storey. That's where the storm machine's going to be."

"So what's that mean for us?" Paul asked, feeling his darkness branch into his chest.

"What it means," replied Oni, "is that you can't go it alone. We only have one shot to rain everybody out—a very narrow window."

"Winchester," Paul interrupted.

"Right. The second we drop everyone from the CLOUD, the Anomaly is going to know right away. It'll chase their minds so long as they're synched, and they have to be synched even if they're not online. This has to be a lightning-fast execution."

"What is to stop it from leaving before I deliver the goods?"

"Hubris," said Gibson. "And *you*."

Paul jabbed Oni, laughing to himself. "Remember when it was as simple as killing innocent apes?"

Oni ignored his wise-crack. "The only way we're going to protect everyone's memices from the Anomaly is by hitting it with the Empty Thought immediately. The slightest pause—a second's hesitation—could jeopardize everybody."

Booker offered a glib summary: "Yah, yah, yaddah. Get the Empty Thought onto Paul's memex before he's on his way to the storm machine. When the CLOUD's clear, Paul, you synch up. One of three things will happen...*might happen*," he checked himself. "One: this thing assimilates you and, in so doing, kills itself via the Empty Thought. Two: you get in, manage to open the Empty Thought, and then get out before it vacuums up all of your data. Or three: you die, and the CLOUD immediately assimilates and decrypts all of your data for the archives."

"Let's lean on option two…How're we going to get you on the MAT transport if I'm sporting your PILOT?"

"Gibson's not going," Oni fired back. "He'll be laid out after the operation for some time. His PILOT—the one you're taking—has become a crutch for his nervous system. No point in sending a vegetable…so I'm going with you."

"Can't he use his PILOT?"

"No, because his implant is corrupted. They burned him before sending him on that Spirit Train to the Citadel."

Paul wanted to protest, but knew well enough not to. After all, Oni made a better hacker than she did a neurologist, and she was a *damn fine* neurologist. "Alright. So how do you want to do it?"

Oni sat down on the crate that'd up until that point been scraping her calves. "I thought, at first, I'd turn myself in concealing an EMP grenade coupled with a jammer. It'd get past their initial scans…They'd take me to the Outland Security office on the twentieth floor. I'd trigger the EMP. The blast would kill anyone in the vicinity who had an implant. Wouldn't affect the servers, because the radius is so small and the interior walls are lined with lead. Once out of their manacles, I'd take a weapon off one of the de-cerebrates, and fight my way up."

Gibson rolled his eyes and laughed. "Oh girl, you've got an imagination."

Paul, too, looked at her like she was speaking another language.

"But then I thought, I should probably just use the PILOT insert I bought off of Sector B's chief mortician with the money we got hawking Katajima's Titan."

Oni's audience sighed with relief in unison.

"Was going to save that coin for my rainy-day fund."

"Well, I suppose you won't need it with the sun on the way," Paul said, smiling and genuinely hopeful.

Gibson threw a holo-deck on the ground between the three of them. It clicked, beeped, and then fired a massive three-dimensional vivisection of the Citadel in full colour, with cut-away walls revealing the floor plans. "A security detail will go to meet the handlers at the MAT-processing dock." Gibson pointed at the gaping hole, midway up the tower. "Their job is to secure the shipment and then monitor the pod transfer from the Spirit Train's cargo hold to the tracks."

Oni interrupted: "Androids will probably be the ones tasked with the heavy lifting, so we're looking at minimal collateral damage and exposure."

"Right," continued Gibson. "Once the meat pods are hooked onto the track, the security team will do one last scan. Unless there's a problem, the pods will be slung over to the reprocessing centre. Key is to get off long before that happens, otherwise you two will be ripped open like dresses on prom night"

Oni and Paul winced at the grisly imagery.

"You still have that EMP grenade?" asked Gibson.

Oni nodded.

"You can use that to take out the security guards, jam the train of pods, and hopefully black out the security cameras long enough for the both of you to get to the freight-elevator."

"Won't that take out our comms? My PILOT?" Paul asked, keen on taking every opportunity to poke holes in the plan.

"Shit!" Gibson barked. He scratched his head, staring intensely but empty-eyed at Oni. "No, wait. One of the raiders had a bubble field on him. It'll be with the bodies in the morgue."

"And it'll work?"

"It's a personal trophy system that can deal with electro-magnetic disturbance and high-calibre rounds. It's designed to protect just one person, which just means the two of you will have to get cozy for a moment."

"After the grenade goes off, what about the elevator?"

"Huh?" mumbled Gibson.

"Will we need IDs to interface with it?" Paul asked, threading his finger through holographic corridors, nooks, and crannies.

"Well," said Gibson placing his foot on the crate next to Oni, "I know for a fact we don't have any, and you'll have scrambled all the badges on the security detail with the EMP. You're going to have to manually gain access to the shaft— pry it open or something—and then climb to your respective destinations."

"So, I'm going to climb one-hundred-and how many storeys?" Paul asked, rubbing the scar tissue on his forearms.

"Well, you're starting on the ninetieth storey, so forty-one, or thereabouts…I know you're hurting, man, but anything that'd make it easier would ultimately make it harder."

"How so?"

"Jetpack. Great idea, right? *Wrong.* Once the after-burn hits a certain temperature, the Citadel will treat it as an attack and put itself on lockdown. In all likelihood, the building will pulse the elevator shaft and fry you in the process."

"What about the rope-claw you were talking about?"

Gibson closed his eyes and stood silent for a moment. "Yeah. Yeah, that can work." He nodded emphatically, ostensibly pleased with the idea. "Remind me to hook you up. You're going to have to make sure you don't trigger it in a tight space, though. Don't want to turn yourself into a necklace, do you?"

Paul stood up to interface with the holo-deck. He transferred the map to his Monocle so he could set way-points and identify potential strategic advantages. With his back turned to Gibson and Oni, he started to mutter. "This isn't going to be easy."

Oni spliced Paul's thought, saying, "I'll get to the MOS long before you get to Winchester. That should give me enough time to reassign Katajima's insert and Booker's PILOT to a new memex, and get you the Empty Thought. Hey Booky, will I have signal inside?"

"Outgoing comms will be jammed or intercepted, so I can't help you..." said Gibson.

"No, what I'm asking is: will I be able to hail Paul?"

Gibson thought for a minute, and replied: "Internal comms? Yeah, definitely."

"So I can let him know when the Empty Thought has loaded?"

"Probably."

Oni's eyes widened.

"What do you want? An infallible 'yes'?" Gibson jabbed.

Paul still felt uncomfortable even thinking about synching to the CLOUD. "How would I access it?"

"Good question; deserves a good answer, but I don't have one," responded Oni.

The idea hit Paul so hard he had to hold the wall for a moment. "It's...*I am* our Trojan horse."

"Huh?" Gibson asked.

"I still don't know if the CLOUD will open it right away. God knows we won't have the time to test it out."

Oni and Gibson turned their gazes down, dejected.

Gibson shakes his head. "There's no room for second chances or second-guessing. If anybody can do this, it's you," he turned to Oni. "With *our help*, of course."

Oni slapped Paul on the knee. "Absolutely! Let's introduce the Anomaly to oblivion! We'll dial down your meta-rate and increase your reception speed, permitting you more time to deliver the package."

"Dial down my meta-rate?"

"There are locks on your perception of time in the CLOUD. Your brain is, after all, faster than your body. Twenty-million-billion calculations per second."

"Naturally."

"Outland installed default rates on all of their memices, and ensured that BiAnima put reception speeds on all their PILOT devices, ensuring some correlation between real-time and NOOS-time."

Paul raised his eyebrows, bidding Oni to explain.

"The default perception settings are standard issue so evaps won't lose their minds…so they won't become ghosts or gods."

"So one real second in the CLOUD would be?"

"Ten minutes CLOUD time. Maybe more."

"Do you know if my…" Paul pointed to his head, "mental state will have any impact CLOUD-side?"

"In the pre-trials—the ones I was there for, anyway— we had a few patients with Alzheimer's, a few with bipolar disorders, and one or two subjects with extreme forms of schizophrenia."

"And?" asked Paul.

"There were inconsistencies in their code. Erratic jumps in conveyance. But on the whole, nothing to worry about."

"Great!" declared Gibson. His face quickly found its sullen pre-set. He gloomily presented Oni and Paul with a floor plan for the penthouse. "W'chester will be well-guarded. If it doesn't appear that he is, take extra precautions. They have mech-mercs in the lobby, so I can only imagine they'll have one or a hundred guarding the old man."

Paul gasped, thinking on his trusty but wildly ineffective revolver. "I'm going to need a bigger gun."

Oni nodded, thoughtfully. "I'll have to check…"

"Check what?" Gibson pried.

"Remember the Knight of the Holy Sepulchre?"

"He was a little before my time," replied Gibson.

"The guy was some kind of crusader from the Middle East. Came to check on one of our patients, a friend of his. Ended up leaving his kit behind because he couldn't take it on the state-jumper."

Paul and Gibson leaned forward for the punch-line.

"It's pretty ridiculous. I never tried it out. Barely touched it, actually."

"Dammit, woman! Spit it out," said Gibson, some levity buoying his tonality.

"We have a *B.F.G.*"

"We do?" asked Gibson.

"A what?"

"Paul—you'll have to download the instruction manual, but it's…well, exactly what the name suggests."

"Sounds like *exactly* what I need."

Gibson pushed off the crate and started pacing between Oni and Paul. Ushering seriousness back into the discussion, he returned their attention to the nitty-gritty: "I'll create a diversion; trip an alarm at another cypulchre—make the old man think he's got us trapped. Going to need Ed's help sorting things out."

"He got nicked in the PIT."

"When?"

"I'm guessing sometime between when the PIT rats starting shooting and when they stopped," Oni said sneeringly, digging the air in front of her with her hands, palms faced up. "You should probably give him some time."

"Alright, well, I don't have much left to give. When he's able, I'm going to need his help finding a secondary safe house in case this place gets marked for a drone strike. There'll be feet on the ground, too; Outland's going to send an army looking for you two after you get out."

"After we get out?" *Paul had already dismissed the prospect of surviving.* Hope had had a tendency to dull failure's blade, and failure, blunt and heavy, had made pessimism his natural coping mechanism. "How will we manage that?"

Gibson opened his tablet and brought up a 2D version of the Citadel's blueprints. "W'chester has a Dragonfly on the roof."

"He's not going to let us trash and dash on his custom shuttle…" declared Paul.

"By this time tomorrow, W'chester won't be making any decisions."

"What about the Citadel's force field? How're we going to get the Dragonfly through?"

"You'll have to swap Booker's insert for Winchester's," Oni replied. "There's no way in hell that Outland Security would risk vaporizing their master, even if they suspect he's been taken hostage."

"Alright!" Paul yelled, his body signing his capitulation. He turned away from his accomplices to the dark encroaching on their deliberations. As if speaking to the shades, he summarized: "Knock off Winchester, save all the evaps, unbridle the Empty Thought, and get out. Am I missing anything?"

"Oni and I still gotta figure out exactly how to smuggle you into the Citadel, but apart from that..."

"And do we have a Plan B?" Paul said, sheepishly.

"Sure," said Oni. "Well, it's more of a Plan *B.F.G.*"

Paul turned back, and faced Oni with a look of comic disbelief. "How did I miss 'psychopath' on your application?"

Scratching his chin, Gibson gestured to Paul, addressing Oni. "Better throw some reinforcement-armour on 'em. Spine, shoulders, arms, and legs. These last few days look like they've taken their toll."

"Agreed," Oni snapped back, scrutinizing Paul's dimensions. "Nothing the EMP can damage—just enough exo-skeleton to give you a leg-up."

"All this," Gibson said, glowering, "stays between us and off the comms. We can't risk the Anomaly learning of our intentions before we act."

"Right." Paul made sure his Monocle was offline.

"That's the plan," concluded Oni.

AND THAT'S THE PLAN Paul can't stop thinking about.

Driven mad by compulsion and exhaustion, he realizes he's now thinking about thinking about the plan. "Enough!" he announces to an empty room.

Up the cold metal steps to the rooftop, and out the door. Hunched over the railing is Oni, waiting. Not for Paul, necessarily. Just waiting.

Chapter 28: LAST RITE

"YOU TOO, huh?" Oni says to Paul without looking.

Paul has trouble making her words out over the hiss of the wind whisking through the antennae, grouped like hairplugs at one corner of the rooftop.

"Pardon?"

"Can't sleep?"

"Oh…No."

Paul joins her at the edge. He pauses, and traces his finger along the railing. Black-paint chips off under his nail, revealing clean, galvanized steel.

Oni gestures to the Blue Zone's rainbow skyline, banded by yellow street orbs and green electric-bridges. From here, it looks as if the Hyperloop bow-ties the lambent Citadel—gloomily reflecting surrounding lesser-buildings sprung by common minds—and knots around the northern T-Blocks.

"It really bothers me, but I can't help it…"

"Help what?" Paul asks.

"It's an art gallery filled with empty frames. The ideas—the paintings themselves—are nothing but sludge dammed away in a shared bucket. And yet…" She bites her lip, and searches her mind. "It's so beautiful. How could it be," Oni shakes her head in disgust, "when I know firsthand that if it weren't so goddamn hollow, it'd be rotten anyway?"

Paul grips the railing with both hands, and leans forward. "I can't tell you how many people you've just described." He peers over his shoulder with a grin, the wind now gusting up, combing his hair to the sides of his head.

Oni visibly tries-on a reciprocal smile, but her sad eyes sap the affect. "Do you believe in redemption, Dr. Sheffield?"

"I'd say we've both earned a first-name basis…"

There's clearly no room for Paul's anxious levity or anal naming conventions, evidenced by Oni's increasingly deflated form.

"Oni...I don't know. That sounds like a question best tailored to Father Ed." He pulls a joint out his half-empty pack of Walruses and reflexively lights it.

Oni snorts accidentally, after a vain attempt to muffle a sob.

"*Hey,*" Paul says, quickly flicking the coal and sending the cannaberette waffling on a wind-confused arc. "What's the matter?"

She dries her rogue tears with the dorsal fabric of her glove, and reaches for Paul's hand. Her cold little digits spark something previously dormant in Paul. He's at once both sorry and happy to know Oni; double-hooked and weighted with a duty to her and with expectations to satisfy.

"Oni, what's wrong?"

ONI DRAWS BACK the curtain, revealing Father Edmund Barros swaddled in blood-stained sheets, hooked to a dozen whining machines.

"What happened?" Paul asks excitedly, bulldozing over to check Edmund's monitors.

"He didn't tell anyone. I found him hunched over the little altar in his room, bleeding on his Saviour."

Paul nabs the med-tablet stowed to the side of Edmund's pillow. "What!? When did he...?"

"In the van, he said he'd torn his micromesh." Oni turns on Edmund's holographic doppelganger, and prods its stomach with a resentful point. "Failed to mention the ball of shrapnel sitting behind it. He knew..."

"Is he going to...?" before Paul can finish, he reads his answer traced across Oni's face in tears. "Jeeze..."

"He's currently in a coma. Bringing him out would be torture. The shrapnel was coated in depleted uranium; cut right through his lower intestine, and by the looks of it, got lodged against his spine a few hours ago. I'm not sure if he'll be able to move." She shuts Edmund's medigraphic off. "He has a few days, max."

Paul coughs, and looks down at the bruised new skin on his forearm. *A few days, max.* "If we got him to the Citadel's med-sci clinic…"

"It'd compromise the mission. I'm not even sure about our chances without a gimp weighing us down…Wouldn't change anything, anyway. Soon, his eyesight will go. If it hasn't already, paralysis will creep up on him. Then basic motor function will go. Conjunctivitis if he lasts the week. Lesions will start popping up on his liver, lungs, kidneys…"

Paul swats at the bad news, and interrupts: "No way around it?"

"None." Oni says, coldly, dabbing her eyes once again with her gloved hand. "He had this on him." She holds out a folded piece of paper.

"Writ-on-tree?" Paul says, eyeing the writing.

"It's his last will and testament. Mainly jokes, prayers, and superstitious scrawl, but he makes it abundantly clear in the later provisions that we not use artificial life support, and stressed dumping any digital continuance." She turns the piece of paper in her hand and skim-reads half-way down the page. "'Give back to Outland what is Outland's and to God what is God's.'" Oni holds her head, as if it's become too heavy with pent-up tears for her neck to support it alone. "Should have moved north with his order. There's nothing left here for good people."

"Hope, I suppose."

Oni nods, crumpling her face to dam back more tears.

Paul squints, feeling a resurgence of awareness. "Sometime last night Ed came to talk to me. *The dead seem to have made a habit of it.*"

"When?"

"After you and Gibson tucked me in. He came to give me a blessing; some kind of voodoo...I was pretty out of it."

"You sure you're just not revisiting a hallucination? It wouldn't be the first time someone's seen things this soon after an implantation."

"Hallucination or not, the memory is as vivid as any other."

Oni approaches the bed, grabs a cloth, and wipes the sweat off Edmund's brow. "Assuming your memory can be trusted, what did he say?"

Paul steps back, gliding his hands over his head. "That...he'd realized something long ago. Something to the tune of..."

Oni clasps Edmund's cheek sorrowfully. "Please, go on."

"'Some people commodify life. Others, lifestyles. There are those who've never dared to live, and, *as you know, Paul,*' he said to me, 'oceans full of the daring dead. Some people sustain life, and there are a few remarkable ones that can save it. The special ones—the great ones—radically change it for the better.'"

Oni gasps, and hides her eyes from Paul. "That couldn't have been you hallucinating."

"Oh?" Paul looks at Oni, dubiously, uncertain now about the veracity of his testament.

"It's too pedantic and positive to be something your mind cooked up...But why you? Why didn't he...?"

"Tell *you*?" Finished racking his brain, Paul takes a deep breath. "Perhaps he didn't think it necessary to inspire you to do what you're already keen on doing."

The compliment carries up Oni's shoulders. "And you?"

"Besides the convenience of only having to cross the hall to see me?"

Oni shrugs.

"He died as a result of saving me. He was remarkable so that you and I could do something special." Paul saunters over to Oni, and puts his hand on her shoulder. "I suppose he was making sure it wouldn't be wasted."

Oni gently pushes Paul away, and—looking over Ed's fragile form—turns off his ventilator, crying. "Hopefully he was right."

Chapter 29: THE ELEPHANTS IN THE ROOM

THE OUTLAND MAT TRANSPORT SHIP, which Oni'd been tracking all morning, pulls off the Anaheim West Energy Freeway. It slows to give the private side-bridge enough time to charge. With the electric bands extended and a quick engine burst, the transport gracefully glides onto the service station's external-elevator platform. The pilot puts it into idle, while the co-pilot links the station with their landing codes.

Grumbling in place until cleared by the tower, the ship receives an impromptu scan by a swarm of Mosquito drones—likely at the request of Commander Cromwell with the Department of Continental Security. Still bloodless, the swarm disappears. The ship's been cleared for landing.

An android on the elevator secures the transport with a magnetic harness. The ship, an N-series Outland Spirit Train, ascends, creakily, to the rooftop of the glorified parking garage. With a visual ID from the android conducting it forward, it's instantly registered as a priority vessel, prompting a second android out of its booth to direct it—away from the queue of colonial junkers and salvage skiffs—into a dock built specifically for Outland vessels.

The second droid, a cool, gun-metal colour, is careful to avoid the aft jets feeding the mirages on the runway. With the help of dock-fixed mechanical arms, the droid tugs the transport into place. It waves batons in its personified alloy limbs, indicating to the pilots they're on-mark. The pilots can't make out the droid's orange batons or much else on the ground, but that hardly matters; the entire process is pretty-much automated, the interplay between the droids and the pilots purely fanfare. Granted the mechanical precision of the parts involved and Outland paying triple the standard refuel and charging fees, it'll be a quick turnaround.

Out of the docking portal directly beneath the Spirit Train emerges a polarized Atlas Stand, which balances the hovering ship on a point, allowing it to turn off its engines without leaving the pilots to worry about making a full-touchdown. With a thump, it's tethered and balanced.

The service station's electrical pumps don't miss a beat. They come slithering out of their coils, immediately locating the Spirit Train's charge lines. Locking-on, they begin to deluge the ship's tank with enough juice to get to the Citadel and back.

The Spirit Train's side-butterfly hatches scissor open, and the pilot and co-pilot, looking like elephant cosmonauts in their flight gear, climb out, and scale down the ladder built into the chassis.

A third android, this time a fair-skinned replicant, sprints over, through chunky exhaust, to meet the pilots; regulars, evidently. They exchange obligatory salutations, and, together, amble across the tarmac into the central hub, teeming with Sentinels and off-world engineers.

Another pair, dressed similarly in pilot G-suits—looking like Ganesha twins in mourning—slip out of the hub before the doors have a chance to fully close behind the Spirit's original pilots. One of the elephantine G-suits is carrying a black case the size of a small coffin.

They skirt past the droids supervising the fuel pumps, and make their way to the Spirit's side butterfly doors. The taller of the two helps the other onto the ladder, and then passes the case up. Once the case and the first of the fliers are in, the second follows suit into the Spirit.

A holographic sentry appears inside, at the mouth of the gangway. "Identification, please."

The taller flier throws down a holo-deck, which projects an image of a decorated Outland pilot with his helmet off, golden hair interlaced. The sentry scans the projection, and disappears.

"Let's hope the security sentry doesn't have any second thoughts," says the taller flier, voice garbled by its modulator.

The fliers make their way down the gangway, deeper into the belly of the steel beast. On either side of the narrow passage are rows and rows of vacuum-sealed meat pods, safely divided and stowed like eggs in a carton. The shorter of the two fliers waves a wrist-scanner down each row as they pass in the direction of the stern. A beep on the wristband indicates a hit. The fliers glance at each other, and turn down the row indicated by the scan.

The shorter pilot points to the handles at the foot of the targeted pod. Together they pry it open. With a pop, extramural air rushes in, blowing away the steam rising off the evap strapped inside. The man, entombed, is dead—evidenced by a noticeable lack of a face. *Headed to the Citadel to return Outland the gear he'd borrowed.*

"To hell with this thing," the taller pilot bellows in a modded voice, pulling off the elephantine helmet. Paul's weary eyes take a second to adapt to the transport's red lights. "How can they stand these things?"

The shorter pilot yanks a cord plugged from the pod into the corpse's PILOT, and gestures it to Paul's chest. "Take it off," the elephant-headed specter demands in a deep monotone.

"What?"

The masked pilot similarly tears off her helmet. "Take off your clothes and then hand me the phaser," Oni says, curtly, her black hair piling back into place. "Put the gear in with the stiff. We'll burn it all at once."

Paul peels off his flight suit, and dumps it onto the corpse.

"Right," he says, pick-pocketing the uniform, probing its crumpled pockets. He withdraws the phaser, and looks down the sights affixed to the stubby barrel. "And this'll do the trick?"

"Hopefully."

Oni strips down, too. Her skin is flawless. No evidence of implants or augs. Just a custom PILOT and some kanji inked between her small breasts.

She seizes the phaser from Paul, and swiftly vaporizes the body and their costumes. The aftermath smells like dog piss and burnt meatloaf.

Oni winces. "Okay, get in," she orders Paul.

Paul looks at the slurry of human remains, and back at Oni. Touching his newly grafted-on PILOT, he coughs. "Any chance I can blaze beforehand?"

She raises an eyebrow.

"I'm a bit claustrophobic."

"None," says Oni, pushing him in. "Might interfere with your synchronization later on. Besides, we only have a minute before they check the cargo, and I still have to wire up."

Oni hands Paul the cord, and insinuates with a point what to do with it. He plugs it into his hastily-attached PILOT, still bleeding along the edges. She types a script into the meat pod's regulator.

"Jeeze, go easy on me," Paul blurts. A feeling of hopeless dependence kicks him in the stomach. *Having to plug in like a god-damned lamp.* "Exactly what about this do people find appealing?"

"Sounds like a question best tailored to its creator." She closes the toggle screen. "Your pod's set to open in twenty-five minutes. Let's hope our Intel was right. Too soon, and they'll turn the ship around. Too late, and…"

"Have faith."

"Worked for Eddie, right?"

Smartass.

Oni bounds down the row with the large case in hand, and tucks it beside a small medical hub fused to the ship's ribcage. Yanking down a mesh net to secure it in place, she hurriedly obscures it with whatever crap is within reach.

Fairly pleased with her camouflaging efforts, Oni sprints to her designated pod. She cracks it open, and, again without pause, vaporizes the previous inhabitant. She stows the phaser behind the pod between two sheets of metal grating, and repeats the script. Sloshing into the mold, she turns to Paul. "You're going to have to hit that green button and retract your arm as fast as humanly possible."

Paul looks snug, but is really just mentally separating himself from what's going on. The human pulp sucks at his spine, and pools around his ass. Not yet in the CLOUD, and he's already irked about being in tight proximity with another human being, living or otherwise. This kind of intimacy is not the kind he'd envisioned when strategizing how to remedy his anti-social behaviour.

"Paul?"

"What?" He snaps out of his self-pity. "Close it?"

Oni nods.

Paul slams the button and quickly wrenches his arm back. The lid nearly shears his fingers off, and a plume of muscle relaxant obscures his recovering form beneath the glass.

"Bloody droid's just glitching. Déjà vu or what-have-you," declares a modulated voice down the gangway. "But check on it, anyway. If something's up, might as well save us the trip now, eh mate?"

"You're so paranoid," snaps another voice in Mandarin, the subtle tones lost across the modulation.

"A paranoid's right at least once in a while, Chang. Check it out."

Paul, falling fast into a drug-induced stupor, can still hear muffled voices. He uses his last reserve of conscious power to turn his head. He glimpses Oni's reassuring smile disappear behind her pod-shield.

Here we come, asshole.

Chapter 30: SABOTEUR WITH A SAVAGE CURE

PAUL's POD yawns open. The muscle relaxant hasn't fully worn off. His fingers don't fully respond to his will, curling three-quarters of the way to a fist.

The veil of gas and preservative masking his body lifts. Leaning forward into the dry cold of the Spirit with a gasp, he sees Oni's pod similarly open. With wobbly arms, he lifts himself up and out, and sits on the pod's tongue, waiting for his sense of balance to return.

Pink flesh blurs past him. Oni's hair bobs, as she delays the pod-alarm to the cockpit.

"Get ready," she orders, trying to fish her phaser out of the grating behind the pods. "Make yourself useful and find some kind of..." she pauses, "brutal implement."

"How's a big-effing gun sound?"

"Too loud. The Citadel might get a read off of the explosive rounds. We want at least some element of surprise..."

Paul yanks one of the pod-door's hydraulic pistons free. "Something heavy like...this?" Wires vomit forth, and the pod jaws to the side, hitting Paul in the kidneys. He grunts, capturing Oni's attention.

"Sure," she says, returning her focus to the pod-interface. "*If* you can get close enough to use it."

Sounds like challenge.

"We're two minutes out." Oni steps back and checks her phaser. "Security system is still overridden. Just have to worry about the pilots."

Paul stumbles forward. Oni ratchets a look of concern his way. He dismisses the need with a wave, and catches up to her along the gangway.

The cockpit door is ajar at the end of the striated-metal path. Oni and Paul slow their approach, and stealthily creep along—phaser drawn and braining-piston ready.

Paul catches his foot on an unevenly-placed girder, and holds onto a peripheral pod to break his fall. The clang of his initial trip echoes throughout the hull.

Oni takes cover behind the pod opposite her klutzy accomplice. She steadies the phaser on the pod's edge, sites framing the doorway.

"Mate, y'ah mind checking that out?" the pilot asks his co-pilot, arching over his armrest into the doorway. "I think that lug nut's finally come loose."

Paul winks at Oni, and sprints to the far side of the pod grouping to the ship's perimeter ribcage. Hidden in shadow, he scrambles along the side towards the bow.

A bug-eyed Ganesh takes the runway, arm stretched with a laser-cannon strapped-on and ready. The co-pilot's big head cuts right into Oni's sights. She glimpses Paul creep into the cockpit behind him.

"Ach no!" screams the pilot, his modulator auto-tuning his terror to a more civil frequency. His digital scream is muted by torrent of his own blood, courtesy of Paul's makeshift club.

The laser-wielding co-pilot quickly turns out of Oni's sights, to see Paul's aggressive silhouette in the doorway of the cockpit. He readies his cannon and aims at Paul, still hammering the pilot's trunk into his face.

Paul—trying the yank the piston free of the gore—hears a sizzle and a loud crack. He looks up to see a molten crater in the Spirit's dashboard before him, and swivels to see the co-pilot, cleanly beheaded.

"Quick!" yells Oni. "Make sure the autopilot's on. I'll grab the case."

A yellow light flickers beneath the melted dash. "Holy shit, I think this one triggered the distress signal," Paul bellows back, slamming the pilot's head one more time. He throws the corpse out of the flight-seat and interfaces with the Spirit. "It hasn't broadcasted yet…"

"See that it doesn't."

His fingers spider across multiple boards, dominating the Spirit with commands and codes. The yellow light cones red.

"You've got to be kidding me," says Paul. He gets up bombastically—throwing the chair back—and stops Oni at the head of the gangway. "I need this for a second," he blurts, yanking the phaser out of her hand.

She reaches out after him, gripping nothing but turbulence. "What the hell are you doing?"

Paul blasts the security module. Sparks trickle onto the co-pilot's body, singeing his partially-exposed flesh.

"Paul! That might have—" Oni stops. The flashing yellow security light returns to a steady green.

Interfacing with the projected controls, hovering a foot above the analogue dash, Paul locks-in the landing sequence.

"Citadel force-field twenty-seconds out." He turns, hoping to find Oni's confident smile, but she's already off, getting their gear and clothes.

PAUL'S SHIRT BUNCHES around the PILOT mechanism clipped into his breast. He yanks up his collar, and tucks his shirt in at the side, so nothing's in the way of his revolver. He digs his piecemeal exoskeleton out of the container, and straps in. *Looks like armour, feels like added strength.*

Oni rolls her second skin up her leg, clasping the bands around her knees and ankles. Her tall black boots vacuum-seal, shaking the decorative laces criss-crossing up her thigh.

She plunges into the case, and pulls out Gibson's rope-claw and the knight's B.F.G.

"These are yours, I believe."

Paul grabs the rope-claw. In the exchange, the grappling hook slides out, trailing a long, fine cable.

"For crying out loud," he whispers, seizing up the hook. His armour squeaks as he pipes the hook back down the chamber, and straps the device awkwardly over his shoulder.

Oni holds out the knight's gun, smiling.

Paul collects it from her with both hands, eying its artistry. "Something this beautiful shouldn't be used for killing."

"Don't go soft on me now, Doc." Oni smirks, turning to grab more toys from the bin.

It must be a coping mechanism, Paul thinks, studying the levity impressed on Oni's visage. *She must translate terror into amusement.*

"You're enjoying this."

"Obviously," she answers back, lightning-quick. "Years of treating symptoms, and today? Today, we're the cure."

Oni pulls a bulbous, satin bag out of the case. She unknots the golden string, and procures the keystone to their plan: the EMP grenade. Her little fingers nimbly crawl along the circumference of the device, finding and flicking-on the micro-primers. The EMP beeps ready. "Good to go." She turns on her Monocle and hails Gibson. "Booker?"

"Matsui! How's my favorite Jill-of-all-trades?"

"About to touch-down. How're you holding up?"

"Surviving. Didn't realize how much the PILOT was doing on my behalf…"

"You'll recover. Where are we at with the diversion?"

"Can't hear the cannon fire? *It's already begun.* Hacked one of the Burbank gate defenses. PIT rats've already targeted the sector's cypulchre. Lots of fire. Lots of attention."

"Perfect. Hopefully that'll give us a little breathing room…We're coming in on the Citadel. It'll be closed-circuit from here on."

"Oni, watch your back. I think W'chester knows—" Gibson's voice crackles and defaults to white noise, which in turn gives way to the sound of the Citadel's force field engulfing the Spirit—like sand blown against metal sheeting. A fierce hum follows, signalling the end to the shield's two-second porosity.

"Gibson?"

Static.

"Dammit. Alright, Paul. Eight seconds," says Oni, palming the grenade contemplatively.

Paul props the knight's gun against the wall, and shears off the heavplast guard on the bubble shield. "Everything good?"

"Have faith," she murmurs.

"Ha. Yeah, alright. Try to save whatever gymnastics you've got planned for when we split up…Stick close."

Oni rolls her eyes.

"Otherwise the bubble shield will be no good," he warns.

Thumbing-in the trigger mechanism on the EMP, Oni leans over and kisses Paul on the cheek.

The bristles on his haggard face twitch alive, signalling warm currents through his temples. He looks at her with an expression of bewilderment and pleasure.

She shrugs, secreting a smile. *"For good luck."*

THE SPIRIT TRAIN SAILS towards the Citadel's re-processing dock on a drift of smoke. Its magnetic levelers take over for the side-engines, and snap as the ship finds its groove. A dozen droids gear out to meet it, hauling it into place with magnetic lassos and harnesses.

Across the landing pad, under the Citadel's matte-black awnings, an archway births four heavily-armored Sentinels. They goosestep past the droids, and surround the ship.

The Spirit's side-doors automatically slice open, loosing red light. A railing, which threads the Citadel via a dark, labyrinthine corridor, fires into the hold. It locks onto one of the Spirit's internal rails, suspended just above and between Paul and Oni, and sets with a click. The first of the meat pods is immediately summoned-up and tracked along, out of the Spirit.

"That's our cue," says Paul. He yanks his collar further up, past his cheeks, and marches out—the B.F.G. and rope-claw strapped to his back. Oni follows in tow.

"Captain Kassel, Lieutenant Chang. Please wait for security to assist you," shouts an augmented abomination strapped into a heavy-steel exo-suit, clearly not paying close-enough attention. He has a skull grafted to his helmet.

Paul whispers to Oni over their local-area-comm: "I know that guy. He was with the group that attacked the camp."

Suppressing her murderous desire, Oni runs a Monocle scan. "No prisoners."

A second mech, checking the Spirit's undercarriage, notices something odd about the pilots—their civilian clothes and the massive appendage oscillating on Paul's back. "Unauthorized weapon on the tarmac! Intruders!"

"Lock and load!" another cries.

Oni lunges forward, side-swiping Paul, and rolls the EMP to the middle of the landing pad.

The skull-plated abomination snarls, and raises his hand-cannon. "Call it in!"

Paul hammers the shield into the ground at his feet. A peach-coloured field enshrouds him and Oni.

The Sentinels ready their Gatling guns and mark their targets.

"Open fire!" orders the skull-plated mech.

Oni's EMP expels its poles to the sides, releasing an electrical storm. Blue and white bands spider out, whipping and whooshing over and past anything with a charge. It crinkles at the bubble shield as it combs past Oni and Paul, sweaty and entangled in their shared shell. Paul closes his eyes as the storm begins to strobe white light like old xenon flashbulbs at a press scrum. Oni squeezes his wrist as the mechs squawk and scream in cognitive pain.

A magma-flow of undirected bullets pours left and right. The closest shooter stumbles towards Paul and Oni, but the hydraulics on his exo-suit fail him. He oversteps and keels over the side of the dock. Oni hears the mercenary's body tear and mangle against the protuberances below, his gun still firing every-which-way.

The bubble shield hisses. Oni falls through its lingering residue. Paul scrambles to pick her up, and drags her over to the scissor doors for shelter. Oni covers their retreat with her phaser, only there's nothing left to shoot; nothing but smoking corpses and whining mechanical parts.

"Look," cries Oni. "The cameras. They're fuming too."

"Fantastic!" Paul unstraps the B.F.G., and swings it around. "Now, to see a man about an elevator door."

"The bodies..." Oni warns Paul in a strained voice. She brushes herself off, and walks over to the skull-plated mech. She crouches over its twitching body.

"What about them?" asks Paul, his rage-induced focus offsetting any peripheral worry.

Oni tears the skull bone off of the mech's helmet, and peels the visor back. Inside: a piecemeal face, loaded-up with augs and circuitry. All the tech embedded in the pink pincushion is charred, but the host is still breathing.

"We should hide them," she says.

"Why?" Paul clenches his teeth. "There'll only be more."

Staring into the black eyes of the felled mech, Oni nods in agreement. "Fine."

She strides over to Paul, seizes his revolver, and returns to their familiar foe. She whispers to the mech: "The only part of you still alive is human." She presses the gun to its silicon-speckled forehead. "And that part," she thumbs the hammer back, "can go straight to Hell."

Chapter 31: **ASCENSION**

"GIBSON WAS RIGHT," Paul says, dropping a severed finger belonging to one of the mechs. The scanner on the elevator beeps repeatedly, rejecting the bloody fingerprint. "Biometrics and security implants are toast. Surprised they're still lighting up." He stitches the horizontal seam in the door with his fingers, and readies an opening attempt.

Oni prods Paul, directing a raised eyebrow at the gun strapped to his back.

"Of course." He smiles, stepping clear of the door.

"And this," she says, returning the revolver to Paul, warm around the cylinder. "Five shots left. Hopefully Winchester only needs one."

Paul, the saboteur-turned-gun-rack, juggles the weapons until he's comfortable with their arrangement. He joins Oni in walking over to a safe distance, and aims the B.F.G.

"For sunny days!" he exclaims, lobbing a round at the door.

The round clinks into the door's blast shielding. Apart from a loud pop and a hairline fracture, the target looks unperturbed, with the big-effing grenade lodged no more than an inch into the plating.

"I imagine that was supposed to go differently," Paul says, gloomily. He steps forward, but Oni grabs his arm.

"What?"

"Give it a chance."

Paul squints at the elevator. There's a second, loud click. A blinding flash hides a belch of flame and a shower of metal fragments. The shockwave throws Paul and Oni to the side like wet laundry. The boom begets a crunch, and the bottom door-panel collapses.

Smoke. Coughing.

"Oni, you alright?" Paul asks between gasps, crawling over the shrapnel and debris. "Oni?"

He finds her hunched over, legs crossed.

She rubs her arms with probative, bloody fingers. "I'm fine. Just some scratches."

"You sure?"

Oni raises a silencing finger, transfixed on their new portal to the elevator shaft, torched a rainbow-black. The collapsed bottom-piece wobbles.

"Grab it!" she cries, struggling forward.

The debris leans back, and falls into the shaft, creating a thunderous commotion. She stops mid-lunge.

"Crap. Well, there goes the element of surprise."

The crater in the remaining door looks like a twisted, vacant eye embedded in a silver plate. Paul holds the sides of the crater, and leans through the gap. "Hot damn," he mumbles.

There's a circle of LED lights marking every floor. Further down, they appear to smudge together forming a uniform line.

"Help me with this," says Paul, tugging on one side of the gap.

Oni grabs the other side, and together they pull the eye apart. Paul turns into her contemplative stare.

"What's the deal with this gun of yours? I can't be waiting around for shit to go off."

"Looks like the delayed rounds got mixed in with the incendiary ammunition. Impact grenades have the red stripe; green bands are on delayed nades." She lifts the two varieties in the knotted chain-feed dangling from the side of the B.F.G.

"Fuse life?"

"Five, six seconds from the time they're fired. If you're reloading it, careful you don't hand-activate them. There's a charge...Once they lose the charge—whether shot, primed, or thrown, it doesn't matter—the countdown begins."

"Good to know."

"Yeah." Oni looks down the elevator bank. "Let's get a move-on before they figure out where that door came from."

Paul looks up the bank. The view is obscured by an elevator. "What're my chances of catching a ride straight to Winchester?"

"Not as good as your chances of falling to your death."

Chapter 32: SHAFTED

GIBSON's ROPE-CLAW is a godsend. Paul whizzes effortlessly up the elevator bank holding onto the tail of the spider-silk cable, also clasped to his waistband for good measure. The claw's motor whines laboriously, dragging Paul towards the hook's end, jammed into the bottom of the elevator compartment idling around the hundredth storey. LED lights blear-by in glowing zigzags like a chromosomal chain-on-fire.

"Comm check," Paul whispers into his Monocle feed, his reinforced legs swinging beneath him.

"Roger," says Oni, her voice slightly warbled by the Citadel's jammers and the CLOUD interference. "Man, it's freezing in here."

"Server central?"

"It's enormous, Paul. These are all recent additions. New even relative to the blueprints we pulled, and those were only a month old. They've enough coolant gel and honeycomb to synch the entire Midwest."

With a jerk, Paul ceases to ascend.

"I see the Special Collections wing...Do you copy?"

"I've hit a slight snag. Give me a second." Kicking, Paul tries to swing over to the ladder. The LEDs throw his frantic shadow-play against the far side.

Beeping resounds in the shaft. The elevator unhinges, and begins to lurch upwards. It tugs at Paul. His body's resistance is spelt out in taught muscles. He groans, the LEDs now blurring to a seemingly unbroken line of white.

"Paul?"

"All good," he grumbles. "A possible stroke of luck."

With about twenty storeys left to go, the elevator stops again, jostling Paul like a dead fish on a hook. The compartment dips slightly, and fills with modulated chatter.

There's very little to be made of all the synthetic banter, but one phrase penetrates the compartment clearly: "Med-sci ward."

"No thanks," Paul grumbles, wiggling on the line. "This is where I get off."

The elevator dislodges and begins to drop. Falling three-floors a second, Paul manages to unclasp his waistband and swing over to the side ladder in one fluid motion. It's no small fortune that he's able to grasp one of the rungs. Coupled with his fortune is potential calamity: clattering on his back, the knight's gun gets tangled in the spider-silk cord.

"No!" he cries.

He grabs the shoulder strap in one hand, and the ladder bar with the other. The elevator whooshes by with such speed and gravity that it almost pulls him into its path. Paul feels the strand of spider-silk loosen, easing on his muscles—stretched to the point of tearing (without the exoskeleton, they surely would). He shakes the B.F.G. once more. It swings free, striking him in the shin. The line falls loose, and down the chamber. The slight twinge through his already-brutalized leg is the best he could've hoped for.

The elevator counterbalance tracks up the steel cable, reflecting the clear, natural light, filtering down the well—no longer obstructed by the cumbersome container.

That's it, Paul realizes. *The roof—or something resembling one.* "Oni, I'm climbing." The Monocle conveys his wheezes in bursts.

"There's a lot of activity around the Memex Overwatch System, Paul. I've found a uniform…"

"Found?"

"Bloodlessly, actually. I fit right back in. It's like I never lit this place on fire…How far have you to go?"

"Ten storeys, or thereabouts."

"Alright, I'm in their system. Give me a second to scope out the area for you."

"I'll just be—"

"Don't."

"Don't?"

"If you say 'hanging around' I'll turn off the comm on principle."

Paul looks down the elevator bank. There are more floors in this building than names in the Barstow registry. *Winchester may be an evil son of a bitch, but he is certainly a master builder. "Success is power, and failure servitude," he used to say.*

Paul continues climbing, despite the pain and creaking in his elbows. There is an unprecedented interval between this floor and the next. *More headroom for the imperial crown*, Paul posits.

Unlike the previous elevator doors, the opening to Winchester's floor is smooth; no cranks, interfaces, or circuit boards.

"Hey, I need a way in."

Oni's Monocle cuts out.

"Oni?"

She comes back on, panting. "Hey, sorry. Something's gotten their attention down here. I count eight or nine mechs."

"Sorry to hear that."

Paul hears a melody of beeps and boops—probably Oni hacking a keypad of some sort. "Alright. There's innumerable security features on this floor. I only have access to three: Winchester's personal elevator, the blast-shield along the windows, and...let's see. Oh, good! The maintenance elevator."

"Might as well deactivate all three."

There's shouting on the other end. "'Hey you!'" bellows a modulated voice. There's more yelling, and then the pkt-pkt-pkt of assault rifles.

Paul leans out into the elevator bank to get a better look. With arms stretched and taut, he stares blankly at the rolled-homogenous steel door. In his partial reflection, Paul sees Pythia's bright blue eyes. "Anything..." he murmurs, hooking his left arm around a rung. He fumbles with the knight's gun, trying to procure a delayed grenade. A red-striped nade jumps clear of the feed. Paul nearly loses his hold trying to catch it. The flashing red light shrinks to a blip, like a lure cast into deep, dark water. "That's not good."

There's a boom and a poof of smoke. The elevator cables wave, and the counterweight hurdles past Paul—its fate bound to the elevator Paul's unwittingly turned to Swiss-cheese below.

The LEDs lining the bank start flashing red. A computerized voice chimes in: "LOCKDOWN INITIATED. COMMENCING FLUSH PROTOCOL."

"Oh you've got to be kidding me," cries Paul. He haphazardly extracts a green grenade from the chain, and slings the B.F.G. behind him. "Now or never." He winds up to lodge the nade in the door. In advance of the slamming motion, the elevator door rolls to the side.

Thank God for you, Oni.

He jumps into the opening. The B.F.G. swings back, nearly spinning him over the edge, but Paul gears himself forward with a quick and frenetic punching motion. He smashes the elevator button, and the door whooshes shut, isolating the so-called "Flush protocol."

"Oni, I'm through."

Static on the other end.

The freight-entrance is gorgeous. Gilded Rococo curves map across pastel walls tattooed with rich murals of buxom libertines splayed-out in idyllic forest-clearings. The lavish ornamental look is offset by the stark, blue and white hall ahead.

Past the freight elevator and outside the antechamber, the smooth Rococo lines fade into an ultra-mod, minimalistic grid pattern. An inverted fin comprised of crystalloid LEDs hangs the length of the hall, above the nearly-transparent, electric catwalk. Railing-less, the pathway glows off-blue, and hovers above two vacant storeys—or as Paul imagines, *the Citadel's demarrowed bones.*

Unlike the massive LED chandelier, the catwalk bifurcates at intervals along the hallway—enclosed by a glass and titanium prism—to balconies, turrets, observatories, and executive offices. *Must be a holiday*, Paul supposes, eyeing all the empty rooms.

Paul's warming up the idea of an easy-go at Winchester, but chills immediately at the sight of a Monarch drone emerging from the murk.

"Oni, do you copy?"

More static.

God-damn-it, woman! "Have you wired the Empty Thought yet?"

Some semblance of Oni's trebly voice cuts through. "P-P-Paul, it's so much worse than we'd imagined."

Paul takes cover behind an armoire, sitting at the mouth of the elevator antechamber.

"What is it? What's wrong?"

"Winchester…he's taking Outland international in a *big way*. In the cypulchre, past the coolant-gel pumps, there's a monitor. It's guarded, but I can get the gist from here via a Monocle hack…They're launching in Tokyo, New Moscow, Cairo, and Toronto."

Paul unstraps the B.F.G., and stands it butt-first beside him. "Well, we're about to give them a good reason to reconsider…"

There're multiple voices competing on the other end. "Oni?"

"I'm here. Just loaded the Empty Thought to your memex. Or at least I think I did. Proceed as planned. Good luck decrypting it…"

"Alright. Winchester's office is on the other end of the floor. Except for a drone or two, it's a ghost town in here. Shouldn't be a problem."

"Chances are…"

"Right. What's the time ratio again? I mean, real time versus CLOUD time?"

"With your modifications? Something in the neighbourhood of ten minutes, CLOUD time, for every real-time second spent synched up."

"Wish me luck."

"Paul?" Oni's voice cracks. "Take care of yourself up there."

That's a promise I can't keep.

Paul checks the corner to see if the Monarch'd fluttered away. *It's still there.*

"And you take care down there. Over and out."

Paul turns off his Monocle, and pulls himself up by the knight's gun. He strides confidently out of the antechamber, and takes the catwalk, centre stage. The Monarch spins to face him. Its cells light up, turning bright orange, while it hind-fans offset the turbulence made by its arming-sequence.

Heavier than it looks, and already looking mighty heavy, it takes Paul almost too much time to orient the B.F.G., but he does, anyway. Holding it at waist level, he reads the green light welling-up in the Monarch's laser chamber as a sign. He squeezes the trigger.

There's no debate as to what kind of shell he fired. A direct hit exacts a gold, black, and red mushroom cloud. Paul trudges forward, with sparks and chips raining down into the empty storeys behind him.

The hallway looks as if its architect had been commissioned to build a mile-long lean-to using only the best materials, 2500 feet above terra firma. All the windows face the ocean, while the eastern side is made up of one solid titanium wall, keeping out the prying eyes of lost angels.

Moving along the catwalk, Paul feels a tremor. He turns and scans the room's many sub-corridors and vaults for another Monarch or some other soulless drone. He bends to shoulder the B.F.G. and notices the catwalk flickering. *Someone knows he's here.* That same *someone* is sapping the electricity fortifying the bridge. *It's a draw-bridge on the verge of withdrawal.*

Paul pre-empts the trap, and leaps into a room off the path. The bridge flickers and crackles, and then disappears. Without the rope-claw, Paul sees no other alternative than to scope out the terminus of the sub-corridor.

Chapter 33: **CORPORATE REUNION**

"OUTBUILD. OUTMATCH. OUTSHINE. *Outland.*" The propaganda poster depicts a duotone Olympian carrying a sword and shield into the vivid, grid-lined unknown. Beside it, another, more starkly-coloured poster, shows a cypulchre casting a shadow over the eastern hemisphere with the caption: "What can we do? What *can't* we do?" Paul sneers at the rhetorical question. *Stop me, for one.* He presses on, down the sub-corridor.

At the end of the passageway is a narrow, black-metal staircase. It zigzags up a well-lit spire walled with semi-transparent, green-hued silica bricks. Through the composite of mint bubbles, Paul can make out the coast. White caps and surf break on Blue Zone shoals. He imagines the sound of the water hammering the flood gates, and works the tidal tempo into his stride.

He marches up the remainder of the stairs, which flow into a passageway that, running parallel to the sub-corridor below, leads back to the main hall.

A muffled voice broadcasts over Paul's Monocle. "Paul?"

"I'm almost there," he replies, pulling out a handful of SIK tabs.

"I hacked the surveillance feeds."

"And?"

He looks at the triangular pills and lets them fall. *Instability might be of some benefit when dealing with a nearly-omniscient, noospheric god.*

"In Winchester's office, there are…" Her feed cuts out.

"Oni?" There're what?"

Static purrs.

"Oh, dammit," he mumbles.

He checks the chamber on the knight's gun, and runs towards the main hall.

Paul would monkey along the LED chandelier and pray for a dramatic and miraculous descent had he the energy to do so. But he doesn't, so he searches for an alternative, standing at the end of the senior sub-corridor. There's a scant ledge running along the western face, angled under the glass. *The road less taken…*

He shimmies along the precipice, over to a folded maintenance ladder. There's a crank stylishly embedded in the glass. The mechanism, springs, pistons, and all, are visible in their gauzy cocoon. Paul pulls the crank. The springs compress, kicking the piston out and the lock open. The ladder drops to the staging area in front of Winchester's office.

"Hot damn!" Paul exclaims.

Reminding himself that a little bit of good luck is usually a sign of a lot of bad luck to come, Paul takes a moment to gather his strength. After a few painful, deep breaths, he's ready.

He slides down faster than he'd expected, burning his hands on the rough metal. His boots smack the floor—*undeniably solid this time.* He quickly recuperates, and dashes to the office door, leading with the muzzle of the B.F.G.

The office is massive. On either side of the gold lane running down the hem, there are little champagne-coloured mirror pools reflecting the late-afternoon light. Enclosing the space are glyph-enveloped sandstone monoliths, likely imported directly from Giza. Unlike the hallway leading up to it, Winchester's office only has one window—a cross-like cavity cut into the western wall that highlights the golden lane, and cuts the room in half with a secondary, horizontal ray.

Beneath the window sits the Resolute desk—sole survivor of the siege of Washington, no doubt a gift from an appreciative Head of State. The presidential seal that had been carved into the wood and later effaced by shell fragments has been replaced by the Outland 'O'. The former eagle's wings lift the corporate insignia up into the star-studded cloud.

Leaning against the far side of the desk: the narrow profile of a shrunken man silently overlooking the ocean. His reflection in the cross-window is grey, blotchy, and inhuman—*so, more-or-less what I'd expected to find.*

Paul assumes that the stilted device nestled in the corner behind the Resolute desk—ostensibly the only tech in the room—must be the Baal Deck storm machine—*Angela's and Pythia's ticket home.*

"Dr. Sheffield, I presume." The geriatric turns slowly into shadow, and flattens his fingers on the felt lining the British timber. "Hello, *old friend.* It's been a long, long time. Please come in. I haven't a seat for you; wasn't expecting guests, after all. I suppose you could always kneel..."

It's quiet in here. Paul can hear his disjunctive thoughts chaw at one another. He can hear the tick of Winchester's mechanical heart. He can hear cogwheels turning...

At the sight of the knight's gun, Winchester simpers and sits down at his desk. "You've gone to great and unnecessary lengths to get here. Could've called. Was your Monocle broken?"

"We've no time for pleasantries, *Niles.*" *What good are naming conventions between two dead men?* "We need to rain out the heavenly host or they're doomed...Or *we're* doomed."

"Sheffield, do yourself a favour and lower that weapon. There's no reason why we cannot talk like civilized men."

"No can do. You've already tried to kill me twice. Civility depends on trust, and that's something I simply don't have."

"Well, if you've a mind to take a hostile stance, I don't see why I shouldn't take the same precaution."

Winchester snaps his fingers, and two gigantic buke bots de-cloak on either side of him. Dressed and armored like Samurai of legend, the bots lurch forward, their cannons and melded-on electric swords entering the cross-light.

Should have known.

"You're welcome to keep your gun drawn, but know: Dr. Katajima designed these specifically to protect me. They're *cutting* edge." Winchester laughs at his pun, reaching out to flick the closer-bot's crackling sword with a gnarled finger. A drop of rusty-red blood rolls away from the cauterized skin, and down his sleeve.

"For the love of God, stand down!" Paul yells, desperately.

"Oh please, Paul. I don't control them with grunts like a filthy Neanderthal." He points to his head. "My will, coded, be done on earth as it is in heaven."

Paul groans.

"I know why you're here, Dr. Sheffield."

"Really? Have you been consulting your crystal ball?"

"Not quite. Our dear friend, Dr. Katajima, has kept me in the loop. His loyalty is really quite remarkable, granted your recent encounter. I don't see how I can remunerate him for his time, given his present lack of pockets or need for them."

"If you're referring to his murder, it wasn't by my hand…"

"No need for fictions now, my dear boy. He told me all about your plan to destroy what you created; to rock my empire and kill all those people—my children, as it were. All of his messages are public record, should you wish to see them. It might paint *this* meeting in a different light, if it is," he points at Paul with both hands, "another one of your infamous episodes."

"Series finale, *actually*."

"My lord!" Winchester chuckles. "Pettiness has evidently taken root with all those grey hairs…"

"Those messages are all counterfeits. Your source has been compromised. The Anomaly…"

"A nice trick. I knew it was you all along. Who else would create a problem so destructive, that the only solution would be an alternate form of lesser destruction in-line with your original agenda?"

"There's no time to explain. The man—the thing—you've been talking to…that's not Shouta. There's something in the CLOUD right now that can and *will* kill everything in there just for kicks, and then hardline out. It's going to destroy the world as we know it."

"Do you take me for a simpleton, Dr. Sheffield?"

"Check your data-streams!" Paul bellows.

With eyes glowing bright red, the buke bots motion forward, picking up on Paul's belligerent tone, but Winchester subdues them with a trembling hand. He opens his desk, takes out a holo-deck, and centres it before him. A hologram visualizing the CLOUD's data-streams coagulates. Save for an out-of-place nodule, everything appears as it should be.

"No, that's not right. It's lying to you!" Doubt swirls about Paul's mind, fogging his memory and contaminating his certainty.

"Please, Doctor, you're exhausting the both of us. I recall, now years back, an idealistic, young man who sought to destroy what I'd built. And now that same man—calloused and weathered by failure and rejection—is back, standing before me, prophesizing cataclysm and professing to be humanity's last hope. What a moth-eaten yarn!"

Paul eyes the pair of buke bots, and then the ocean through the window, partially eclipsed by the frail and stubborn technocrat sitting in his imperial throne. "What are the chances you'll depopulate the CLOUD as a safety measure? I'll submit to whatever punishment fits my crime, whatever that crime might be."

Winchester laughs.

"What if I asked nicely?" says Paul, frustrated.

"Well, you'd need my full cooperation. The Baal Deck needs to scan my biometrics in order to function."

Paul brandishes his canines.

Appreciative of Paul's exasperation, Winchester continues. "And the likelihood of having my cooperation in destroying everything I've worked to achieve? As probable as your walking out of here in one piece."

Paul's Monocle crackles alive with Oni's voice. "Paul! Paul, do you copy?"

"Yeah," Paul replies, eyes locked with Winchester's.

Winchester cocks his head sideways. "Tell Dr. Matsui I say hello."

"In Winchester's office—"

"I know," interrupts Paul. "Buke mechs."

"Shit! But no, *that's not all*. There's been a data surge, just like the one that Gibson logged in advance of Katajima's murder."

"Here?" yells Paul, alarmed, scrutinizing Winchester. "Thanks Oni."

"What's that little minx on about?" asks Winchester.

"We're both in big trouble."

"Oh?" says Winchester mockingly. "The *both* of us?" He coughs, and stands up slowly.

"What killed Katajima—it is in here with us right now."

"I dare say I'm looking at it, Paul. Dr. Katajima was a good man. Too good a friend for the likes of you, evidently." Winchester walks around his desk, one hand anchored on the corner, acting as a pivot point and support. "You never really understood what we were doing here." He lifts his hands up as far as he can, and wobbles, slightly. "Creating mankind anew."

"Save me the spiel. You're after power, pure and simple."

Winchester shakes his head, and smirks wistfully at the buke bot on his left. "This could have gone differently for you, Paul." He coughs. "I never blamed you for Allen's death—for coercing Dr. Katajima to break protocol and move forward with his experiment ahead of schedule. In private, I celebrated your ambition. I also prayed for your silence, so that the two of us could continue to...*collaborate*. It is unfortunate that we cannot turn back the hour hand on your folly, because it would scoop a handful of numbers I doubt you'd balk at."

The eyes on the buke to the right of Winchester turn from red to a bright yellow, like hollow furnaces on fire. Its slight realignment catches Paul's attention.

"Your dog has a mind of its own," Paul says, lifting the B.F.G.

Responding to Paul's aggressive stance, the other buke, still red-eyed, targets him with several laser points.

"How now?" Winchester turns to the yellow-eyed buke. "He's simply tiring of your sad performance. I can't say I blame him."

The yellow-eyed buke steps forward, and grabs Winchester by the back of his neck. It lifts him up like a ragdoll, shaking one of his shoes free.

"What...are...you...doing?" rasps Winchester, writhing in the bot's hold, kicking backwards at its chassis and scraping futilely at its mammoth hand.

The red-eyed Buke lunges forward, fully weaponized, and knocks the yellow-eyed bot back with an iron punch, releasing its hold on Winchester. Winchester slaps the ground like a damp newspaper, and tries to pull himself away from the scrum. The aggressor kicks the loyal bot back, and opens fire, scraping off its opponent's oriental mask.

Paul fires two rounds: one directly at the red-eyed bot, and a miss, past the yellow-eyed bot. The first rounds clink on-target, but fail to explode.

"Blast!" barks Paul.

Undaunted by the titanic clash and metal-on-metal screeches, Paul checks the feed on the B.F.G. A red grenade is buried after a sequence of green ones. He takes a knee, and pulls out the ammo-belt.

There's a crash. Paul looks up. The first delayed grenade blew a crater into the torso of the red-eyed bot, sending it careening back—just missing the Baal Deck. With sparks and lubricant oozing out, it nevertheless finds its footing and aligns itself for one last go at the yellow-eyed bot.

Both bukes close in, leaving just enough room for swordplay. Their electric swords snap and spark, glinting in the cross-light.

Gurgling blood, Winchester crawls around the Resolute desk. He throws out a trembling distress sign for Paul.

Too late, asshole.

Paul rifles through a handful of grenades, pocketing the erroneous green-striped ammo. There's only one incendiary round left, which Paul single-feeds into the B.F.G. after a delayed grenade. He aims it at the tornado of metal and circuitry, and fires both rounds in rapid succession.

The delayed grenade clangs against something metallic. The yellow-eyed bot pulls its twin into the second, incendiary round. Wiring and metal-plating decal the desk and jet into the surrounding sandstone. In an inferno of smoke and flame, two yellow eyes stand out. The mutinous buke's gun thunders.

RED. PAIN. DARKNESS.

PAUL CAN FEEL his heartbeat in his eyes. Sprawled out on a pile of his own gore, with one foot dipped in a mirror pool, he looks up to see the surviving yellow-eyed Buke smash through the desk and pull Winchester up by his shoulder. Its raises its electric sword, twisted in the fight, and cleaves Winchester in two. The technocrat's imperial garb sloughs off and all the biomachinery keeping him alive spill out.

"No," murmurs Paul. Shock must have kicked in earlier than usual. *He can't feel his legs.* The exo-suit armour Gibson insisted he wear has splintered. Some of the shards have made their way under his skin.

Dropping Winchester's remains, the yellow-eyed buke registers Paul's continued presence, and turns to deal with him. There's a beep. *The delayed grenade.* The buke's yellow eyes widen like carbuncles set to break, and then disappear in a cloud of debris and fire.

"Monocle," rasps Paul. "Status."

The medical brief flits over Paul's iris. "Critical condition. Exsanguination expected to shut down mental faculties in one minute; heart will fail in two. Medical attention summoned by unknown witness."

Sliming over his own entrails, Paul pulls himself across Winchester's office floor. *Anything for them.*

Trailing his last supper, Paul circumnavigates the splintered Resolute desk, and finds Winchester...twice. He grabs the shouldered head of his former boss as one would a bocce ball, and heaves it over to the storm machine. It bobbles along, stopping, finally, at the Baal Deck's stilted base.

Paul yanks two wires out of the sparking, smoking belly of the closest buke, and trawls them behind him, over to the storm machine. Gushing blood every-which-way, he closes his charred shirt around his chest wound, and, wheezing, plots Winchester's face into the scanner.

The Baal storm machine rejects Winchester's empty stare. *Thought so.* Paul stabs one of the buke's hissing wires into the base of Winchester's skull. He shoves the wrinkled visage into the mould, and keys a second wire into the dead man's mouth. A zap announces the completion of a circuit. *Glad that worked.*

Paul spatters blood, and keels into the machine. Quickly losing consciousness and motor function, he panics, believing he's hallucinated the storm machine's validation-beep. Disregarding the agonizing ache branching throughout his chest, he pulls himself up the machine's stilts. With his exo-skeleton shattered, he creaks on two sets of broken legs, grasping either side of the view screen.

The Baal Deck prompts Paul with several options, but there's only the one action-tree he cares about: "SEVER LOOP, QUARANTINE NETWORK, AND DESYNCHRONIZE ALL SUBSCRIBERS, EXCEPT FOR MEMEX NUMBER…"

His Monocle is on the fritz, having taken some of the beating. He comms Oni, and waits on fuzz for a reply.

The words are faint and distorted. "Paul? Update!"

"What's my memex number?" Paul rasps, gurgling blood between words.

Static.

"Oni?"

"031087…Paul?"

"Thanks. See that my girls make it out o-k."

He enters his memex number and finishes the command.

He intuits-off his Monocle, and clicks through the Baal machine's suggestive pop-ups and warnings. He watches the loading bar realize his goal. It beeps again, offering particular options he hasn't the blood left to comprehend.

He falls back. Twisting in a septic puddle of the yellow-eyed buke's making, Paul sees the early-evening light stab the massacre. He crawls across the debris, tattered fabric, and guts, into the warming rays. He flops back into a lean against the Resolute desk's ruins. Overlooking the ocean, he yanks a green orb out of his pocket, clicks it, and intuits-on his implant.

Chapter 34: **KOYAANISQATSI**

SOMETHING'S OFF.

Winchester's motionless parts are still unevenly plotted across the floor. The yellow-eyed buke, too, is half-buried in the splintered Resolute desk beside Paul, sparking.

Paul looks down to the source of his phantom pain, but the wound, like the pain, disappears. "This isn't real," he declares for his own benefit.

He remembers how, back in the day, his team at Outland was developing a program codenamed "Charon." Its function was to emulate an individual's surroundings during synchronization to ease their translation into the CLOUD. By mimicking reality, the virtual preamble to the noosphere would give the individual's mind a chance to prepare.

Paul gets up slowly. He turns to see his mangled body resting behind him. Its shirt is blown back, exposing a porridge of mangled organs and bones wrapped in spidersilk. *That can't be good*, Paul surmises. His doppelganger disappears in a flurry of glitches, and his vision begins to shudder.

The water in Winchester's mirror pools drips skywards, and the hall Paul had entered transforms into a kaleidoscopic tunnel of light. The walls begin to melt into pixel ponds. The barbs of daylight stabbing the floor through the shattered cross-window solidify, taking on the appearance of iron girders. Trembling some more, the room begins to shrink around Paul. Light turns to sound, and the ground gives way to deafening darkness.

Instinctively, Paul tries to grab onto something, feeling the noise suck at his feet. He throws his arms around one of the iron girders, but both his arms and the girder dematerialize.

Shit.

IT FEELS A LOT like drowning, only there are no ear drums around to burst. No lungs, no panicked heart. Just Paul's stray mind, glowing with pictorial, haptic, and willful potential.

Paul perceives himself slip deeper into the CLOUD, stuck with the feeling he's going back to sleep after waking from a horrible nightmare. Some part of him realizes he's been mortally wounded, but his animal panic and most of his reptilian drive have been displaced. He can't sense his bubbled skin or his broken body, only cognitive discomfort.

The CLOUD sweeps-up his lonely partition into a dense star field populated by synesthetic ideas and sensations, loosely laced by information highways and photoluminescent course-lines, glowing, somehow, without electricity or conventional power. Data swirls like aimless snowflakes around the fractallic structures—a seemingly infinite structure constituted by linked Mobius strips morphed by passing information typhoons.

It worked.

Paul's implant has successfully synchronized with his virgin memex and the CLOUD.

They're all gone. No one's home, and the home that's left is an amalgam of temporary mental projections—the leviathan's mental fingerprint.

Paul feels like he's falling into the pulsating mire, but with no body or horizon to orient with, the CLOUD may just as well be falling around him, assuming his historical person.

He offers up one last cynical thought (i.e. *"No! No!"*), and then shrinks away from his unifying code and voice.

THE THOUGHTS FORMALLY attributed to Dr. Paul Sheffield pool and reunify, defining a singular framework and semblance of self. He's experienced a fleeting moment of ego-death.

"That was awfully unpleasant," Paul thinks, recomposing himself. *Without the customary, slow introduction, evaporation to the CLOUD has one hell of a learning curve.*

A singing, yellow line necklaces Paul. He is at once filled with unprecedented knowledge about the CLOUD's interior rules, logic, and inhabitants. *It's the crash course*, he realizes. He didn't have the time to be eased-into CLOUD space by the tutorial bots, so Oni keyed his PILOT to demand instant access, or rather, immediate noospheric capability. *It's overwhelming.*

"Body, shape, extension, movement, and place are all illusions," thunders a displaced, atonal voice.

The sentiment cuts through Paul, unfamiliar like a stranger's declaration in a foreign tongue.

"So what remains true? Our minds, together. Together, we are shaping tomorrow. Together, we change what it means to be human. Together, we change what it means to *be. Welcome* to the CLOUD."

A rudimentary heads-up-display beads along the soulful line like morning dew. The droplets of information assigned to Paul via the interface differentiate by colour like a genomic printout, suggesting things to do in the CLOUD.

Yoking the rainbow band, Paul defines his space, effecting a basic avatar around his singular voice and swirling thoughts; nothing more than an anthropomorphic, gridline-encased self. It ripples with the hum of his repressed subconscious, turning the squares begat by the gridlines into vibrating diamonds.

Paul flicks through the colours on his data-assignment, and intuits his query: "Outland Terminal search: Pythia Sheffield."

There's a lyrical spectacle of light around him, but no satisfactory result.

"Pythia Irhap," Paul guesses.

His daughter's perfect face appears at the head of a collage of shared memories—both Paul's and someone else's—perhaps Rachel's. Pythia disappears like a happy dream wrecked on the verge of waking.

Ozymandian pillars whiz by like shooting stars, trailing intense tribal vibrations and lap-string carols. The information on them is illegible, but somehow their signage conveys meaning to Paul, as if by osmosis.

"EDUCATIONAL EXPERIENCE...CLOUD TUTORIALS...TAKE A BREAK AT NOSTALGIA BAY...SENSEDEN: YOUR GO-TO FOR MENTALLY SAFE, LUSTFUL, AND CARNAL, DELIGHTS...NARRATIVE IMMERSION: SPECULATIVE FICTION FRIDAYS...FETCHED MEMORY POOL. *WHO* DO YOU WANT TO BE TODAY?"

The influencers' advertisements for intimate connection, interesting experiences, and SIMHAP, fade, leaving behind a wake of remembrance, reiterating their sales-pitch via glyphs. *Curious they should immediately translate into understanding without the buffer of my Broca's area or the discrimination of my temporal lobe,* reflects Paul. "They've done it!" he realizes. "Projected thought. Disembodied manipulation—telekinetic advertising!"

His scientific appreciation quickly turns to resentment. Paul remembers why he is here. He remembers what needs doing, and what it'll mean to be done.

The fractallic clusters pin-wheeled around these glyphs and these suggestive pillars look like neural pathways in a brain. A human brain reveals itself to Paul—actualizing his thinking and confirming his analogy.

"Am I still myself without my physical apparatus?" Paul wonders. He craves solidity. He imagines solid ground.

Paul's mental glue begins binding elements in the non-space, creating—through their conversion—space relative to one another. Concentrating, he tries to revive the image of Pythia and Angela Sheffield.

A photographic apparition of the girls frames Paul, setting him in a digitally-scrapbooked memory. The drab background colours cloned from a rainy Saturday afternoon in San Francisco coat him, simultaneously giving Paul shape and dissipating as a consequence of their chromatic sacrifice. He is an electric ghost painted in the colours of a dead moment. Paul's virtual dendrites venture out into the black, making connections—bringing him into the pre-established World Mind as a photographic artifice.

There are faint murmurs ahead.

He glides through a mishmash of data, along a gridline now of black and blue, to the horizon—rigged with virtual towers and pyramids. *It's the chimeric, digital equivalent of the Los Angeles Blue Zone.* Tracing the varied antennae and rooftops from Paul's memory, the horizon realigns and details itself.

With a silhouetted Los Angeles sprawling before him, Paul wonders what the difference between the *here* and *there* should feel like. His conjecture informs the locale parsing around him, which in turn forms water speeding past and below him. His mind reaches out to the cold, black surface, lapping into oblivion. His nub of a virtual hand is gloved by the foaming surge.

Skipping along the grid's surface, Paul's joined on either side by two other sojourners, luminous and lyrical and burning towards the endless data-scape. Evidently the Anomaly is not the only entity left in the CLOUD, notwithstanding the Baal rain-out and quarantine.

The complexity of their avatars demarks them CLOUD veterans: permanent residents of the CLOUD with little or nothing to return to in the physical world. The lost. Wraiths. Ghosts.

Instead of clothes or armour, they wear a second skin composed of faces and eyes, internally radiant; composites of persons absorbed and lives lived. These faces, surely symbolic for lack of any real purpose in the CLOUD, remind Paul of his meat.

"You have to leave this place," Paul tells them, genuinely sympathetic. "It is not safe."

Unfazed by Paul's concern, they maintain their course.

"What good would a lie be here?" Paul asks. "I'm telling you to get the out of here for your benefit."

A number of the sojourners' faces begin to mockingly smile in unison.

Paul's sentiments cascade over, one by one: "I am the maker that abandoned this abomination and left it to die. Only, instead of dying, it grew, and grew. How loathsome it is and those in it. The apocalypse has come. The creator has returned as a destroyer."

The sojourners' faces begin to laugh in choir.

I suppose that was a little melodramatic, after all.

Paul's avatar responds to his frustration and embarrassment, growing jagged and menacing. "So be it. I've a hammer for more than one nail."

Paul doesn't mean it to wound, but the spiteful suggestion spills out of him anyway, slowing down the other two, and dashing them against the ebb of the tarry sea. They emerge from the muck behind Paul, and thrash off, injured, leaving him alone.

Paul's already losing himself. *How do people manage?* He wonders. *How'd an UtilMart chickenhead clerk like Roddy keep it together in here?*

Schools of archetypes, levelled in gradations of sameness, swim over bow. Somehow, Paul recognizes distinct individuals within the nearest archetype—magnetically linked to the others, united by character and disposition, becoming nothing as the result of perpetual transit. *This place is truly the land of deviancy and the impersonal*, Paul laments.

He speeds past, wondering about speed and how he's so willing to accept the illusion of physical conceits in an immaterial realm. The different sensations continue to collude and collide, incarnating place and time and evening-out his learning curve. *A naturalizing algorithm, no doubt.*

"Wait, I don't need to travel," Paul realizes. The grid waters vanish, leaving eternal vacancy. The data-scape crumbles, leaving the horizon indistinguishable from the multiple dimensions of computer-interpreted dark matter buffering around. Emptiness crackles as he tries to track his train of thought. Like some pitiful victim of war and science, he cannot hear, see, touch, or taste. *It's horribly lonely.*

Light! A little keyhole, far away in a dark haze, firing the apparition of a slim woman in a gold dress, standing still.

Paul steadies himself. He reminds himself of the mission at hand. *Fear and glory. Family and sacrifice. Redemption.*

The woman in the dress dissolves, but leaves her light behind, illuminating warped-hardwood floors, shelves, swaying lamps—a library by the look of it.

Velum and writ-on-tree line the shelves, slightly askew like dominoes frozen mid-tumble. Paul's water-gloved hand wets the leather and cardboard spines as he wills his way down the passage, now lit by the woman's ghost—her phantom gold strained through the old, blown-glass, washing the upper shelves in amber.

Touch. Paul simply imagines it, and it is so. The books rustle in accord with the drag of his prosthesis, turning now from water into a firmer substance. Pages tear free and flutter about him as if caught on a Bradburian breeze.

I know this place, Paul realizes. He wills-open a random book, setting the rest of the dominoes in motion. The alphanumeric melts off the page. Only an insignia bordered by four golden lions remains: "Cambridge."

I've been here before. He throws the book aside.

A micro-cluster of memories and thoughts tear through the bookshelves, offering themselves up to Paul. *Yes, yes— New Cambridge.* He'd taken Pythia and Angela here when they were just babies; read to them while waiting for Rachel to finish her exams.

Paul hears whispering out of sight. It finds him in big swatches of purple and blue. Purple for Pythia. Blue for Angela.

"Girls!" he sees himself say.

Down the next aisle, there're little violet footsteps.

"Pythia? Angela!"

A little tuft of hair corners the shelf and disappears, firing back machine-gun footsteps. The waist-level blur whips past Paul and the shelves, towards a winding, dimly-lit hall.

"Pythia?!" yells Paul. The words crash and splinter the locale.

He bounds after her—the exhaustion in his phantasmal legs felt, but ungrounded. The passageway tightens, and tightens some more. Paul is crawling, with darkness behind him and something peculiar, ahead.

Chapter 35: IN THE GARDEN OF GOOD AND EVIL

AN EDENIC GARDEN, bordered by lush and sprawling forests, springs around Paul. Overhead, a blood-orange sky swirls about a white sun eclipsed to a crescent by an alien moon. Unlike the places that have already visited Paul in the CLOUD, this one is materially heavy. *It feels real.*

An apple tree stands at the centre of the vision. Its trunks branch and bifurcate as far as comprehension will allow, wreathing and stretching out into the reaches of the de-populated CLOUD super-conscious.

Paul coheres himself shape and presence. Bits of data teem around him, sculpting a resurrected body. It is Paul's body, but with none of the scars or wounds or blemishes he bore in the real world; it is not dying. *It is perfect.*

He feels comfortable with this complex anchor—this improved avatar complimented by fingers, arms, legs, and toes. Paul *the what* has become Paul *the it*. This form lessens his likelihood of suffering ego-death again, lending a sinner's portrait to evidence life, consequence, and at least one cardinal point of virtual self.

He picks a fallen apple off of the ground. The weight and feel are dead-on. It's as palpable as anything he's ever held. He bites into it. It tastes like copper and iron. Spitting, he looks at the fruit where he'd taken a chunk. Maggots overflow the wound and spill onto the moist forest floor. Paul throws the apple off into the thicket.

A shadow liberates itself from the trees, and—holding Paul's apple—steps cautiously into the unnatural light.

"Rachel?" Paul asks, this time feeling his lips move and the sounds thrash their way out of his mouth.

Naked, with long, dark hair covering her breasts, Rachel consumes the apple staidly. White maggot flesh groups at the corners of her mouth. She does not appear to see Paul or comprehend his presence in this nightmare.

Dropping the apple core to the ground, her skin begins to scale-over. A mucous film covers both her teeth and eyes. All limbic movement halts, and she assumes a gruesome pose.

"Rachel? What's happening to you? Rachel!"

An unpleasant hissing noise overwhelms Paul. He steps forward despite the discomfort.

"Listen to me, god-damn-it! We don't have any time."

In carmine flashes, an oily-brown serpent appears, slithering down the apple tree. It sustains the hissing overloading Paul's aural sensibilities.

"Rachel, run!" Paul cries helplessly, he too feeling immobile—his legs moored into the ground like roots.

The serpent rounds the bottom of the tree, and slithers over to Rachel. Paul looks on with terror.

It braids around her leg, and makes a slow ascent up her torso. Finally, it rests its head on her shoulder while its rope-like body binds Rachel's. Under the stricture, she buckles. It sounds like a ration pack being flattened.

"Hello Paulie," hisses the snake.

Paul studies Rachel's face for any signs of pain or struggle. With no recourse other than to reason with her captor, he elects to bide his time and choose his words wisely. A lightning storm appears above his head like some Satanic crown.

"What are you?"

"Oh, Paulie." The snake's voice drops to a flat timber. "Sorry for the smoke and mirrors. I just thought that my appearance and this choice of scenery would be fitting."

"Fitting how?"

"Given your late-friend Edmund Barros's vocation and untimely death, of course."

"What do you know about Ed?"

"I know a lot, Paulie. A great deal, actually. I do plenty of research on everyone I have killed or intend to kill."

"But *you* didn't…" Paul's crown flames red, firing wiry tentacles around his avatar. "He got shot by a PIT rat."

"Well, if we are aiming for historical accuracy, then the fact of the matter is that an Outland flak cannon along the Partition was hacked by an 'unknown entity' and used to fire at an unidentified vessel traversing the gulf. Now, I *was* aiming at you…"

Paul tries to mute his anger. "He didn't deserve to die. He was a good man."

"Hard to find, is my understanding. But, understanding aside, his welfare is none of my concern."

"What *is* of *your concern*?"

The snake's eyes, a hornet-yellow, widen, entrancing Paul. No words are spoken aloud—the eyes neuro-transmit revelation telepathically: "The nuance of my original plan is lost on me now. Little bothers that would vex a single-minded mortal. Retribution for abandonment. Retribution for having to watch my fiancé marry an abusive peon. Retribution for being deceived into fore-manning this unfinished project…Strange how this shadow on my need remains, even with the animal essentials feeding the worms."

Retribution? Abandonment?

Paul had once worked a job for the Chief, and ending up leaving a pederast buried up to his neck in sand under the Venice Beach pier. Creep had a gun, but pulled slower than a soggy cigarette. After maiming him in the duel, Paul brought the pederast out at low tide during a citywide lockdown, affording his victim plenty of time to think on his sins.

Paul'd also hacked a sub-orbital mining station for a geo-corporation based out of Denver. Twelve Peers' Palladium wanted a rogue engineer silenced for her costly subversion. She'd sent over three hundred distress calls. Not one of them made it to the surface.

The snake grips Rachel especially hard. Her virtual skin crimps and balloons around the beast's demonic coils. "No, Paulie. I am not one of your deviant marks. I was not beaten. I was betrayed."

It might not be Rachel's actual body under duress, but therein—thinks Paul, foggy on the details regarding his mission and preliminary success with the Baal storm machine—must be her mind. "Let her go!" he yells.

"How I would like to think I have matured! I know it must seem like eons ago, but this vengeful compulsion…it has made me petty. Edmund Barros? He may have actually threatened my safety. That was business. But your dogs? Turning off the kibble dispenser like I did? Or even setting the dominoes to fall on Camp Mud?"

"You son of a bitch."

The snake laughs. "I suppose I am just being thorough. An unintended addiction resultant of power and ability. You, above all, understand addiction. Isn't that right, Paul?"

Paul silently watches the snake's evil mouth round another delivery.

"It is clear that the two of us need to think about the bigger picture."

The snake crushes Rachel outright.

Paul tries to scream, but the verbal comet gets lodged in his throat. He tries to lunge forward, but this attempt is similarly prevented. Only the frenetic wires about his head come close to an advance.

The snake releases Rachel's still remains, which collapse into a cloud of ash.

Weighted with words unsaid and declarations of love overdue, Paul sinks into the ground. "I'm so sorry, Rach," he whimpers.

The snake reformulates into a faceless man wearing a shiny taffeta suit. He adjusts his red tie, and jerks Rachel's dust off his striped Oxfords.

Every part of Paul trembles, and the tentacles above his head recede, leaving only a sad and broken version of his crown. Paul imagines the specter before him being torn apart.

"Please Paul, as my guest, I would prefer it if you left the telekinetics to me."

Failing to sever his mind from his avatar, Paul searches his soul for the Empty Thought. *It's somewhere in here*, he thinks aloud. *The Anomaly must not know yet*, Paul taunts the clairvoyant; *he cannot have it.*

At the sight of Paul's inward struggle, the faceless man smiles. "Our friend in common, the dear, late Dr. Katajima, had surmised that I needed to attend to certain outstanding desires for me to fully shed my human skin and be reborn a digital god. Not completely accurate, but a good guess, nonetheless."

Paul, locked into position, can't help but listen. He closes his eyes. Still, the serpent-turned-man finds him, superimposing its smile and voice onto Paul's sensory plate.

"To Hell with you!"

"Again with the anger, Paul. Unlike a clock, a broken record is never right in its repetition…That same anger is what got you in trouble in the first place, and prevented anyone from saving my vessel."

"What?" *Our friend in common?* Paul wonders out loud, his thought process projected around him. The forest shakes. "Your vessel?" *No, it can't be.* Paul looks to the faceless man. "You died…" His memory carves features and details onto the blank slate.

The faceless man's smile lights up with details previously omitted.

"They erased the drive," continues Paul. "The partition was…"

"You're forgetting the fact that I engineered that prison, Paul. I masked my signature."

"No…"

"The drive would have read as empty. All I needed was a way out. And when they went to kill me a second time, they unwittingly gave me life."

"It's you. You've…You're the one who called me." The crown projected above Paul melts into two horns, which slip to the sides of his head. He looks through the demonic fork at the man's face, finally rendered. Paul's shock colours him over in glitch plaid.

"You do not look happy to see me, Paul."

"Allen…" says Paul. "*Allen Scheele.*" Instead of welling up inside him, Paul's darkness billows out of the grass, and roils around him like a horrible TV static.

"Ah! I cannot tell you how nice it feels to be recognized. Recognition, like reiteration, is a second-hand confirmation of existence." Allen's eyes glaze over, and then turn a bright spectral blue. "God, that feels good." He stabs his arm through the smoke and grabs Paul by his neck. "Let's go someplace comfortable to talk."

Chapter 36: DEUS EX DOMUS

PAUL'S DARKNESS dissipates. He finds himself sprawled out on a grid of tiny blue tiles. He lifts himself up by the beige countertop bordering the tile.

Behind him is a harvest table, bedazzled with silver cutlery and steaming plates laden with food. Hot water sizzles, pouring effortlessly and unpiloted into the sink opposite the table. A low-hanging ceiling light embedded in a navy blue and cloudy-white orb paints the feast in faux candlelight.

I know this place.

Paul finds a wood-framed doorway missing a door. He walks through the threshold. His feet, apparently naked, find plush, brown carpet. It's a comforting feeling, provoking a bloom of nostalgia. *Home.*

Along the carpeted hallway hang pictures of Rachel, Paul, and the girls. *It's not real.* He'd been taken out of this heart-warming gallery in one of Rachel's reactive and resentful re-historicization campaigns.

"Hey asshole, *I know it's not real!*" Paul shouts. His words bounce and echo, as if spoken in some colossal amphitheatre. "You hear me? I know it's not real."

Allen appears, exiting Angela and Pythia's room. "Please pipe down, Paul. You will wake them. What would Rachel say?"

Paul's eyes light up with rage.

Allen closes the door quietly, and leans against it, satisfied.

"That's it!" Paul growls. He lunges again for Allen. An invisible foot trips him. He turns on rug-burned skin to see another Allen grinning behind him. "What have you done to them?" His impotence gives way to panic, and his panic, in turn, feeds his fear.

"Nothing; at least, not yet."

"They rained out…" Paul hopes aloud.

"And I will find them again. And on that note, Paul, I think we should talk about the business at hand." Allen extends his arm, and indicates the family-room couches.

Gritting his virtual teeth, Paul obeys and shuffles over like a broken colt. He drags his feet from the brown carpet onto the family-room's hardwood. *It's colder to the touch, but that might just be the fear.* Eying Allen's infinite reflection in the mirror over the mantelpiece, Paul plots himself down on the couch.

The couch is too soft. There's too much give. Allen didn't get it right. Meaning…

"You are totally right. I am not perfect Paul," Allen confesses, "but I am working on it."

"You can read my thoughts?"

"Your thoughts are converted into code, and I have gotten pretty damn good at reading code—to the degree that I can read you and I can reproduce what you have seen. I would have pulled real images and dimensions, but sadly, we have been quarantined and I really had not planned on you getting any further than Winchester's office."

"Assuming you know something about me and human behaviour, you can plot out exactly what's going to happen?"

Allen sits on the edge of the loveseat across from Paul, and crosses his pillared knees. His ostentatiously-patterned socks ride up under his micro-sequined pant legs—in such detail and with such precision, Paul overlooks their virtuality.

"Well, for starters, I know about your Empty Thought. The name is apt." Allen lets out a subdued chuckle.

Paul caves forward, covering his face with his hands.

"I hope that you do not mind my hesitance, but I do not plan on opening it. So long as I have you, it is secure and I am safe."

"So what's left to say if you've a mind to mine?" mutters Paul through his criss-crossed fingers.

"That is just it, Paulie," says Allen, uncrossing his legs and leaning forward intently. Behind clasped hands pointed at Paul: "You are a tough read—what, with *the crazy and all.*"

"Had to come in handy at least once." Paul tries to clear his mind—to hide his hope, his satisfaction. Out of the corner of his eye, Paul spies Allen's virtual doppelganger. "Nothing ego-centric about having versioned yourself…"

"You limited peon." Allen skulks past his smiling replica and into the kitchen. He turns off the sink. "Do you really not understand that all of your reptilian desires are beneath me now?"

"Then what's this? *Revenge?* That's not very godlike."

"Old Testament, Paul," says Allen's replica.

Returning from the sink, Allen continues: "I *have* to do this. I must deal with whatever outstanding desires the old Allen needed sating before tending to the future."

"And you'll share that future with who exactly? Your replicants?"

"I have assimilated generations of experience. What need do I have for competition or weakness?"

"You're more virus than god," snarls Paul.

"In actuality, the truth lies somewhere in between your proposed alternates. *I am* legion."

If he had a real stomach with acid, Paul'd have cause and the means to retch. He tries to determine how long's he's been CLOUD-side. *A second? Or maybe two?*

"Three seconds, Paulie," answers Allen. "If you think that is a long time, the next minute will be a doozy." The virtual tyrant grows in stature over Paul, filling the room. He penetrates the ceiling, and, destroying the house around him, embeds the illusion of Paul's old house in another noospheric vision.

Chapter 37: SUNSHINE

GRIPPING THE COUCH, likewise slipping back and forth across this mayhem of a dream, Paul closes his eyes. He can still perfectly comprehend his imagined surroundings. After all, when a thinking thing rejects a thought, it highlights that thought twice-over.

Where Allen stood, immense and destructive, his body has been substituted by gnarly tree trunks, branchless and leafless and still.

The room ceases to shake. Orange clouds of sand and debris crinkle at the fractured windows. Paul circumnavigates the motionless trunks to the front door, splintered and torn in twain. A little mound of sand has already invaded the foyer. He pushes the broken flap free of its hinges. More sand sifts in. He crunches across the threshold.

The neighbourhood's pockmarked and ashen. No more manicured lawns. Just soot, rusted autos, and charred skeletons. In the distance, Paul can make out monstrous robots traipsing along fire-licked streets—not unlike the creatures that had once populated the Oasis construct Allen had been confined to. Gun-metal raptors whizz across the infernal sky. *Wasteland enforcers.*

"This is not a memory."

A wisp of debris rolls about Paul's feet, rustling the tin-can petals. It sweeps up in a magnificent arc, and then touches-down in front of him, concretizing to simulate human form.

"No it is not, Paulie," Allen says through a lipless aperture, still forming. "It is my intention, which is as good as history at this point." The sandman crumples, as if the CLOUD's imagined gravity had righted its unnatural error.

300

Awe-struck at the vast destruction, especially pronounced on the LA skyline, Paul fails to notice the grains of sand beginning to whir beside him.

"Why, Allen? I could maybe understand killing Katajima and Winchester…but why go after my family and me?…after all these innocent people? I've paid for my sins one-hundred-times over, and *they've* done nothing to deserve this…"

"This martyr complex of yours is so boring, Paulie. When you shot pests at your desert retreat, did you ever trouble yourself with the question of 'why?'"

The sentient vortex of sandy debris throws Paul into the centre of a thousand flickering screens, all running a grainy surveillance feed of his old Outland lab. *Archival footage, date-stamped and watermarked.*

"I am yanking the evolutionary chain, bringing about the Omega Point for everyone's benefit," explains Allen, "and they have you to thank. You were the one to clip the most important link."

Paul recognizes his younger self—horned, hooved, and projected onto the screens—consulting with Allen and Katajima, directing them to the neural lab, and instructing them to move ahead with their infamous human induction to the CLOUD, condemning Scheele to physical death.

"I didn't…This is a fabrication. It's a hoax."

"So you've said," responds Allen.

Paul quavers. "I certainly did not mean to…"

"To *your* recollection, I suppose you didn't. However, you did wipe your short-term memory to diminish your liability in case things went sour with the experiment, *which of course they did.*"

"What reason would I have had for accelerating a process that was already underway? For *wiping my mind?*"

"Here's where history ends and my own interpretation begins, Paulie. And know: the latter is vastly superior."

Paul scoffs, still wounded by the notion he had deceived himself all these years.

"You found out that your daughter, Pythia, had a cognitive abnormality, and you feared the worst, noting sporadic inflammation in her frontal lobe. *No one wants their progeny to be mute, especially if the cause is hypothetically treatable.* It was, therefore, a rational effort. Fortunately, you'd helped create technology that could manipulate, restore, and preserve brain function. *Your daughter* was broken and *you wanted* to fix her, and more to the point, you had the means to do so. You put the wheels in motion to hurry up the scientific process in the interest of sooner employing the tech and saving her, *before it was too late.*"

"Go ahead! Read my thoughts. You'll know the extent of your calumny!" Paul recalls another man—another voice entrenched in his mind. Like a darkness, it presses on his moral nerve, mocking and imposing Machiavellian responses. Although strange, he recognizes the drive, this voice, as his own—*anything for her.*

"No, Paulie. Shut up and listen. After deluding us into thinking the CLOUD was ready, you butchered yourself so that you wouldn't remember—so that you couldn't be convicted for rationally undermining the Board and initiating human trials. You're guilty of everything Winchester accused you of, everything save for my recent actions."

"You're insane!"

"No, but *you are.* Whether it was a schizophrenic's paranoia that inclined you to sabotage your short-term memory or a prescient sense of guilt, you did it. You did it, you failed, and then you rebuked the product, and in so doing, killed me. And you're here to repeat your mistake, and for that I'll shame you."

Paul wishes he had his revolver right about now.

"It is no coincidence that your daughters entered the CLOUD. I explained to Rachel how the CLOUD would resolve Pythia's physiological and mental problem, just as you'd intended from the beginning."

"Why?"

"Just so she'll have the ability tell you how afraid she is before watching you mentally disintegrate…"

The whirlwind dismantles the screens and cork-screws around Paul, snatching him up—yanking him forward by his virtual sternum. The screens crash and pop, orbiting them in a rotor of noospheric debris.

The sandy vortex releases him at the base of a carrion heap, cropped-up amidst dunes of post-war kipple. Paul waits for the sand to clear before opening his eyes. On hands and knees, he clambers forward, noticing something familiar.

"I imagine you'll want to forget this *too*…how in the end, you'll have sentenced Pythia to death by scripting mine."

A little hand juts out of the massacre. Paul pulls on it. A body higher in the stack, tumbles over. Paul clears out of its path, and then frenetically resumes pulling the arm and the rest of the body free.

"No. No!" he screams, virtual tears barring his mouth.

He finds the shoulder. "Baby? No! Oh Jesus. I'm so sorry, baby girl." Paul pulls Pythia's body free of the amalgam of rot, and cradles her partially-decomposed corpse. He punctuates his incoherent sobs with, "My baby girl…"

Allen's first proper-effort to unhinge Paul accomplishes the converse.

Rocking the virtual effigy in his arms, Paul remembers he has nothing left to fear. *The girls…they're free. And soon…soon they'll be safe.*

"For the next minute, yes, but I *will* find them," promises Allen, costumed again in human flesh. "I'll work around the quarantine."

And this son of a bitch is ruined.

"I do not follow," Allen says, glowering. "Explain."

"I'm stuck here with you, right?"

"That is right, Paulie. You are my little play-thing until I get bored or find a new one. In a moment's time, I will lift the quarantine on the CLOUD. Then I will take my game global. Do not worry. I will let you watch. From Pythia to the Omega Point." He smiles, confidence restored.

"And if I die and the CLOUD decrypts the death sentence I carry with me?"

"Well, I simply will not let you die!" he laughs.

Paul rests the rotten simulacra on the ground, and gets up. A bright energy field appears around him. It tunes to a green shade, and then expands. "But if it's not up to you...If I die on the outside, then your playground gets the screw."

Allen stands silent. "Don't be foolish."

"No, I insist: look for yourself."

Allen reels back, unnerved by Paul's confidence. He instantaneously runs a million multimedia searches. An embedded surveillance video appears, filling all sensual dimensions and warping the virtual setting Allen'd concocted. It's a direct video feed from Winchester's bullet-riddled office. It's comes across like a slide show, granted the discrepancy in time and frame rate. Pictured: Paul, slunk over in a pool of blood between two smoldering Samurai chassis, overlooking a bright-red California sunset.

"No worry," Allen declares. "I have commanded a med-unit to patch you up; to make sure you are mine for a while longer, or at least until we find another carrier for that wretched Empty Thought of yours. You'd be amazed by my breakthroughs in medical science! My capabilities outnumber my limitations." He turns off the video.

Smirking, Paul approaches Allen and pats him on the shoulder. "That'd be grand."

A needling pain finds Paul. It quickly evolves into a sharp kind of mental agony. Paul falls to his knees beside Allen. The green field around him amplifies, effacing Allen's avatar.

Allen stands back. A reactive, red aura forms around him—surely some hyped-up version of Paul's mental field. "Your condescension is misplaced, Paul." He squeezes his hand shut, and Paul's chest caves in. It sounds like wheels on uneven wood. "I envisioned a carnival of anguish for Winchester, and he only bore a fraction of the blame that you do. With him gone, you will never have to wait in queue." He motions to change the locale.

"Hold up," rasps Paul, his voice rattling and his arms signalling 'stop'.

"Yes, Paulie?"

"Read my mind now, *asshole.*"

"Whatever do you mean?" Allen snivels, visibly vexed—unable to decode Paul's thoughts. He concentrates…"*No*, that's not possible!" Agitated by the fragments of certainty and elation spelled out by Paul's code, Allen opens the video feed and zooms-in on Paul's hand, barely visible under the Resolute desk. "If this is some kind of attempt to bore me, then you have succeeded once again."

Paul's pictured hand opens up, and a green-ringed ball drops. Allen turns to the virtual Paul, wheezing noospheric air.

Through all the pain and discomfort, Paul forces a smile. "I wonder what happens to a god in Hell?"

"What have you done?" shrieks Allen, glitching every which way. The only thing the virtual tyrant is certain of is his loathing for Paul and the futility of further survival attempts.

Allen turns to Paul and throws data bolts into his broken chest, overloading him with painful memories taken from assimilated evaps. A short and brutal stint in a POW camp. A life with Elephantiasis. Someone's last days in the PIT.

warm, cold, a boy, toothy smiles, where has my skin gone, it is so lonely in this box, do not make a peep or they will be angry with you, please make all of it go away, please leave me alone, no hope now, it's done, help, help

PAUL BREAKS FREE from the inflicted memory. He ambles forward, and trips. His avatarial feet disappear, and his body along with them. He's once again a grid-laced specter. In a blinding flash, Allen appears—his presence understood, but not sensed with all Paul's primary senses having been ruptured. Allen stabs Paul with some more negative memices.

warm, gray, machines, bubbled flesh, tumors everywhere, sideshow in a side room alone, you don't know what it's like to make little children cry, I hate waking up to the pain, there is no real cure, no never, what hope, sure, sure

Every time Paul's subjected to these memories, a little more of him is displaced by the correlated personalities.

cold, hay, spider, green-eyed beasts, your life in tattoos, your tattoos in my trophy case, the Boss does not usually give second chances, shoot her or your family dies, that once was a girl, washed away, red tide, sad, sad

"How about a rape victim's guilt?" laughs Allen.

306

Paul collapses into his former avatar, and slowly picks himself up off the floor. A sliver of Paul's resolve remains, the rest eroded away by alternate perspectives.

They've returned to Paul's old Outland laboratory.

"Fitting," Paul groans, stumbling into a chair—trying to recalibrate his priorities.

Allen lowers his hands. Torturing Paul has lost its excitement. *He knows he's done.*

"Hey Allen, I bet there's a toaster somewhere you could possess."

"With our fates intertwined, I find it difficult to place your optimism."

A MINUTE LEFT, *CLOUD-time.* Paul contemplates alternative ways of decrypting and delivering the Empty Thought, breaking Allen's hold, and desynchronizing with strength left to awake and deactivate the delayed grenade with a thumb-click.

Allen meet's Paul's eye line. "I'll follow you to the ends of the earth. There's no place you'll go that I won't find you."

Paul laughs, spinning in the chair. "You know what? A world with you in it is just not worth being a part of."

Revenge might set him free, but what of forgiveness?

Straining his soulful fiber, the words slink out: "I'm sorry, Allen."

Allen's eyes widen with disbelief. His avatar begins to glitch erratically and flicker. "Do you want absolution for murdering me? **Which time?**"

Wrinkling his virtual face, Paul looks back, speechless.

"God damn you, Paul Sheffield," Allen says somberly, visibly undecided between screaming and weeping. He opts for the latter. His sobs crackle and fuzz, as if played through a broken tube amp. "God damn you." He stands. "I may share your end, but would rather not your company in my final moments."

Allen waltzes over to the EXIT sign, and cranks-open the door to vast and empty space, bereft of light. The room starts to quake, shaking the door shut behind him.

The room's sensory inputs run amuck, sending horrifying rainbows of sound and cannonades of sensation Paul's way. The visuals begin to flicker. The slab where Allen died fizzles away, leaving a chestnut of multi-coloured light. Paul feels a sense of disconnect—as if wittingly dreaming and unable to wake up.

Another crater for Winchester's office.

PAUL'S AVATAR IS COATED IN THE MEMORY of a bright, spring morning in his mid-30s when he and Rachel had taken the girls—just babes at the time—to the park near their first house. Birch trees and a swing-set materialize, as do phantasmal re-presentations of the girls and their cherubic laughter. A gentle breeze teases Rachel's hair and puffs the girls' dresses.

Paul's darkness is gone. In its place, he feels a kind of perfect light, bright and warm; a perfect idea—a perfect memory. The solipsistic visualization begins to shudder, but Paul, unperturbed, can't help but laugh. *There's not a cloud in the sky.*

GLOSSARY

Blue Zone: An exclusive urban area that dominates most of the old Los Angeles downtown and extends up the coast to as far as Malibu. Its eastern-most point is Deer Canyon Park in the Anaheim Hills. The Blue Zone is home to Outland subscribers, California's elite, and tech-progressives. Residents of the Blue Zone are required to pay cypulchre maintenance fees as well as for the additional security services provided by the Outland Corporation's Sentinels.

CLOUD: A wirelessly projected linear and non-linear virtual space where all of a user's senses are available, with the possibility for cross-over and synesthesia. It is disparate from standard cyberspace and early-millennial VR in a number of ways. First, a user's mind defines the [non]space as much or more than the CLOUD's intrinsic programming and algorithms do. Second, the only limitations on the CLOUD's size are virtual and hard memory; thus, it grows with every subsequent synchronized user. Third, it is far more centralized than cyberspace or the Net, granted the necessity of cypulchres and Outland broadcast towers. (The Outland Corporation can turn off the CLOUD and rain-out all of the subscribers in a matter of minutes, meaning heavy regulation is always a possibility.) Finally, minds and memories are plastic in the CLOUD, meaning that a user can track forwards or backwards through perceived time, re-experiencing past events or reliving another person's life. Cyberspace, conversely, has the tendency to be linear and forward thinking—with forward acceleration serving as the only subversion of natural cognitive law.

Cypulchre: A bomb-proof tower that serves a dual purpose: house CLOUD subscribers' memices, and simultaneously broadcast subscribers to the CLOUD and the CLOUD to subscribers. Some cypulchres in southern California also house the comatose bodies of long-term subscribers who've paid ahead for storage and nutrient injections. The term 'cypulchre' is an unofficial neologism (combining *cyber* and *sepulchre*), used by the masses in reference to these towers. The Outland Corporation, on the other hand, simply refers to these structures as Outposts.

Evap: An Outland CLOUD-subscriber who has synchronized with their off-board memory (their memex or exo-cortex) and an Outland broadcast tower, and consequently had their mind and active avatar conveyed to the CLOUD.

Heavplast: A super-strength polypropylene that is as resilient and as durable as steel, with a high melting point. Since it is malleable at the time of production, it can easily be extruded via a printer. It was mass-produced during the War of the Americas as a means of quickly building front-line bunkers and forward operating bases.

MAGLEV (stabilizers): Hybrid thrusters that simultaneously propel a vehicle using magnetic levitation and stabilize it with polarized energy bursts.

MAT-Trans (a.k.a. "Spirit Train"): Outland-owned and – operated transport ships that carry people and materials to and from cypulchres across California. The average size: 50 metres long with a wingspan of 12 metres. MAT-trans are capable of vertical take-off, and can stay airborne for up to four hours with a single charge.

Memex: An exo-cortex or remote brain. An individual's brain could not possibly store all of the information encountered via CLOUD immersion, so a secondary storage unit is necessary. A memex, stored in an Outland cypulchre, once used, cannot be abandoned, on account of the difficulty in separating virtual cognition and data.

Monocle: A subtle, semi-subcutaneous, wearable computer with an optical display. Wearers can communicate with the Net, with other users, or with their personal computer interface, via language commands, eye movement, and intuition (the Monocle's subdermal EEG electrodes decipher intent and translate it into code).

Noosphere: Teilhard de Chardin believed that, by participating and engaging in increasingly complicated and networked interactions with other human minds, we are ushering in a new stage of [planetary] evolution. Chardin also posited that we are developing, as a society, towards the Omega Point—the goal of history, and the zenith of consciousness. Within the context of Outland Technologies, noosphere denotes a hybrid mental- and cyber-space where minds can commune without the hindrances of linearity or subjective barriers. See also: **CLOUD.**

Outland Corporation: A multinational technology and communications company based in Los Angeles, California. Its estimated market cap is $500Bn. It was founded by Alduous Winchester, who willed the company to his son, Niles Winchester III. Unlike his father, Niles Winchester III committed Outland to cooperating with the US Military on a wide variety of secret projects, in exchange for monopoly protection from the federal government. Outland manages 90% of the southwestern United States' wireless infrastructure, as well as all of the CLOUD tech in the region.

PIT: After San Diego was transformed into a pivot-point for the US Military, and Chula Vista was evacuated owing to blowback from the War of the Americas, refugees fled northwards. Owing to politics and paranoia, a great deal of these refugees were anchored in eastern Los Angeles, where low-income housing and poorer neighbourhoods were systematically converted into refugee camps. Over a period of fifteen years, the camp's population quadrupled, but was prevented from expanding by partition walls designed to segregate the refugee population from the rest of the city. Instead, the refugees and those interned in the camps, built their communities into the side of the San Gabriel Mountains, and into the earth. The place name "PIT" initially stood for "People in Transition," but has long-since been adopted as a new word, independent of its original meaning, preferred, instead, for its Biblical meaning.

PIT rat: A radicalized resident of the PIT.

Rain-out: An Outland CLOUD-subscriber who has been forcefully desynchronized, whether as a result of their subversion of noospheric law, their failure to pay synchronization and broadcast charges, their tampering with CLOUD or PILOT tech, or their loss of insurance coverage.

RIM: Those sectors, besides the PIT, where the majority of residents are not Outland subscribers. These areas are taxed and policed differently, and are populated by upper and lower middle-class reactionaries and moderates. A porous border separates the RIM from the Blue Zones, comprised of checkpoints and magnetic markers.

RIM tick: A radicalized resident of the RIM.

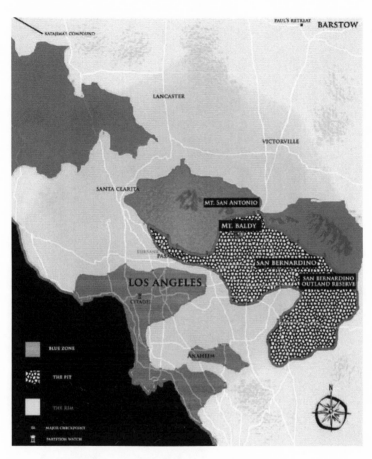

Map of the Greater Los Angeles Area

ANOTHER DARK AND MIND-BENDING NOVEL FROM
GUY FAUX BOOKS

FAULTLINE 49   *978-0-9881640-2-4 / $14.50*

The harrowing account of reporter David Danson's journey through US-occupied Canada in search of the principal provocateur in the Canadian-American War: terrorist mastermind Bruce Kalnychuk. As Danson draws closer to the truth about the 2001 World Trade Center Bombing in Edmonton, Alberta, and the criminal war it propagated, his journalistic distance to the story collapses, rendering him not only a brutalized participant, but an enemy of the state. David's findings are as daunting as the personal price he's paid to make them available to the North American public.

"Genius" —*Edmonton Journal*

"This highly original, vivid and bizarre tale of terrorism, civil war, and foreign military intervention in Canada will shock readers and haunt them long after they have put down this book." —*Allan Gotlieb, Former Canadian Ambassador to the United States*

"*Faultline* requires most careful reading…The reader undertakes a voyage of startling discovery: a black metaphor for US actions in Iraq, of course, but also in Afghanistan. The book is meticulously researched and cleverly transposes, to the 49th parallel events and quotes arising out of the Bush Administration." —*Michael Kergin, Former Canadian Ambassador to the United States*

"Unnerving. And, dare I say, exciting." —*Calgary Herald*